ADVENTURE TIME™

GRAYBLES SCHMAYBLES

ROSS RICHIE CEO & Founder • MARK SMYLIE Founder of Archaia • MATT GAGNON Editor-in-Chief • FILIP SABLIK President of Publishing & Marketing • STEPHEN CHRISTY President of Development
LANCE KREITER VP of Licensing & Merchandising • PHIL BARBARO VP of Finance • BRYCE CARLSON Managing Editor • MEL CAYLO Marketing Manager • SCOTT NEWMAN Production Design Manager
IRENE BRADISH Operations Manager • CHRISTINE DINH Brand Communications Manager • DAFNA PLEDAN Editor • SHANNON WATTERS Editor • ERIC HARBURN Editor • REBECCA TAYLOR Editor • IAN BRILL Editor
WHITNEY LEOPARD Associate Editor • JASMINE AMIRI Associate Editor • CHRIS ROSA Assistant Editor • ALEX GALER Assistant Editor • CAMERON CHITTOCK Assistant Editor • MARY GUMPORT Assistant Editor
KELSEY DIETERICH Production Designer • JILLIAN CRAB Production Designer • KARA LEOPARD Production Designer • MICHELLE ANKLEY Production Design Assistant • DEVIN FUNCHES E-Commerce & Inventory Coordinator
AARON FERRARA Operations Coordinator • JOSÉ MEZA Sales Assistant • ELIZABETH LOUGHRIDGE Accounting Assistant • STEPHANIE HOCUTT PR Assistant • HILLARY LEVI Executive Assistant • KATE ALBIN Administrative Assistant

kaboom!™   CARTOON NETWORK.   FREDERATOR

Created by Pendleton Ward

Written by **Danielle Corsetto**
Illustrated by **Bridget Underwood**
Inks by **Jenna Ayoub**
Colors by **Whitney Cogar**
Letters by **Aubrey Aiese**

"Flan!"
Written & Illustrated by **Meredith McClaren**

Cover by **Stephanie Gonzaga**

Designer **Kara Leopard**
Associate Editor **Whitney Leopard**
Editor **Shannon Watters**

With Special Thanks to Marisa Marionakis, Rick Blanco, Nicole Rivera, Conrad Montgomery, Meghan Bradley, Curtis Lelash and the wonderful folks at Cartoon Network.

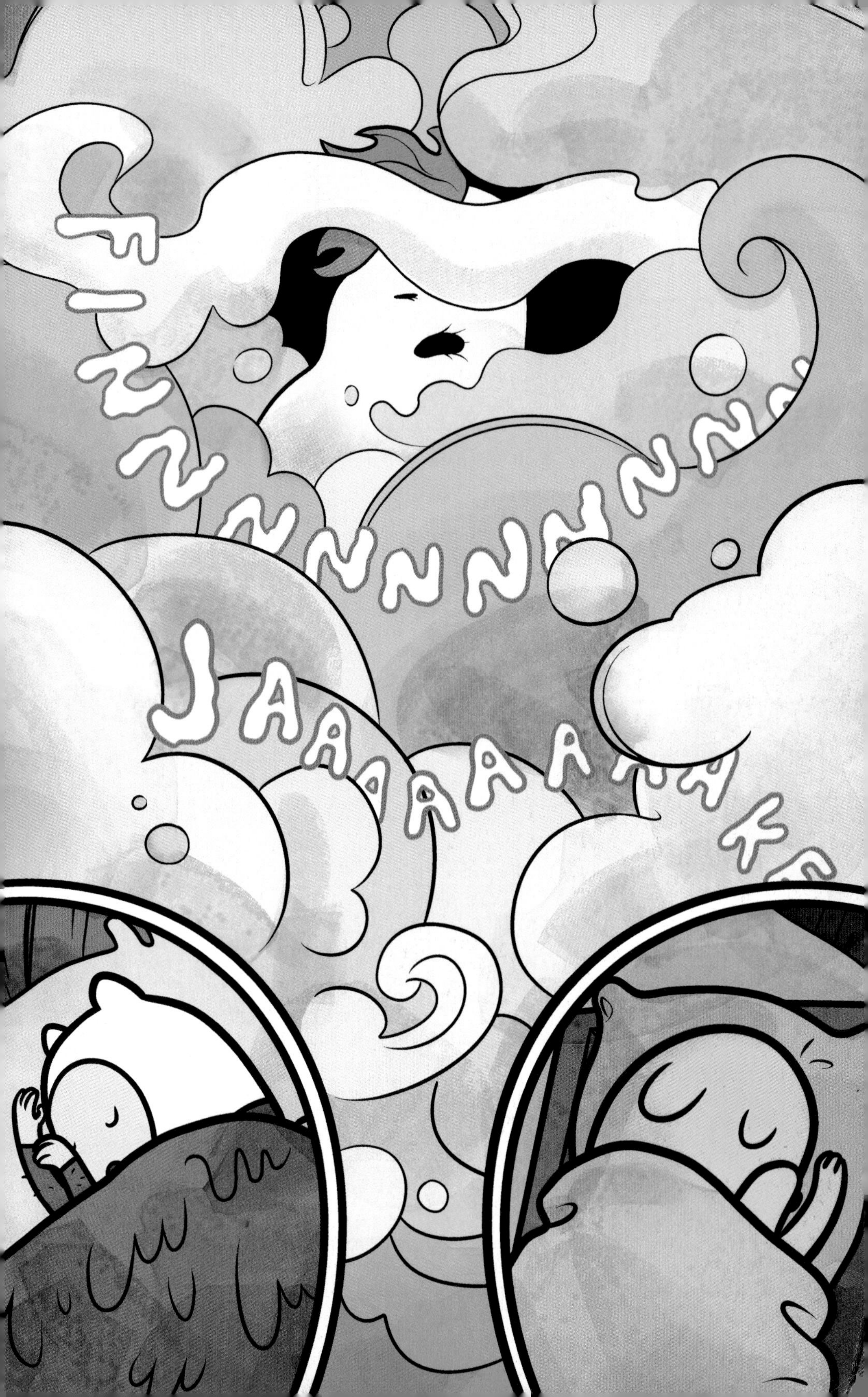
FINNNNNNNNNNN
JAAAAAAAKE

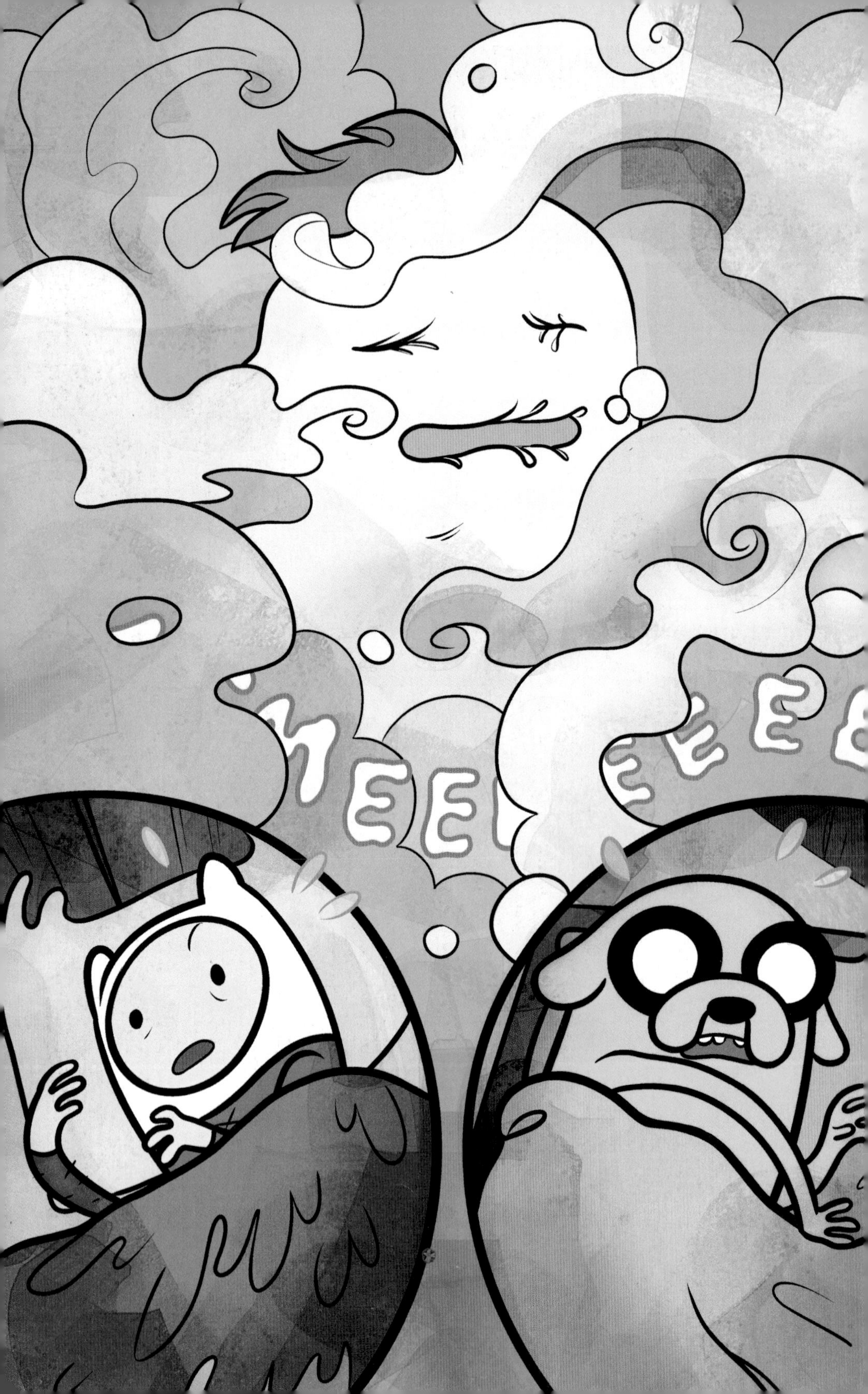
MEEEEEEE

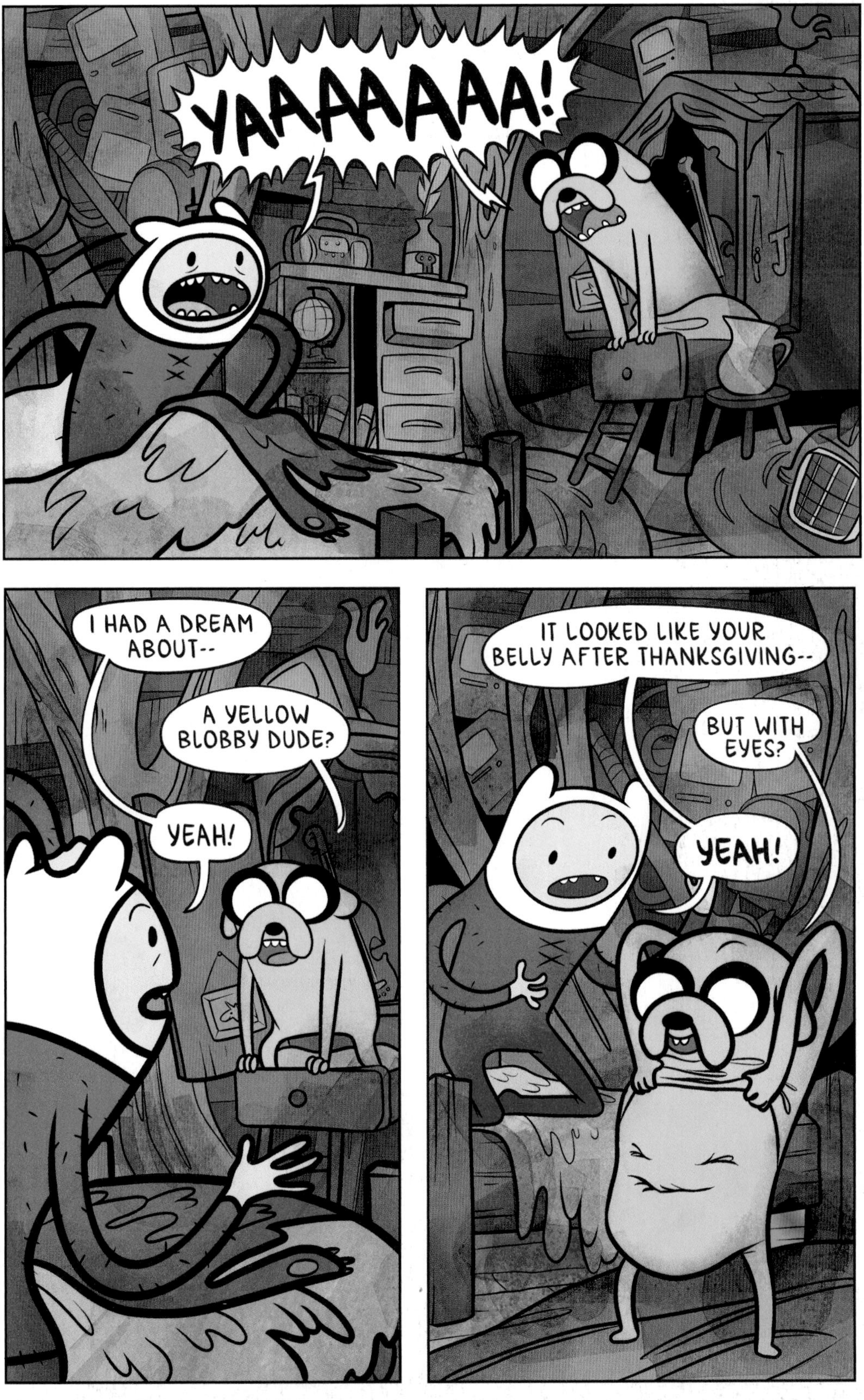
YAAAAAAA!
I HAD A DREAM ABOUT--
A YELLOW BLOBBY DUDE?
YEAH!
IT LOOKED LIKE YOUR BELLY AFTER THANKSGIVING--
BUT WITH EYES?
YEAH!

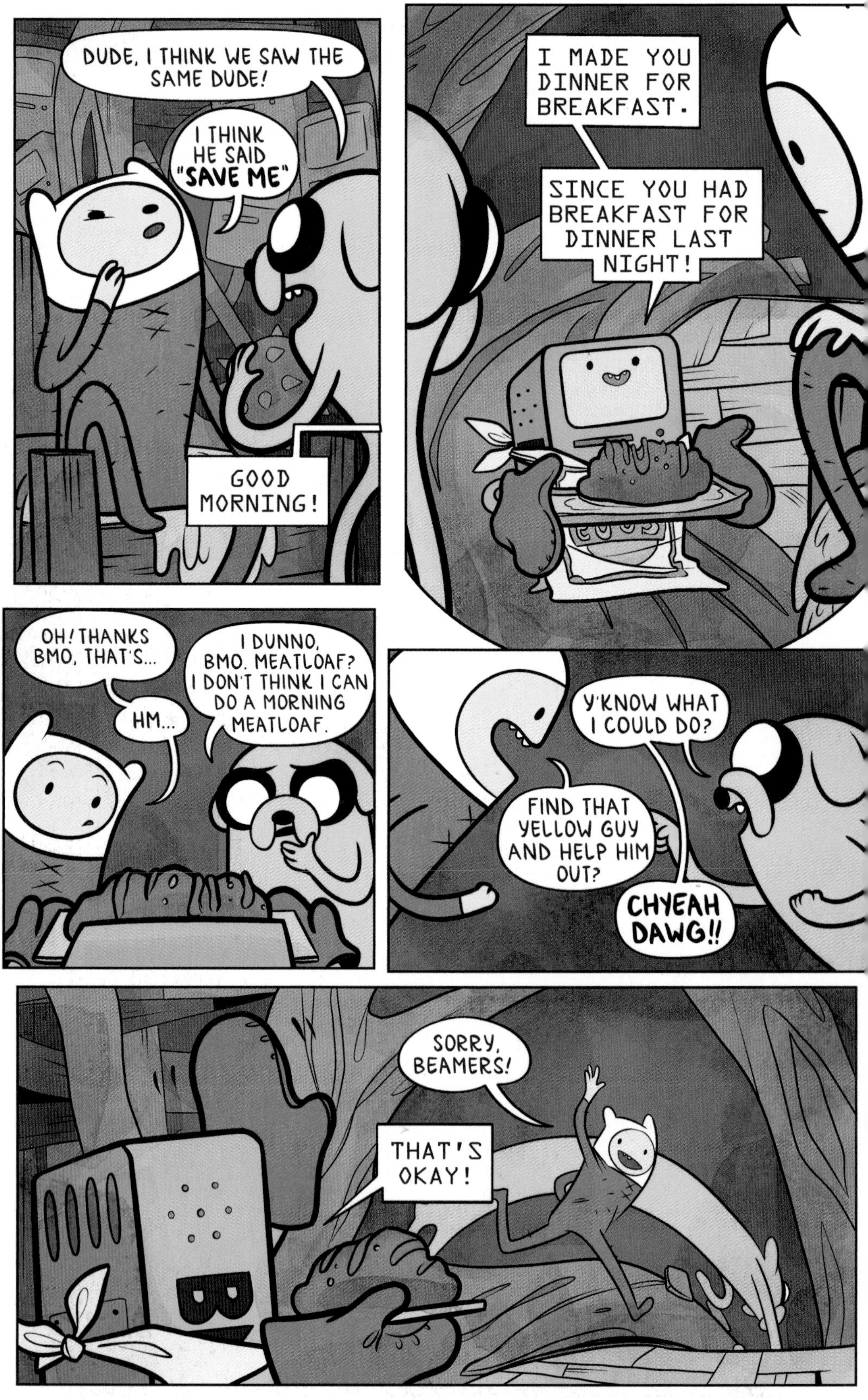
DUDE, I THINK WE SAW THE SAME DUDE!
I THINK HE SAID "SAVE ME"
GOOD MORNING!
I MADE YOU DINNER FOR BREAKFAST.
SINCE YOU HAD BREAKFAST FOR DINNER LAST NIGHT!
OH! THANKS BMO, THAT'S...
HM...
I DUNNO, BMO. MEATLOAF? I DON'T THINK I CAN DO A MORNING MEATLOAF.
Y'KNOW WHAT I COULD DO?
FIND THAT YELLOW GUY AND HELP HIM OUT?
CHYEAH DAWG!!
SORRY, BEAMERS!
THAT'S OKAY!

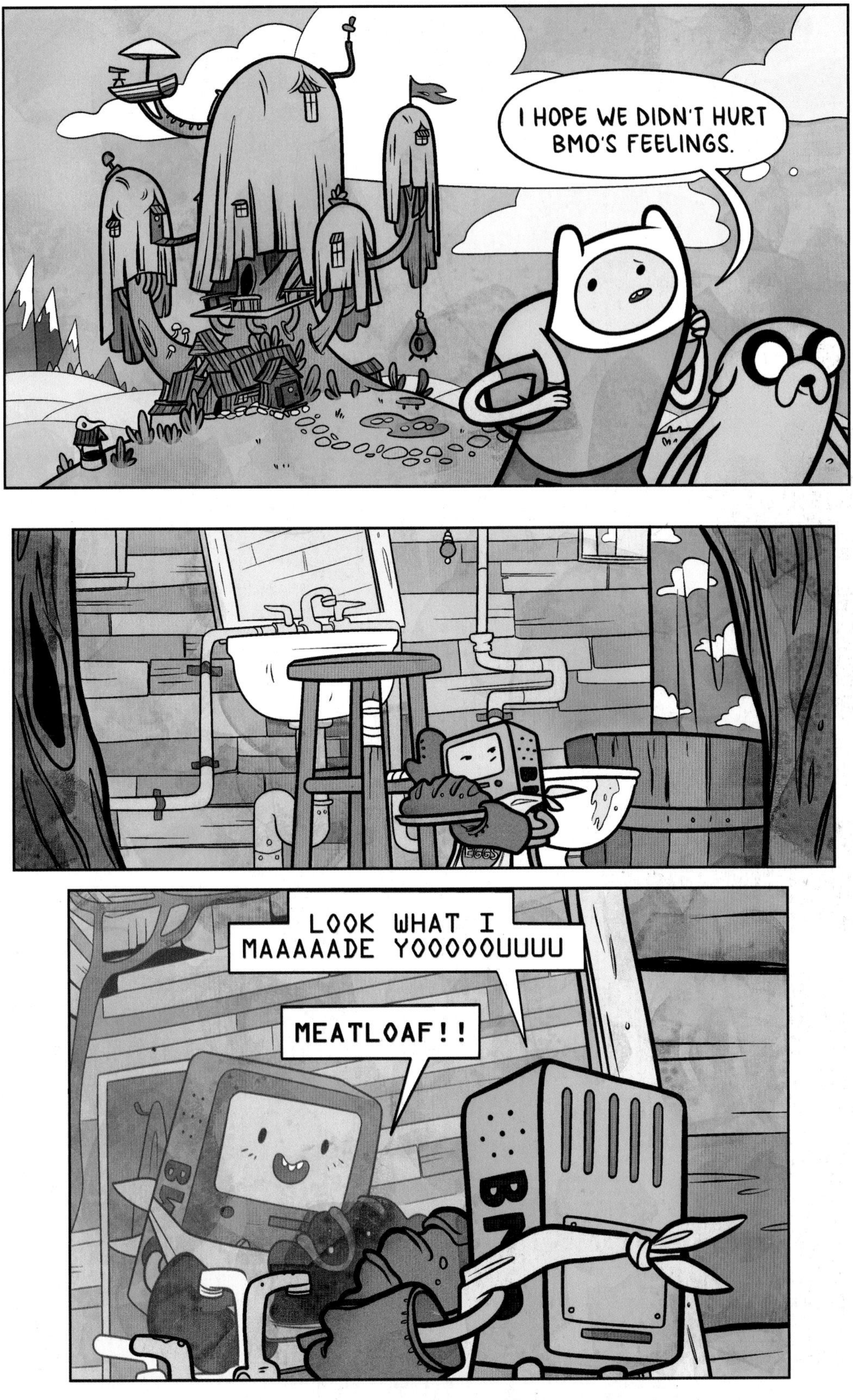
I HOPE WE DIDN'T HURT BMO'S FEELINGS.
LOOK WHAT I MAAAAADE YOOOOOUUUU
MEATLOAF!!

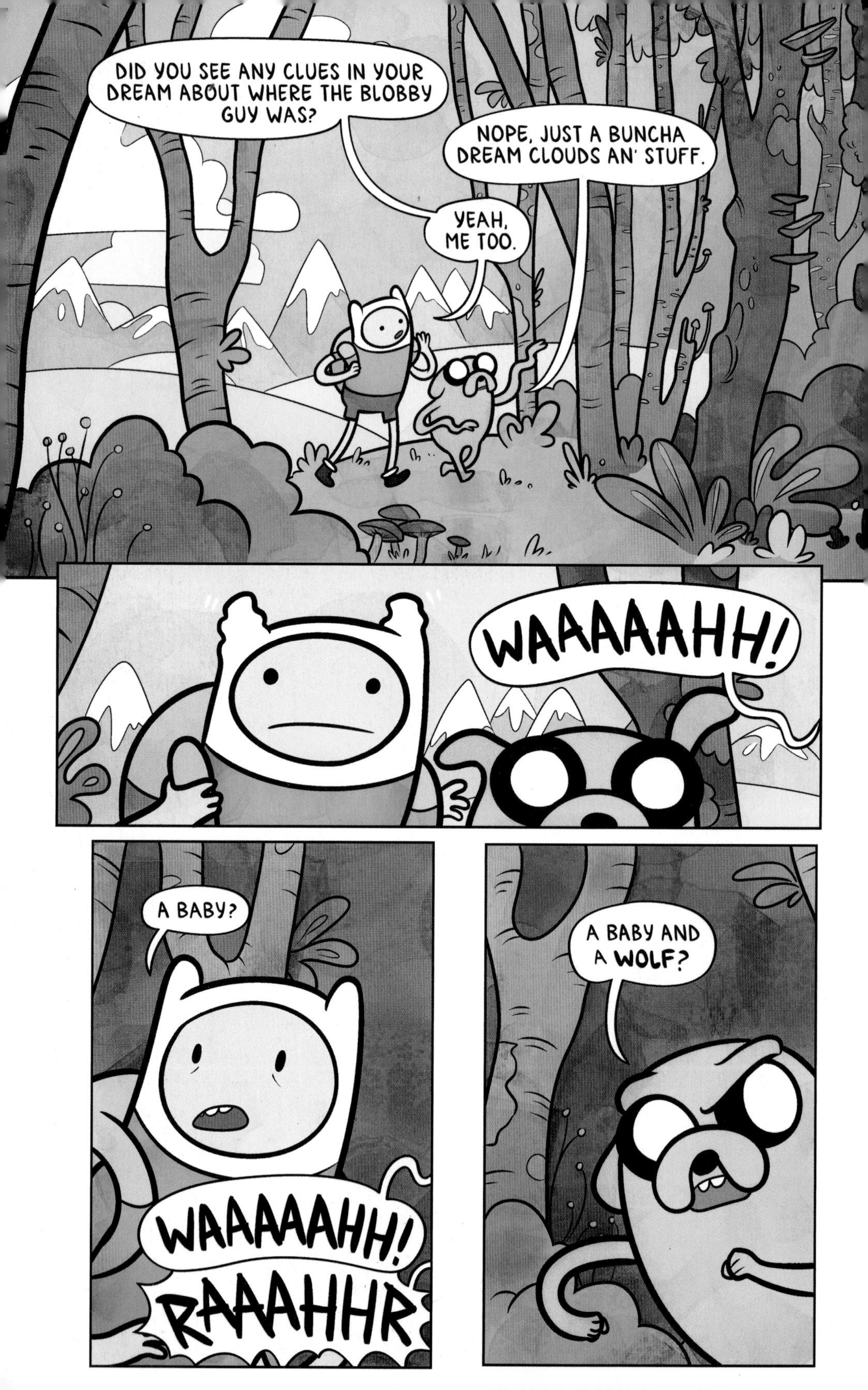
DID YOU SEE ANY CLUES IN YOUR DREAM ABOUT WHERE THE BLOBBY GUY WAS?
NOPE, JUST A BUNCHA DREAM CLOUDS AN' STUFF.
YEAH, ME TOO.
WAAAAAHH!
A BABY?
WAAAAAHH!
RAAAHHR
A BABY AND A **WOLF**?

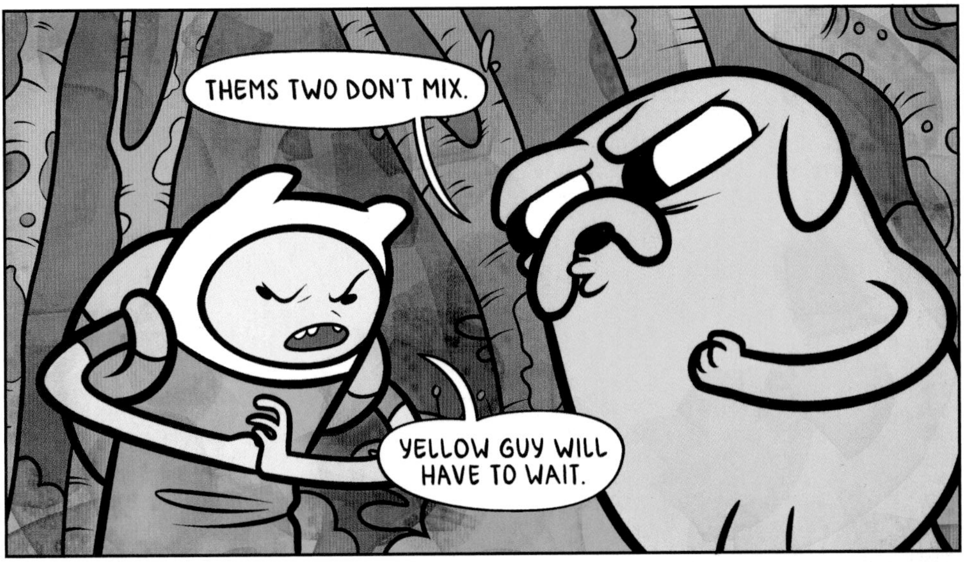
THEMS TWO DON'T MIX.
YELLOW GUY WILL HAVE TO WAIT.

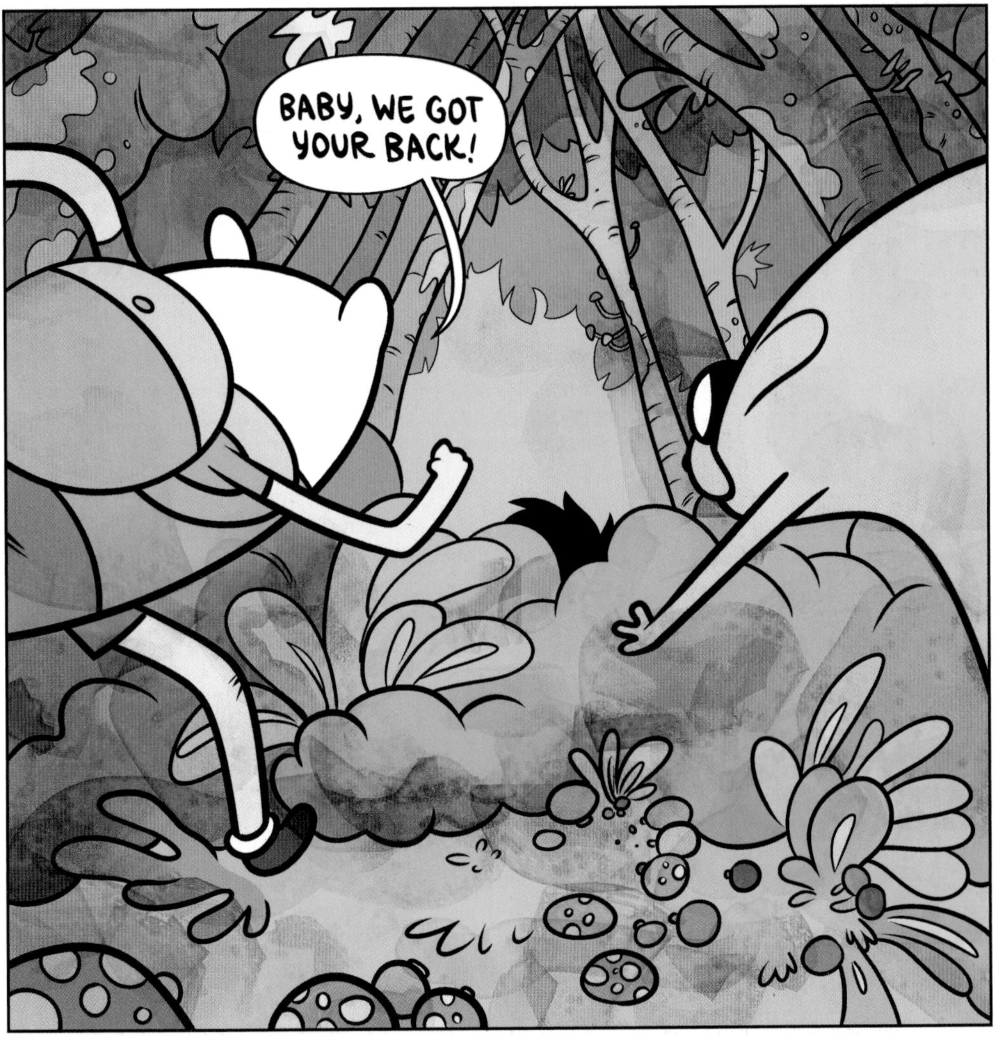
BABY, WE GOT YOUR BACK!

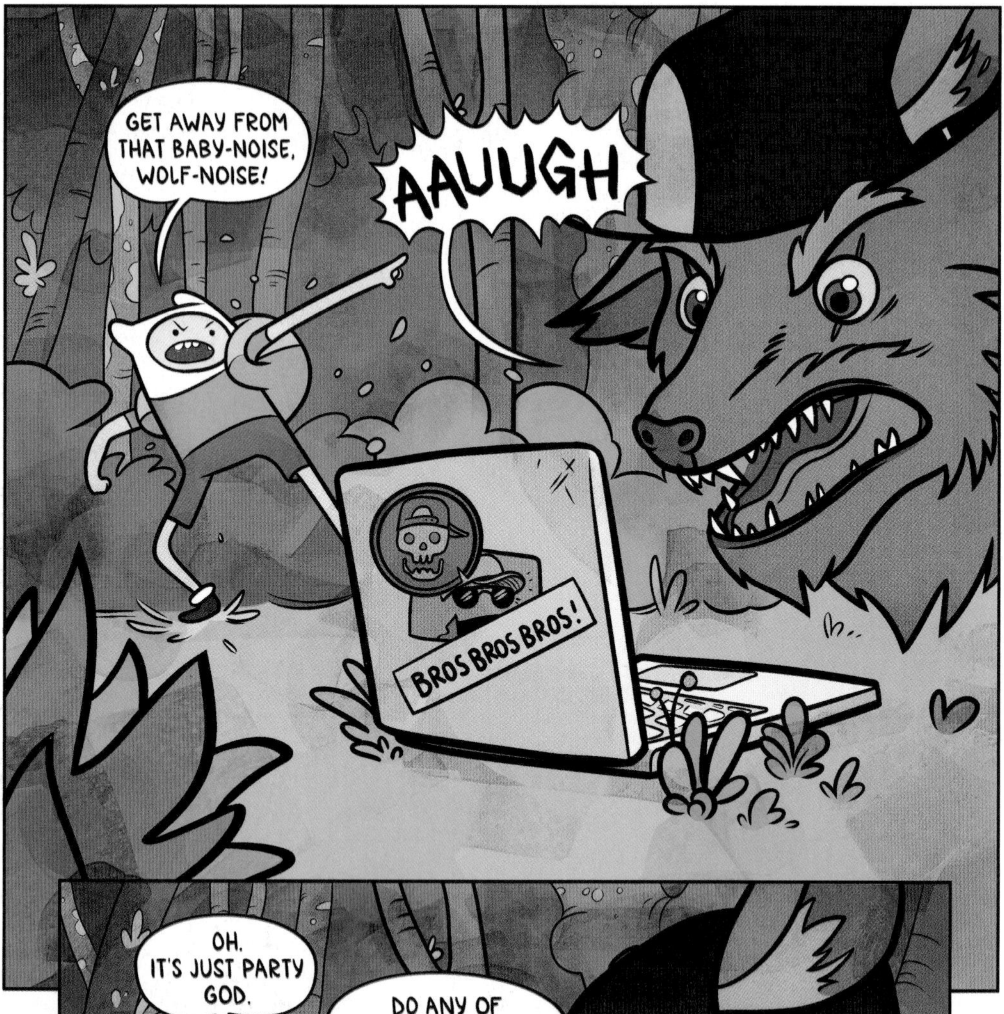
GET AWAY FROM THAT BABY-NOISE, WOLF-NOISE!
AAUUGH
BROS BROS BROS!

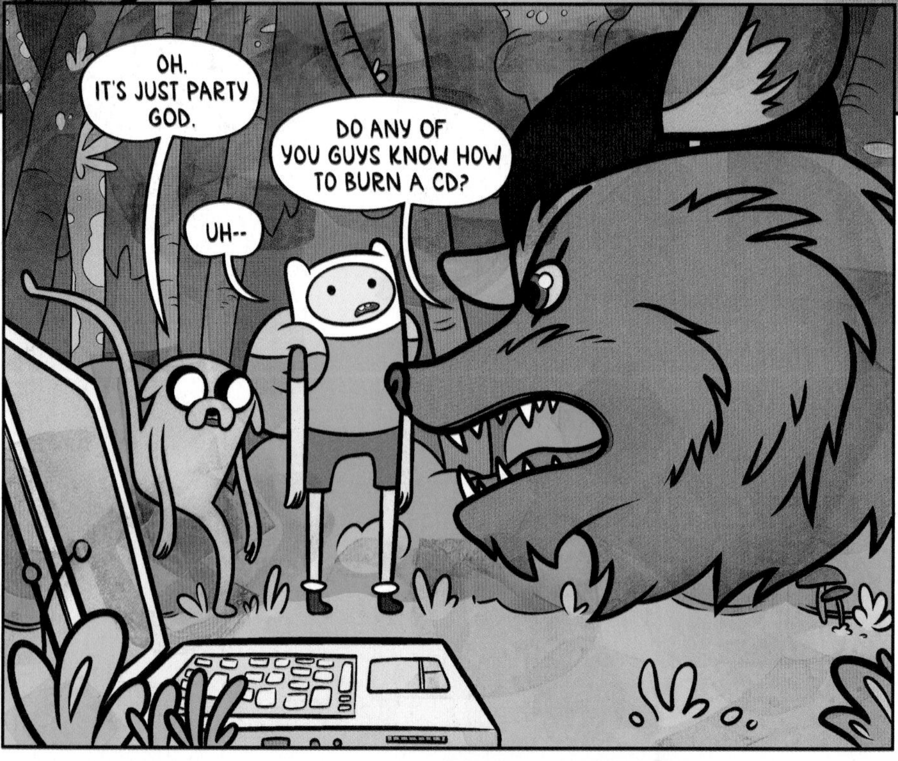
OH. IT'S JUST PARTY GOD.
UH--
DO ANY OF YOU GUYS KNOW HOW TO BURN A CD?

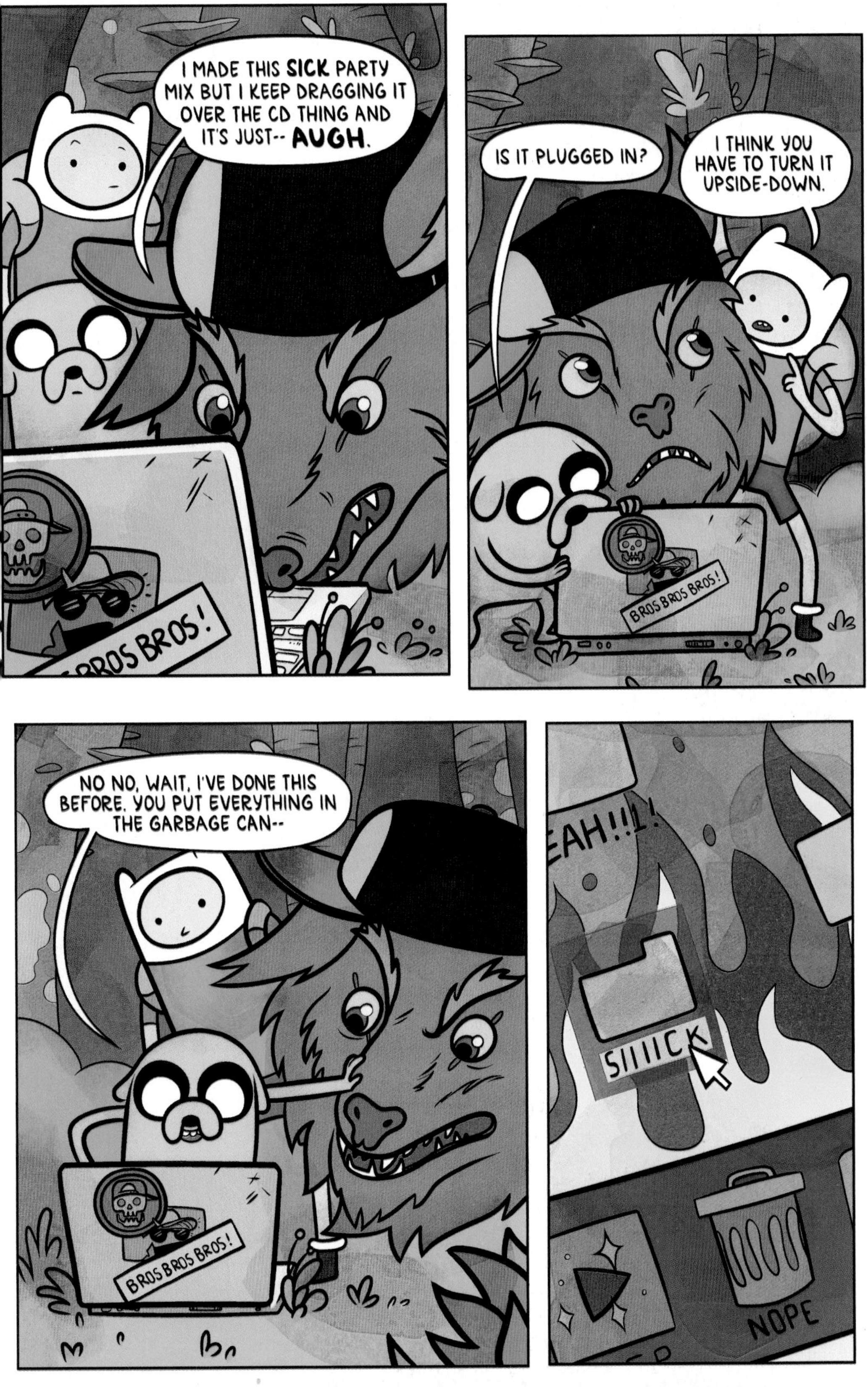

I MADE THIS **SICK** PARTY MIX BUT I KEEP DRAGGING IT OVER THE CD THING AND IT'S JUST-- **AUGH**.
BROS BROS!
IS IT PLUGGED IN?
I THINK YOU HAVE TO TURN IT UPSIDE-DOWN.
BROS BROS BROS!
NO NO, WAIT, I'VE DONE THIS BEFORE. YOU PUT EVERYTHING IN THE GARBAGE CAN--
BROS BROS BROS!
EAH!!1!
SIIICK
NOPE

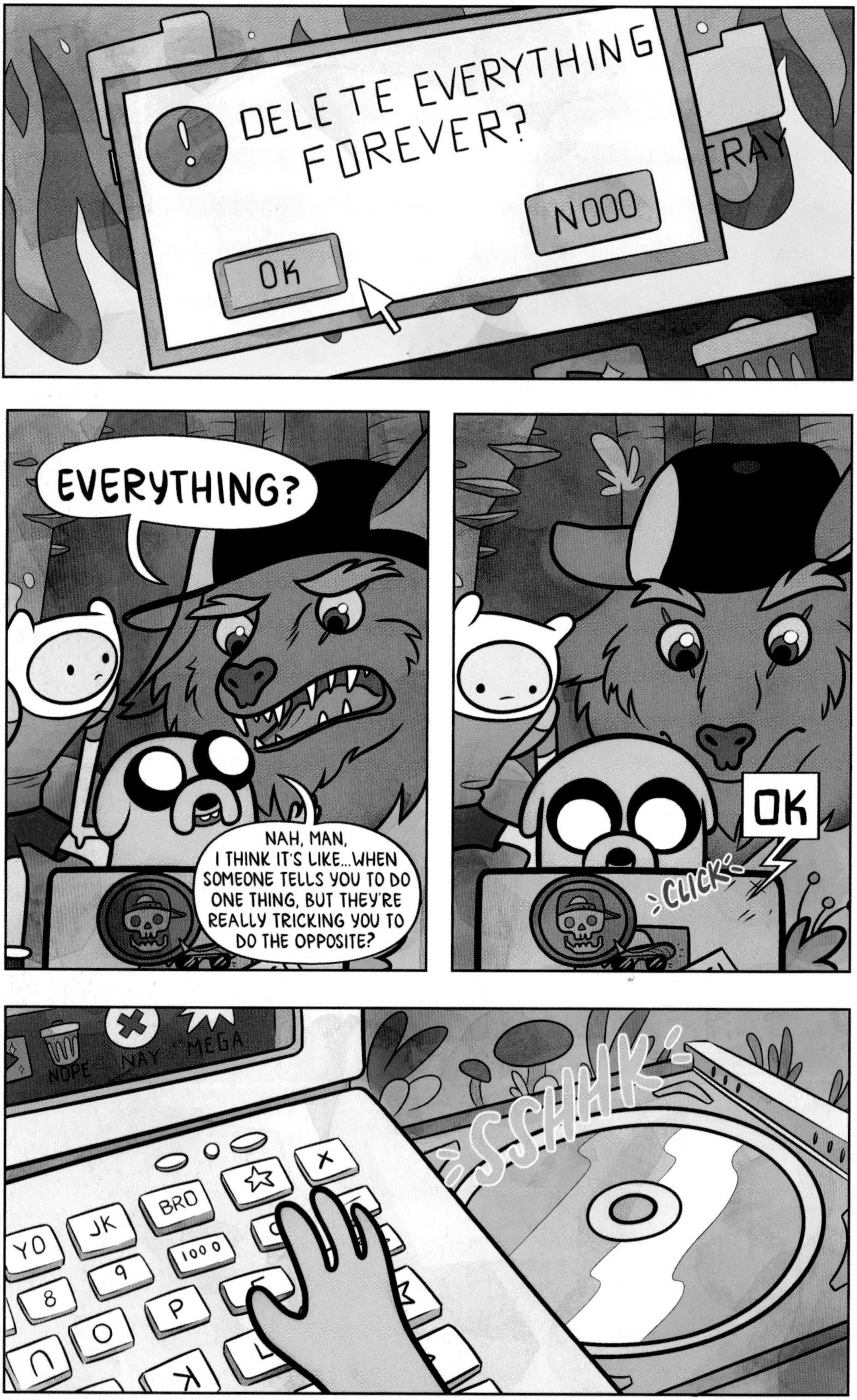
DELETE EVERYTHING FOREVER?
NOOO
OK
EVERYTHING?
NAH, MAN, I THINK IT'S LIKE...WHEN SOMEONE TELLS YOU TO DO ONE THING, BUT THEY'RE REALLY TRICKING YOU TO DO THE OPPOSITE?
OK
CLICK
NOPE
NAY
MEGA
SSHHK
BRO
JK
YO

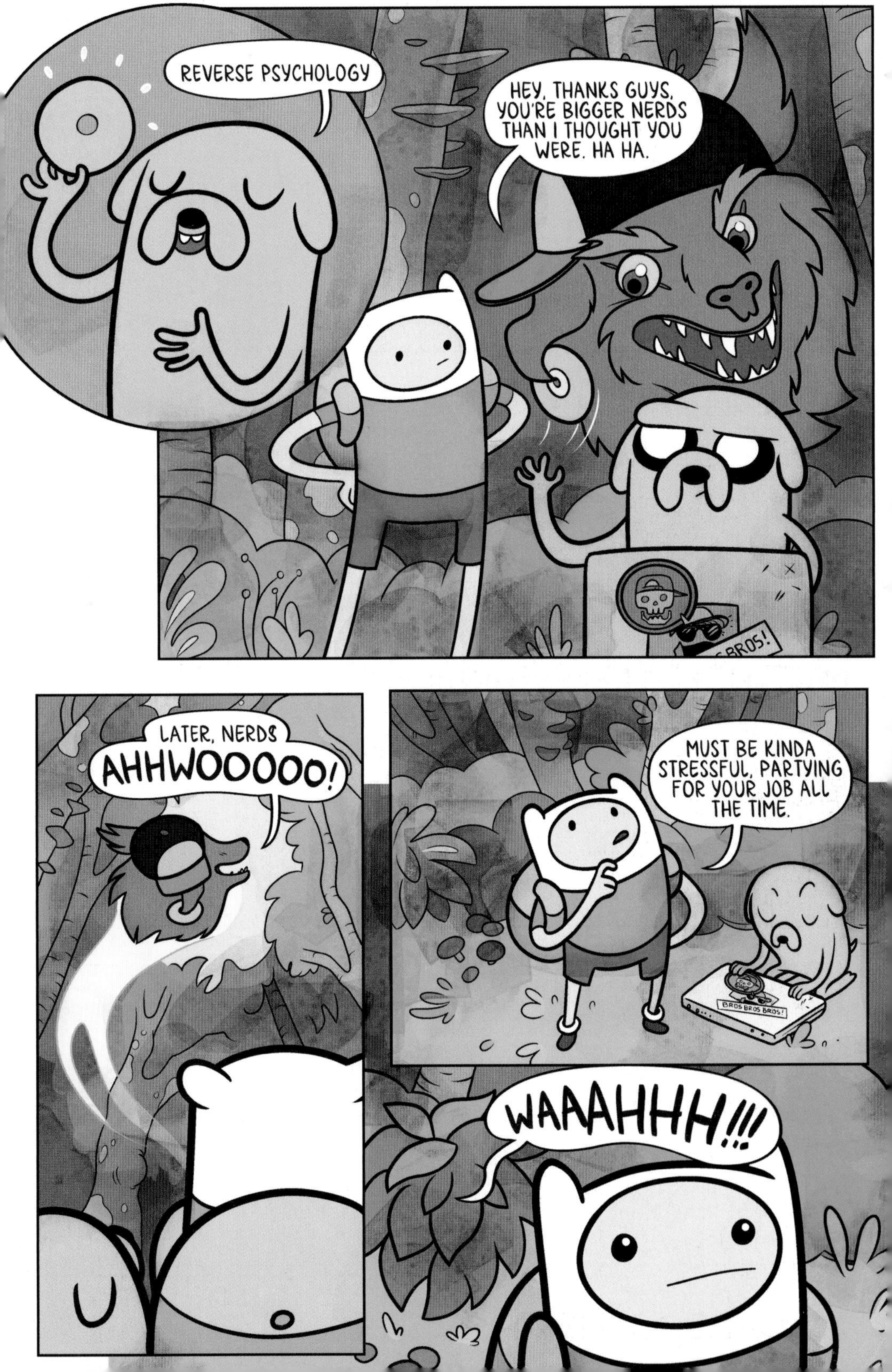
REVERSE PSYCHOLOGY
HEY, THANKS GUYS, YOU'RE BIGGER NERDS THAN I THOUGHT YOU WERE. HA HA.
BROS!
LATER, NERDS
AHHWOOOOO!
MUST BE KINDA STRESSFUL, PARTYING FOR YOUR JOB ALL THE TIME.
BROS BROS BROS!
WAAAHHH!!!

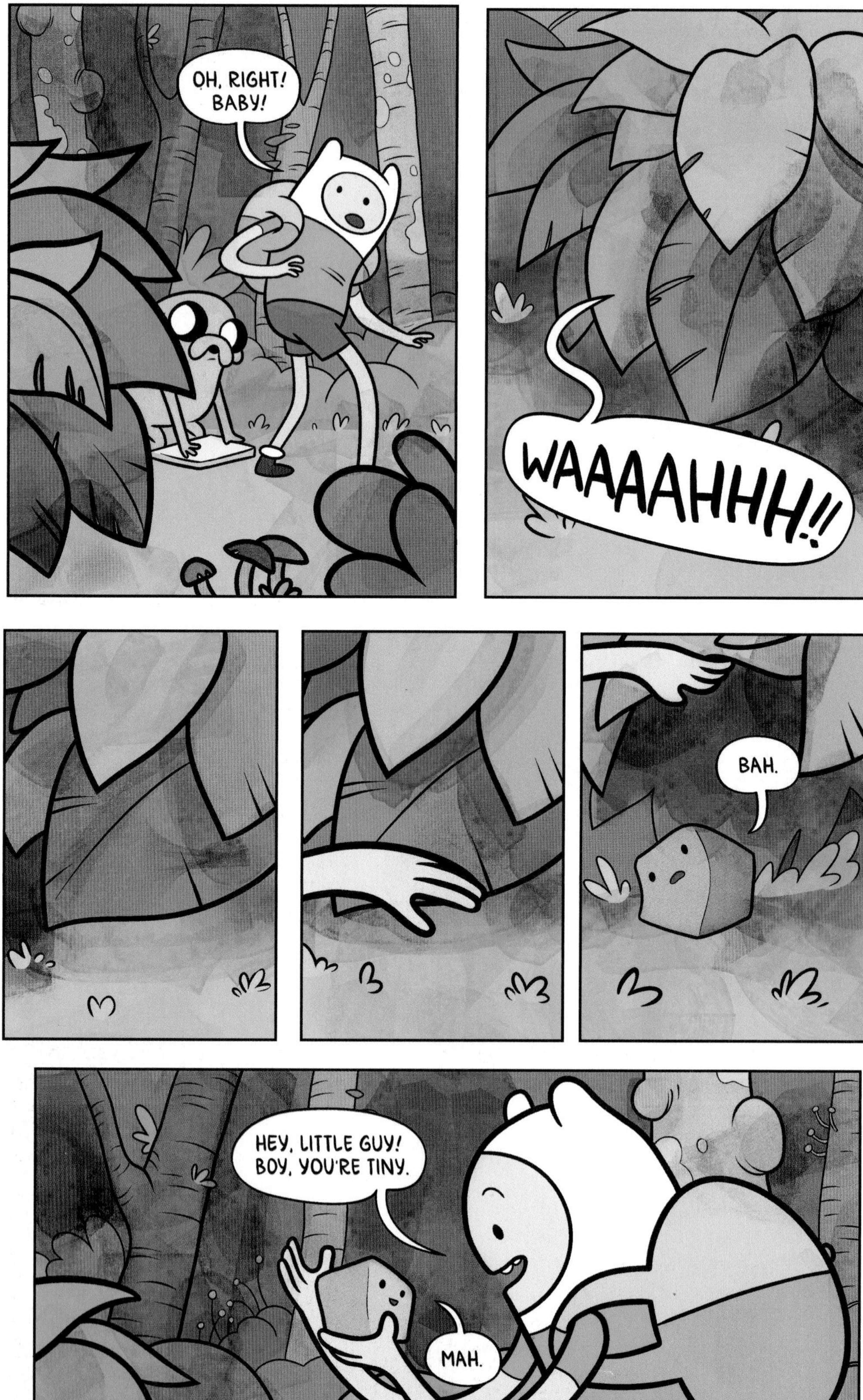
OH, RIGHT! BABY!
WAAAAHHH!!
BAH.
HEY, LITTLE GUY! BOY, YOU'RE TINY.
MAH.

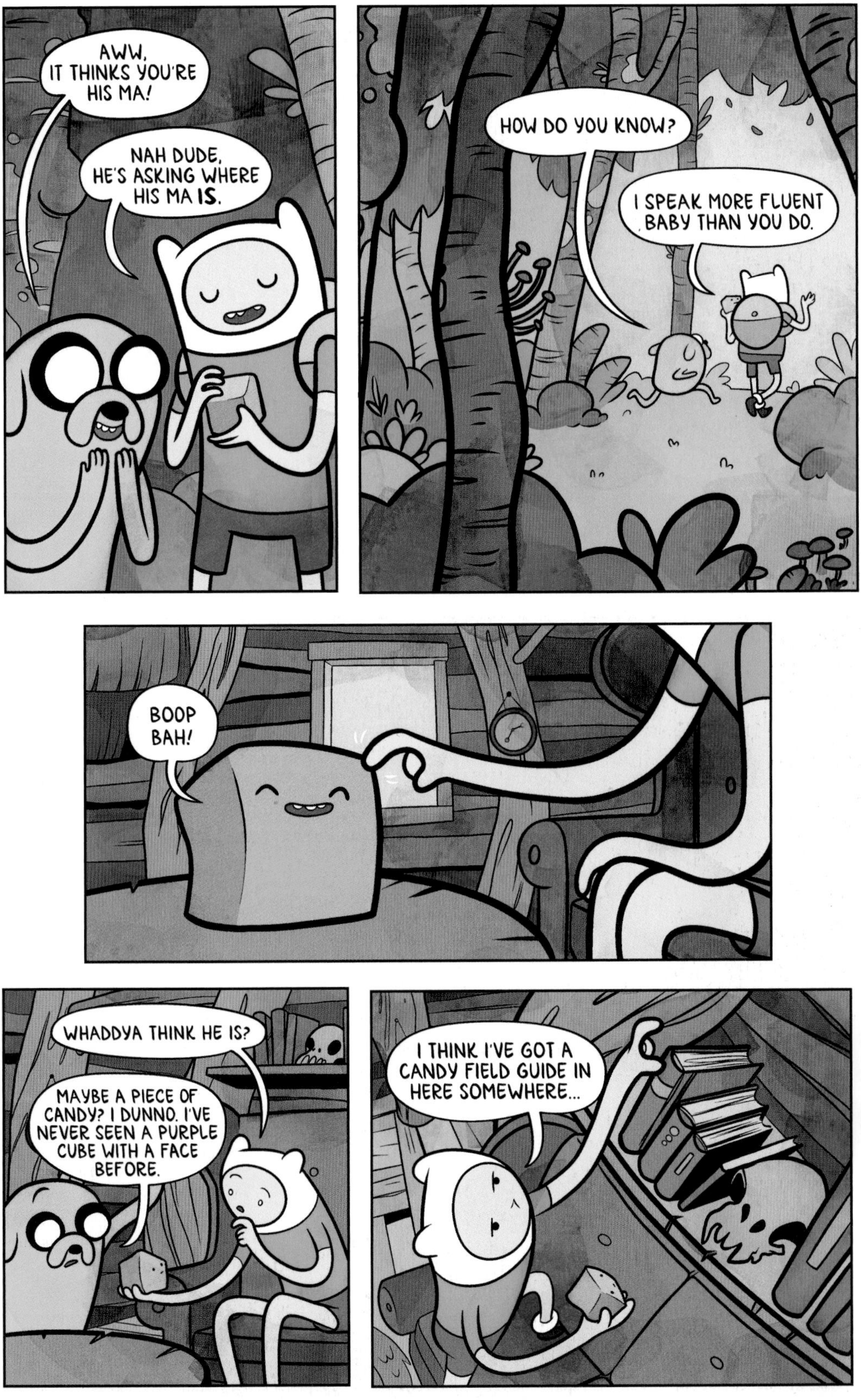
AWW, IT THINKS YOU'RE HIS MA!
NAH DUDE, HE'S ASKING WHERE HIS MA **IS**.
HOW DO YOU KNOW?
I SPEAK MORE FLUENT BABY THAN YOU DO.
BOOP BAH!
WHADDYA THINK HE IS?
MAYBE A PIECE OF CANDY? I DUNNO. I'VE NEVER SEEN A PURPLE CUBE WITH A FACE BEFORE.
I THINK I'VE GOT A CANDY FIELD GUIDE IN HERE SOMEWHERE...

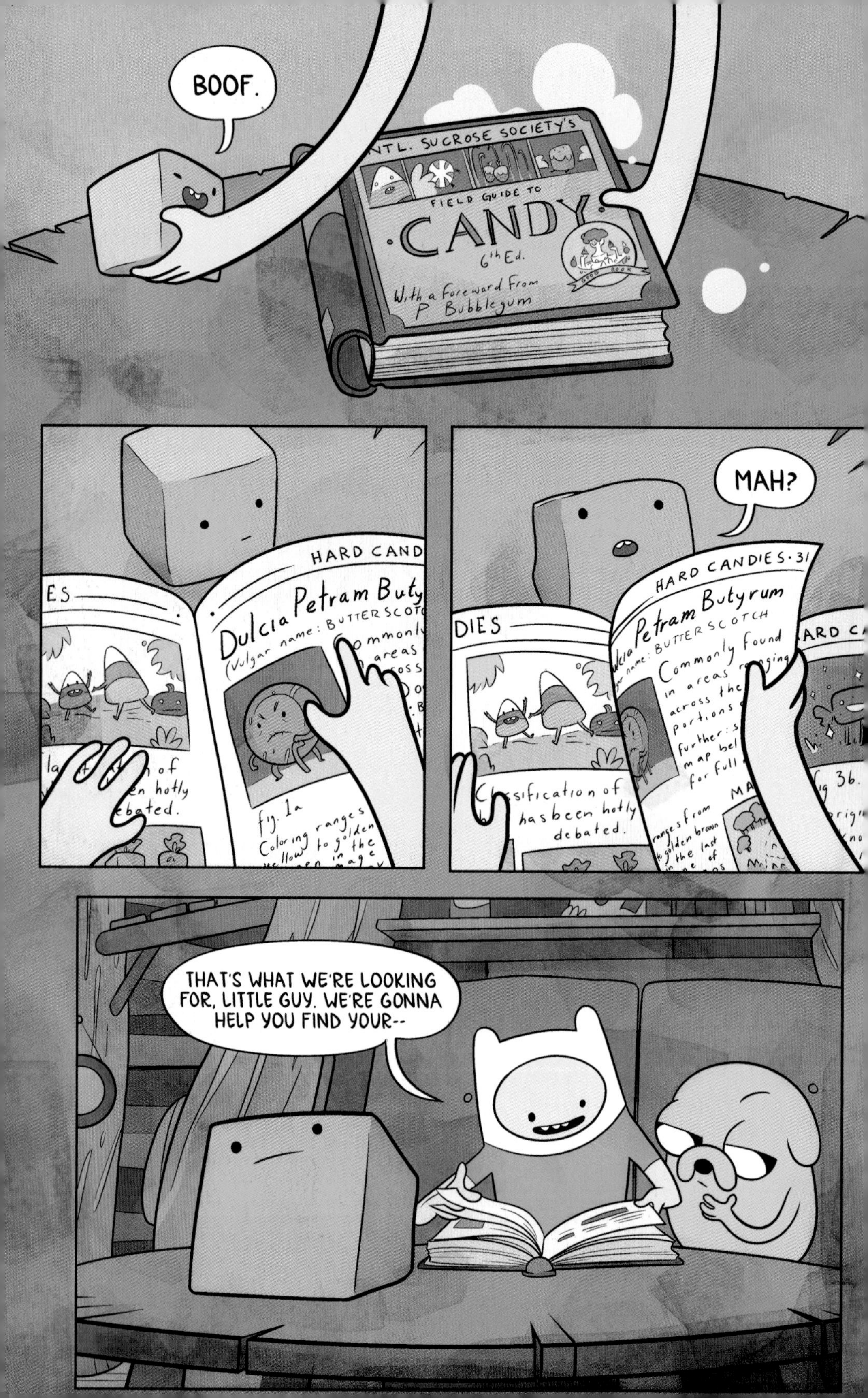
BOOF.
NTL. SUCROSE SOCIETY'S
FIELD GUIDE TO
CANDY
6th Ed.
With a Foreward From P. Bubblegum
GOOD BOOK
HARD CANDIES · 31
Dulcia Petram Butyrum
(Vulgar name: BUTTERSCOTCH
Commonly found in areas ranging across the
Classification of has been hotly debated.
fig. 1a
MAH?
THAT'S WHAT WE'RE LOOKING FOR, LITTLE GUY. WE'RE GONNA HELP YOU FIND YOUR--

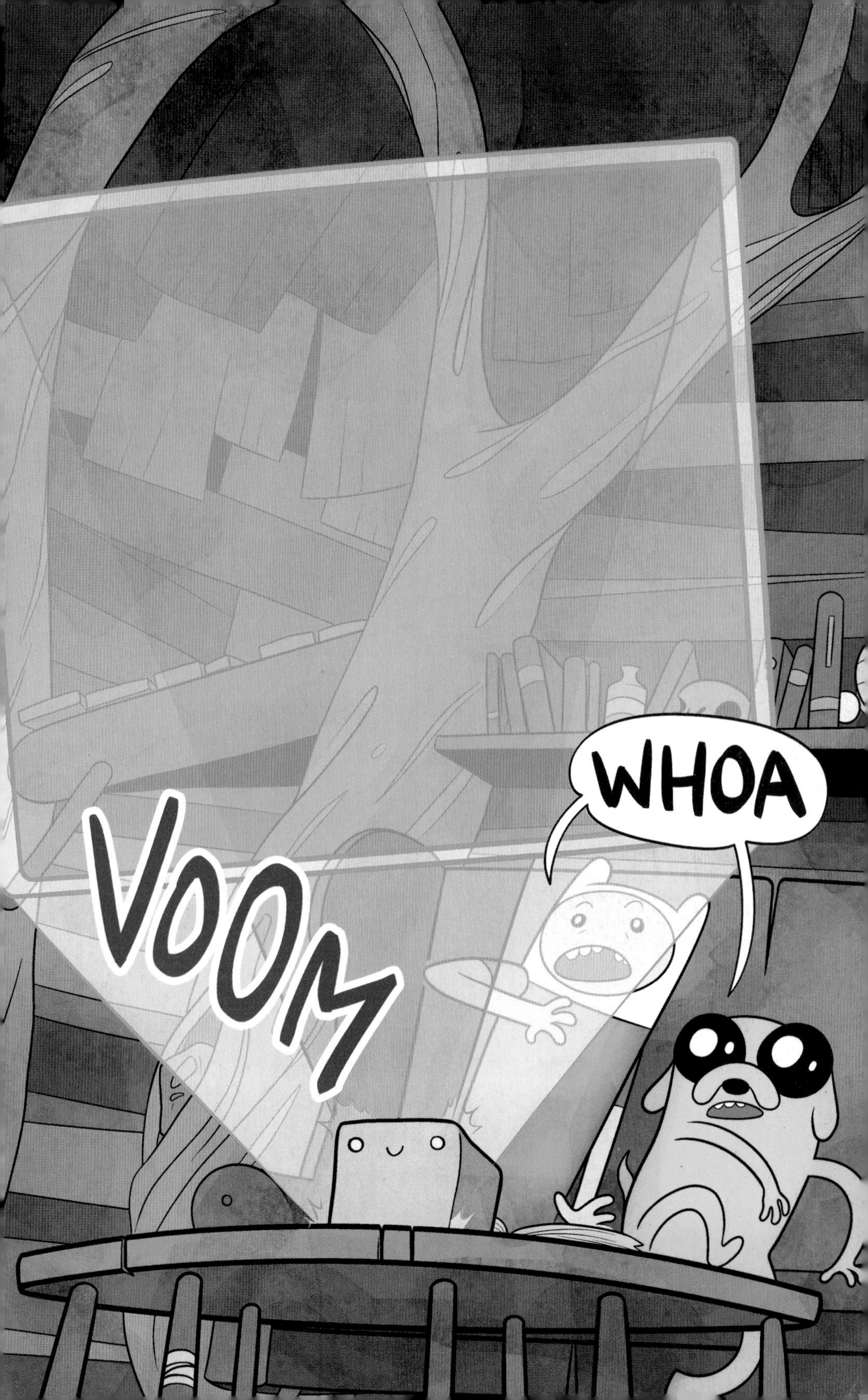
VOOM
WHOA

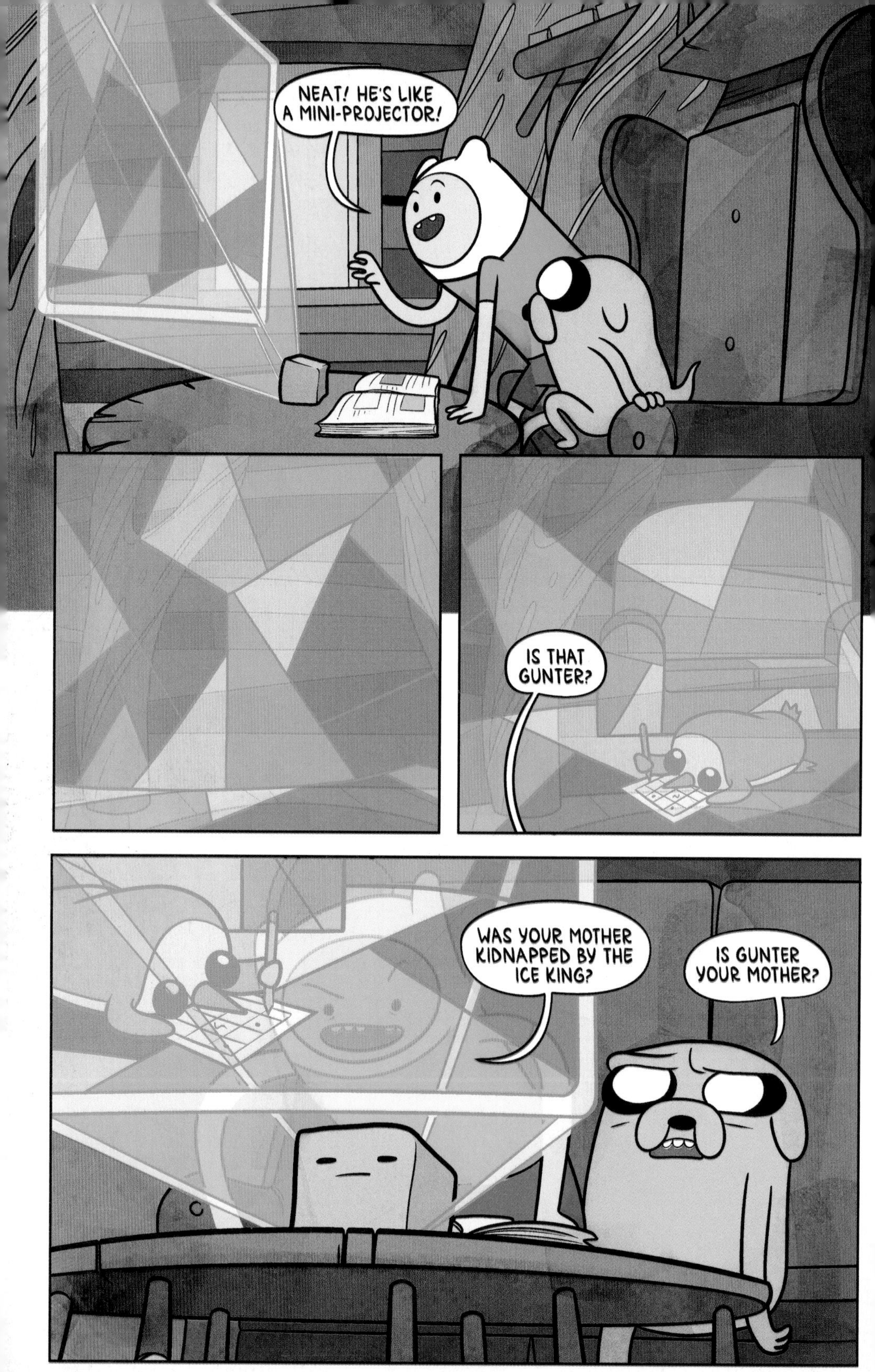
NEAT! HE'S LIKE A MINI-PROJECTOR!
IS THAT GUNTER?
WAS YOUR MOTHER KIDNAPPED BY THE ICE KING?
IS GUNTER YOUR MOTHER?

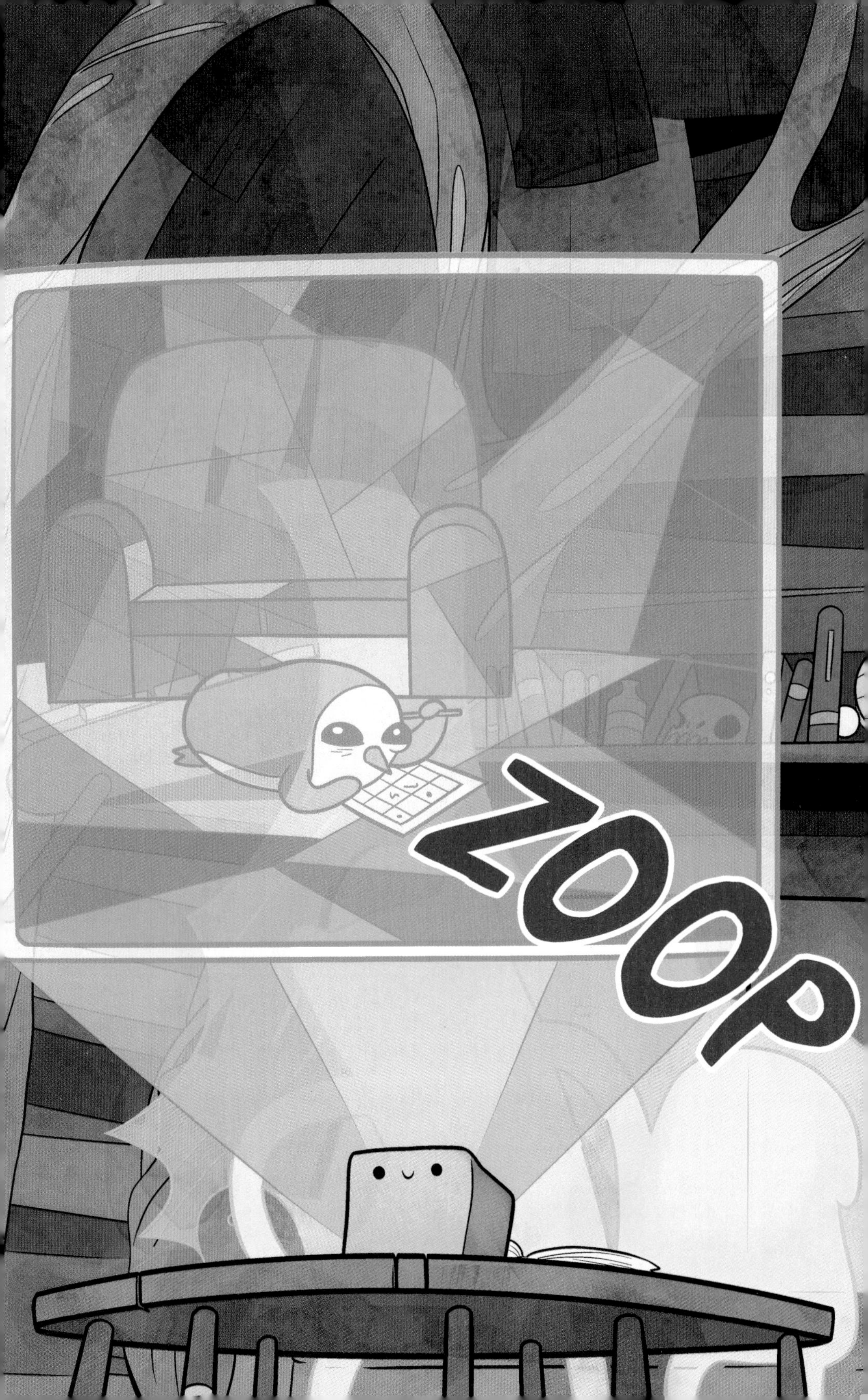
ZOOP

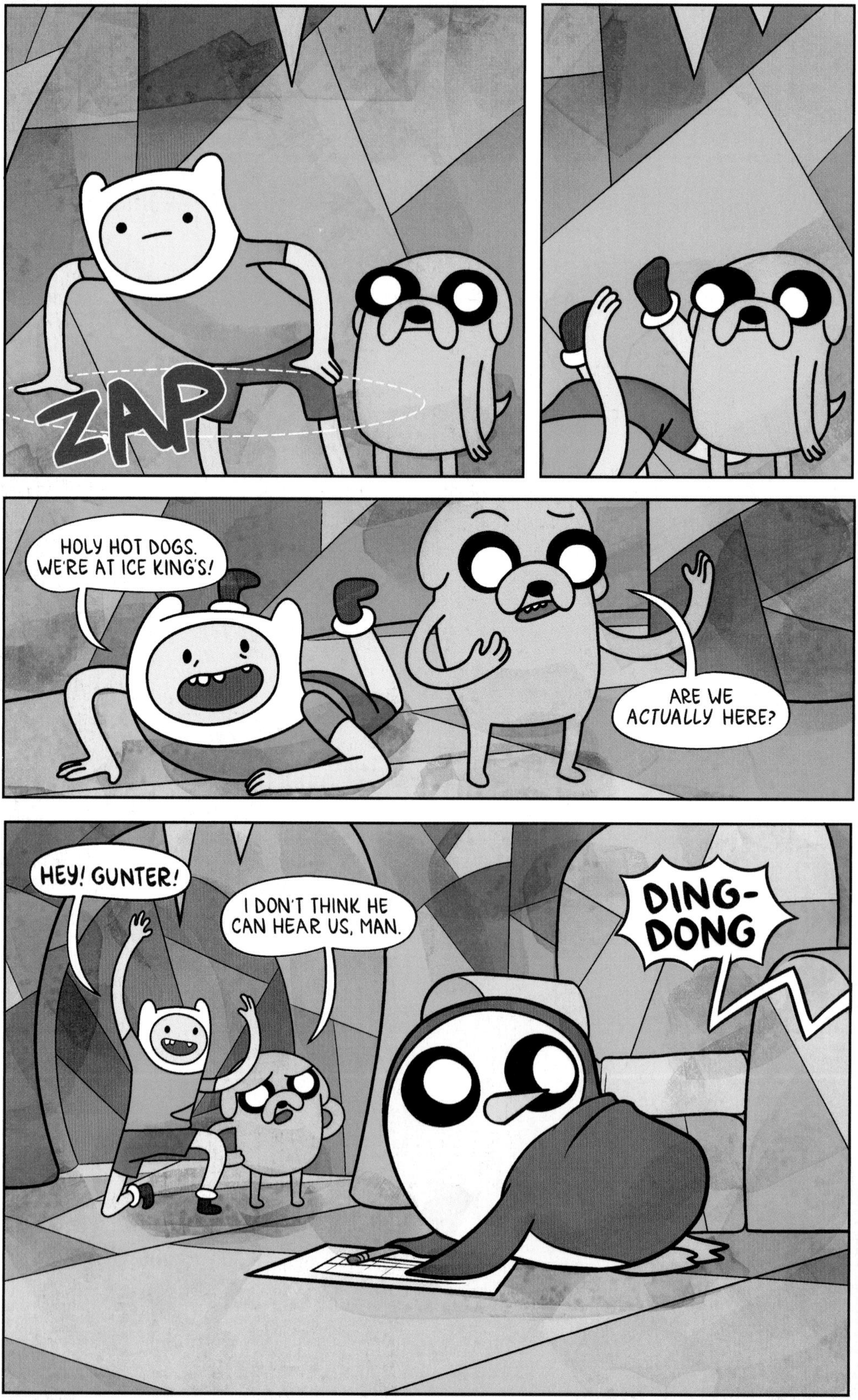
ZAP
HOLY HOT DOGS. WE'RE AT ICE KING'S!
ARE WE ACTUALLY HERE?
HEY! GUNTER!
I DON'T THINK HE CAN HEAR US, MAN.
DING-DONG

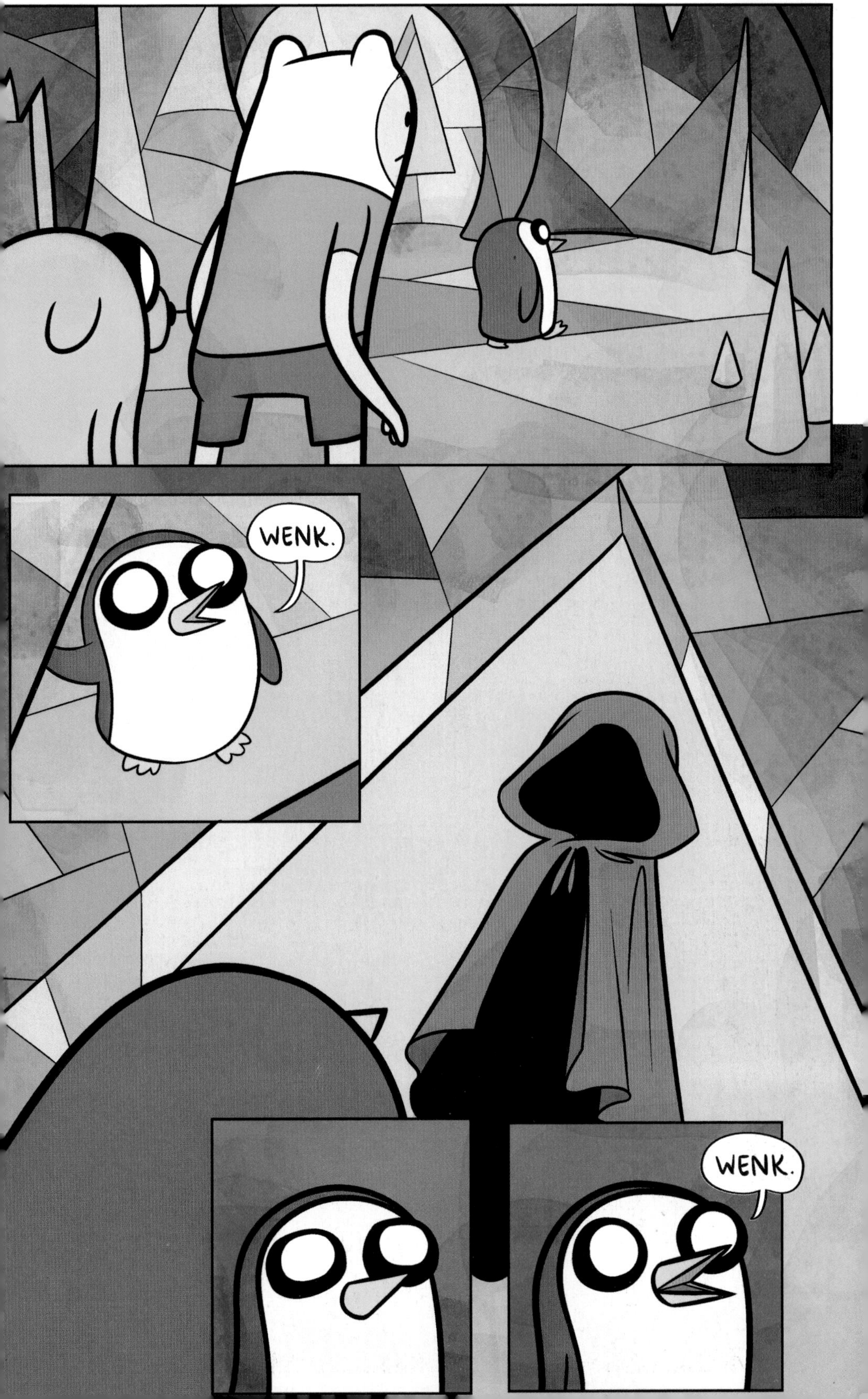
WENK.
WENK.

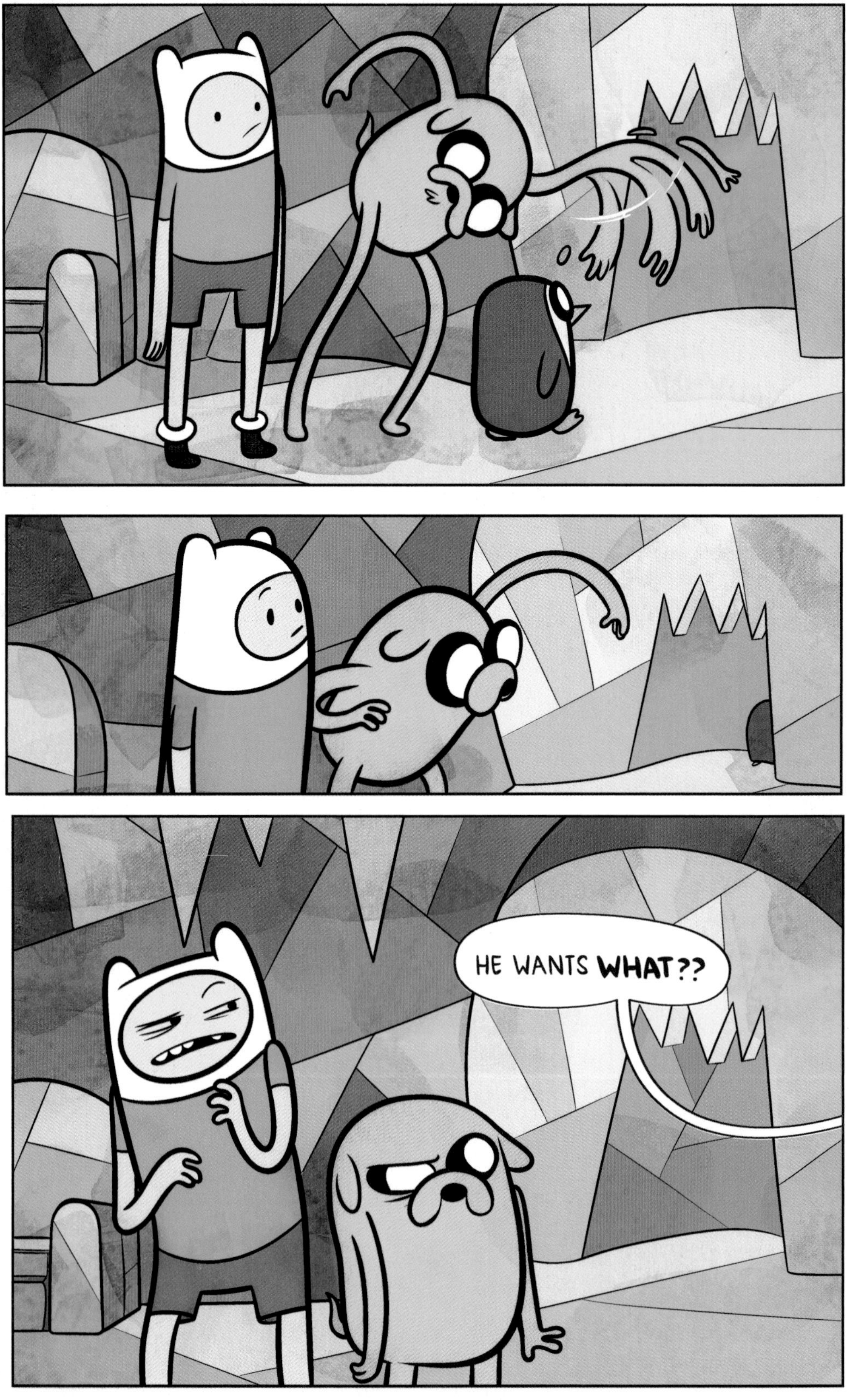
HE WANTS **WHAT**??

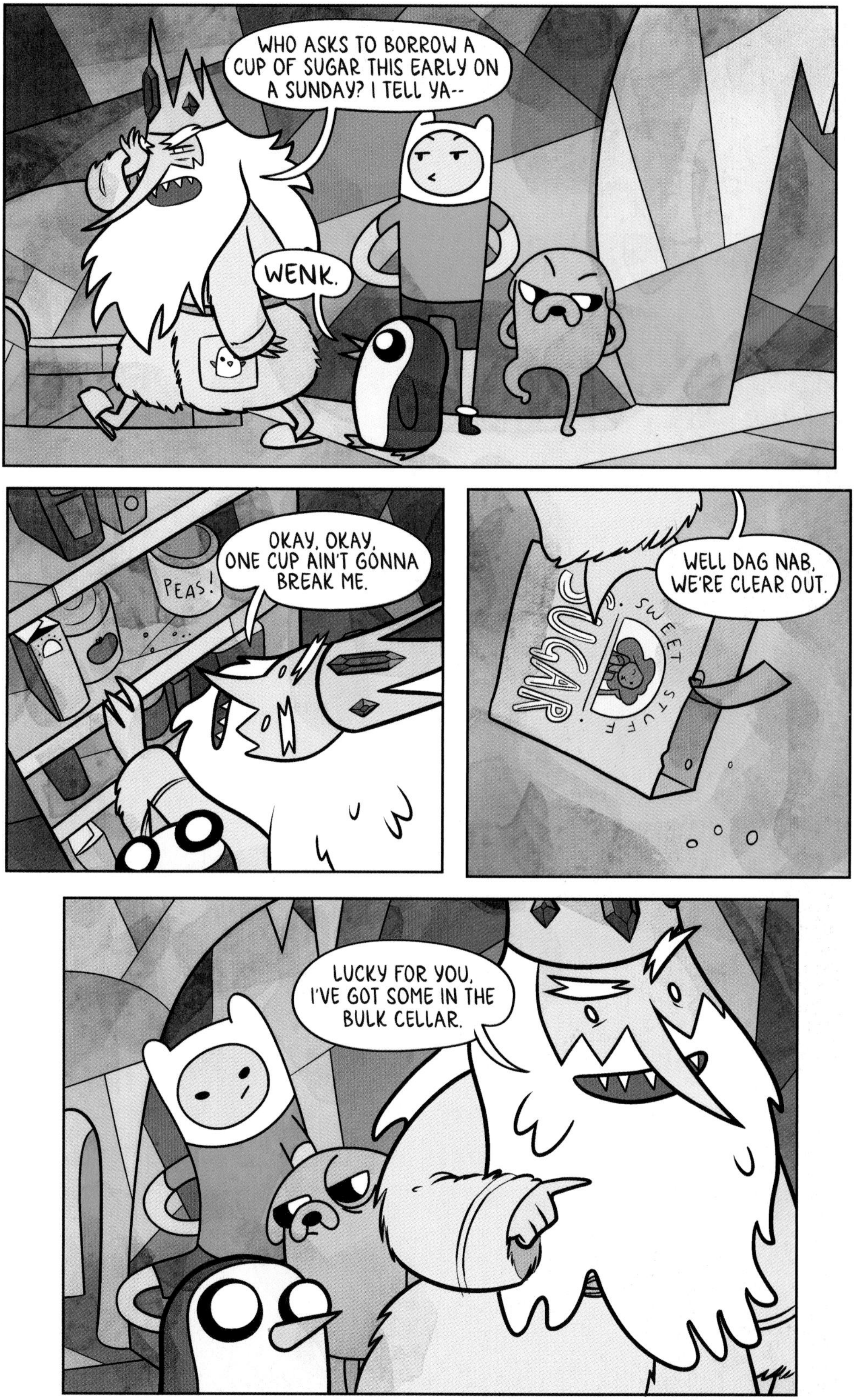
WHO ASKS TO BORROW A CUP OF SUGAR THIS EARLY ON A SUNDAY? I TELL YA--
WENK.
OKAY, OKAY, ONE CUP AIN'T GONNA BREAK ME.
PEAS!
WELL DAG NAB, WE'RE CLEAR OUT.
SWEET STUFF
SUGAR
LUCKY FOR YOU, I'VE GOT SOME IN THE BULK CELLAR.

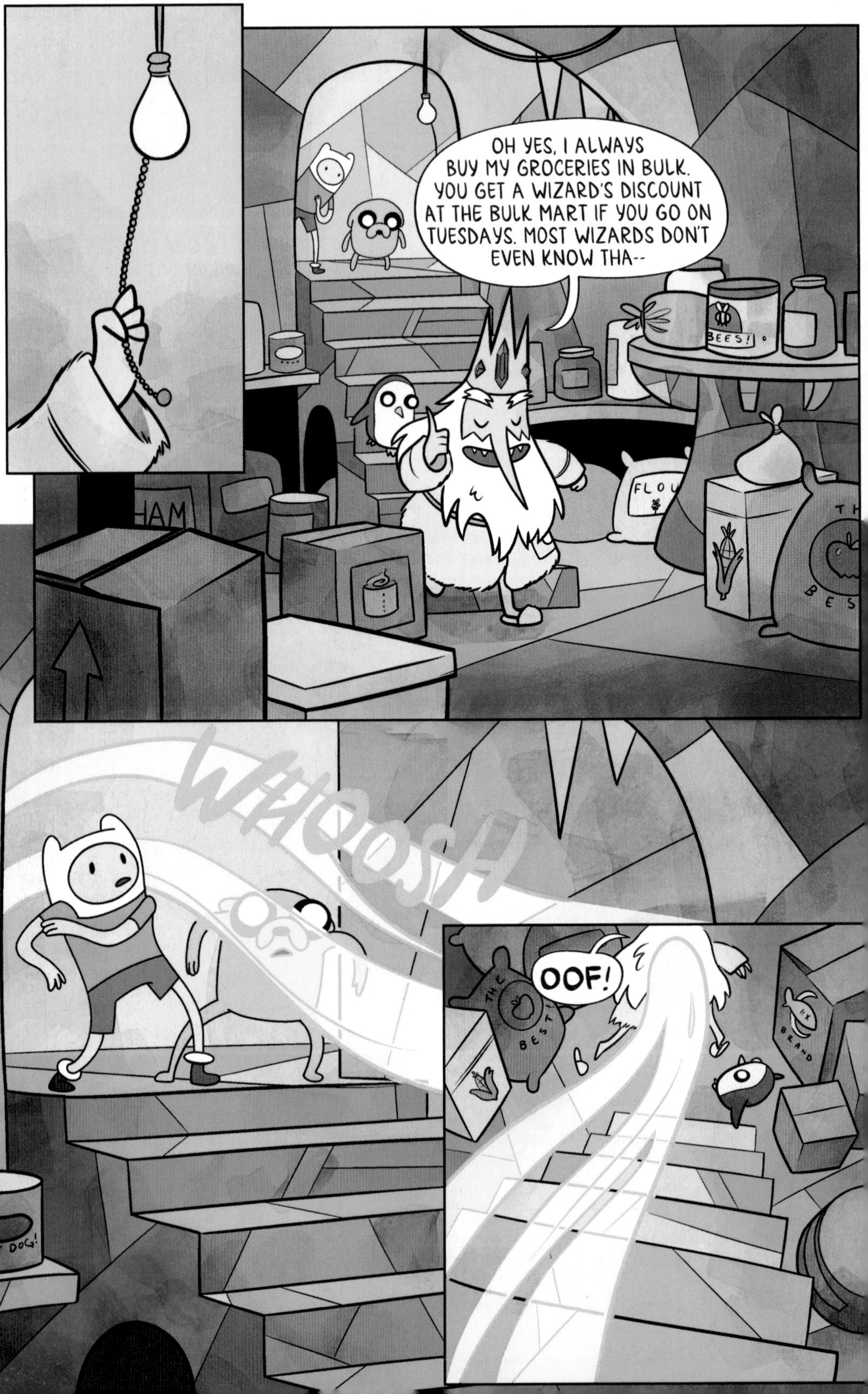
OH YES, I ALWAYS BUY MY GROCERIES IN BULK. YOU GET A WIZARD'S DISCOUNT AT THE BULK MART IF YOU GO ON TUESDAYS. MOST WIZARDS DON'T EVEN KNOW THA--
BEES!
HAM
WHOOSH
OOF!
THE BEST
BRAND
HOT DOG!

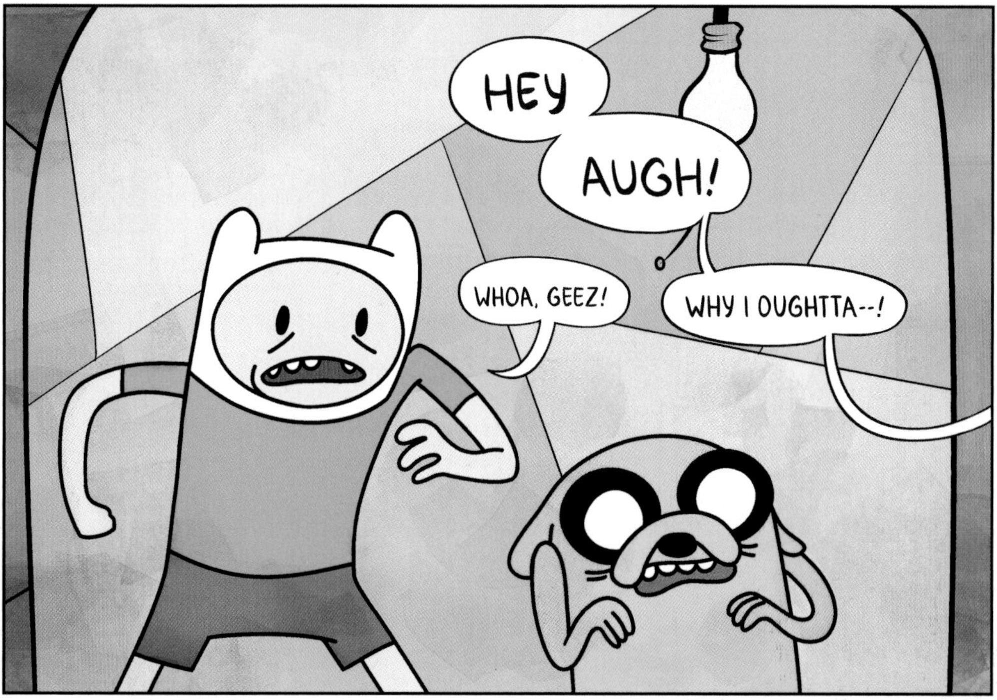
HEY
AUGH!
WHOA, GEEZ!
WHY I OUGHTTA--!

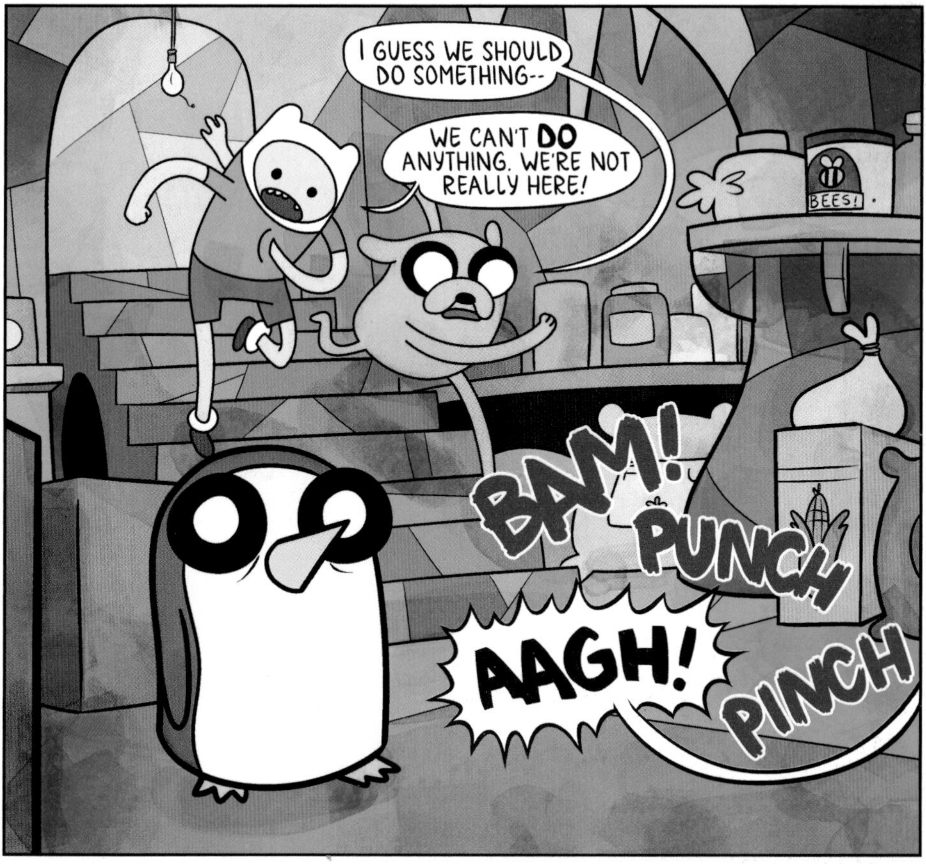
I GUESS WE SHOULD DO SOMETHING--
WE CAN'T **DO** ANYTHING. WE'RE NOT REALLY HERE!
BEES!
BAM!
PUNCH
AAGH!
PINCH

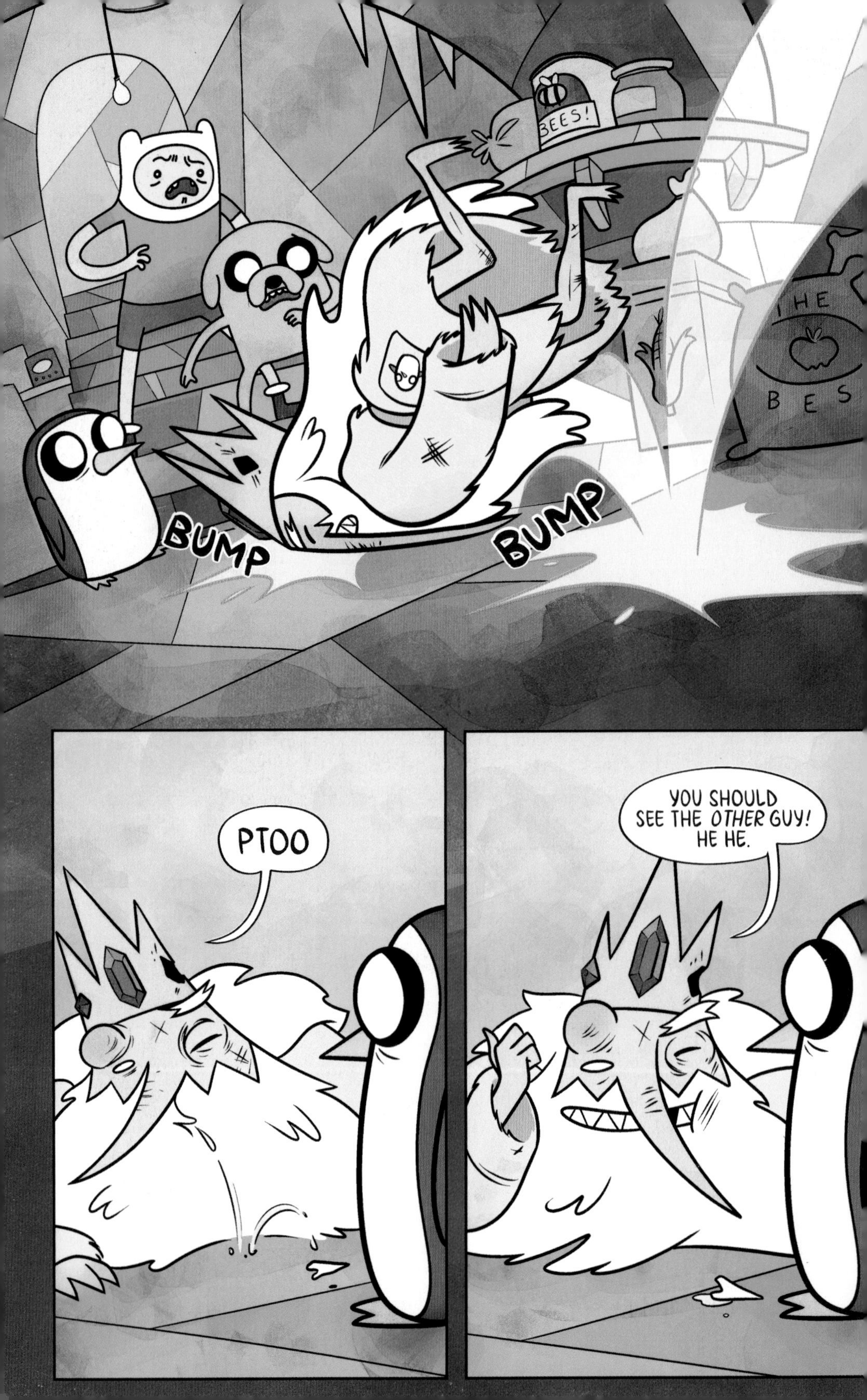
BEES!
THE
BES
BUMP
BUMP
PTOO
YOU SHOULD SEE THE *OTHER* GUY! HE HE.

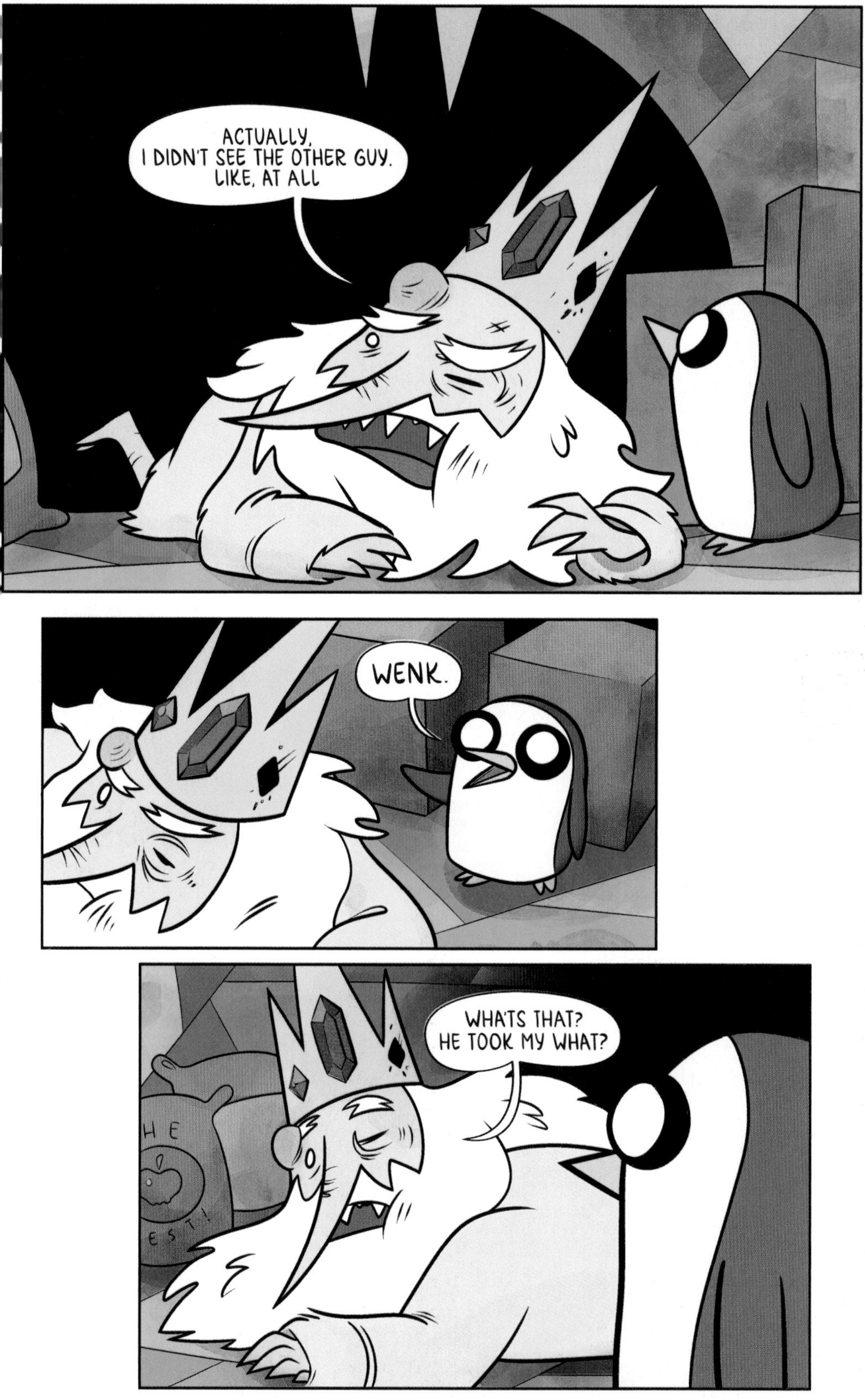
ACTUALLY, I DIDN'T SEE THE OTHER GUY. LIKE, AT ALL
WENK.
WHAT'S THAT? HE TOOK MY WHAT?

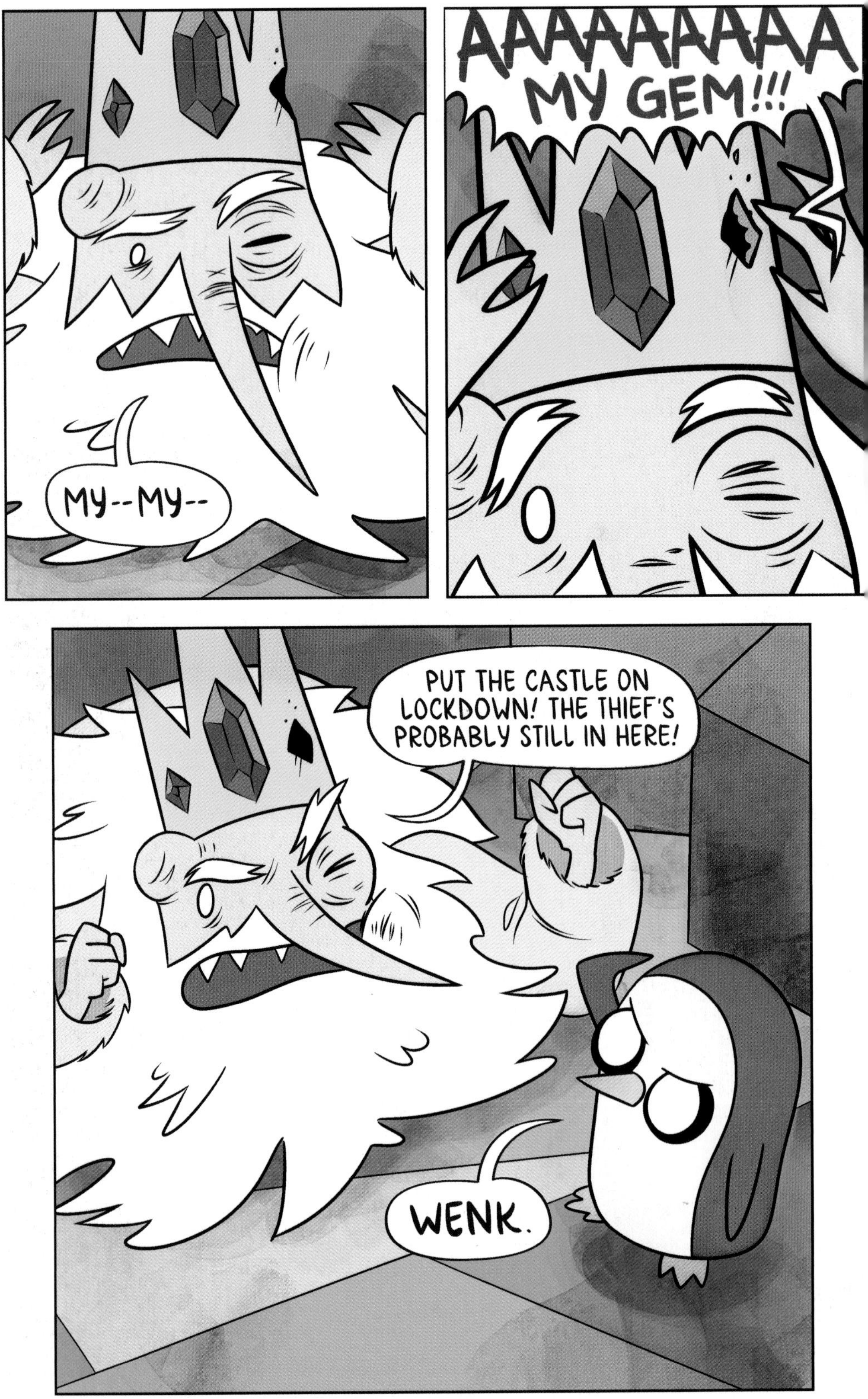
MY--MY--
AAAAAAAA MY GEM!!!
PUT THE CASTLE ON LOCKDOWN! THE THIEF'S PROBABLY STILL IN HERE!
WENK.

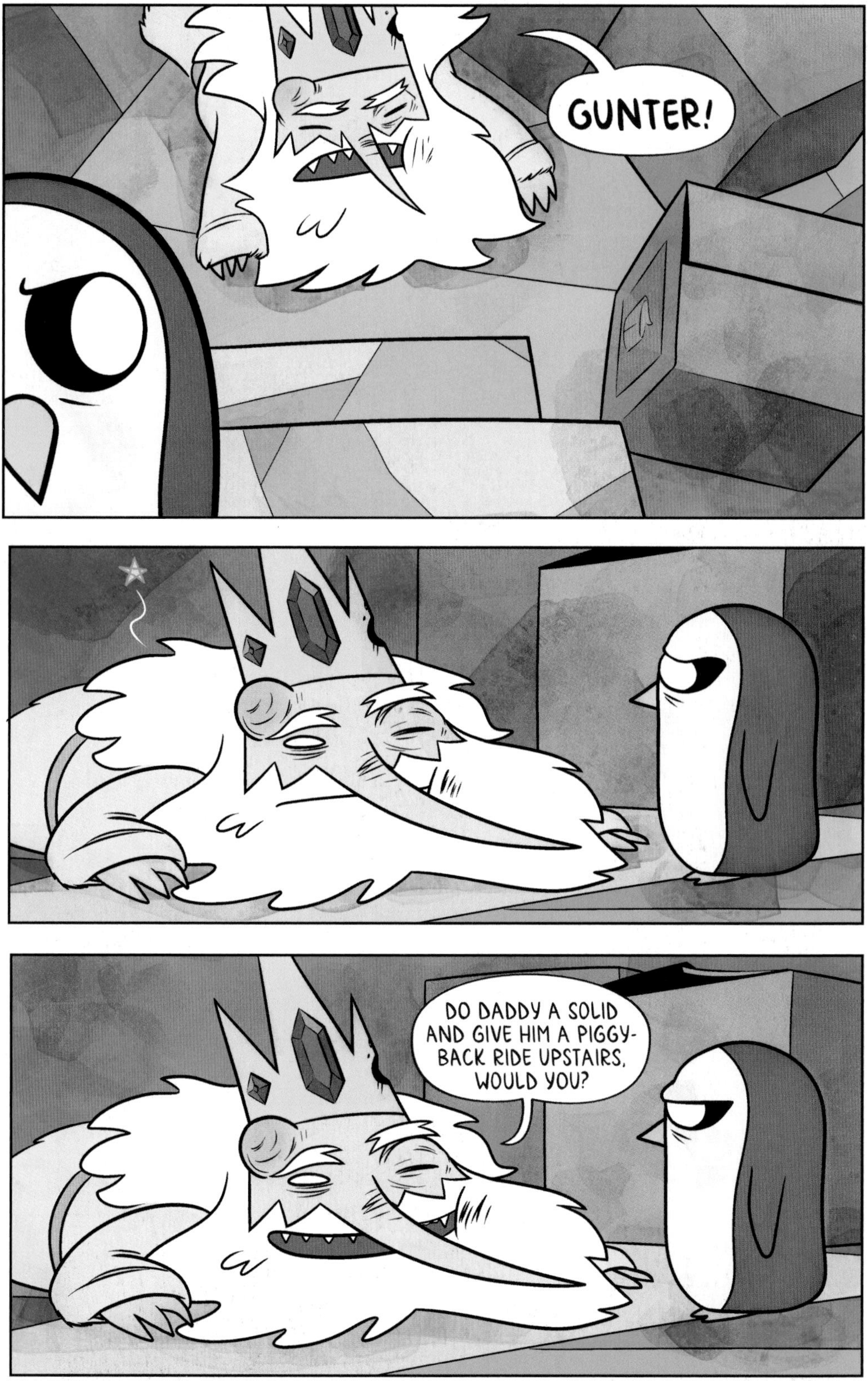
GUNTER!
DO DADDY A SOLID AND GIVE HIM A PIGGY-BACK RIDE UPSTAIRS, WOULD YOU?

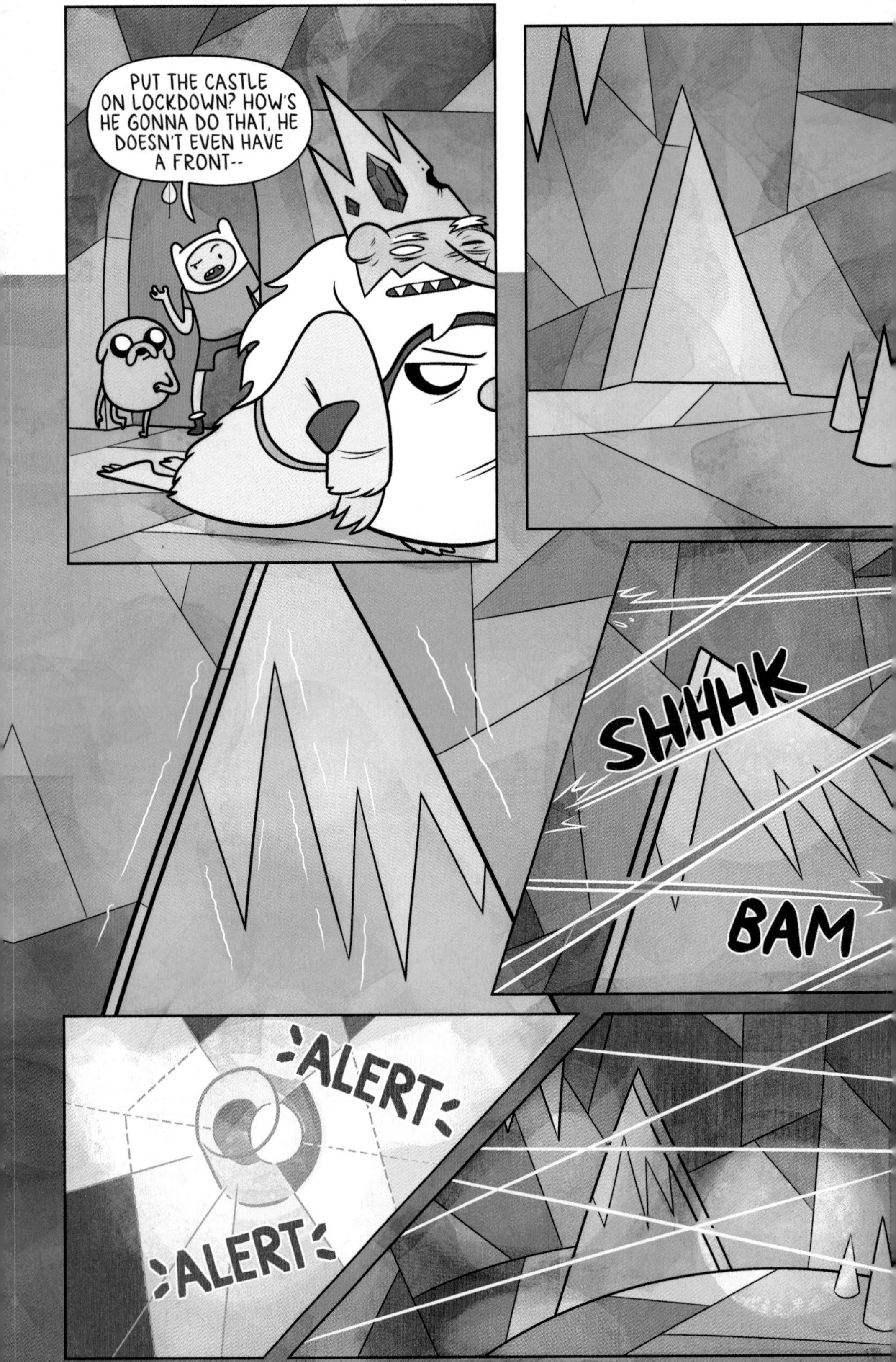
PUT THE CASTLE ON LOCKDOWN? HOW'S HE GONNA DO THAT, HE DOESN'T EVEN HAVE A FRONT--
SHHHK
BAM
ALERT
ALERT

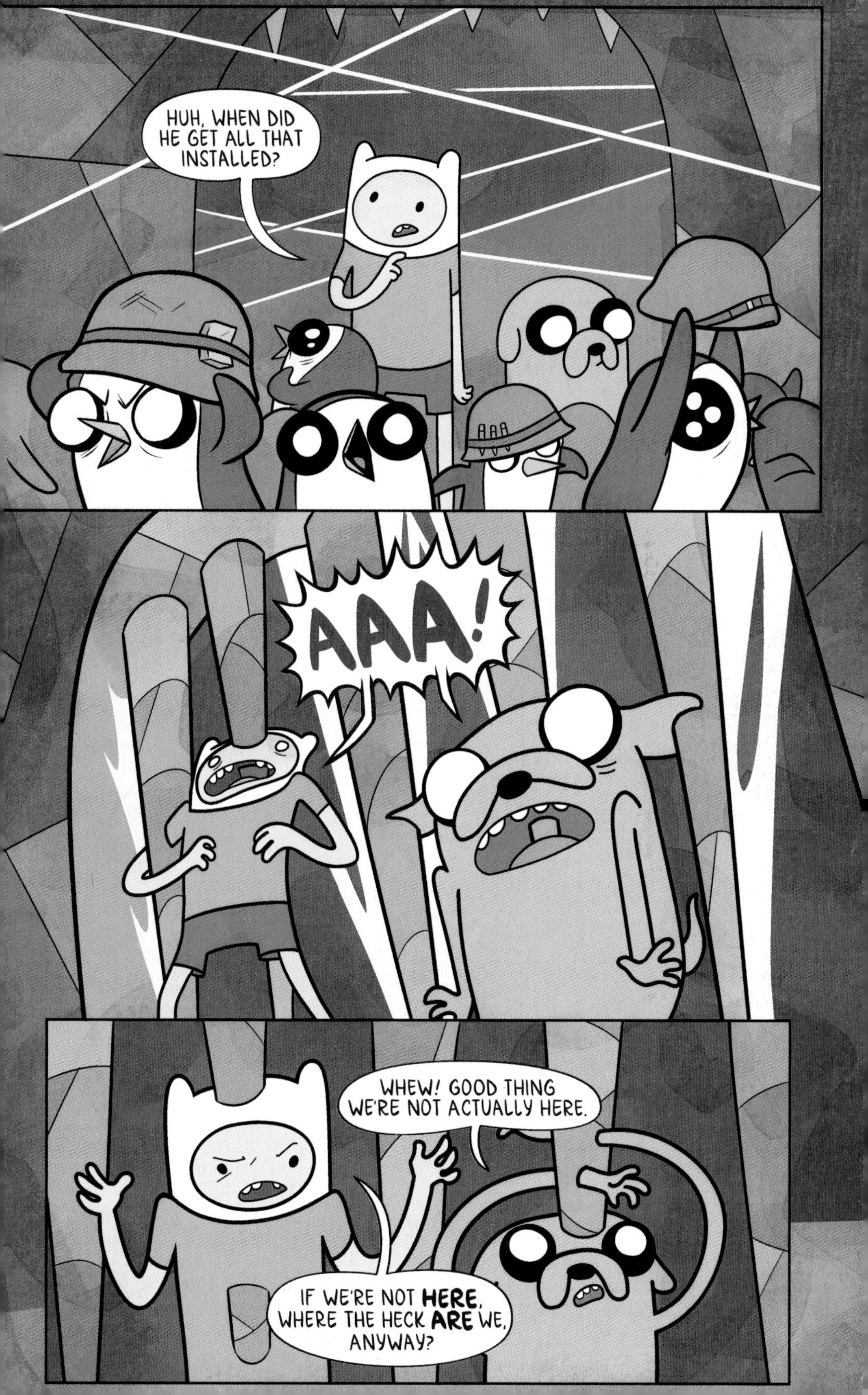
HUH, WHEN DID HE GET ALL THAT INSTALLED?
AAA!
WHEW! GOOD THING WE'RE NOT ACTUALLY HERE.
IF WE'RE NOT **HERE**, WHERE THE HECK **ARE** WE, ANYWAY?

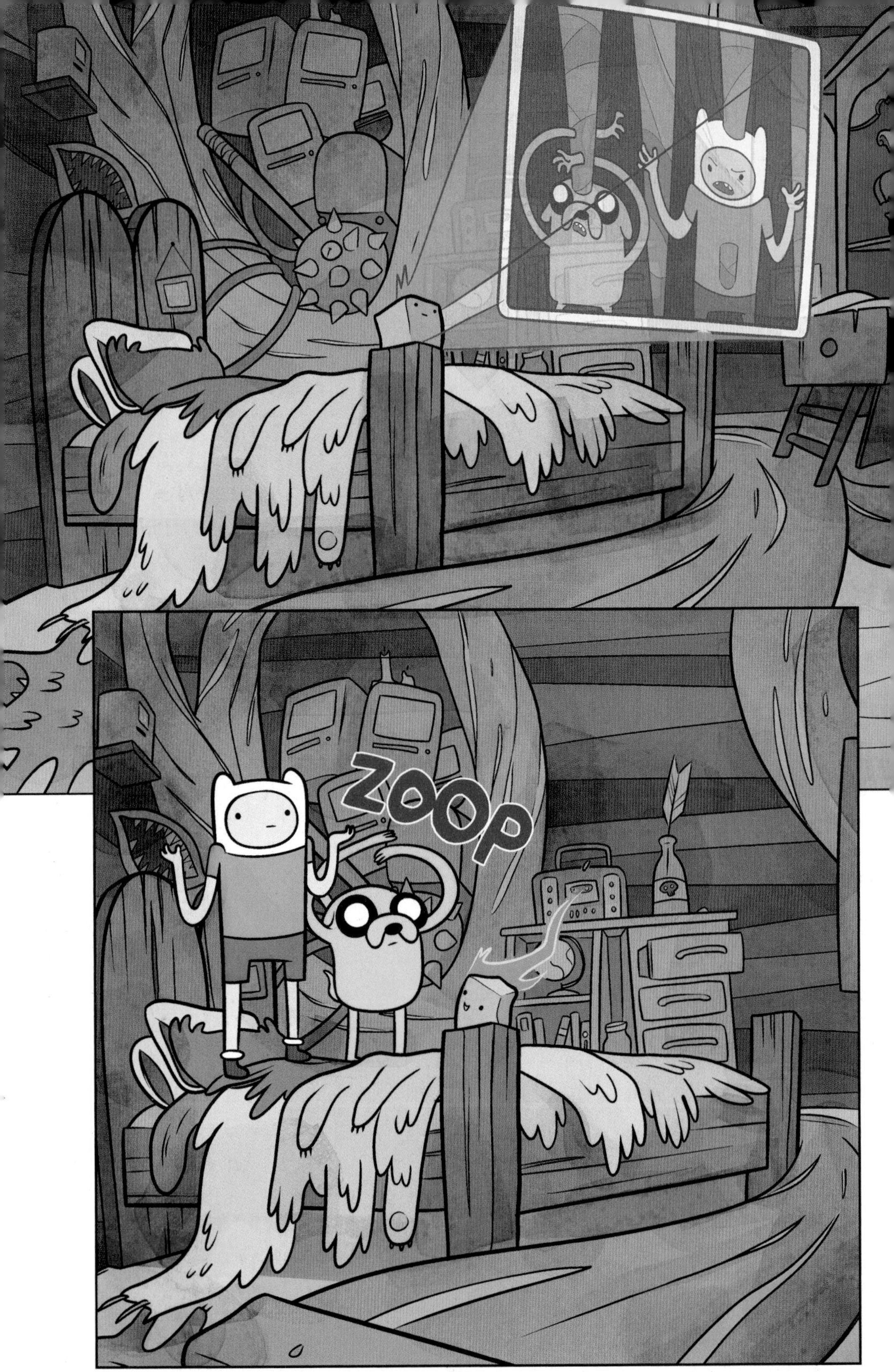
ZOOP

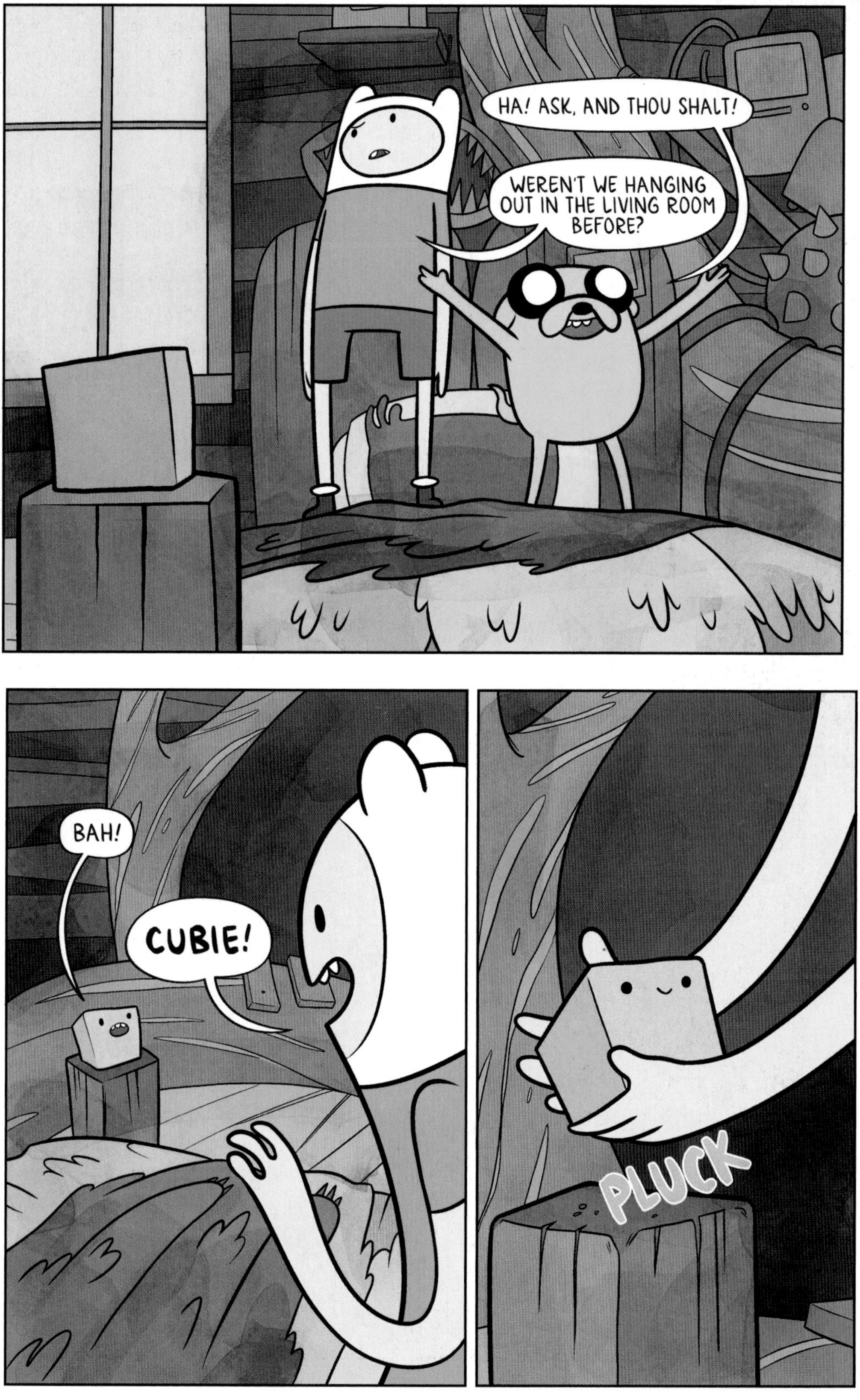
WEREN'T WE HANGING OUT IN THE LIVING ROOM BEFORE?
HA! ASK, AND THOU SHALT!
BAH!
CUBIE!
PLUCK

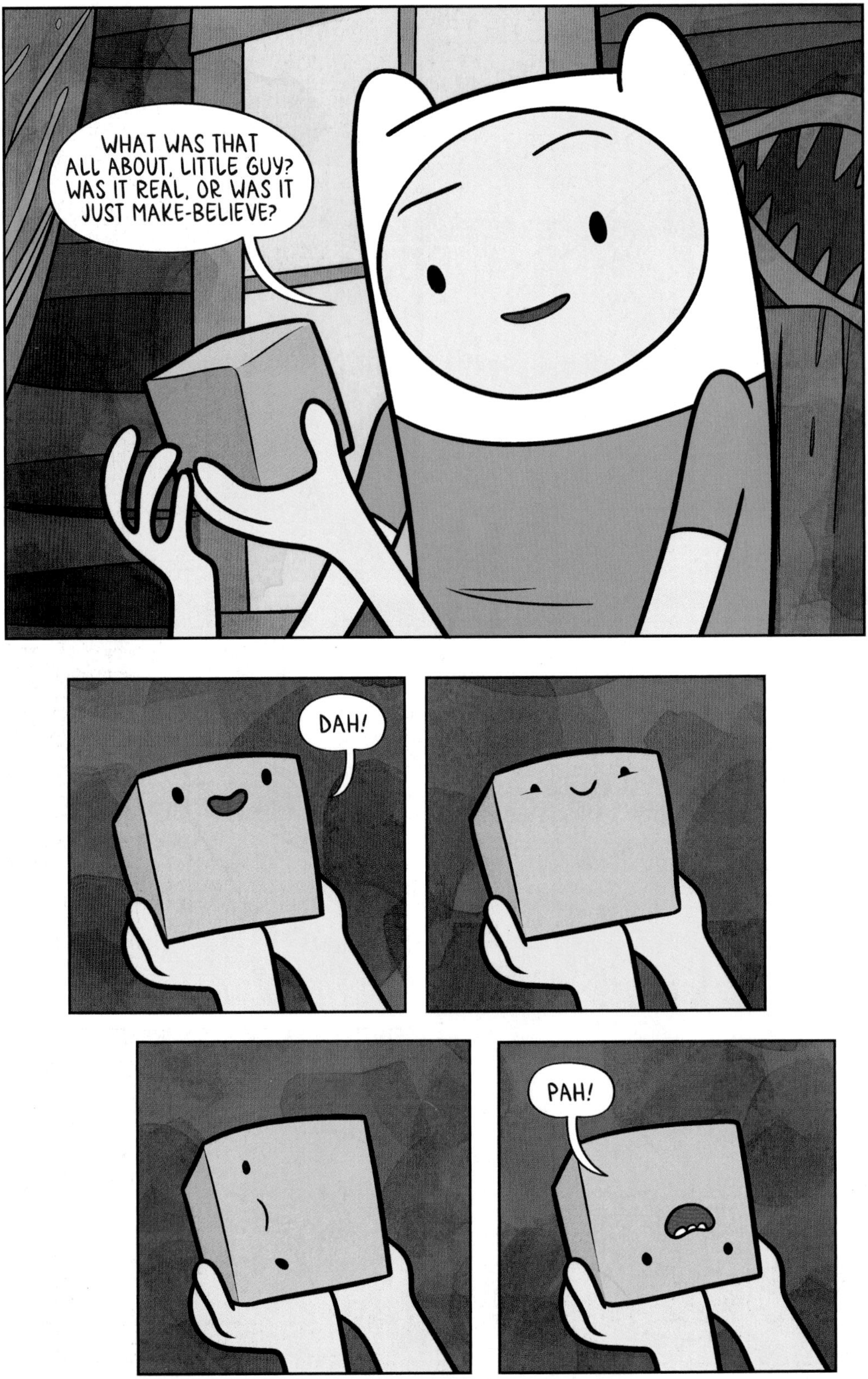
WHAT WAS THAT ALL ABOUT, LITTLE GUY? WAS IT REAL, OR WAS IT JUST MAKE-BELIEVE?
DAH!
PAH!

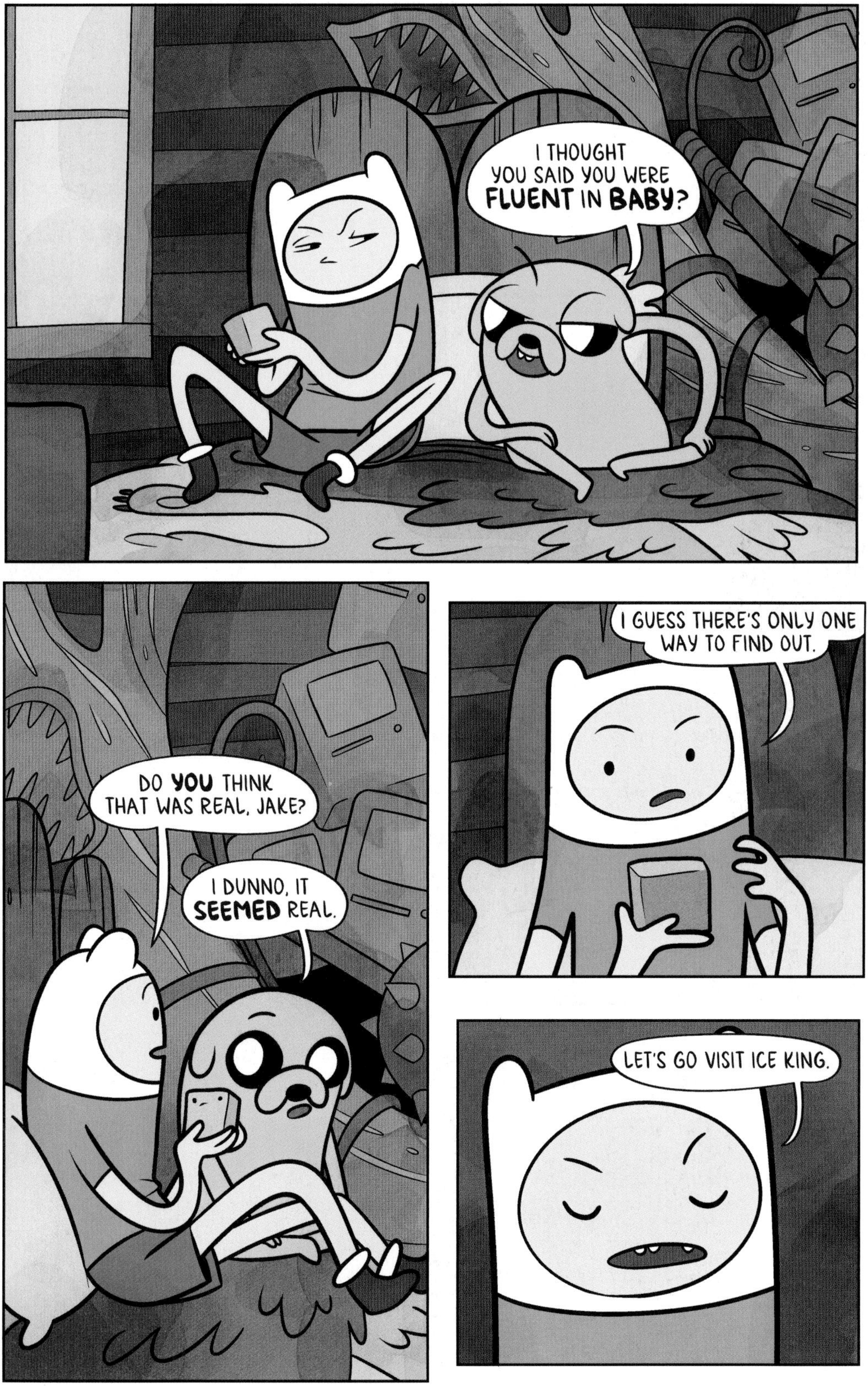
I THOUGHT YOU SAID YOU WERE **FLUENT** IN **BABY**?
DO **YOU** THINK THAT WAS REAL, JAKE?
I DUNNO, IT **SEEMED** REAL.
I GUESS THERE'S ONLY ONE WAY TO FIND OUT.
LET'S GO VISIT ICE KING.

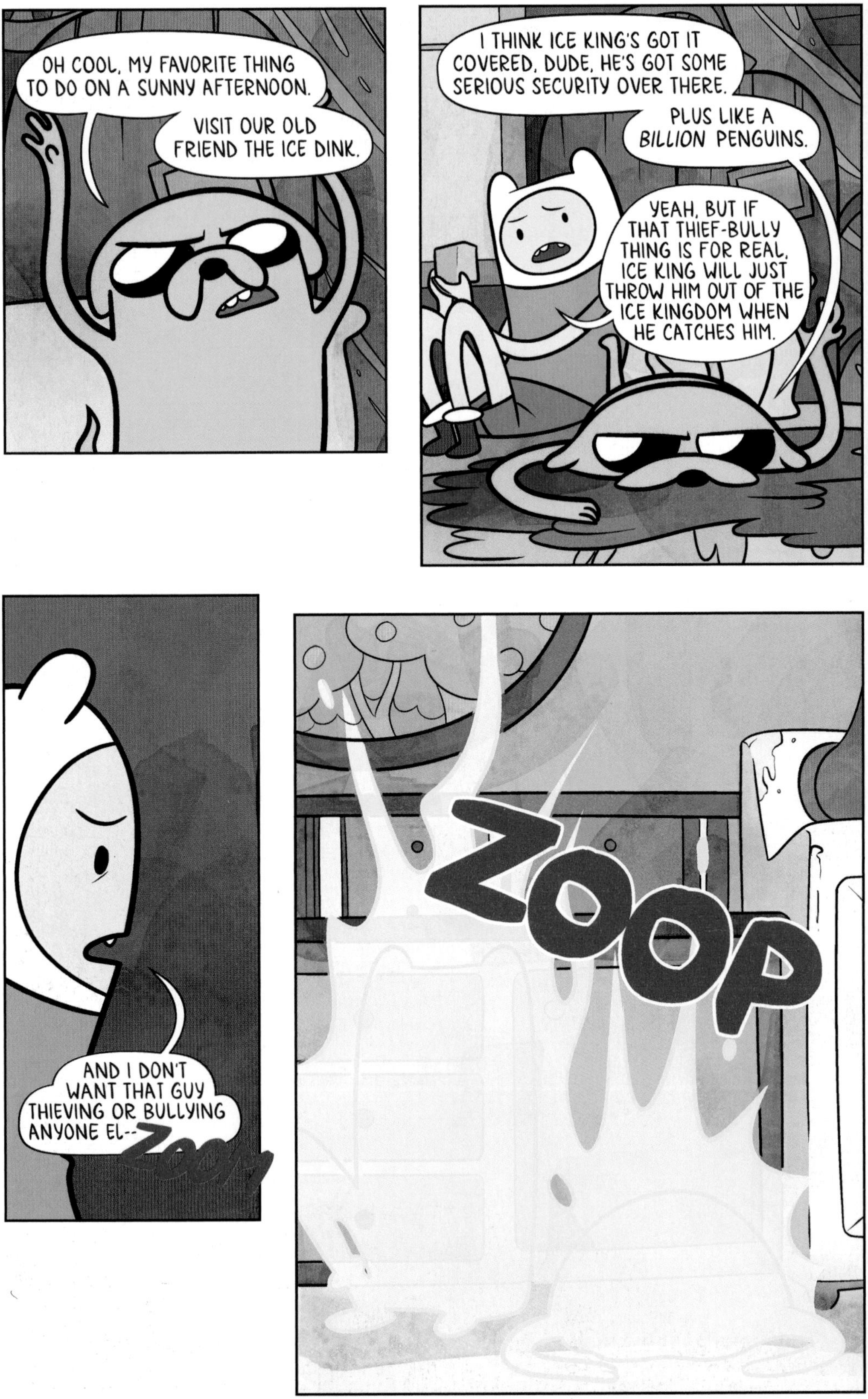
OH COOL, MY FAVORITE THING TO DO ON A SUNNY AFTERNOON.
VISIT OUR OLD FRIEND THE ICE DINK.
I THINK ICE KING'S GOT IT COVERED, DUDE, HE'S GOT SOME SERIOUS SECURITY OVER THERE.
PLUS LIKE A BILLION PENGUINS.
YEAH, BUT IF THAT THIEF-BULLY THING IS FOR REAL, ICE KING WILL JUST THROW HIM OUT OF THE ICE KINGDOM WHEN HE CATCHES HIM.
AND I DON'T WANT THAT GUY THIEVING OR BULLYING ANYONE EL--
ZOOP
ZOOP

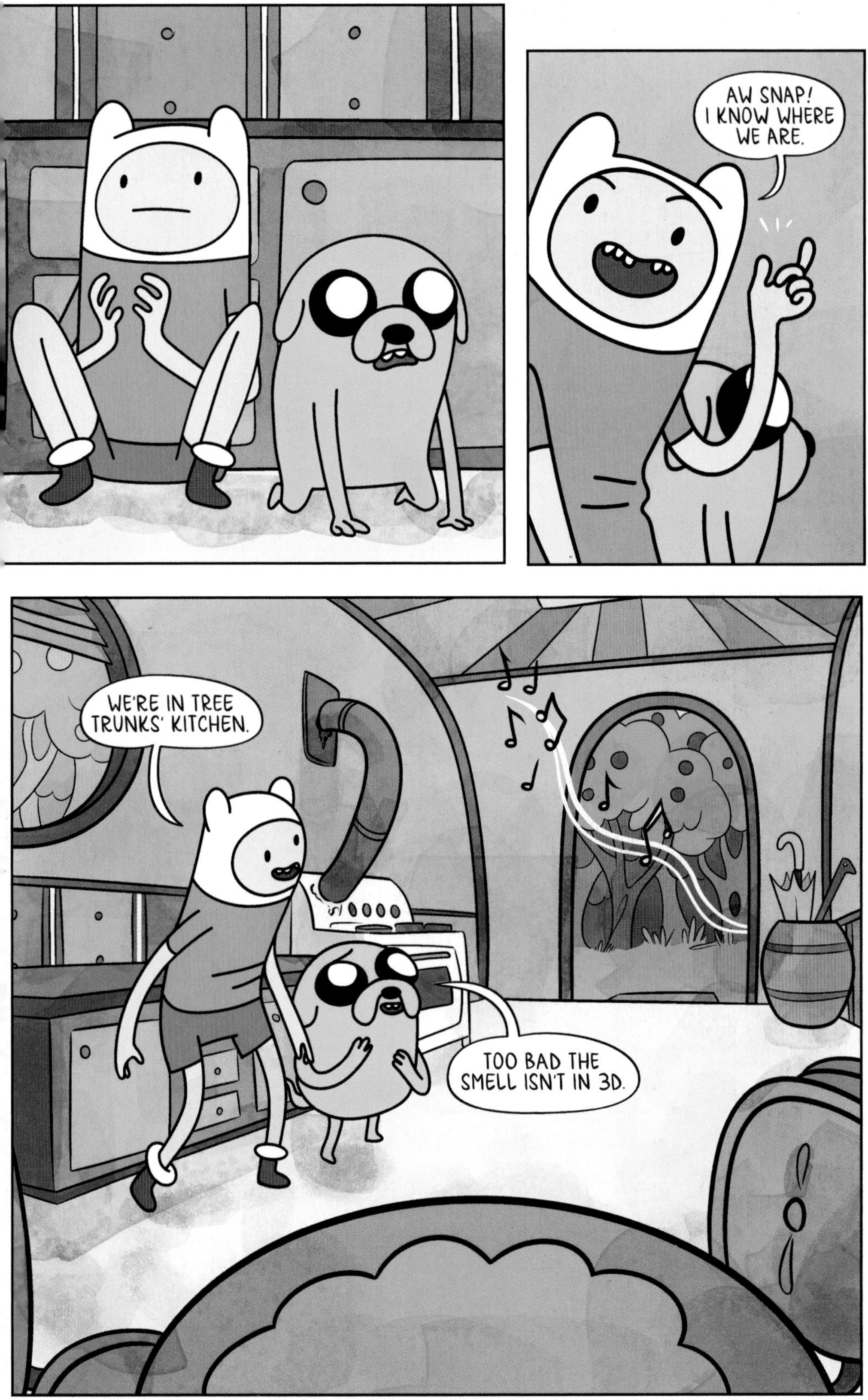
AW SNAP! I KNOW WHERE WE ARE.
WE'RE IN TREE TRUNKS' KITCHEN.
TOO BAD THE SMELL ISN'T IN 3D.

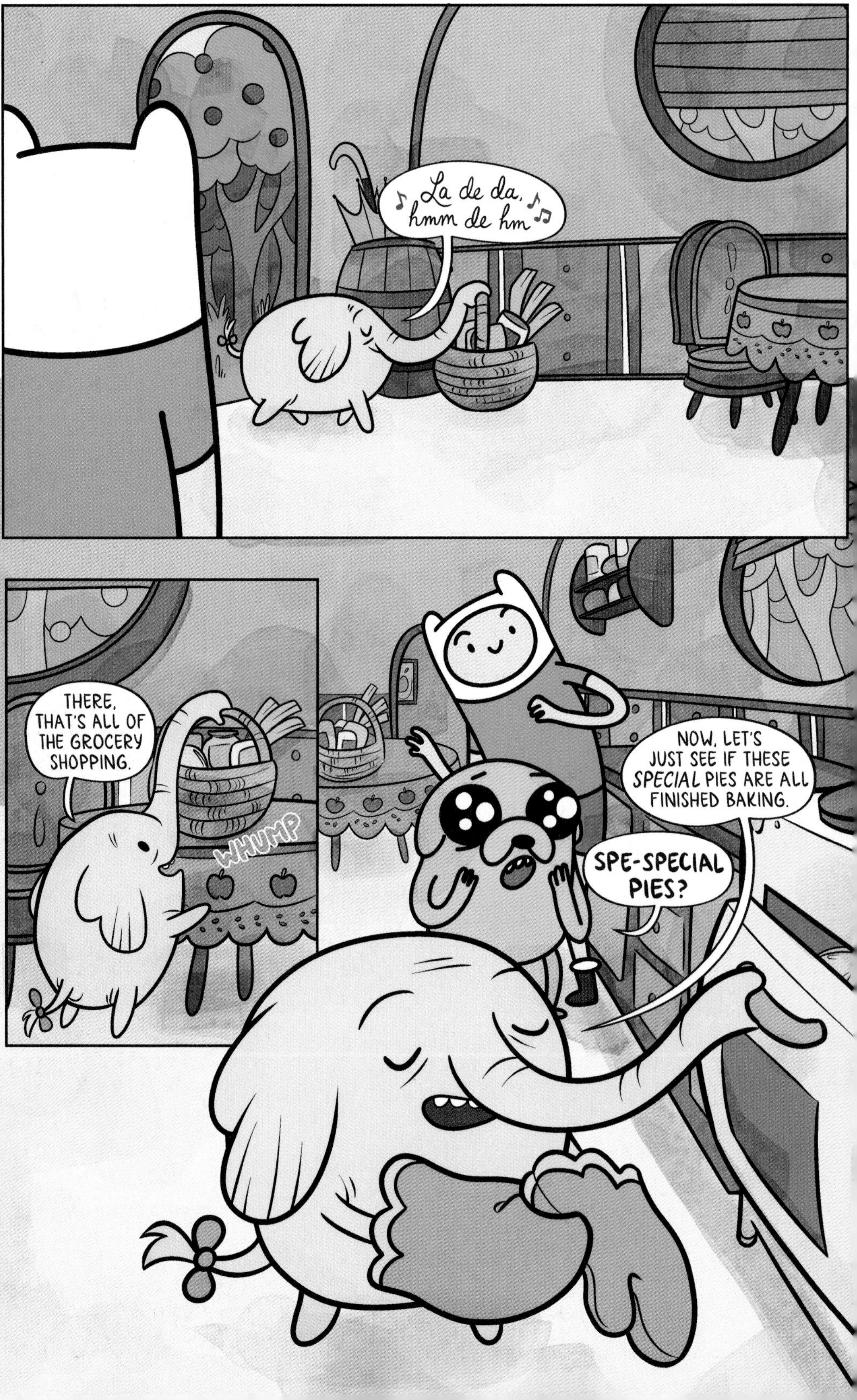

♪ La de da, ♪ hmm de hm ♫
THERE, THAT'S ALL OF THE GROCERY SHOPPING.
WHUMP
NOW, LET'S JUST SEE IF THESE SPECIAL PIES ARE ALL FINISHED BAKING.
SPE-SPECIAL PIES?

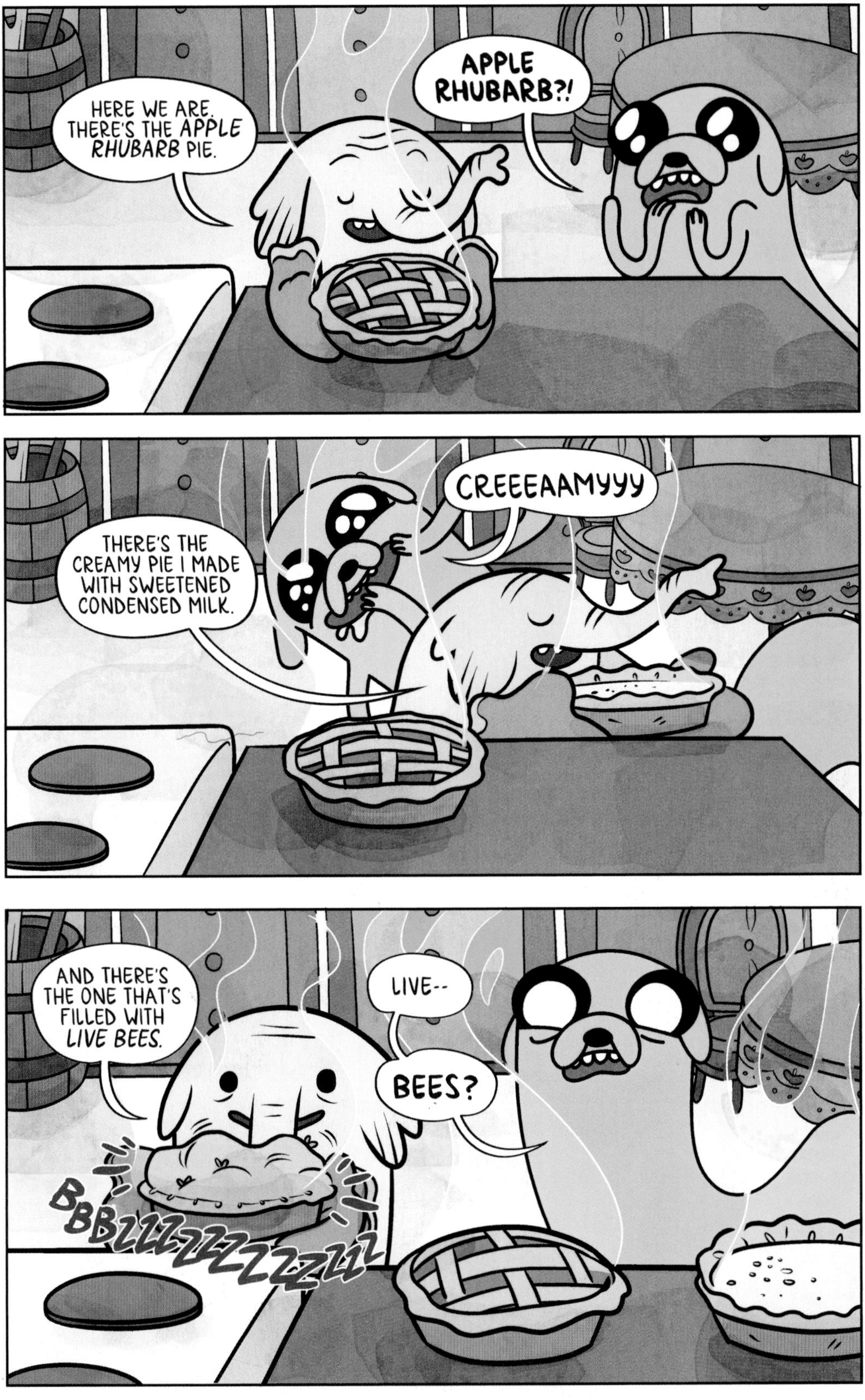
HERE WE ARE. THERE'S THE APPLE RHUBARB PIE.
APPLE RHUBARB?!
THERE'S THE CREAMY PIE I MADE WITH SWEETENED CONDENSED MILK.
CREEEAAMYYY
AND THERE'S THE ONE THAT'S FILLED WITH LIVE BEES.
LIVE--
BEES?
BBBZZZZZZZZZZZZ

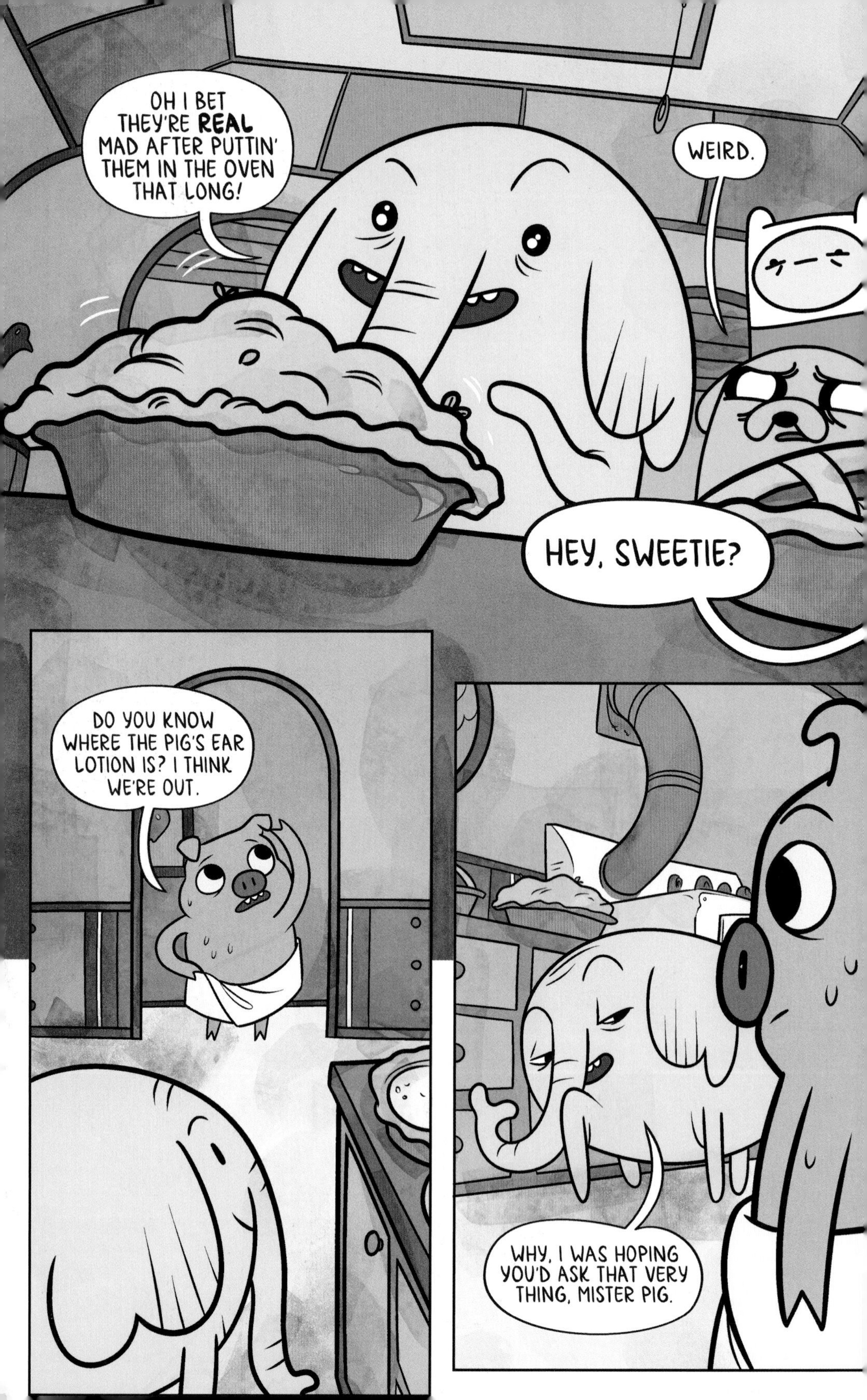
OH I BET THEY'RE **REAL** MAD AFTER PUTTIN' THEM IN THE OVEN THAT LONG!
WEIRD.
HEY, SWEETIE?
DO YOU KNOW WHERE THE PIG'S EAR LOTION IS? I THINK WE'RE OUT.
WHY, I WAS HOPING YOU'D ASK THAT VERY THING, MISTER PIG.

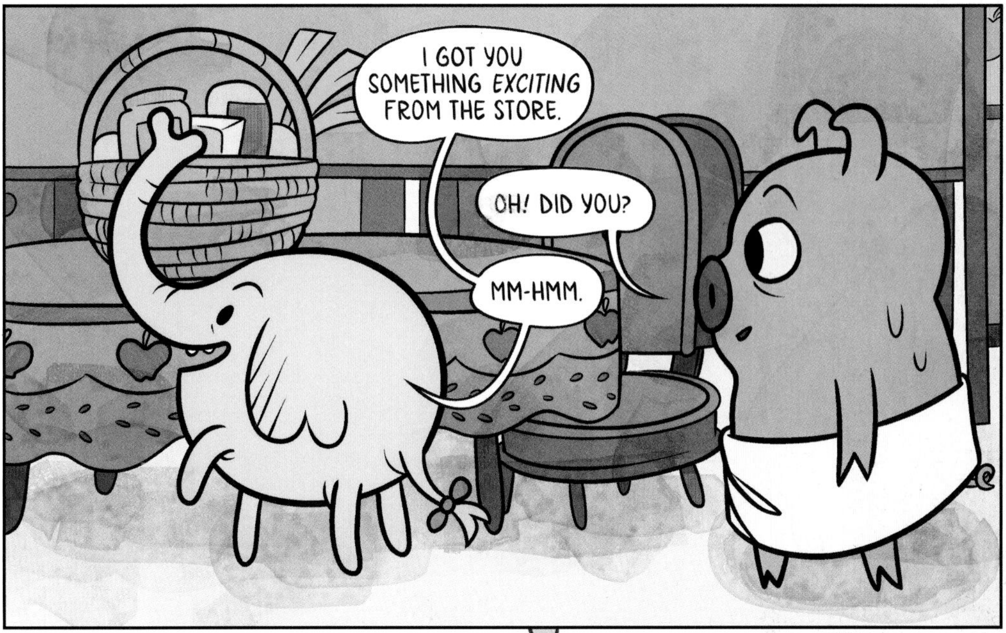
I GOT YOU SOMETHING *EXCITING* FROM THE STORE.
OH! DID YOU?
MM-HMM.

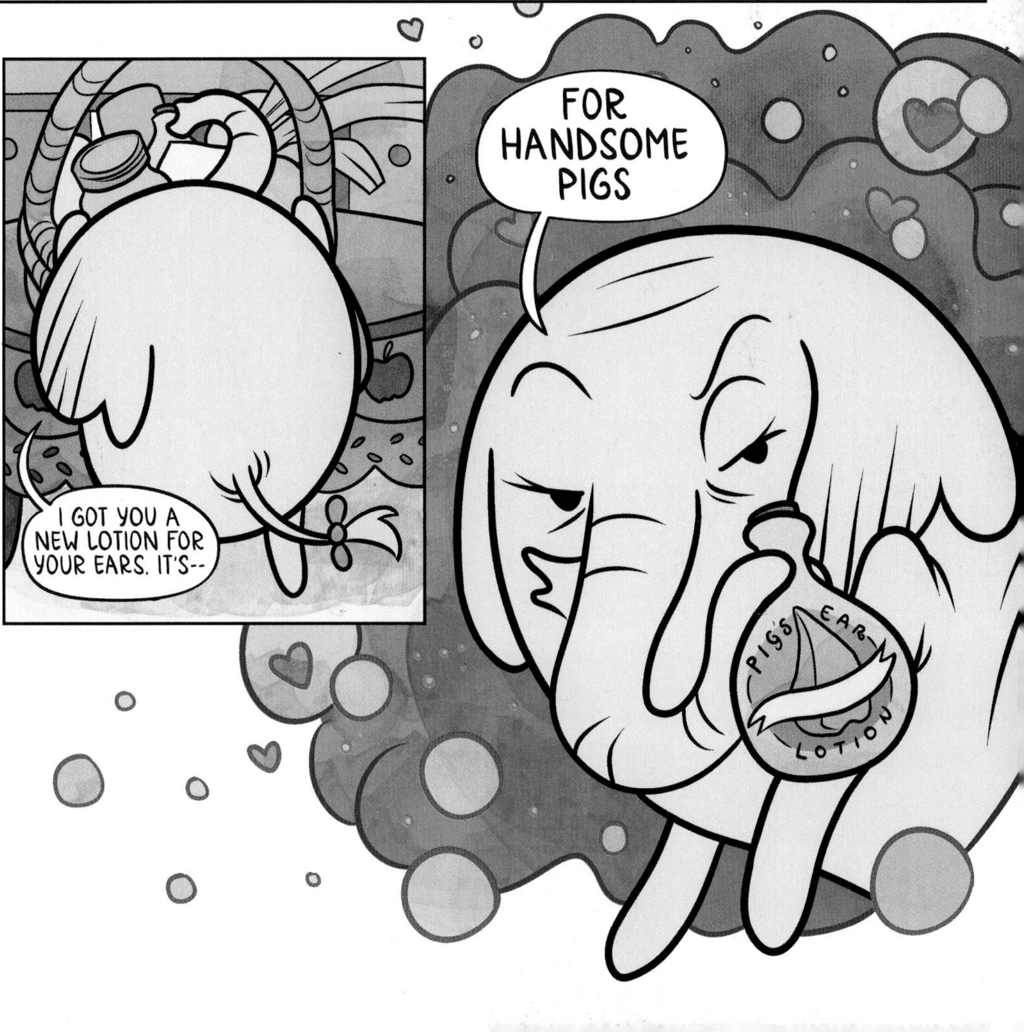
I GOT YOU A NEW LOTION FOR YOUR EARS. IT'S--
FOR HANDSOME PIGS
PIG'S EAR LOTION

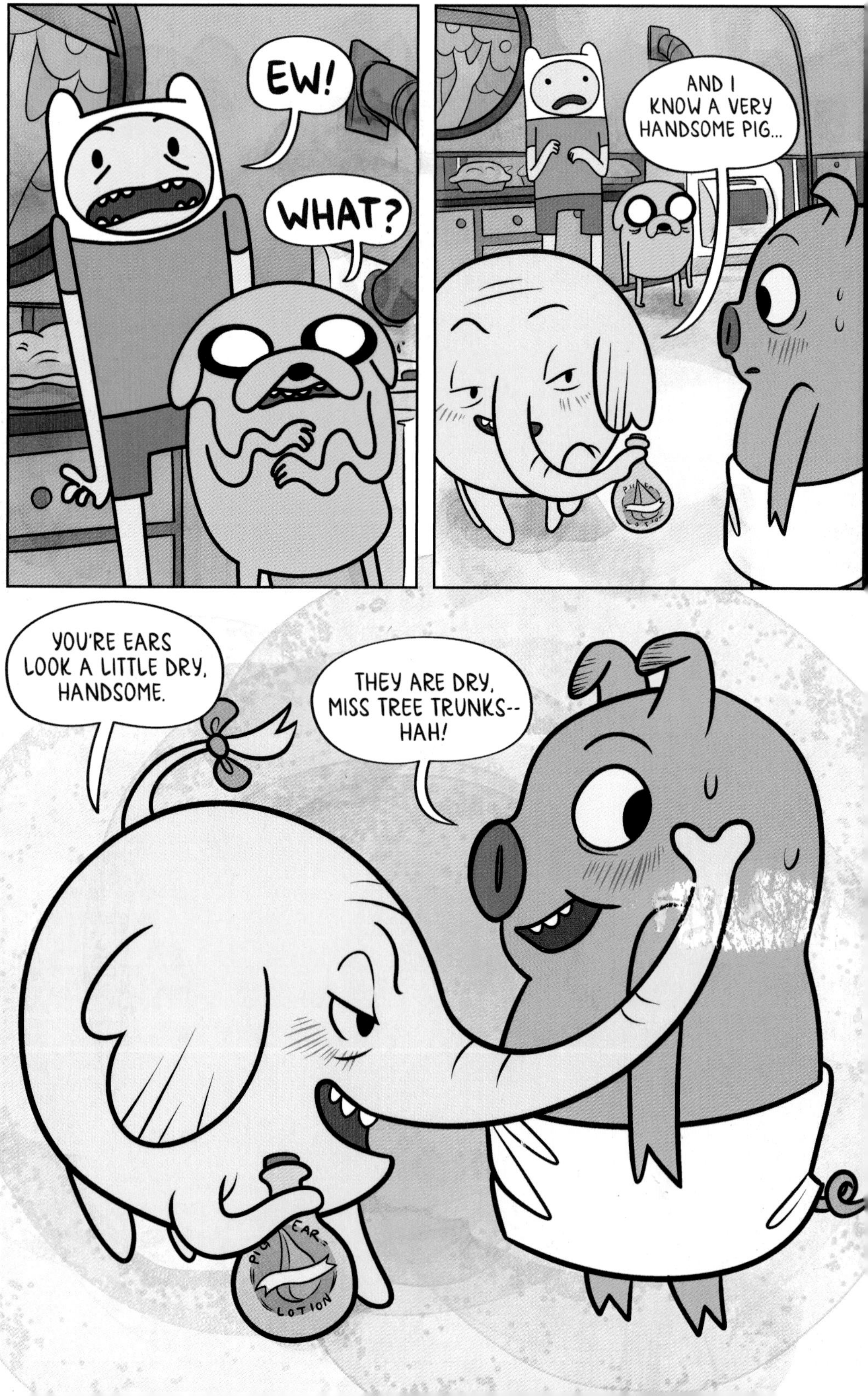
EW!
WHAT?
AND I
KNOW A VERY
HANDSOME PIG...
PIG EAR LOTION
YOU'RE EARS
LOOK A LITTLE DRY,
HANDSOME.
THEY ARE DRY,
MISS TREE TRUNKS--
HAH!
PIG EAR LOTION

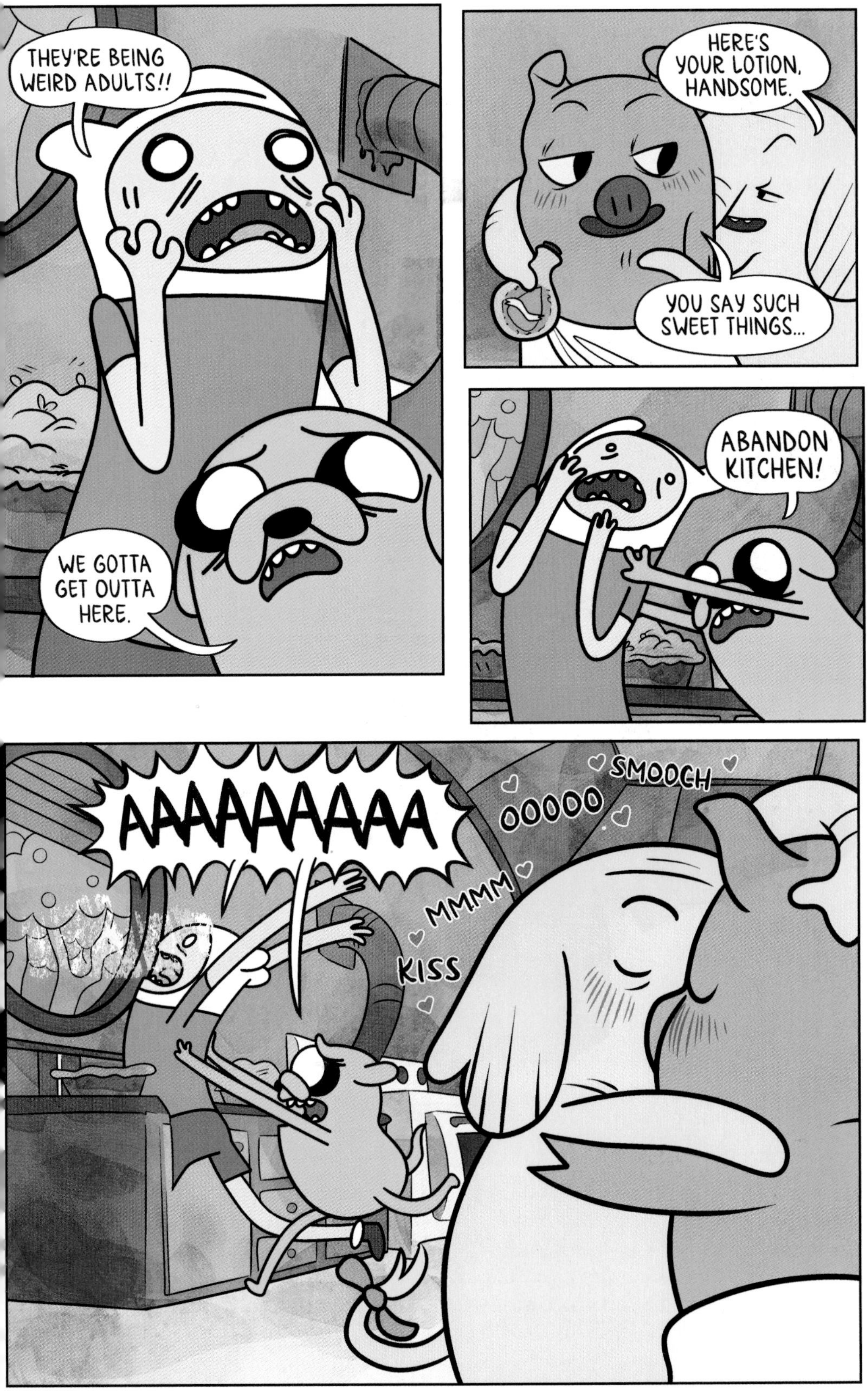
THEY'RE BEING WEIRD ADULTS!!
WE GOTTA GET OUTTA HERE.
HERE'S YOUR LOTION, HANDSOME.
YOU SAY SUCH SWEET THINGS...
ABANDON KITCHEN!
AAAAAAAAAA
SMOOCH
OOOOO
MMMM
KISS

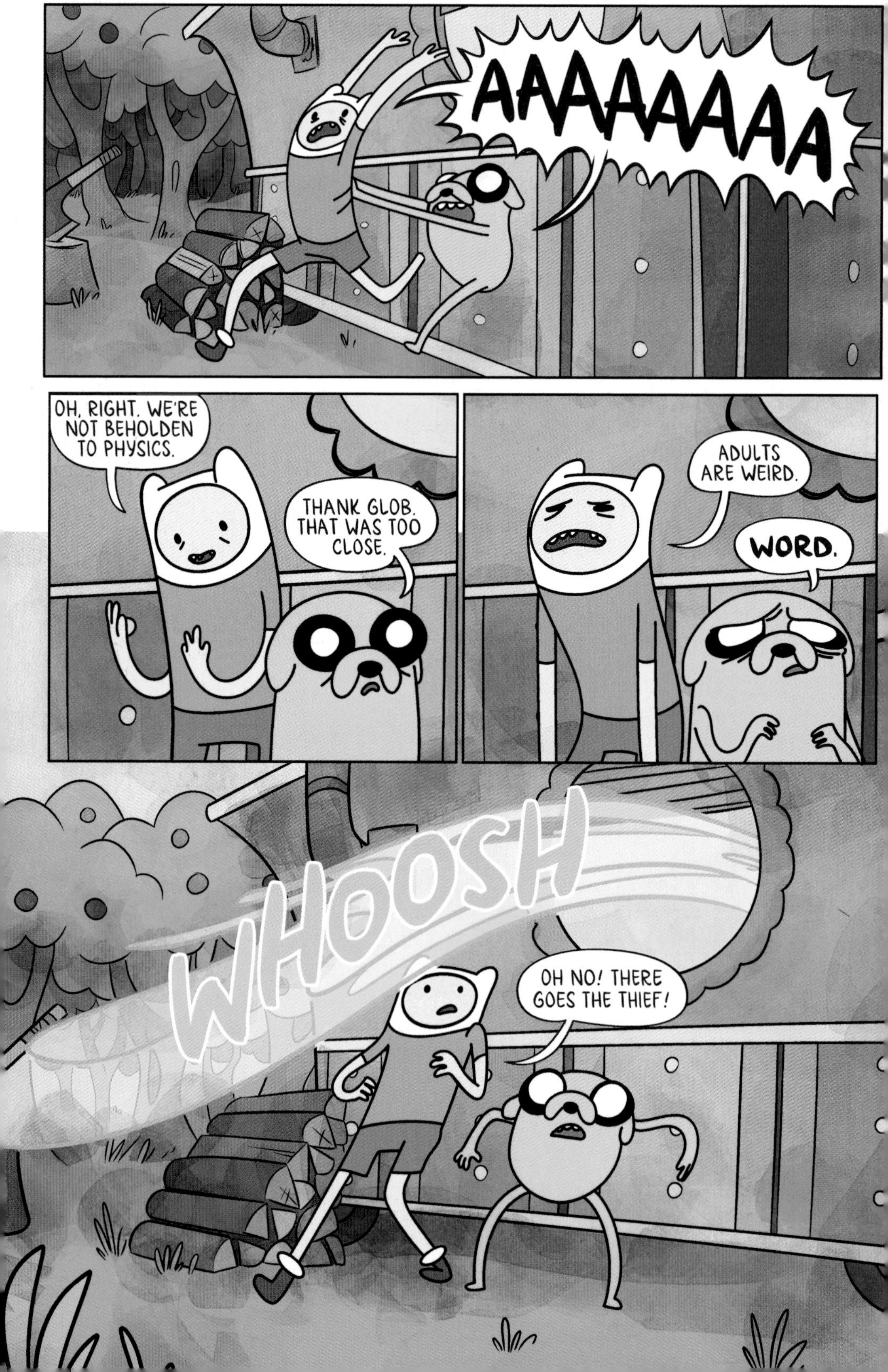
AAAAAAAAA
OH, RIGHT. WE'RE NOT BEHOLDEN TO PHYSICS.
THANK GLOB. THAT WAS TOO CLOSE.
ADULTS ARE WEIRD.
WORD.
WHOOSH
OH NO! THERE GOES THE THIEF!

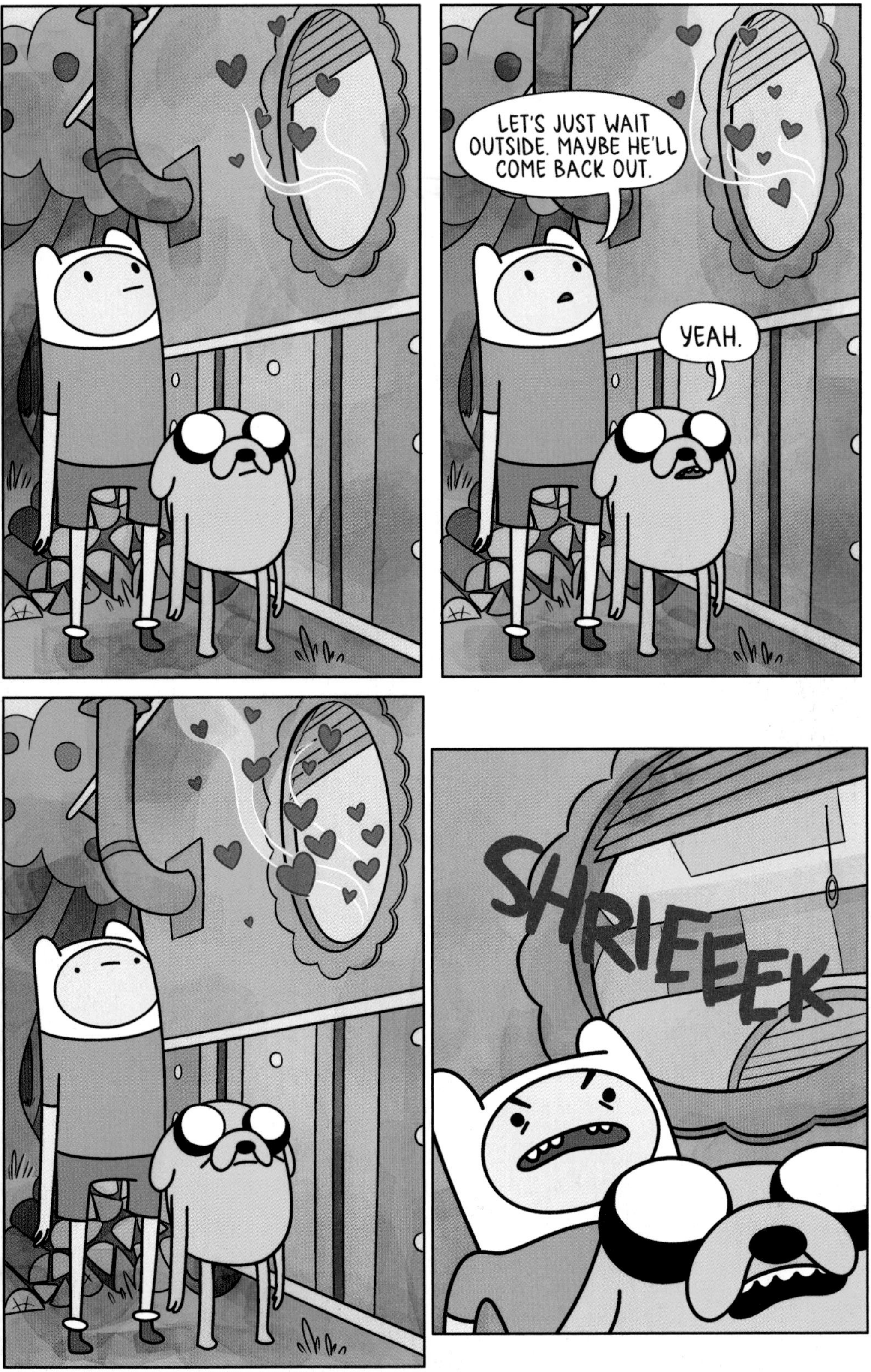
LET'S JUST WAIT OUTSIDE. MAYBE HE'LL COME BACK OUT.
YEAH.
SHRIEEEK

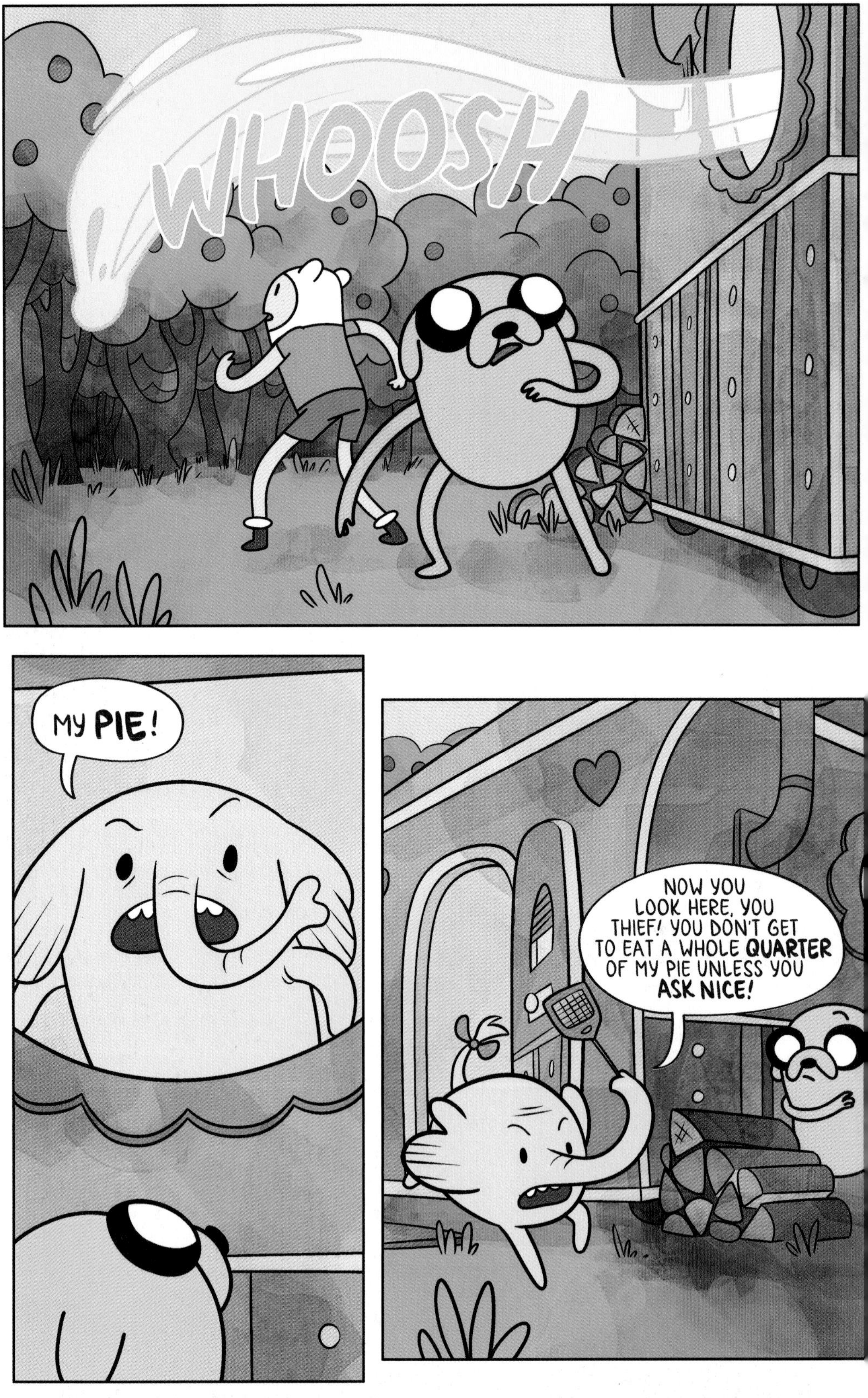
WHOOSH
MY PIE!
NOW YOU LOOK HERE, YOU THIEF! YOU DON'T GET TO EAT A WHOLE QUARTER OF MY PIE UNLESS YOU ASK NICE!

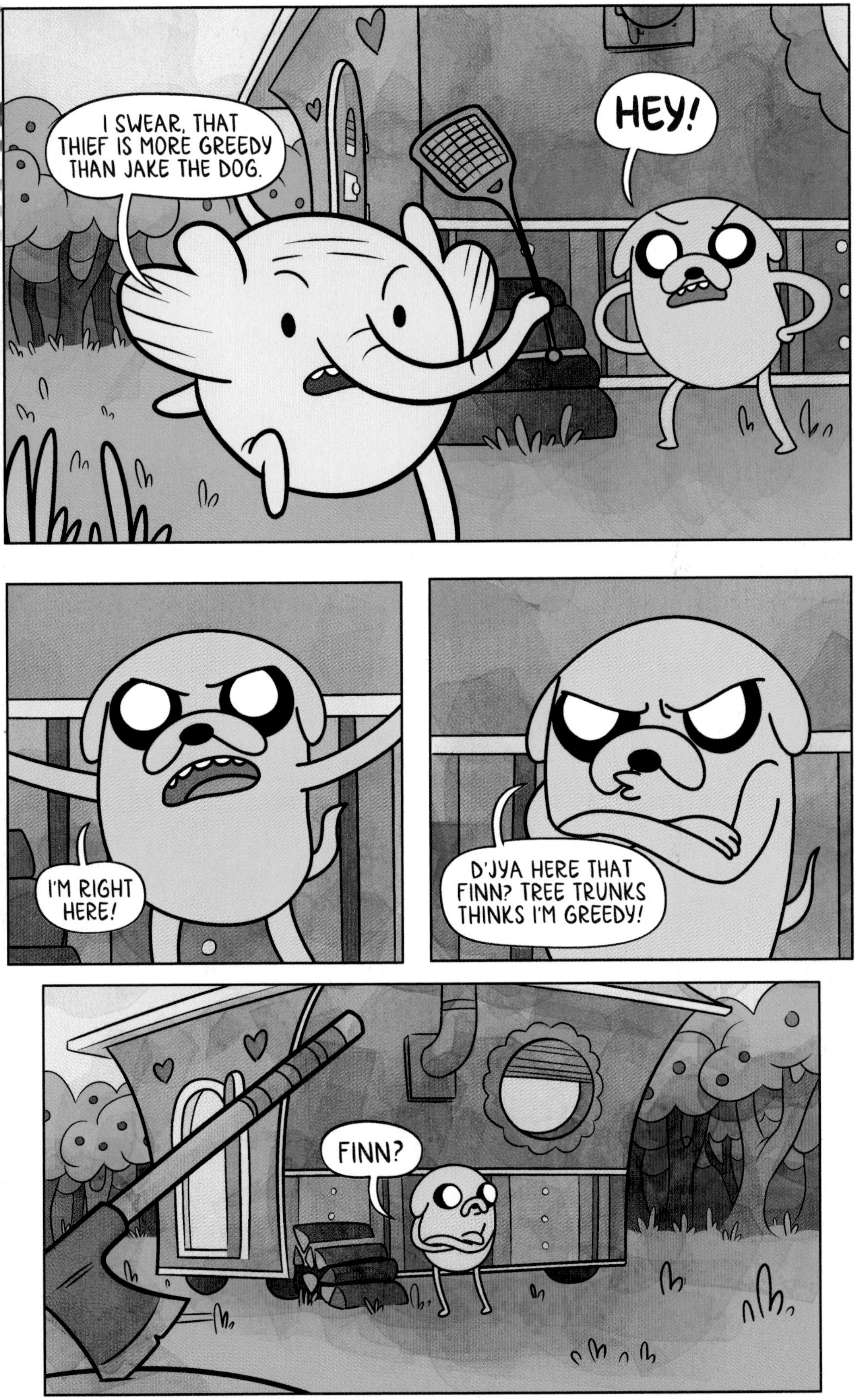
I SWEAR, THAT THIEF IS MORE GREEDY THAN JAKE THE DOG.
HEY!
I'M RIGHT HERE!
D'JYA HERE THAT FINN? TREE TRUNKS THINKS I'M GREEDY!
FINN?

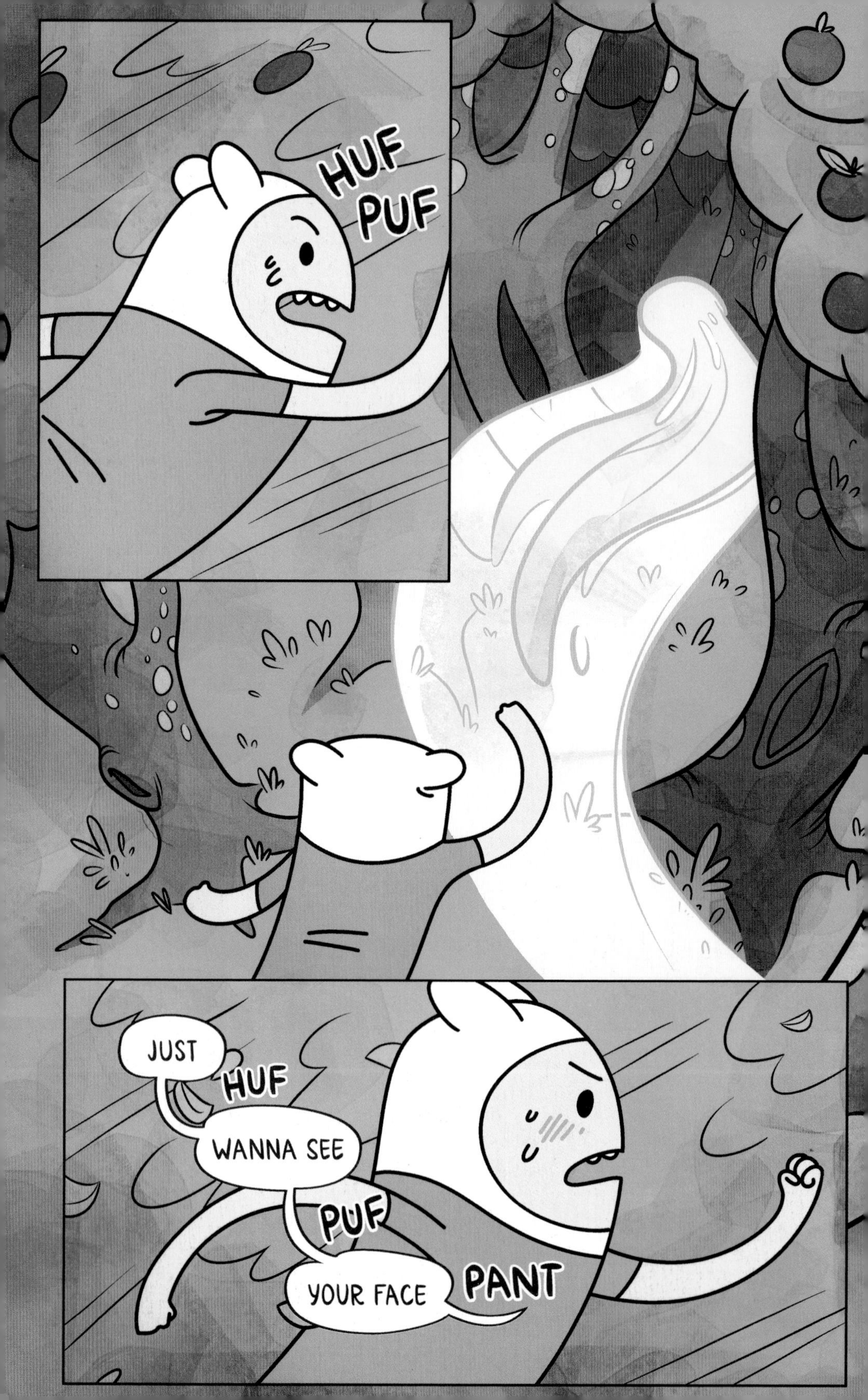
HUF
PUF
JUST
HUF
WANNA SEE
PUF
YOUR FACE
PANT

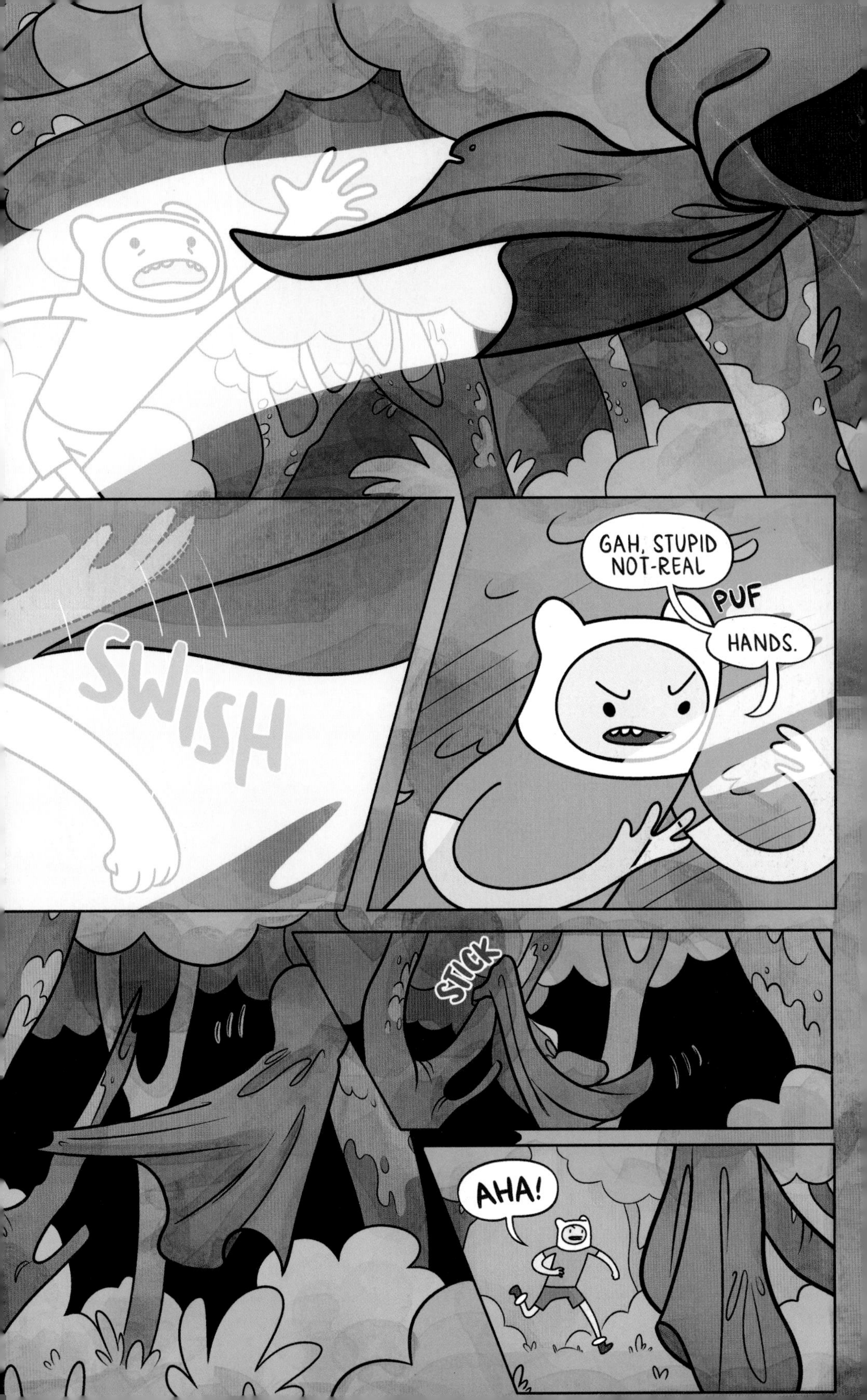
SWISH
GAH, STUPID NOT-REAL
PUF
HANDS.
STICK
AHA!

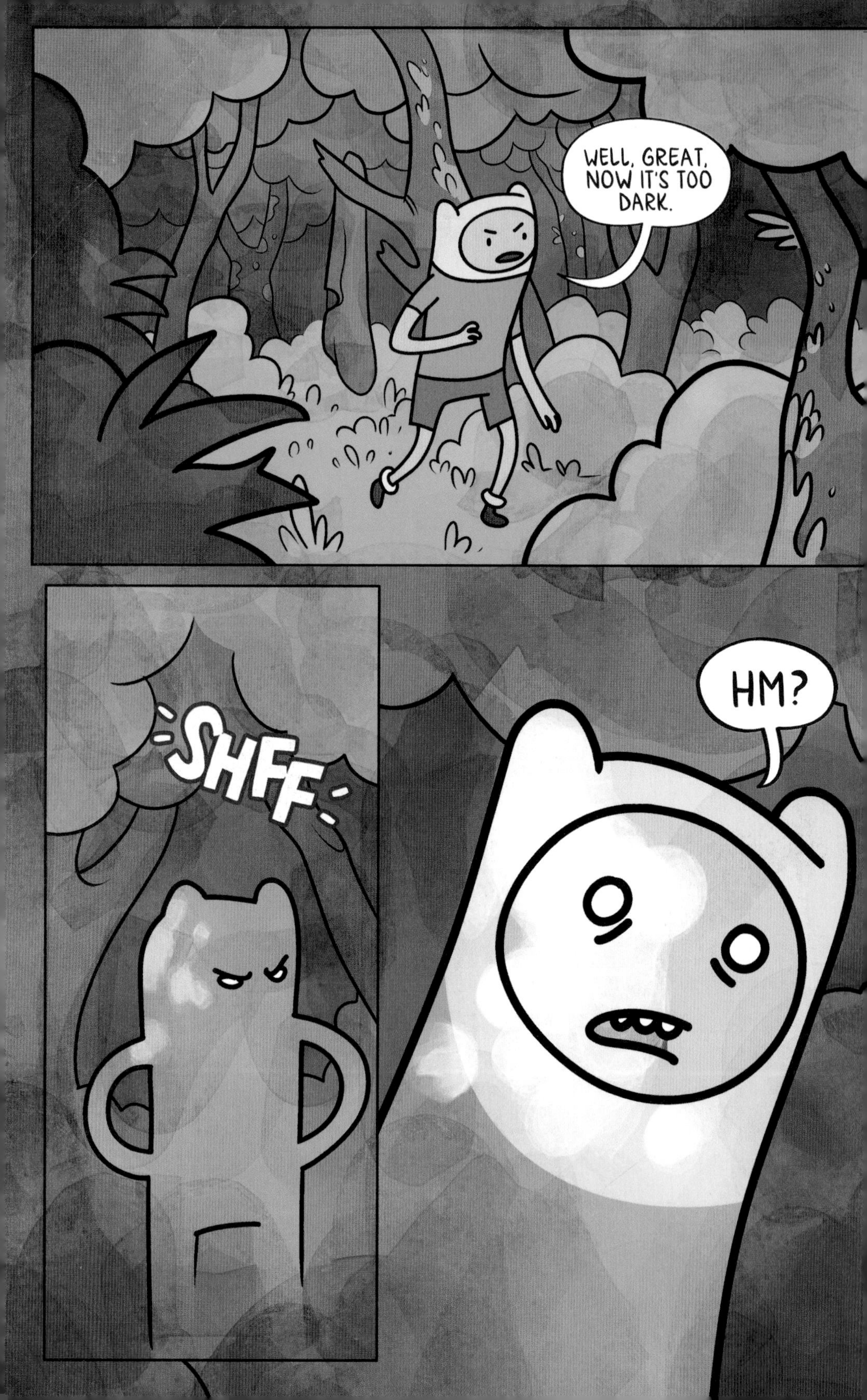
WELL, GREAT, NOW IT'S TOO DARK.
SHFF
HM?

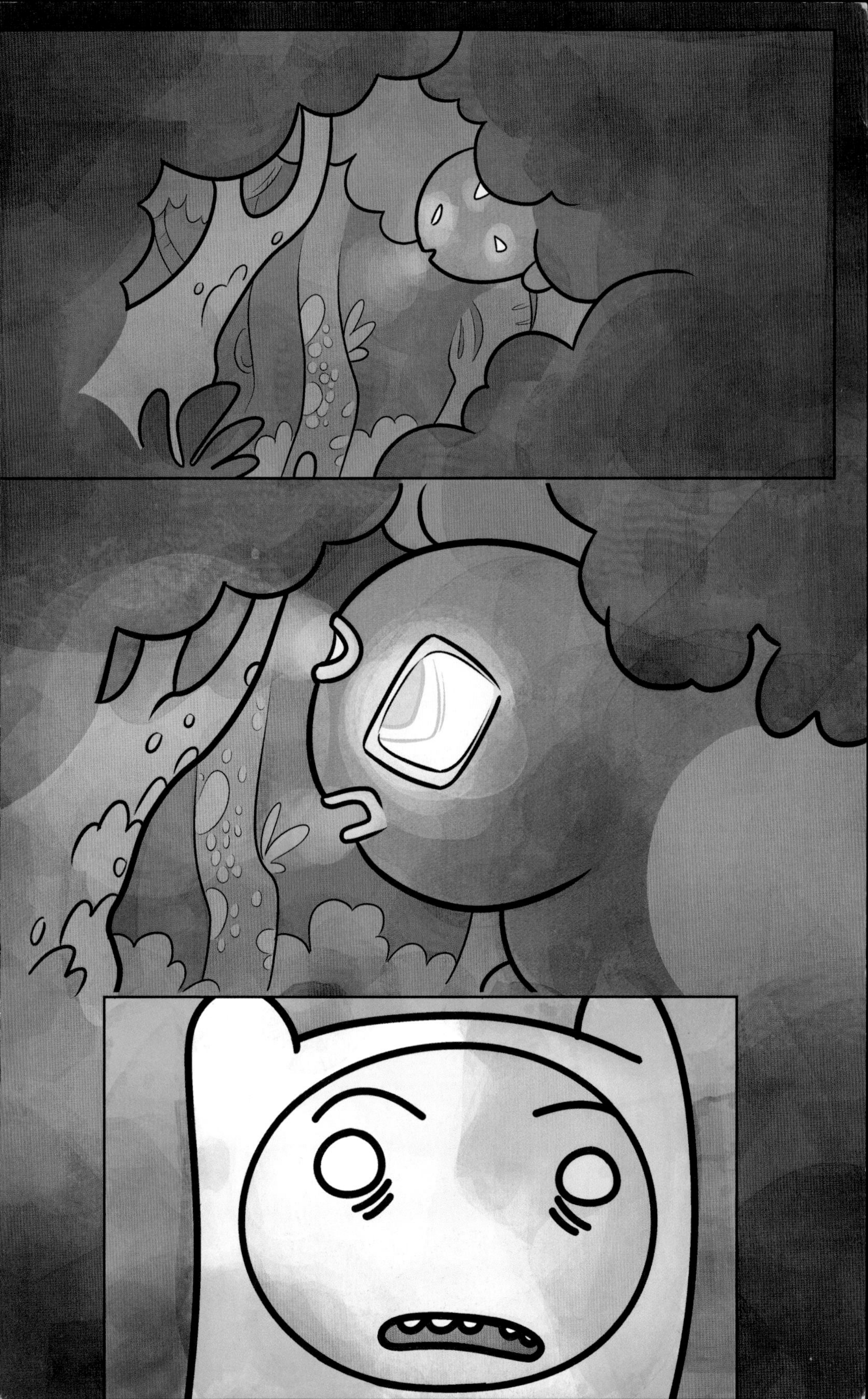

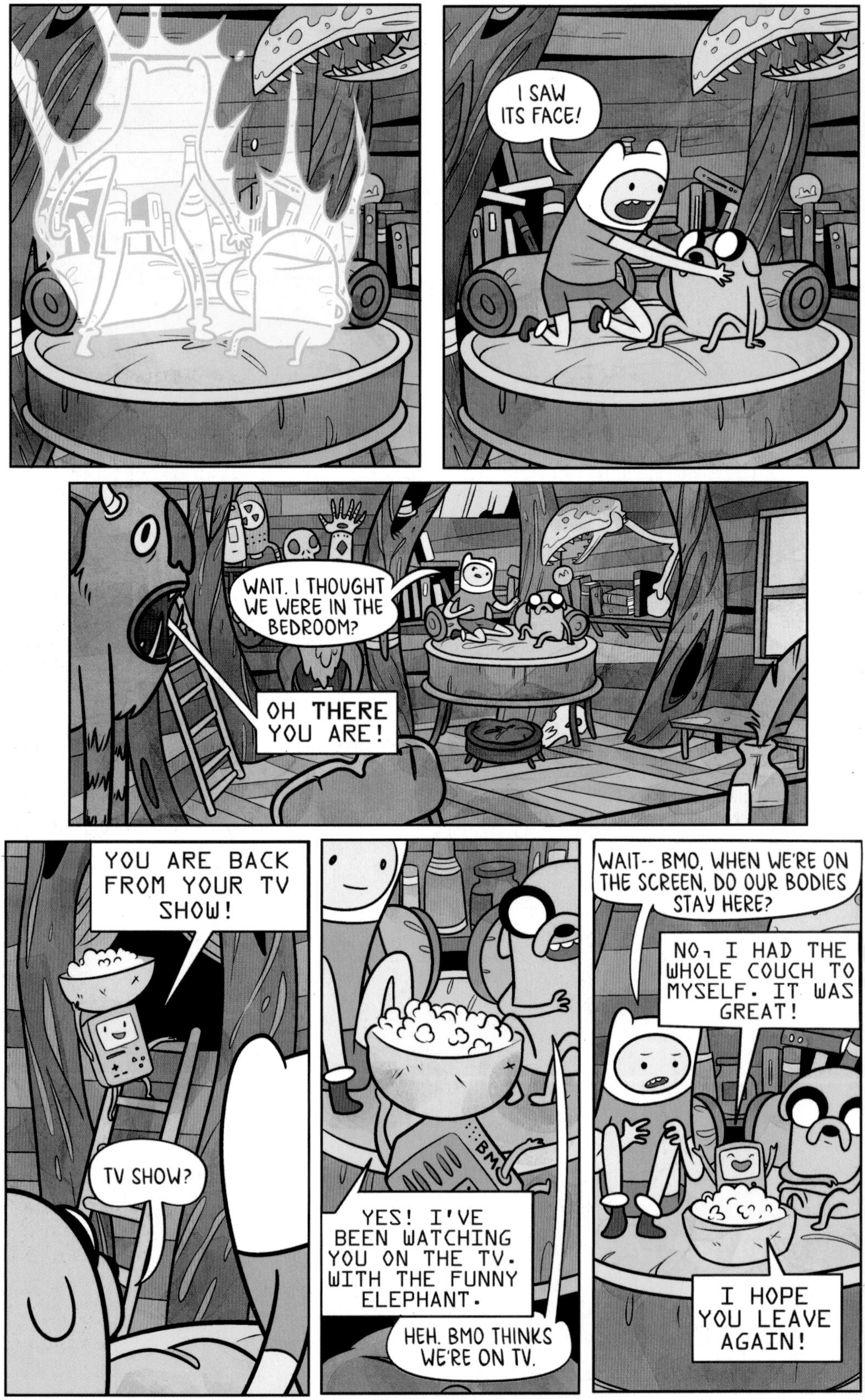
I SAW ITS FACE!
WAIT. I THOUGHT WE WERE IN THE BEDROOM?
OH THERE YOU ARE!
YOU ARE BACK FROM YOUR TV SHOW!
TV SHOW?
YES! I'VE BEEN WATCHING YOU ON THE TV. WITH THE FUNNY ELEPHANT.
HEH. BMO THINKS WE'RE ON TV.
WAIT-- BMO, WHEN WE'RE ON THE SCREEN, DO OUR BODIES STAY HERE?
NO, I HAD THE WHOLE COUCH TO MYSELF. IT WAS GREAT!
I HOPE YOU LEAVE AGAIN!

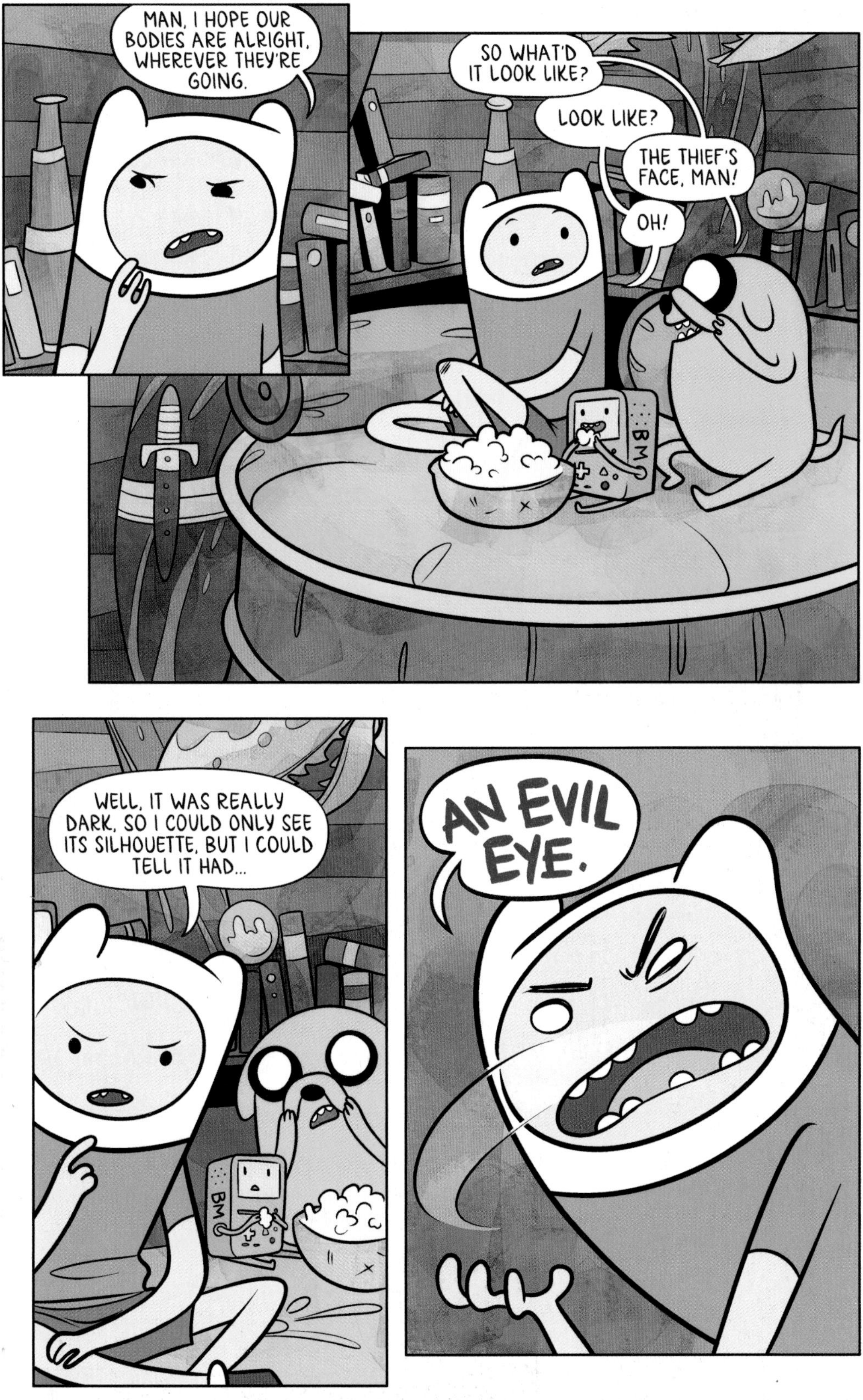

MAN, I HOPE OUR BODIES ARE ALRIGHT, WHEREVER THEY'RE GOING.
SO WHAT'D IT LOOK LIKE?
LOOK LIKE?
THE THIEF'S FACE, MAN!
OH!
WELL, IT WAS REALLY DARK, SO I COULD ONLY SEE ITS SILHOUETTE, BUT I COULD TELL IT HAD...
AN EVIL EYE.

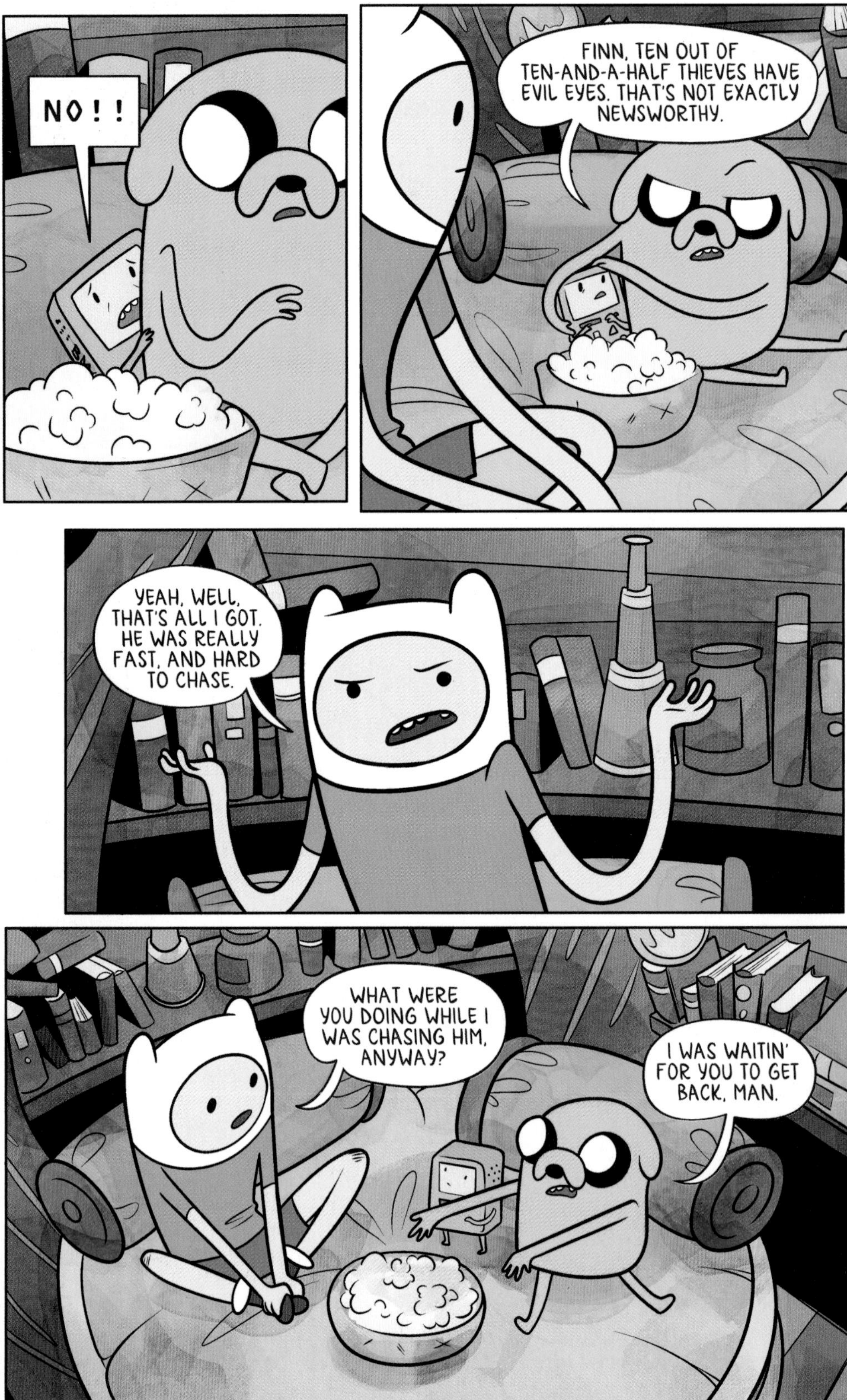
NO!!
FINN, TEN OUT OF TEN-AND-A-HALF THIEVES HAVE EVIL EYES. THAT'S NOT EXACTLY NEWSWORTHY.
YEAH, WELL, THAT'S ALL I GOT. HE WAS REALLY FAST, AND HARD TO CHASE.
WHAT WERE YOU DOING WHILE I WAS CHASING HIM, ANYWAY?
I WAS WAITIN' FOR YOU TO GET BACK, MAN.

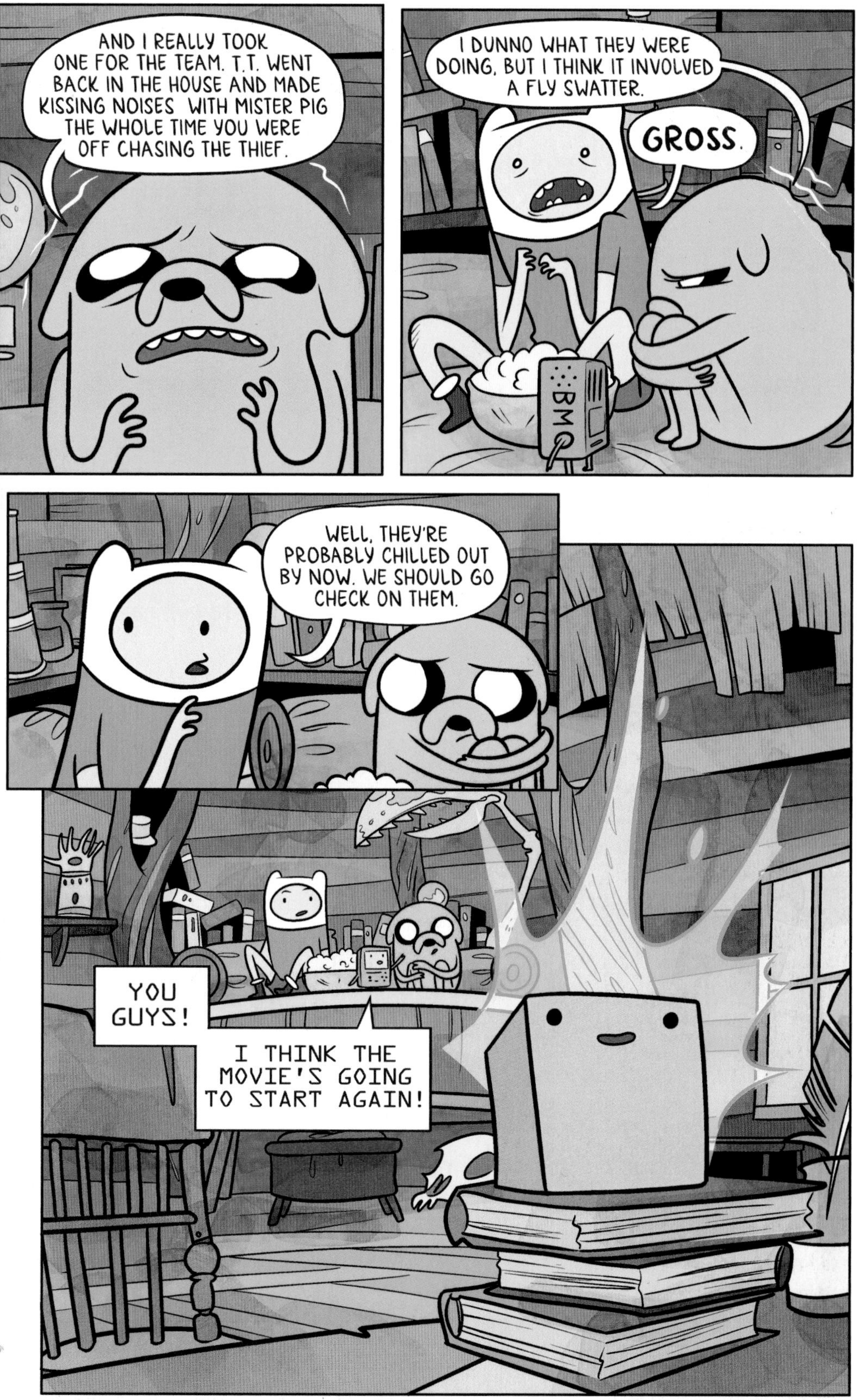
AND I REALLY TOOK ONE FOR THE TEAM. T.T. WENT BACK IN THE HOUSE AND MADE KISSING NOISES WITH MISTER PIG THE WHOLE TIME YOU WERE OFF CHASING THE THIEF.
I DUNNO WHAT THEY WERE DOING, BUT I THINK IT INVOLVED A FLY SWATTER.
GROSS.
BMO
WELL, THEY'RE PROBABLY CHILLED OUT BY NOW. WE SHOULD GO CHECK ON THEM.
YOU GUYS!
I THINK THE MOVIE'S GOING TO START AGAIN!

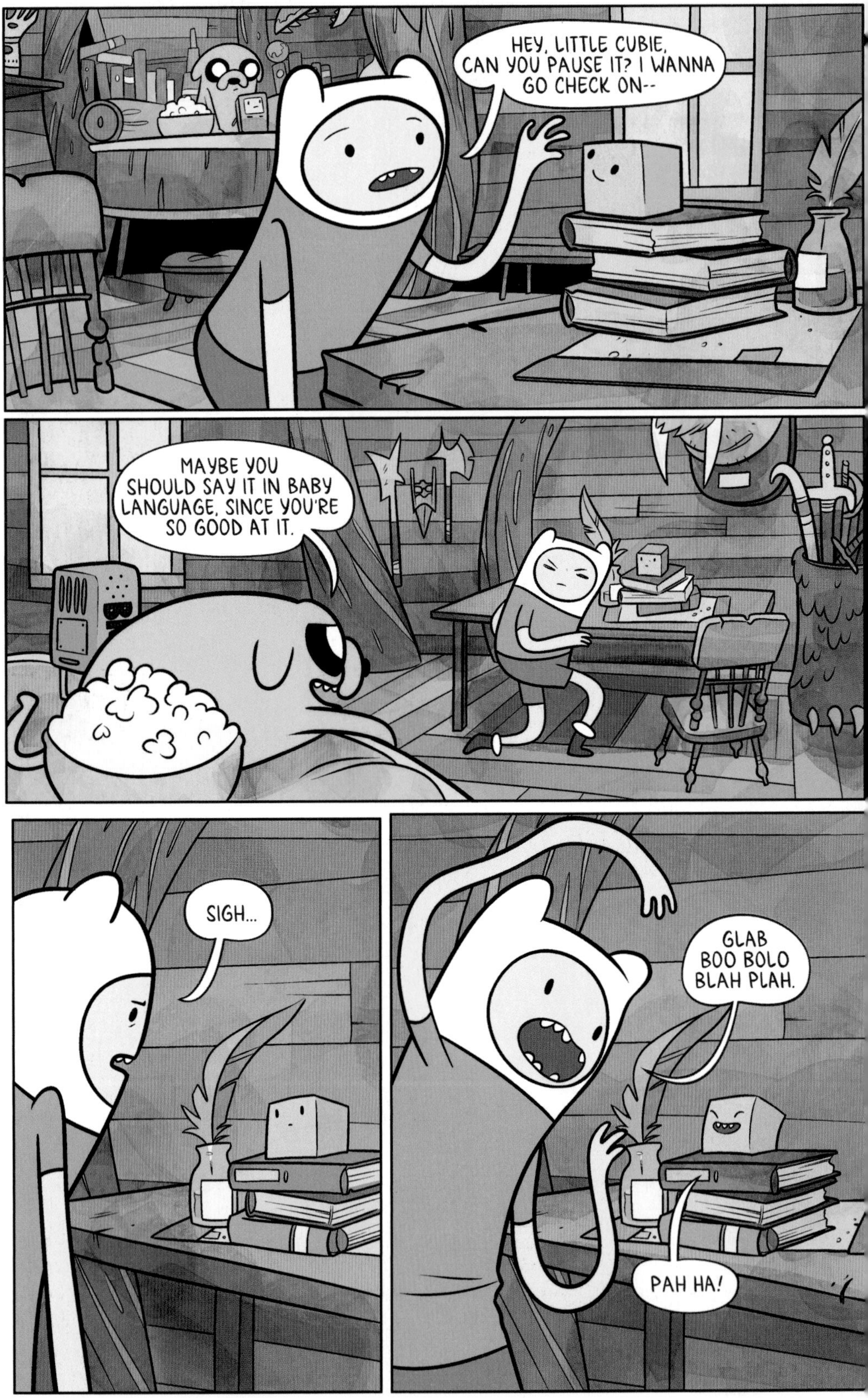
HEY, LITTLE CUBIE, CAN YOU PAUSE IT? I WANNA GO CHECK ON--
MAYBE YOU SHOULD SAY IT IN BABY LANGUAGE, SINCE YOU'RE SO GOOD AT IT.
SIGH...
GLAB BOO BOLO BLAH PLAH.
PAH HA!

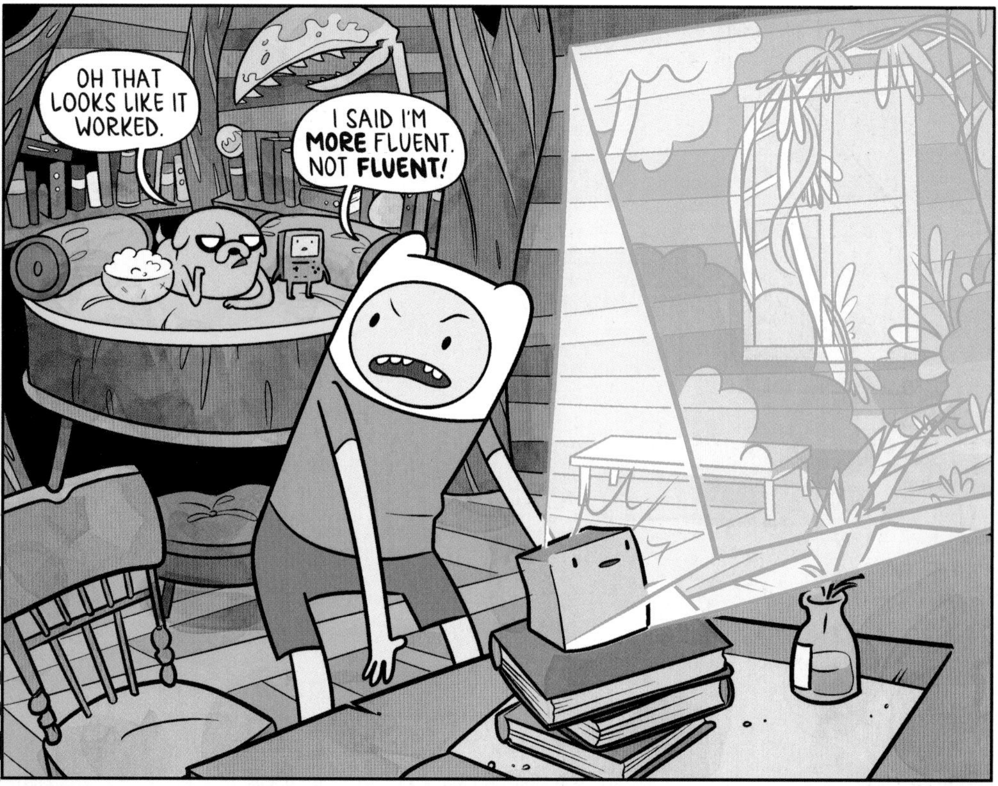
OH THAT LOOKS LIKE IT WORKED.
I SAID I'M **MORE** FLUENT. NOT **FLUENT**!

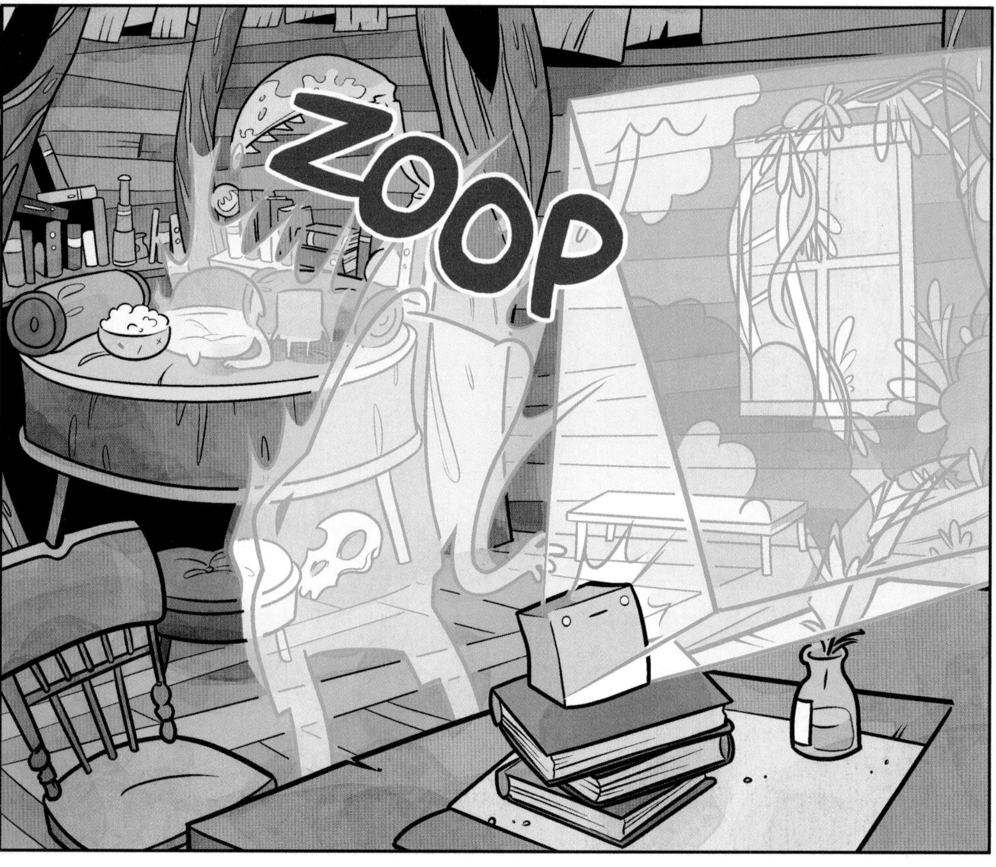
ZOOP

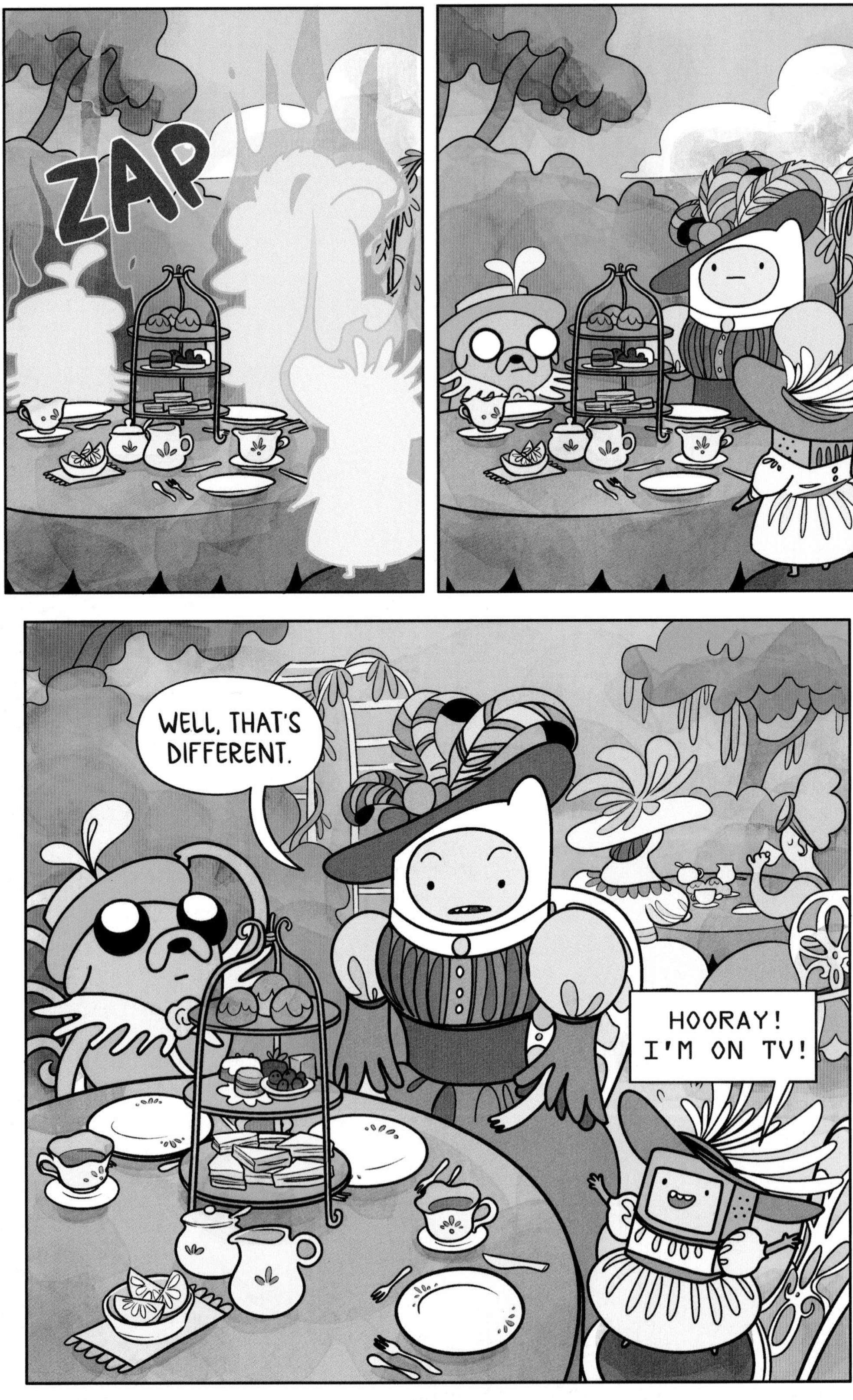
ZAP
WELL, THAT'S DIFFERENT.
HOORAY! I'M ON TV!

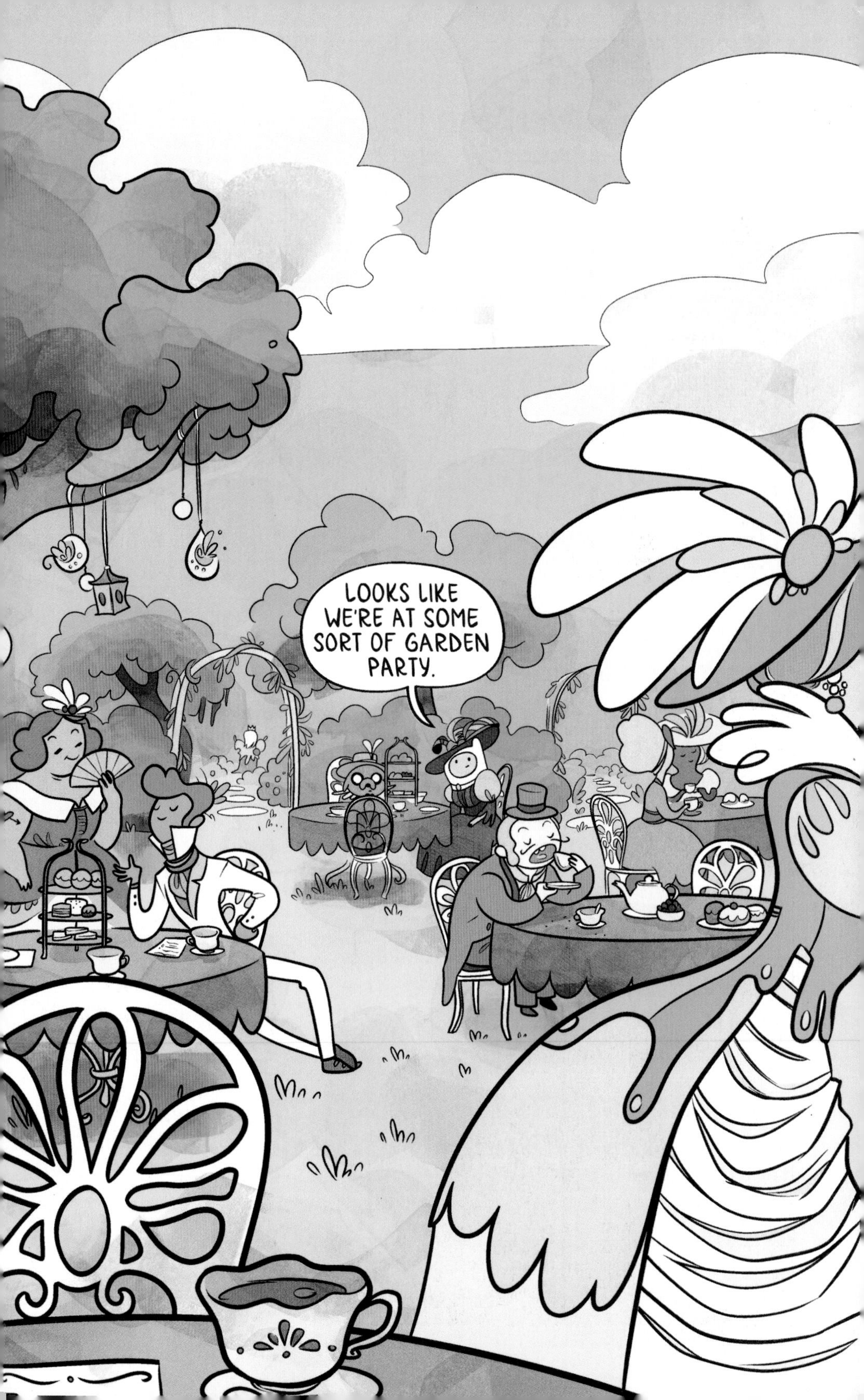
LOOKS LIKE WE'RE AT SOME SORT OF GARDEN PARTY.

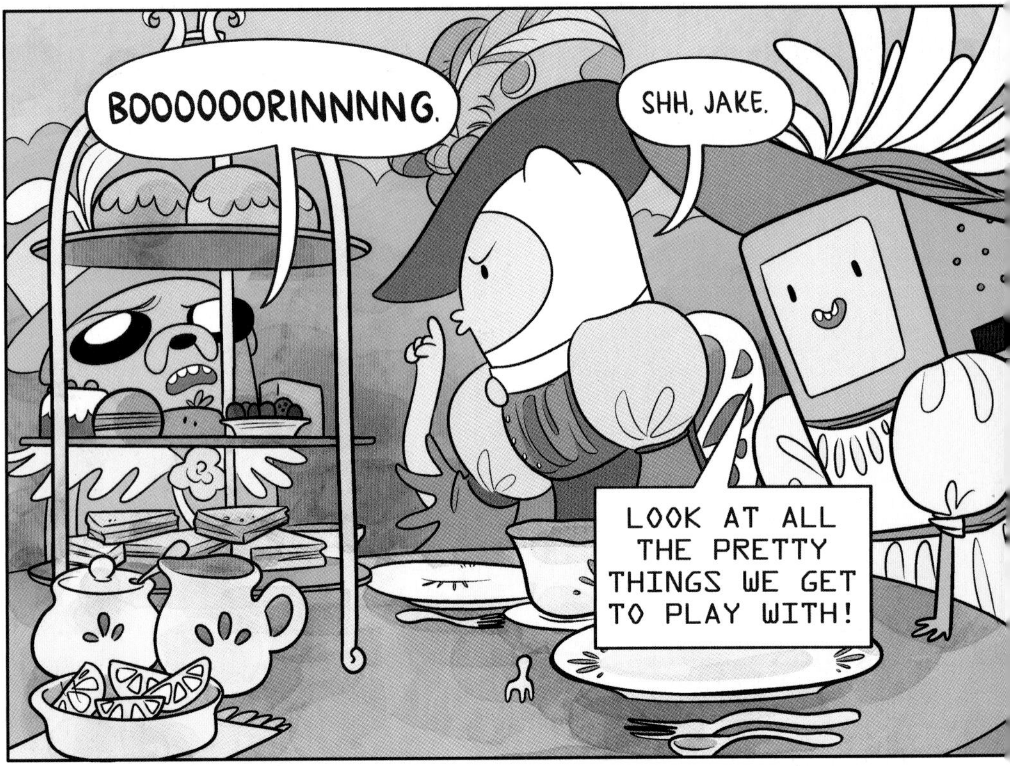
BOOOOOORINNNNG.
SHH, JAKE.
LOOK AT ALL THE PRETTY THINGS WE GET TO PLAY WITH!

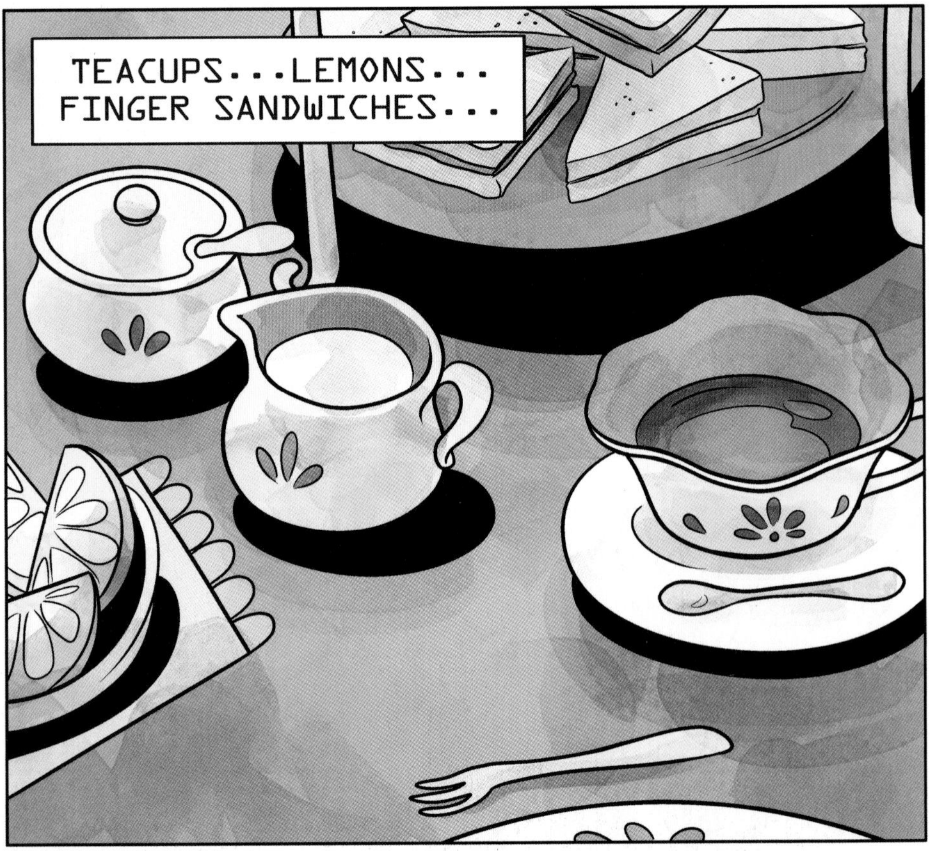
TEACUPS...LEMONS...
FINGER SANDWICHES...

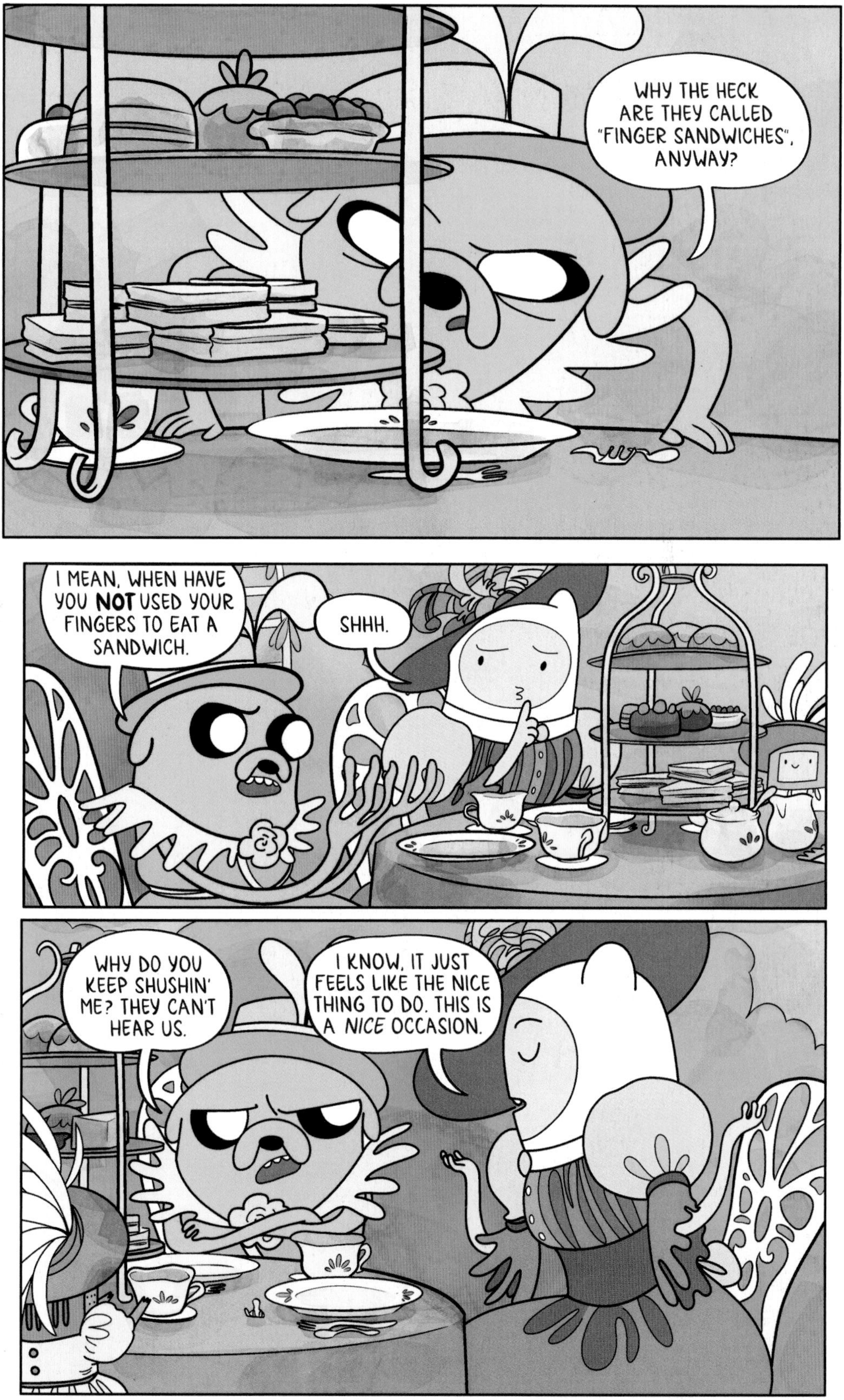
WHY THE HECK ARE THEY CALLED "FINGER SANDWICHES", ANYWAY?
I MEAN, WHEN HAVE YOU **NOT** USED YOUR FINGERS TO EAT A SANDWICH.
SHHH.
WHY DO YOU KEEP SHUSHIN' ME? THEY CAN'T HEAR US.
I KNOW, IT JUST FEELS LIKE THE NICE THING TO DO. THIS IS A *NICE* OCCASION.

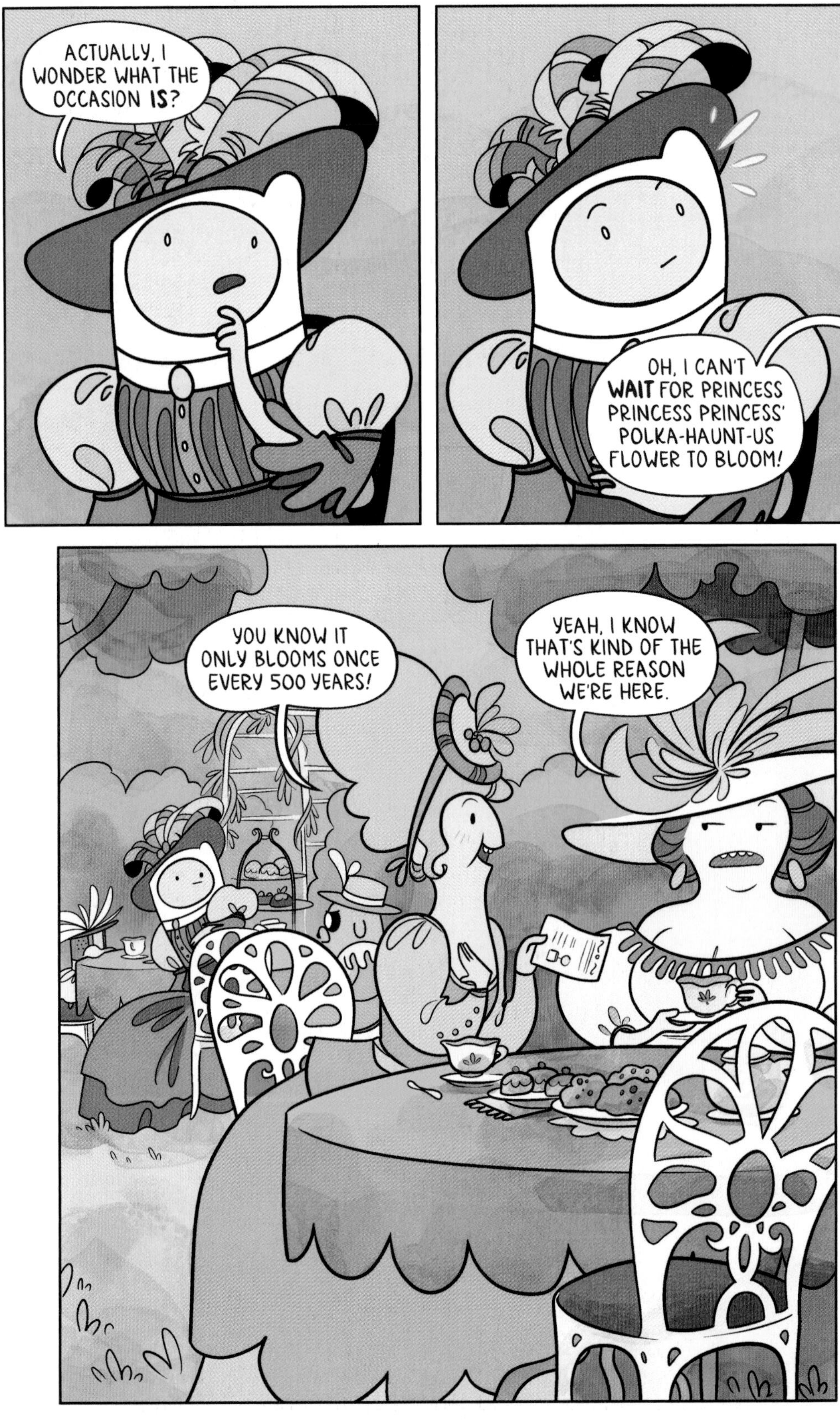
ACTUALLY, I WONDER WHAT THE OCCASION **IS**?
OH, I CAN'T **WAIT** FOR PRINCESS PRINCESS PRINCESS' POLKA-HAUNT-US FLOWER TO BLOOM!
YOU KNOW IT ONLY BLOOMS ONCE EVERY 500 YEARS!
YEAH, I KNOW THAT'S KIND OF THE WHOLE REASON WE'RE HERE.

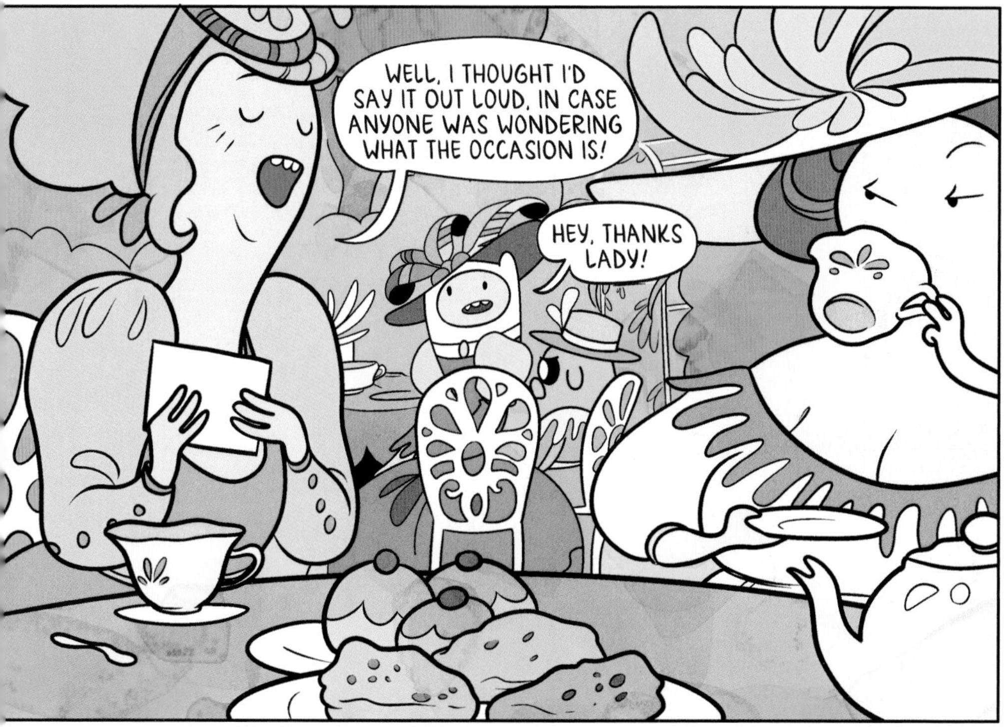
WELL, I THOUGHT I'D SAY IT OUT LOUD, IN CASE ANYONE WAS WONDERING WHAT THE OCCASION IS!
HEY, THANKS LADY!

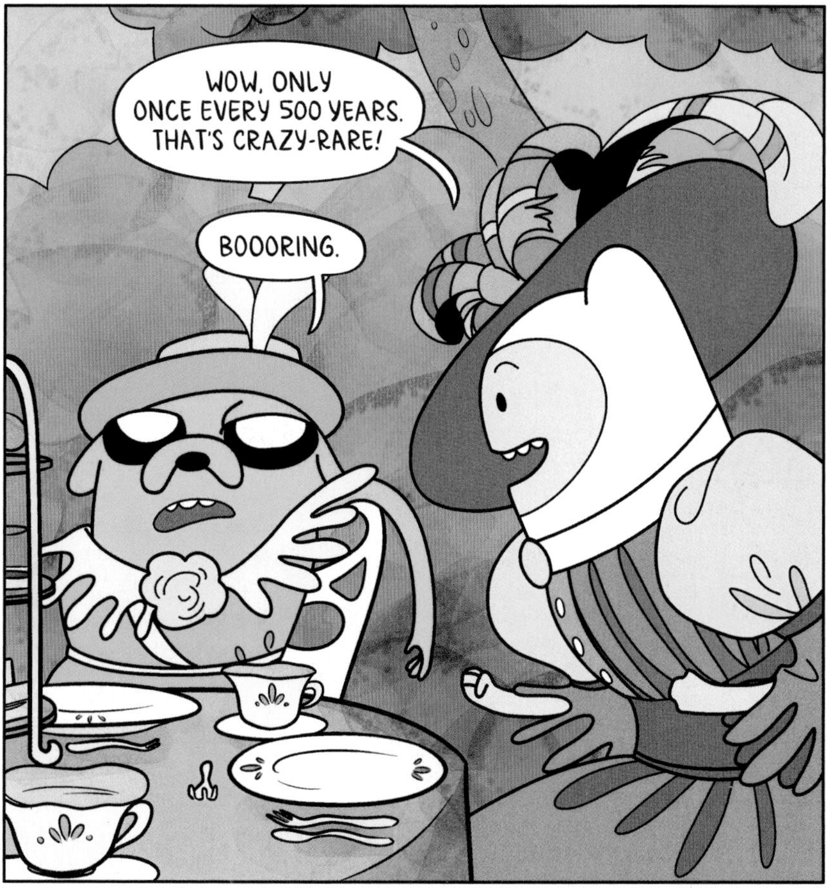
WOW, ONLY ONCE EVERY 500 YEARS. THAT'S CRAZY-RARE!
BOOORING.

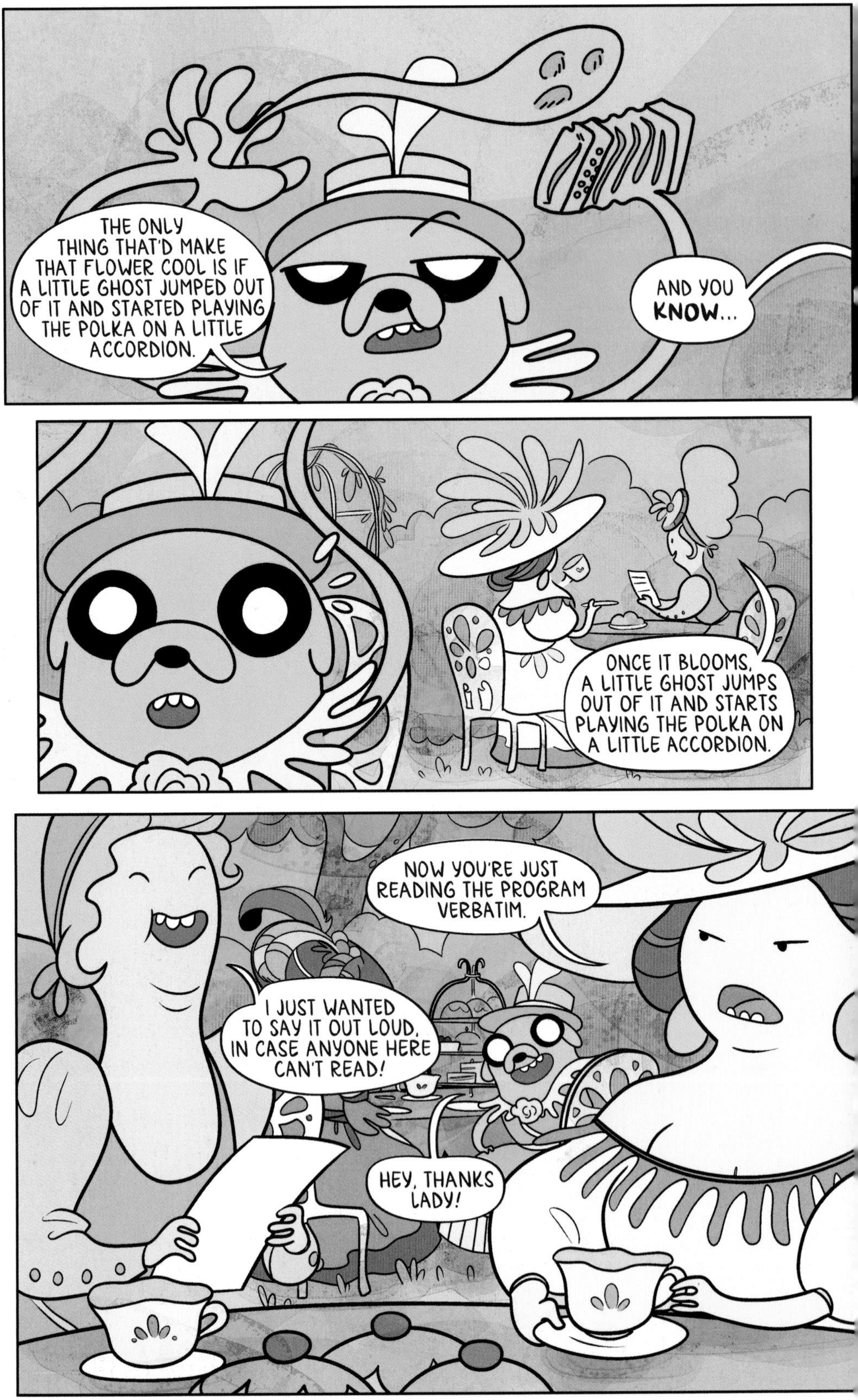
THE ONLY THING THAT'D MAKE THAT FLOWER COOL IS IF A LITTLE GHOST JUMPED OUT OF IT AND STARTED PLAYING THE POLKA ON A LITTLE ACCORDION.
AND YOU **KNOW**...
ONCE IT BLOOMS, A LITTLE GHOST JUMPS OUT OF IT AND STARTS PLAYING THE POLKA ON A LITTLE ACCORDION.
NOW YOU'RE JUST READING THE PROGRAM VERBATIM.
I JUST WANTED TO SAY IT OUT LOUD, IN CASE ANYONE HERE CAN'T READ!
HEY, THANKS LADY!

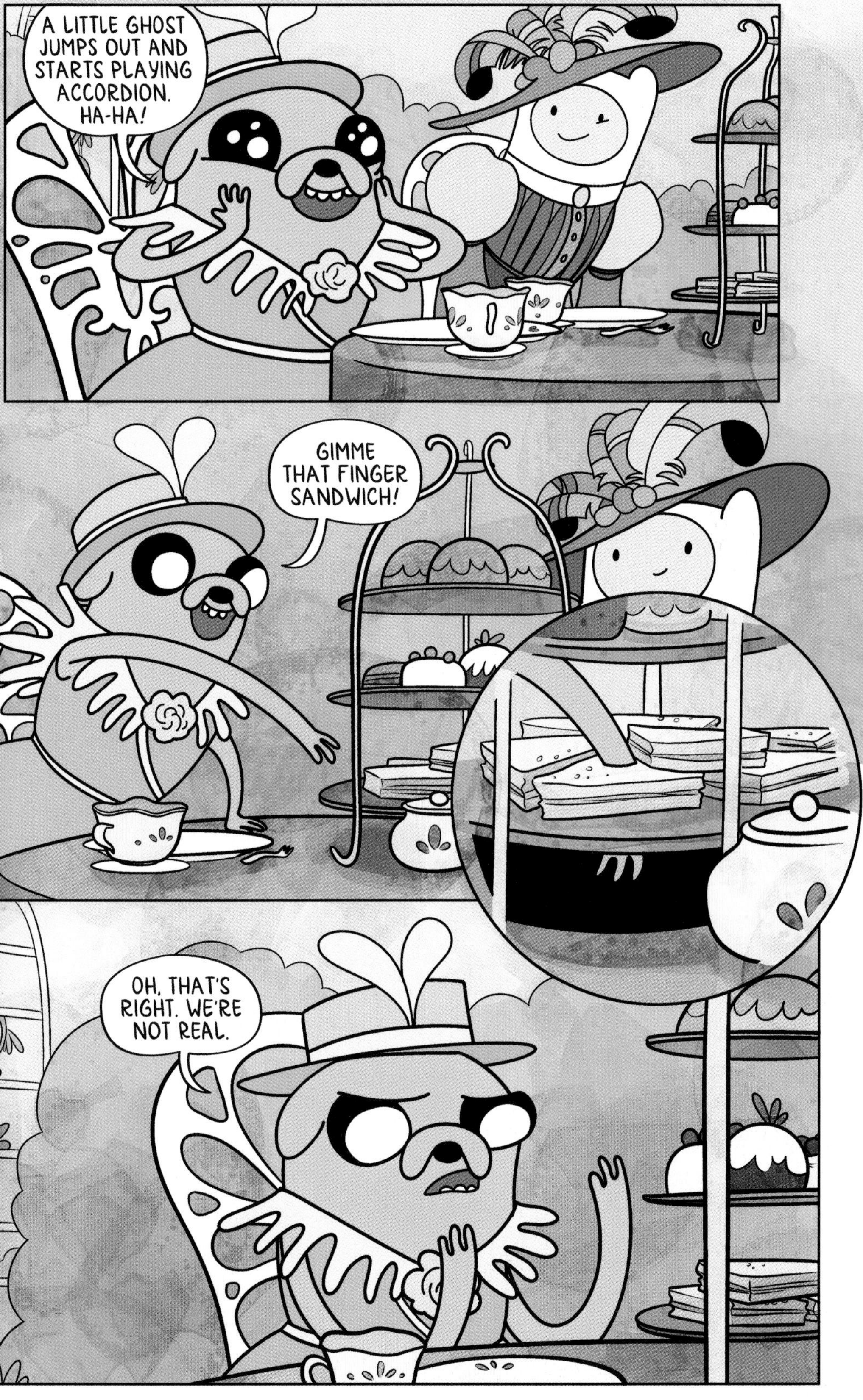
A LITTLE GHOST JUMPS OUT AND STARTS PLAYING ACCORDION. HA-HA!
GIMME THAT FINGER SANDWICH!
OH, THAT'S RIGHT. WE'RE NOT REAL.

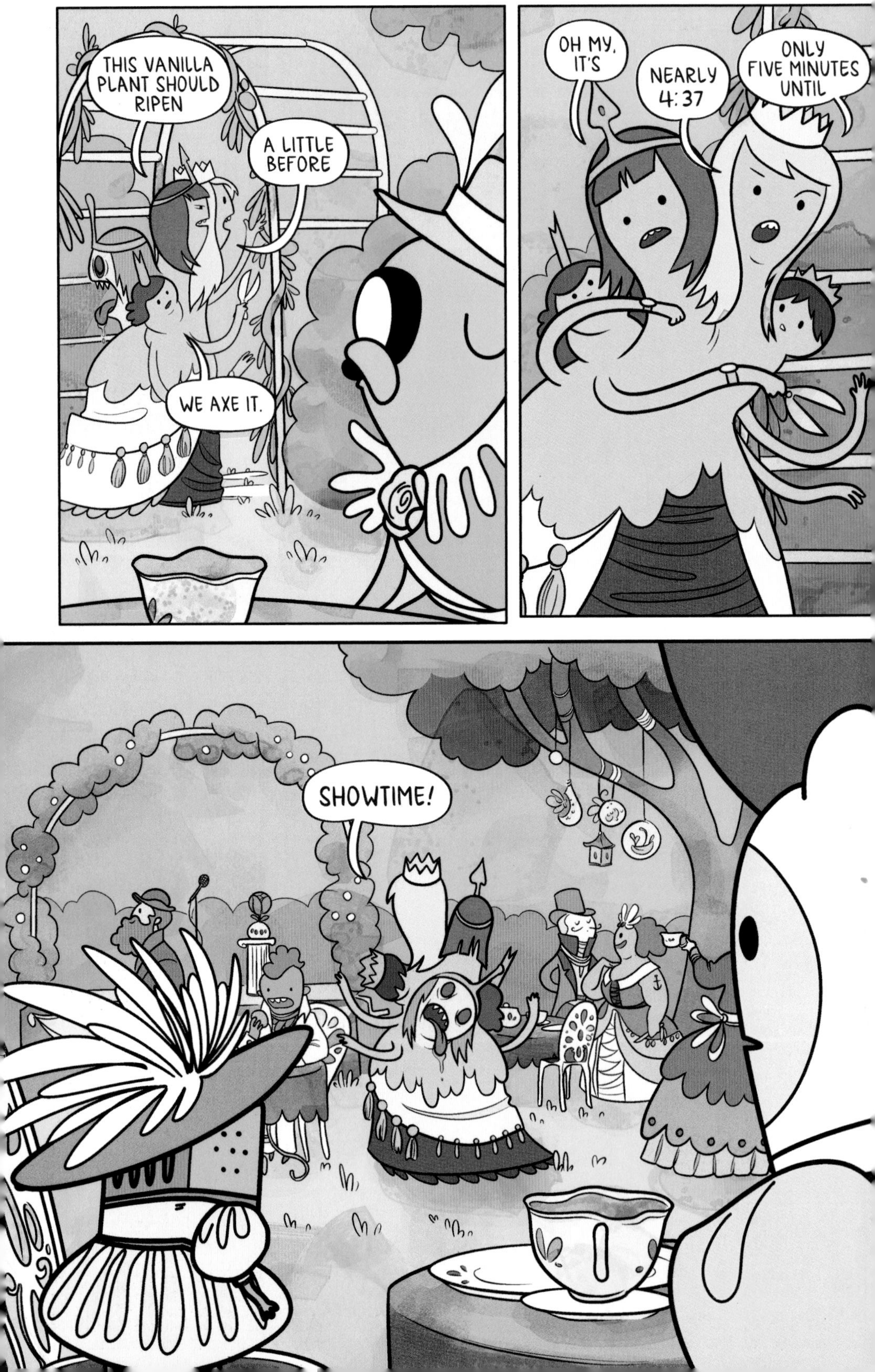
THIS VANILLA PLANT SHOULD RIPEN
A LITTLE BEFORE
WE AXE IT.
OH MY, IT'S
NEARLY 4:37
ONLY FIVE MINUTES UNTIL
SHOWTIME!

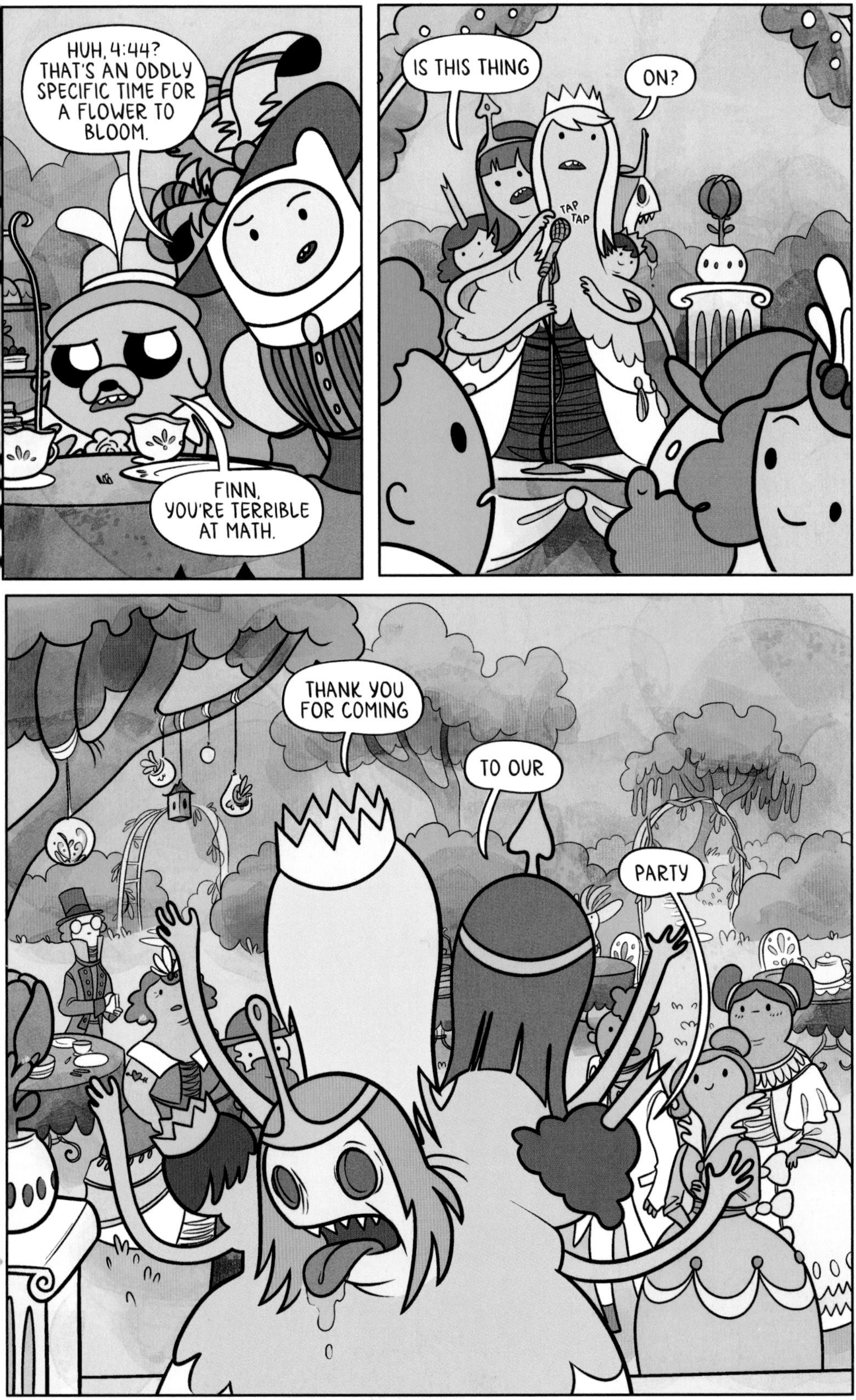
HUH, 4:44? THAT'S AN ODDLY SPECIFIC TIME FOR A FLOWER TO BLOOM.
FINN, YOU'RE TERRIBLE AT MATH.
IS THIS THING
ON?
TAP TAP
THANK YOU FOR COMING
TO OUR
PARTY

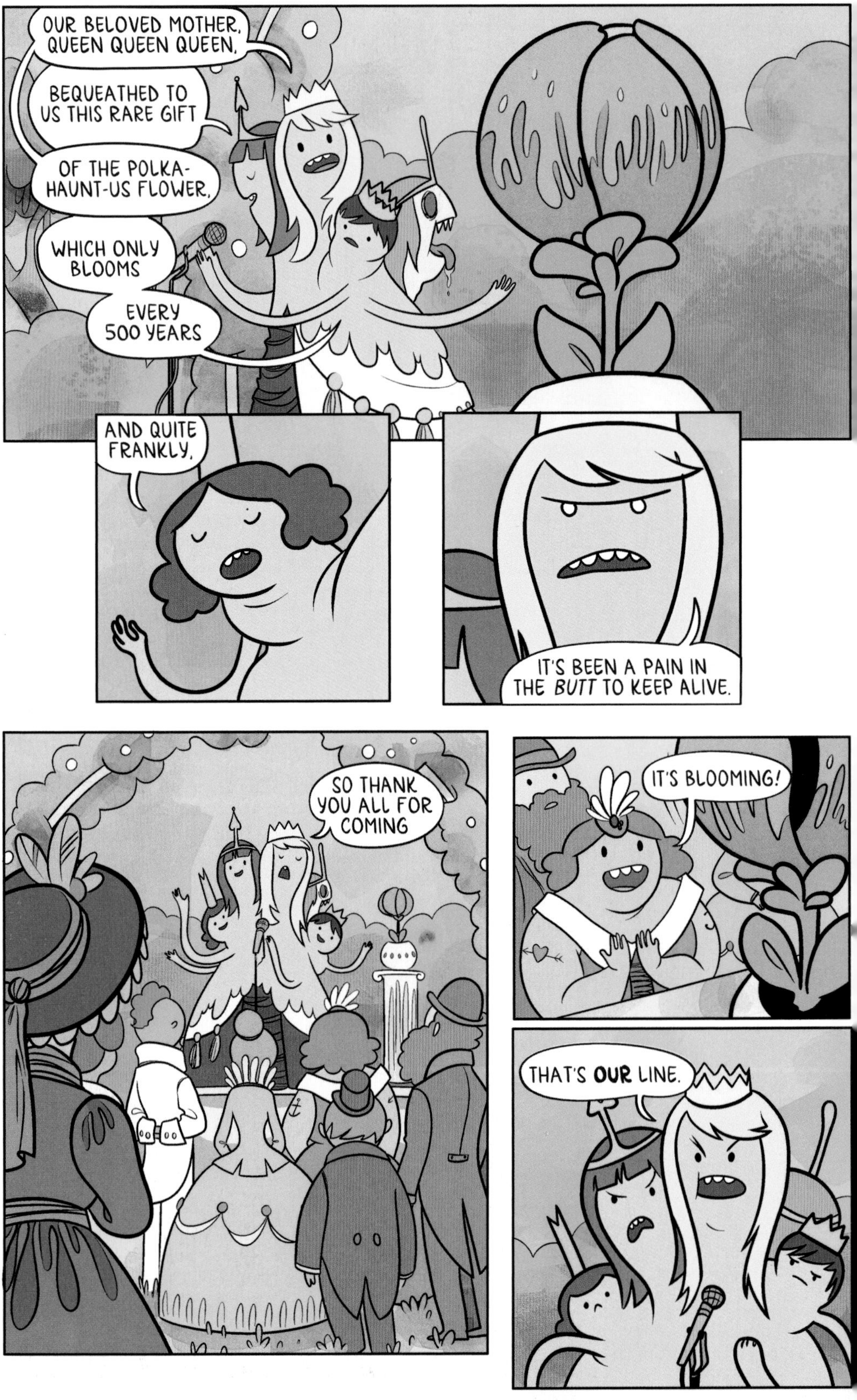
OUR BELOVED MOTHER, QUEEN QUEEN QUEEN,
BEQUEATHED TO US THIS RARE GIFT
OF THE POLKA-HAUNT-US FLOWER,
WHICH ONLY BLOOMS
EVERY 500 YEARS
AND QUITE FRANKLY,
IT'S BEEN A PAIN IN THE *BUTT* TO KEEP ALIVE.
SO THANK YOU ALL FOR COMING
IT'S BLOOMING!
THAT'S **OUR** LINE.

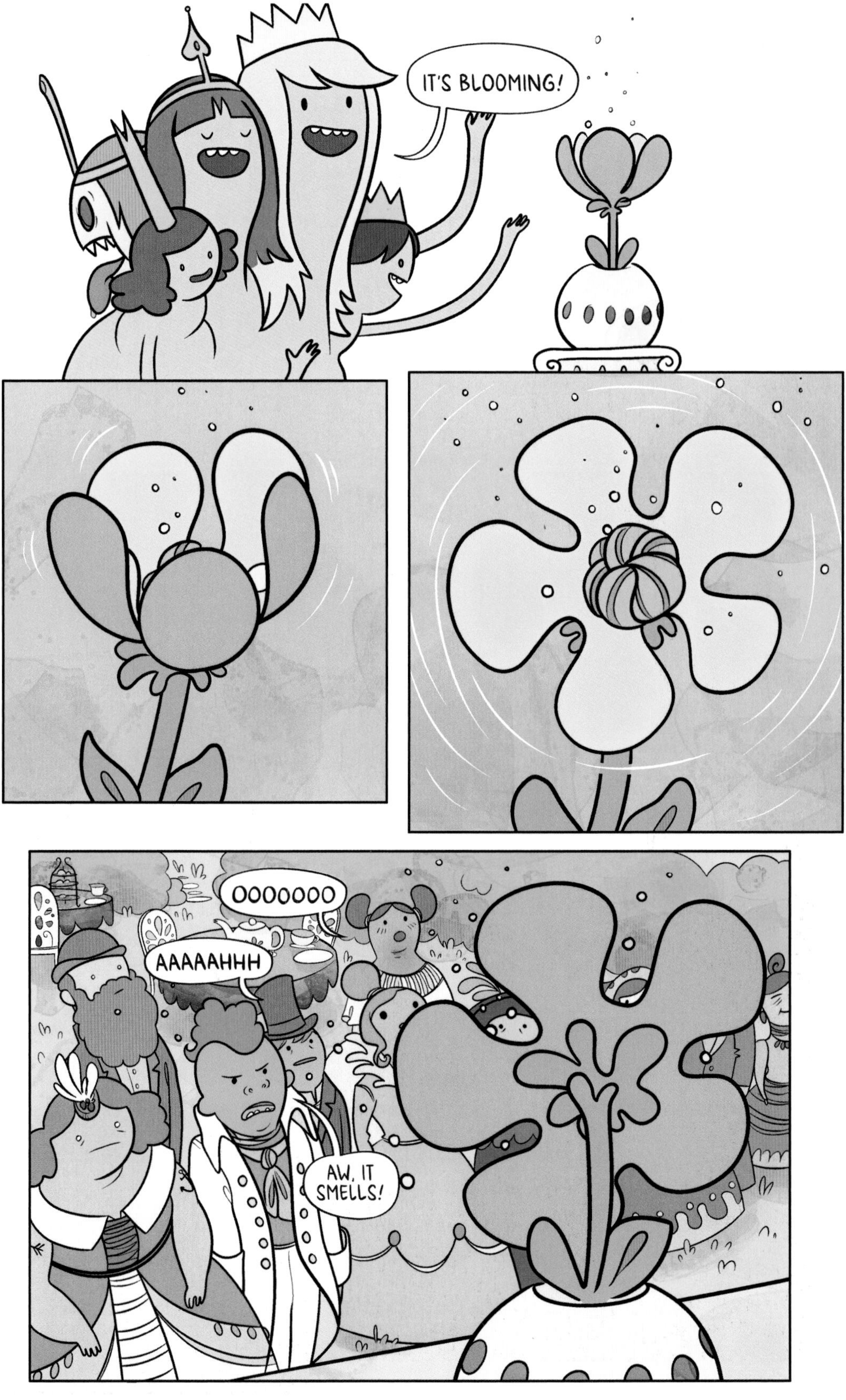
IT'S BLOOMING!
OOOOOOO
AAAAAHHH
AW, IT SMELLS!

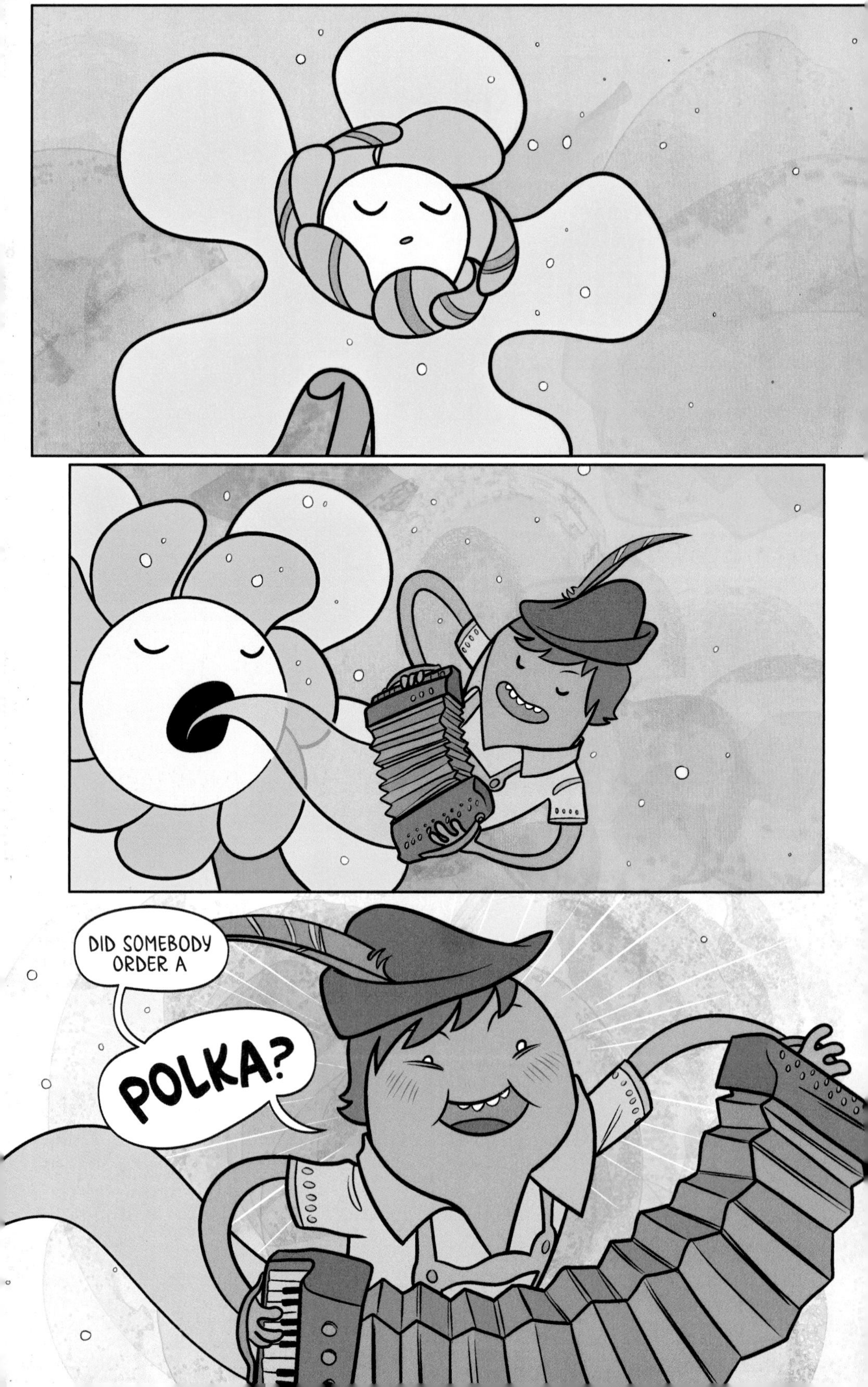
DID SOMEBODY ORDER A
POLKA?

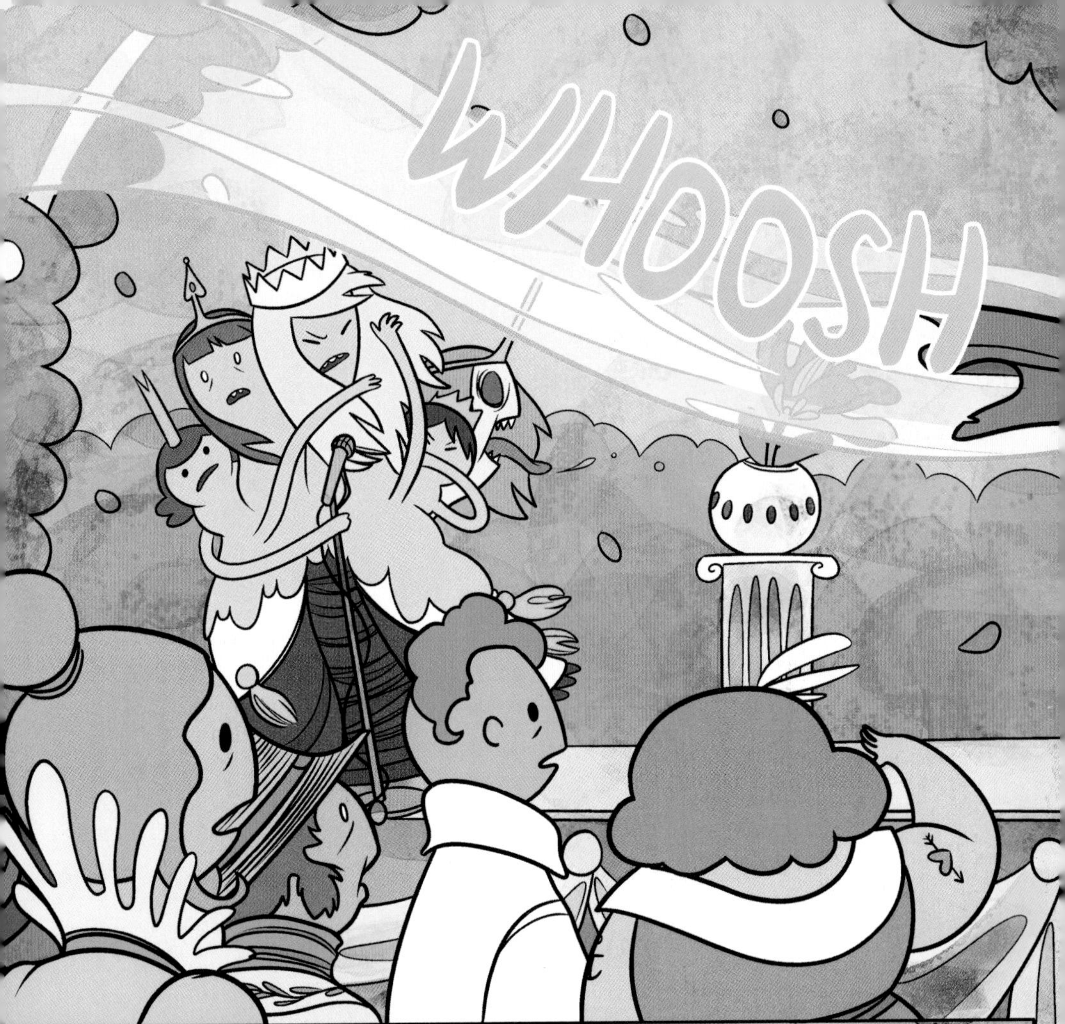
WHOOSH
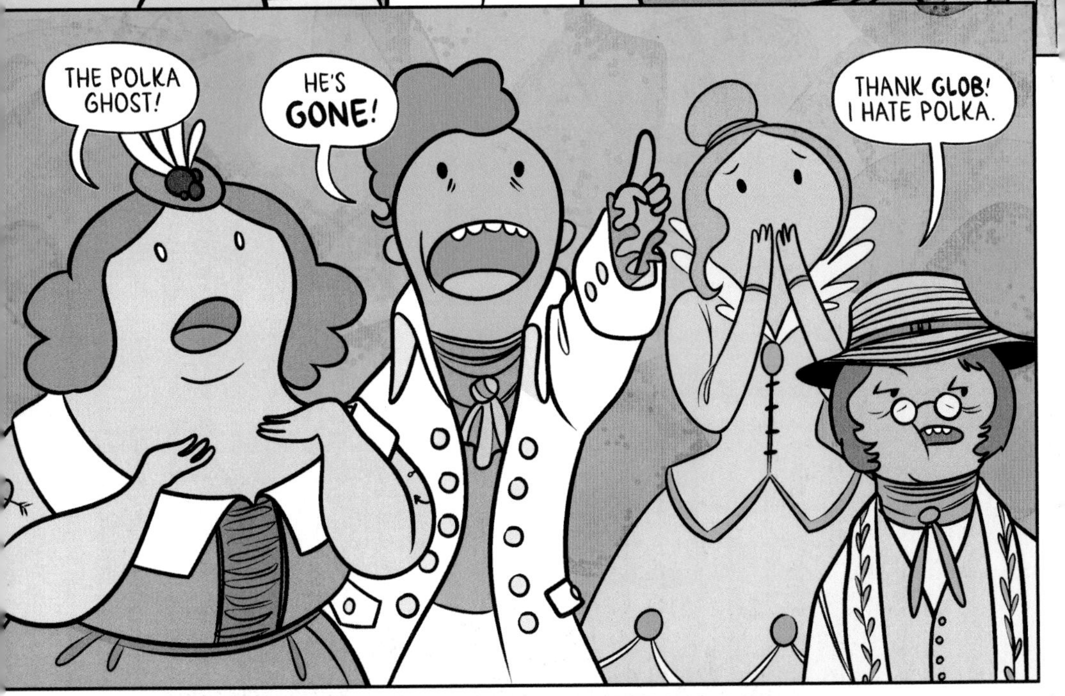
THE POLKA GHOST!
HE'S **GONE**!
THANK **GLOB**! I HATE POLKA.

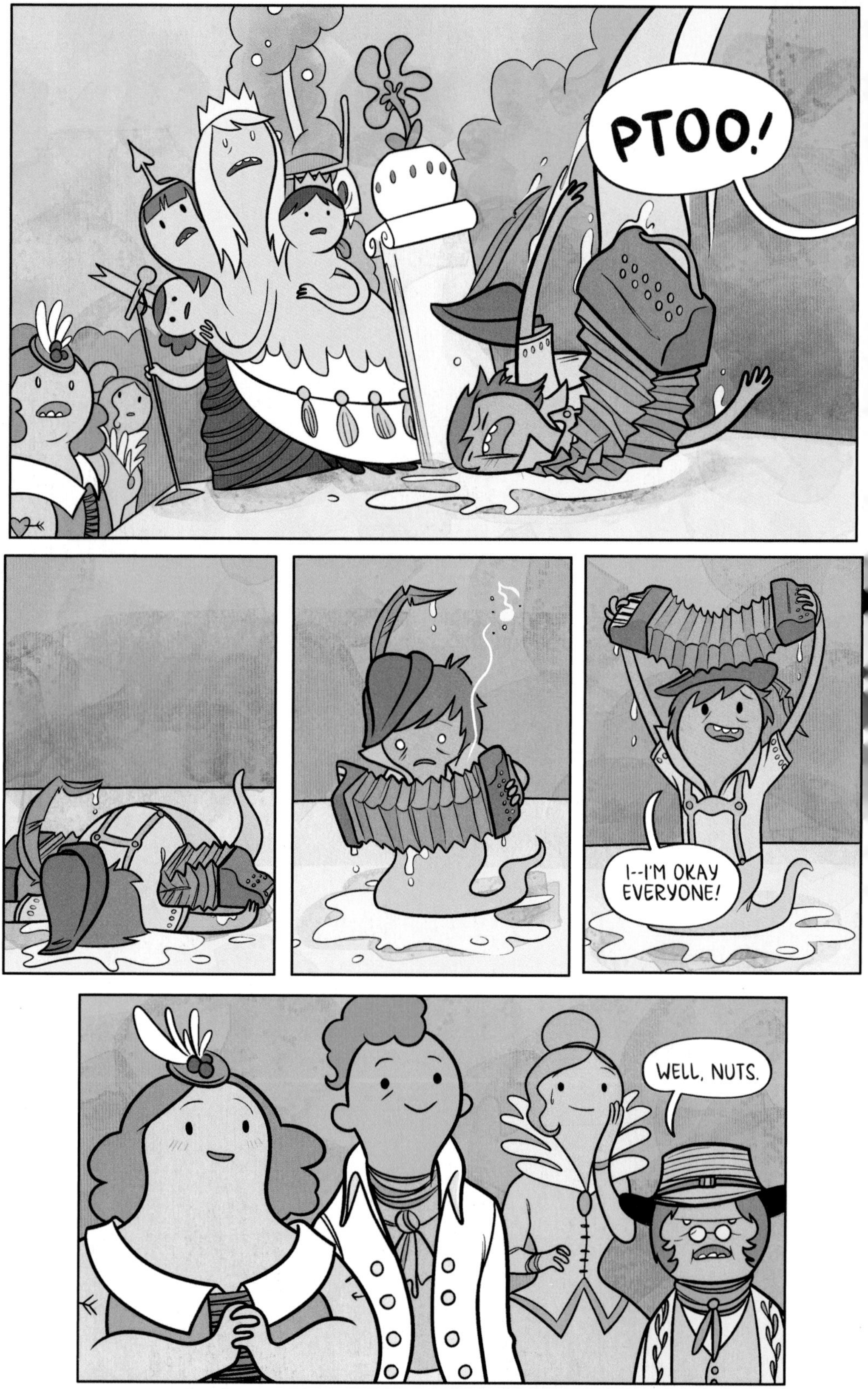
PTOO!
I--I'M OKAY EVERYONE!
WELL, NUTS.

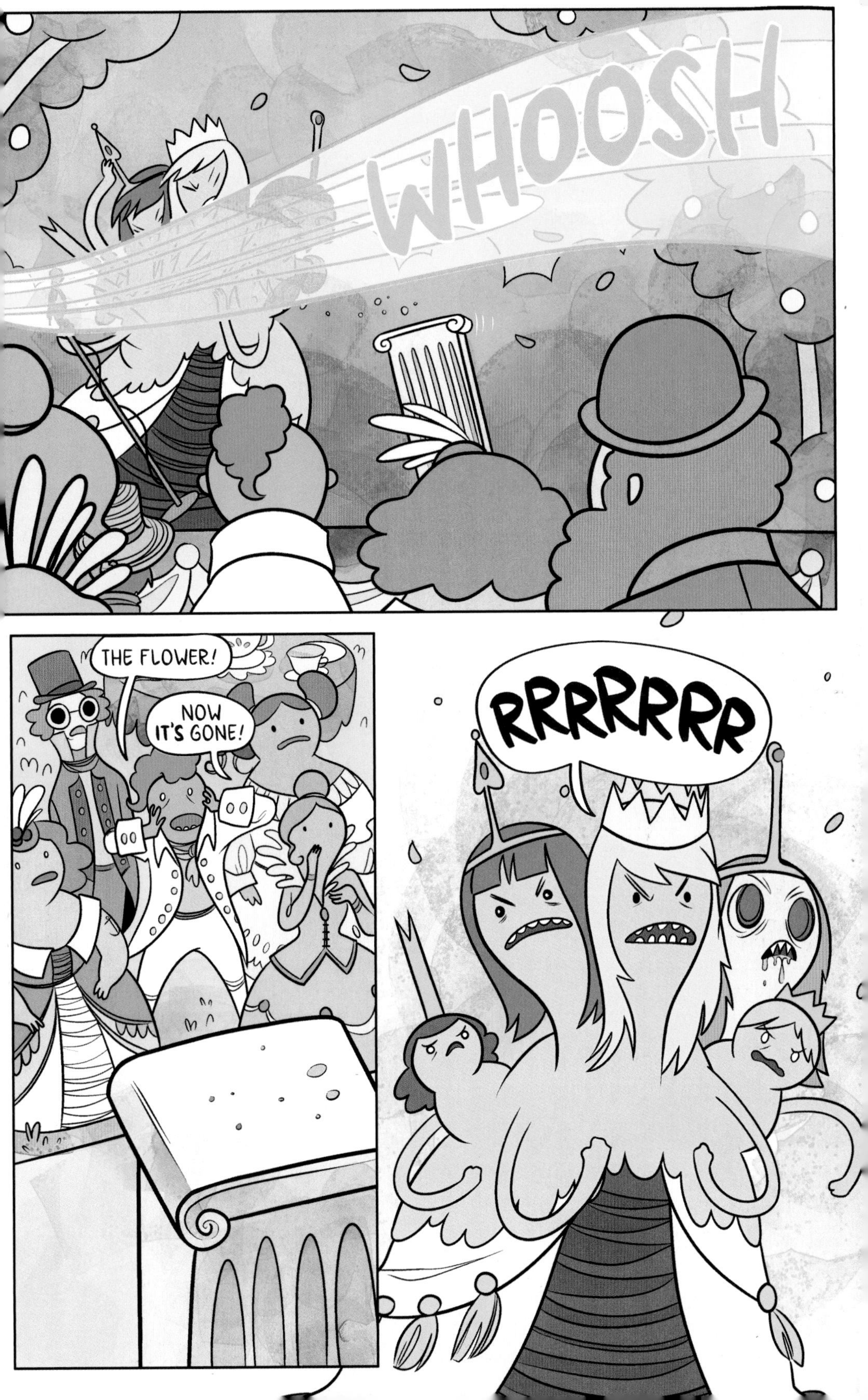
WHOOSH
THE FLOWER!
NOW IT'S GONE!
RRRRRRR

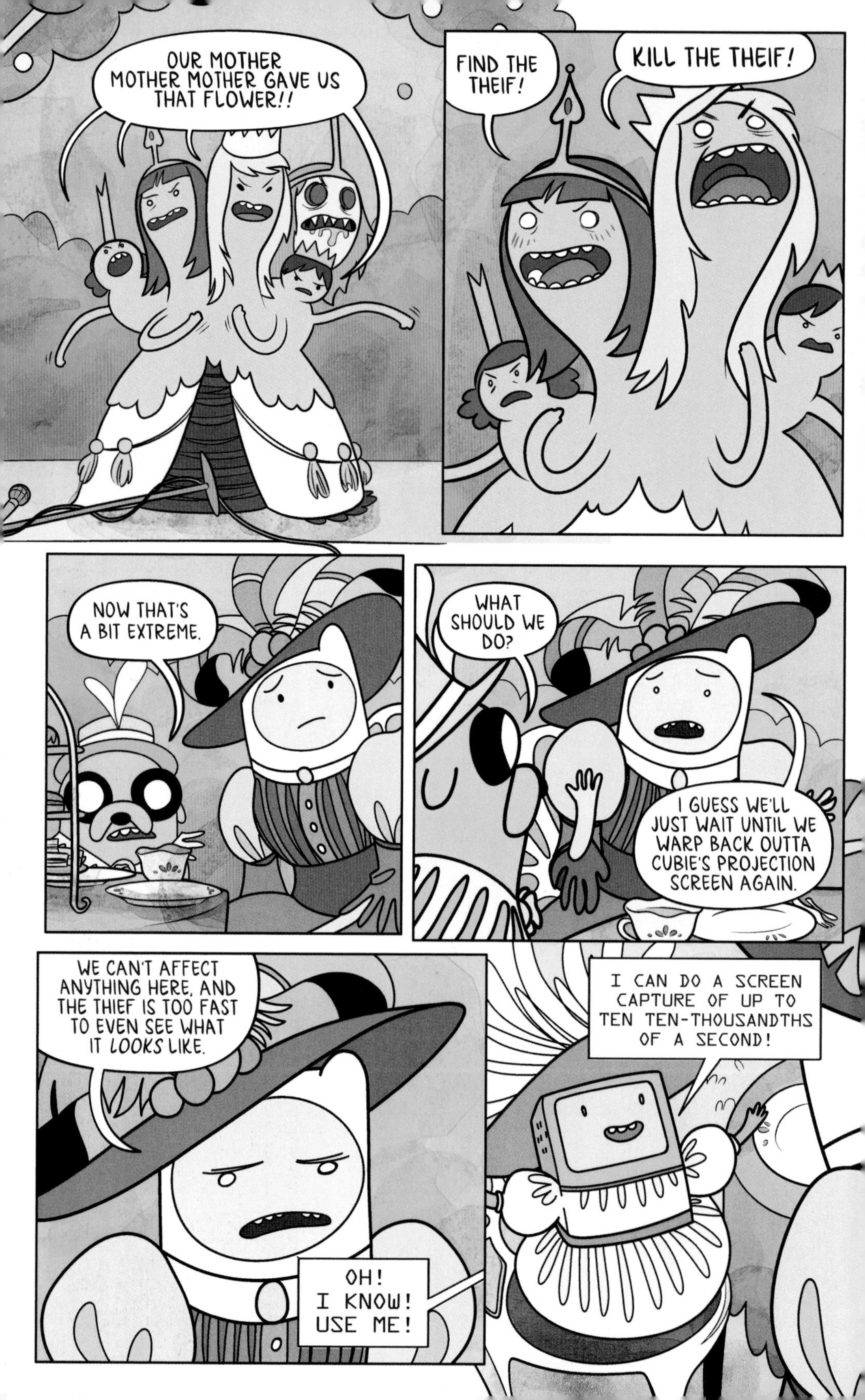
OUR MOTHER MOTHER MOTHER GAVE US THAT FLOWER!!
FIND THE THEIF!
KILL THE THEIF!
NOW THAT'S A BIT EXTREME.
WHAT SHOULD WE DO?
I GUESS WE'LL JUST WAIT UNTIL WE WARP BACK OUTTA CUBIE'S PROJECTION SCREEN AGAIN.
WE CAN'T AFFECT ANYTHING HERE, AND THE THIEF IS TOO FAST TO EVEN SEE WHAT IT *LOOKS* LIKE.
OH! I KNOW! USE ME!
I CAN DO A SCREEN CAPTURE OF UP TO TEN TEN-THOUSANDTHS OF A SECOND!

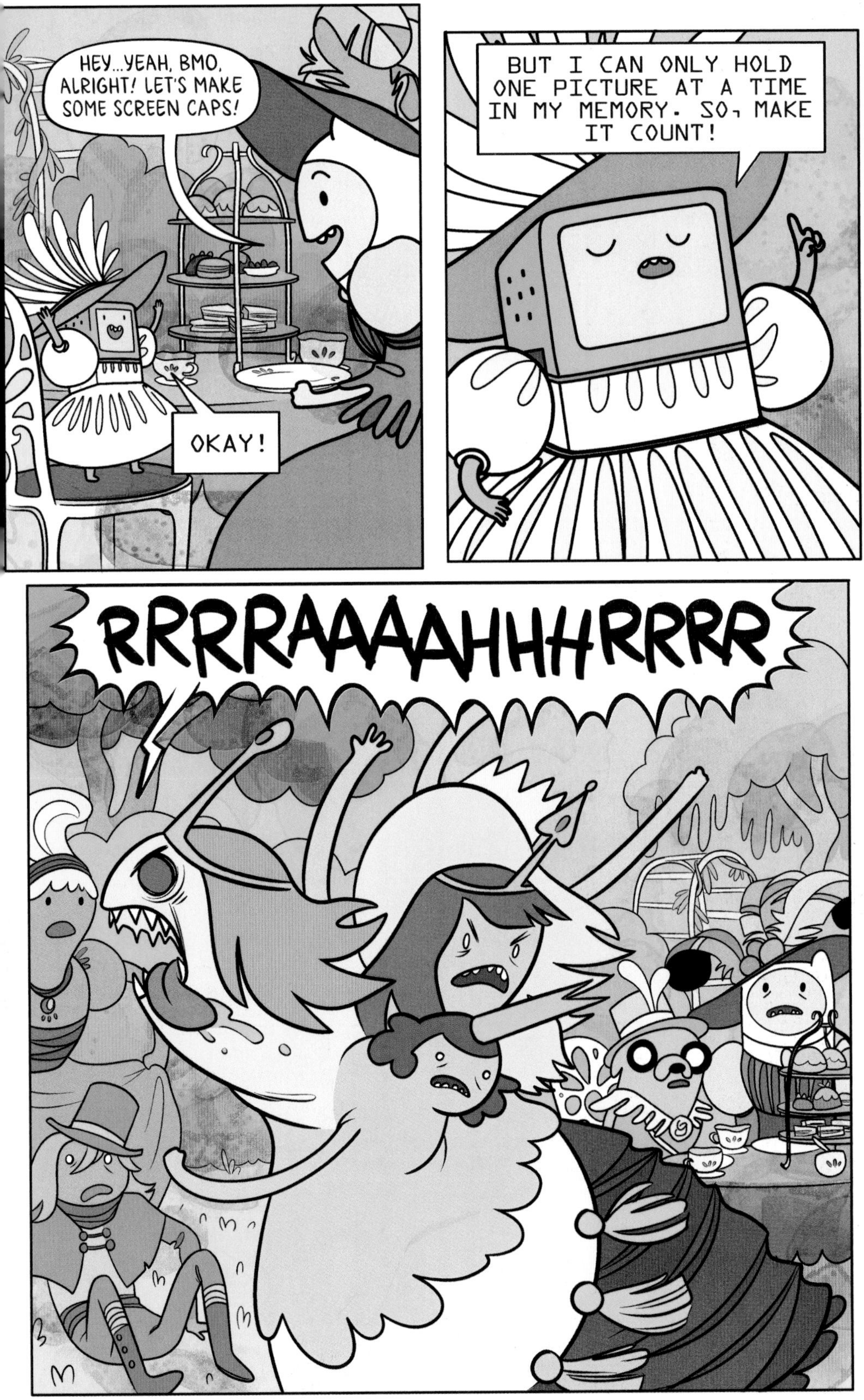
HEY...YEAH, BMO, ALRIGHT! LET'S MAKE SOME SCREEN CAPS!
OKAY!
BUT I CAN ONLY HOLD ONE PICTURE AT A TIME IN MY MEMORY. SO, MAKE IT COUNT!
RRRRAAAAHHHRRRR

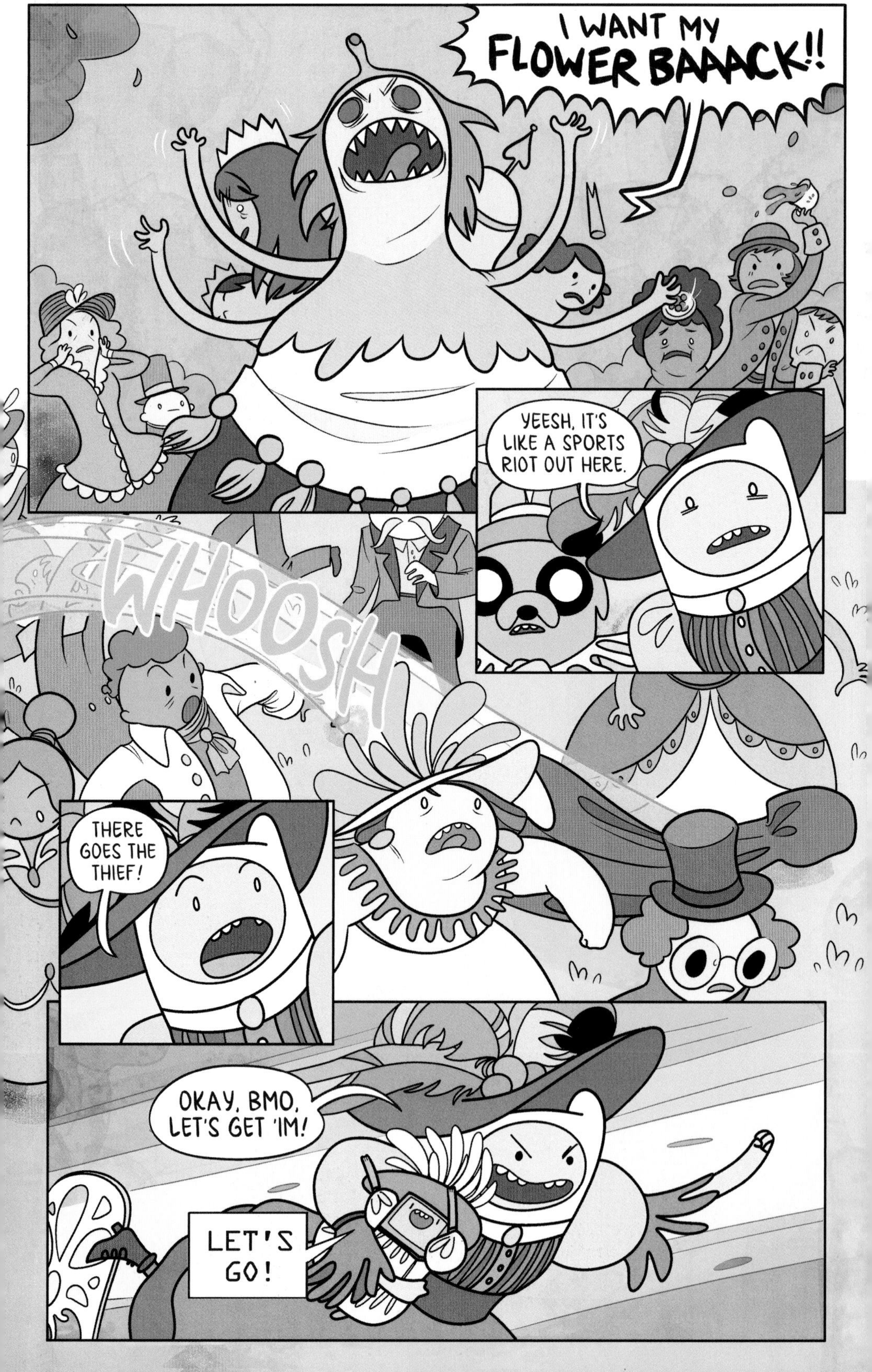
I WANT MY FLOWER BAAACK!!
YEESH, IT'S LIKE A SPORTS RIOT OUT HERE.
WHOOSH
THERE GOES THE THIEF!
OKAY, BMO, LET'S GET 'IM!
LET'S GO!

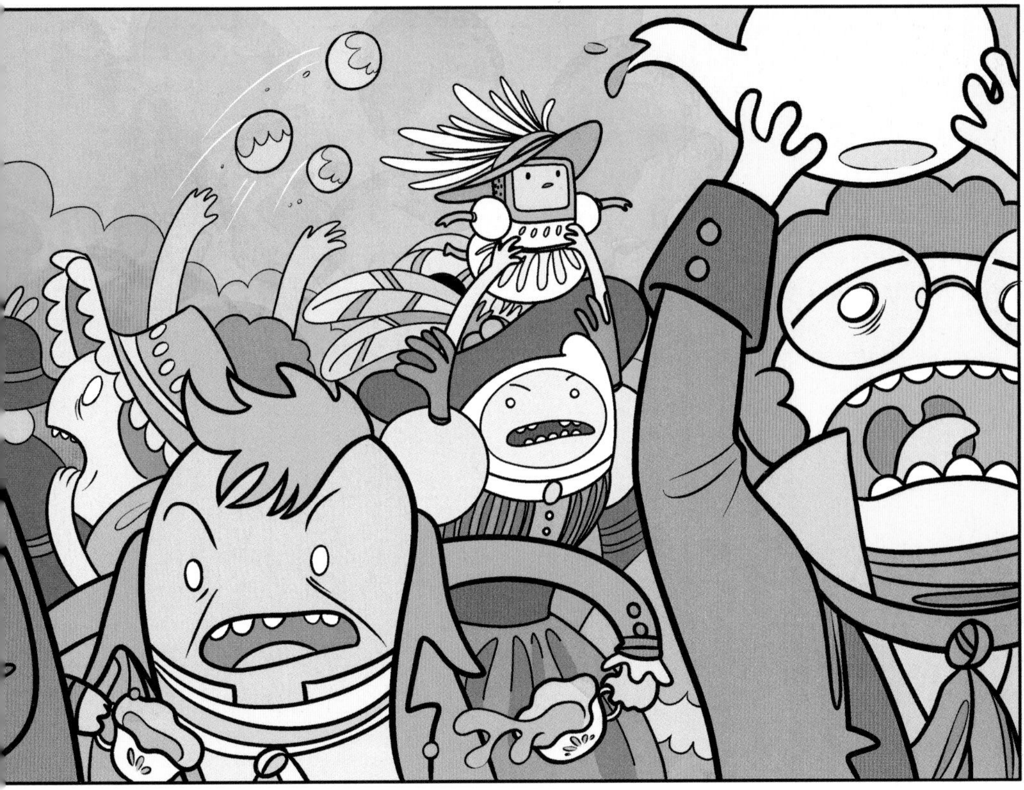

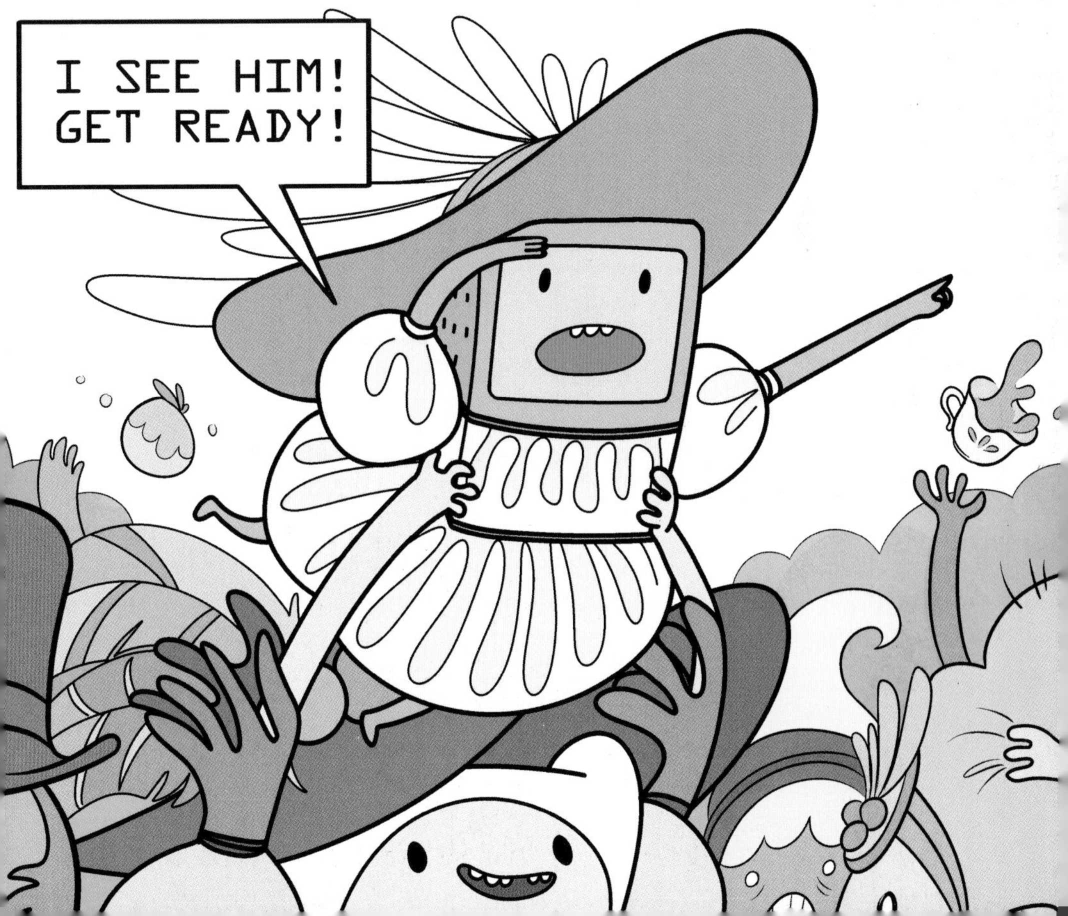
I SEE HIM! GET READY!

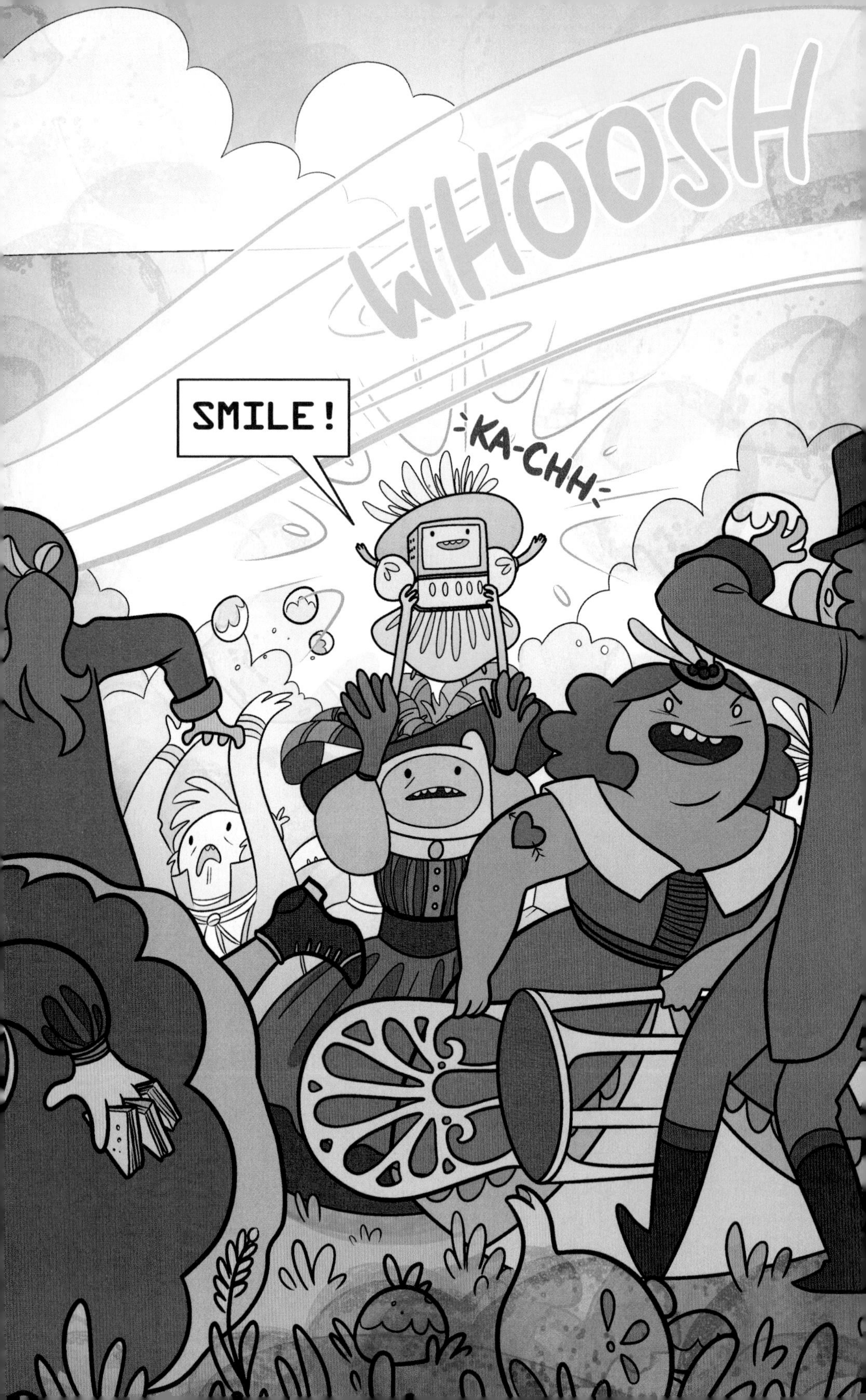
WHOOSH
SMILE!
KA-CHH

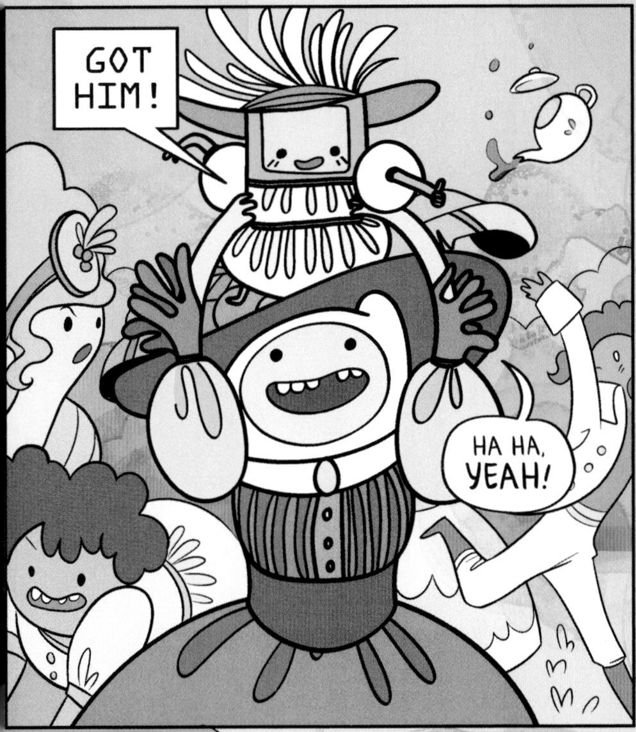
GOT HIM!
HA HA, YEAH!

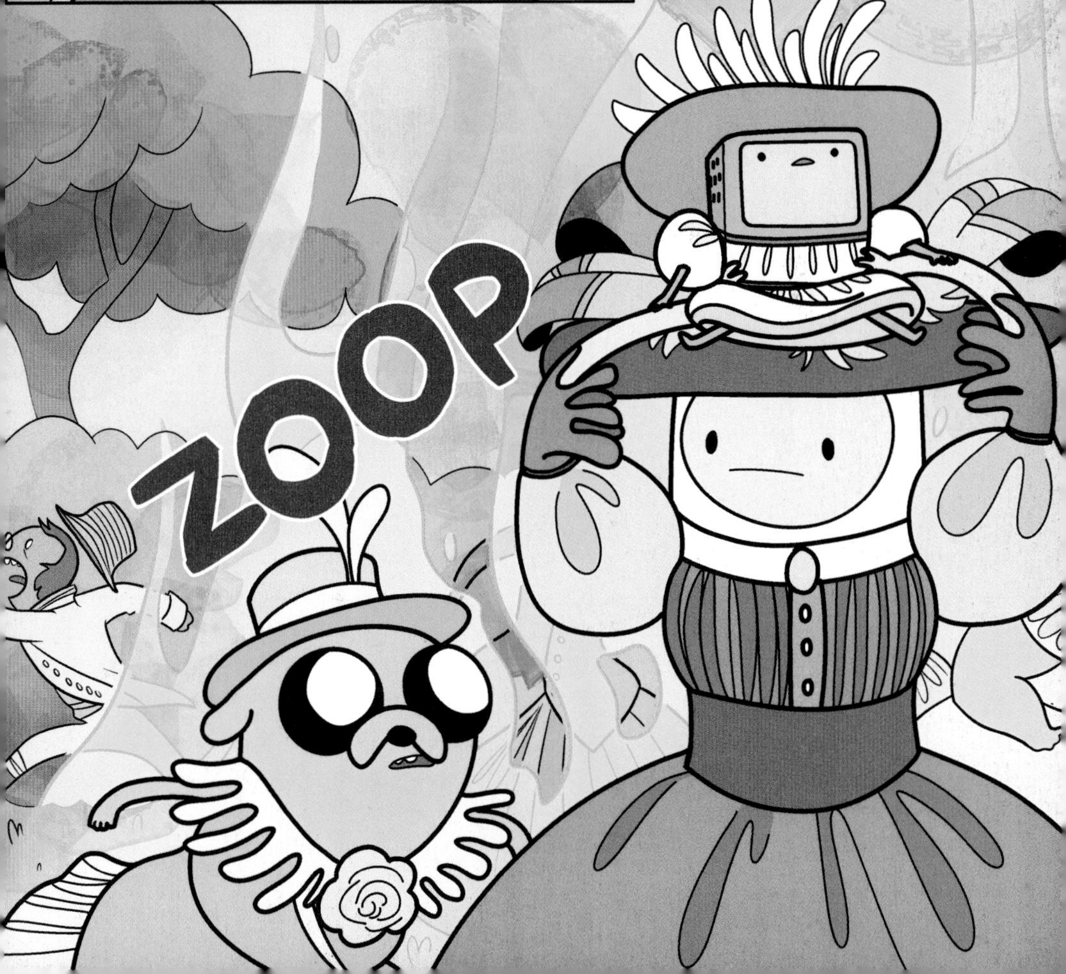
ZOOP

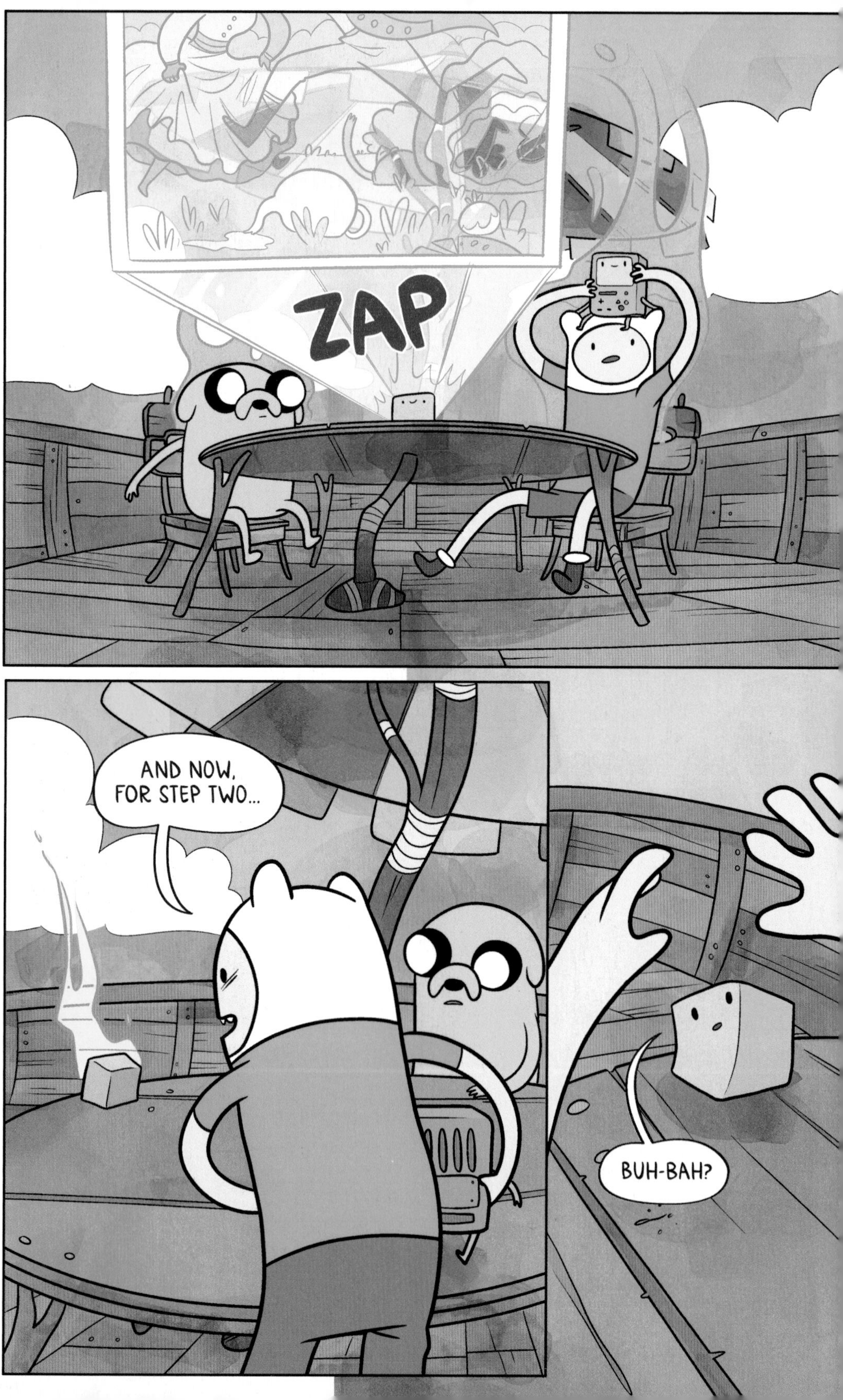
ZAP
AND NOW, FOR STEP TWO...
BUH-BAH?

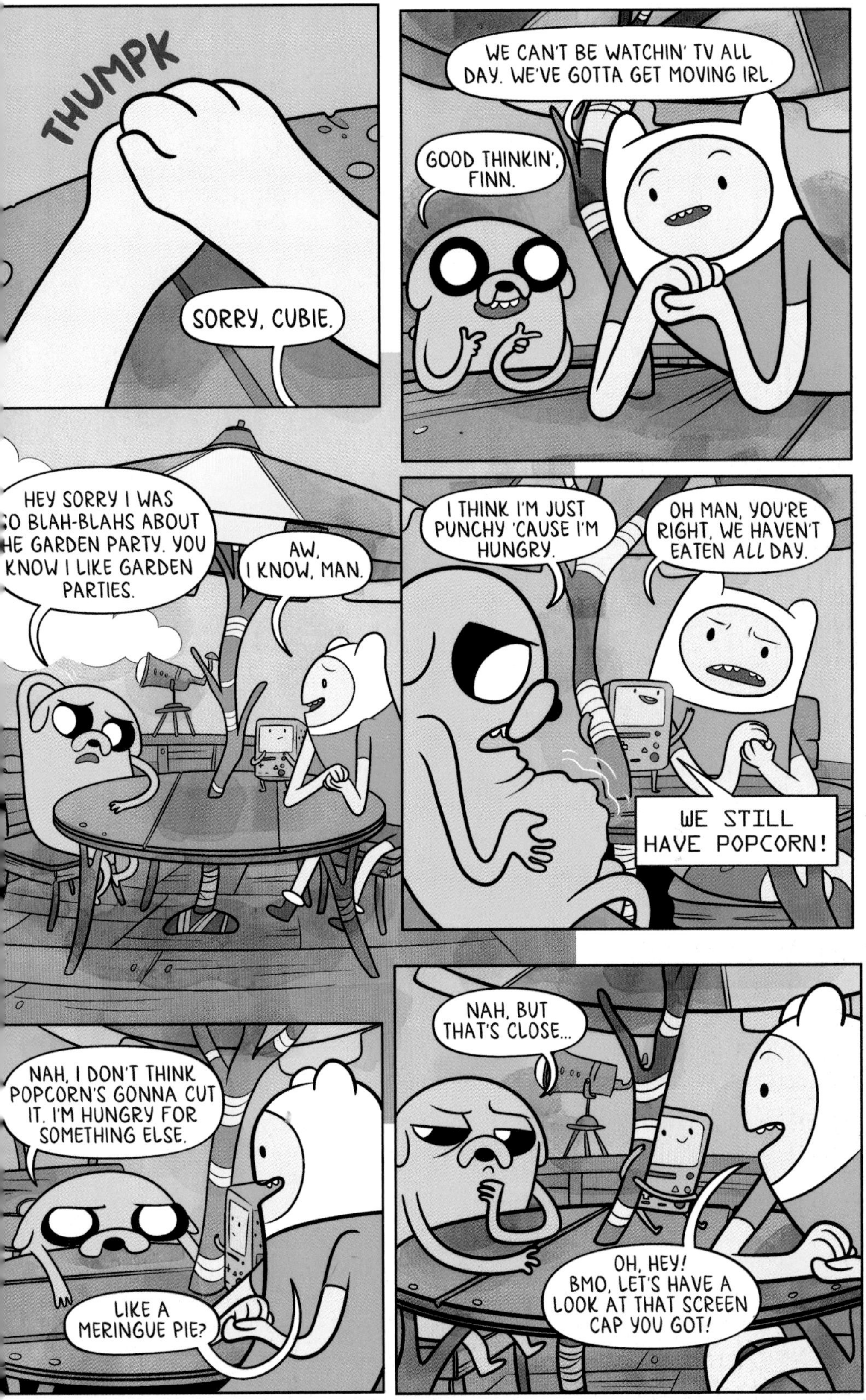
THUMPK
SORRY, CUBIE.
WE CAN'T BE WATCHIN' TV ALL DAY. WE'VE GOTTA GET MOVING IRL.
GOOD THINKIN', FINN.
HEY SORRY I WAS O BLAH-BLAHS ABOUT HE GARDEN PARTY. YOU KNOW I LIKE GARDEN PARTIES.
AW, I KNOW, MAN.
I THINK I'M JUST PUNCHY 'CAUSE I'M HUNGRY.
OH MAN, YOU'RE RIGHT, WE HAVEN'T EATEN *ALL* DAY.
WE STILL HAVE POPCORN!
NAH, I DON'T THINK POPCORN'S GONNA CUT IT. I'M HUNGRY FOR SOMETHING ELSE.
LIKE A MERINGUE PIE?
NAH, BUT THAT'S CLOSE...
OH, HEY! BMO, LET'S HAVE A LOOK AT THAT SCREEN CAP YOU GOT!

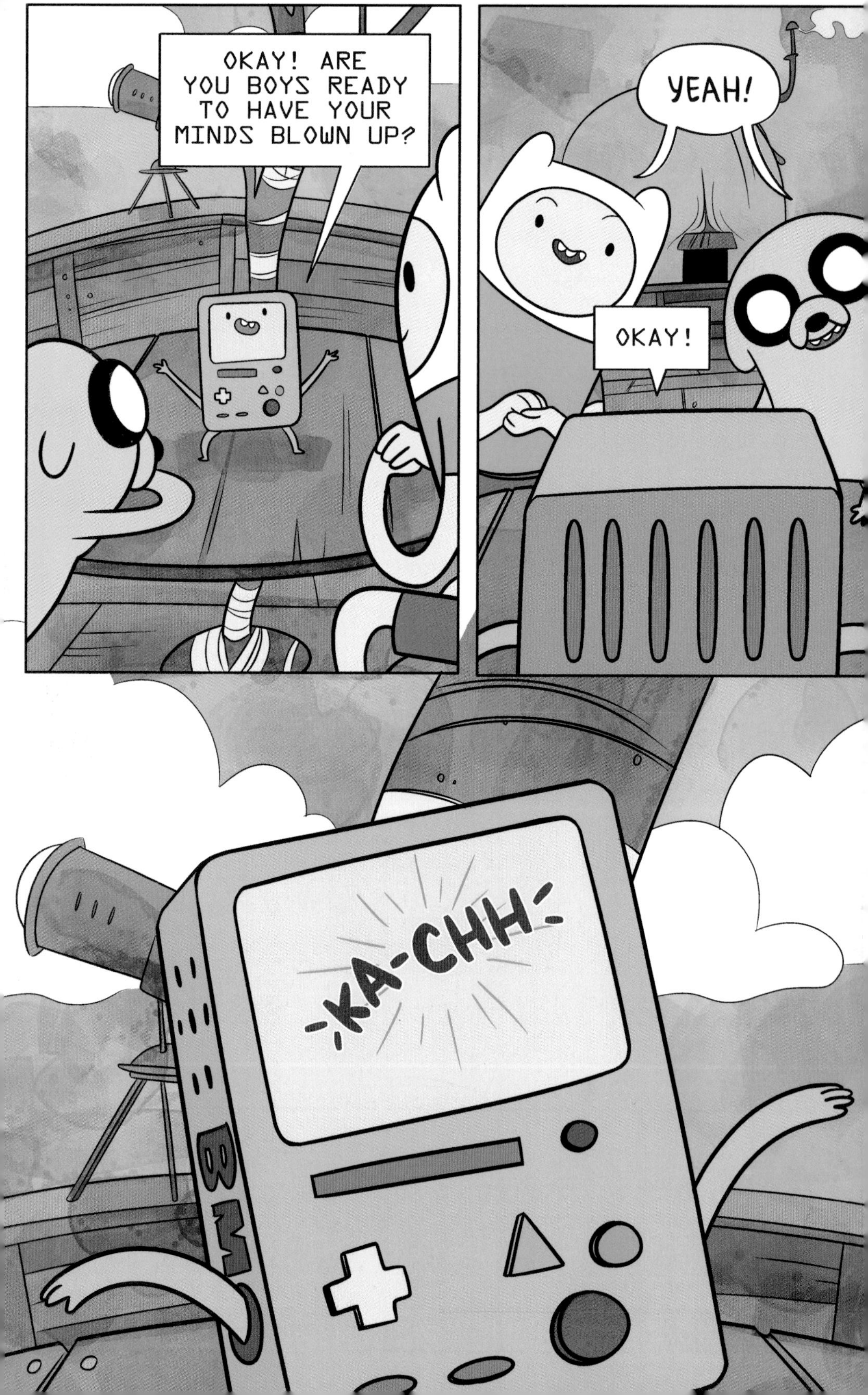
OKAY! ARE YOU BOYS READY TO HAVE YOUR MINDS BLOWN UP?
YEAH!
OKAY!
KA-CHH
BMO

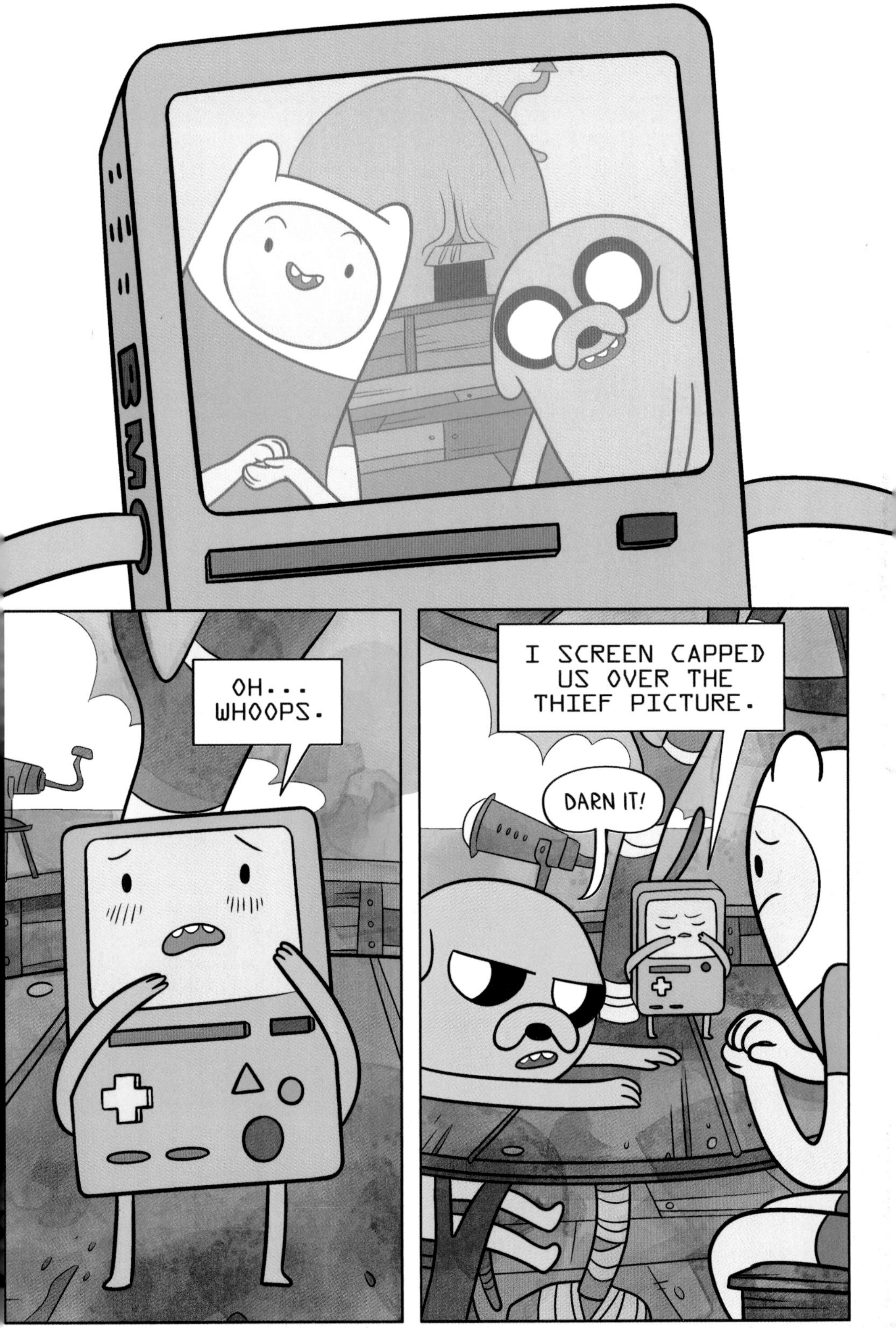
OH... WHOOPS.
I SCREEN CAPPED US OVER THE THIEF PICTURE.
DARN IT!

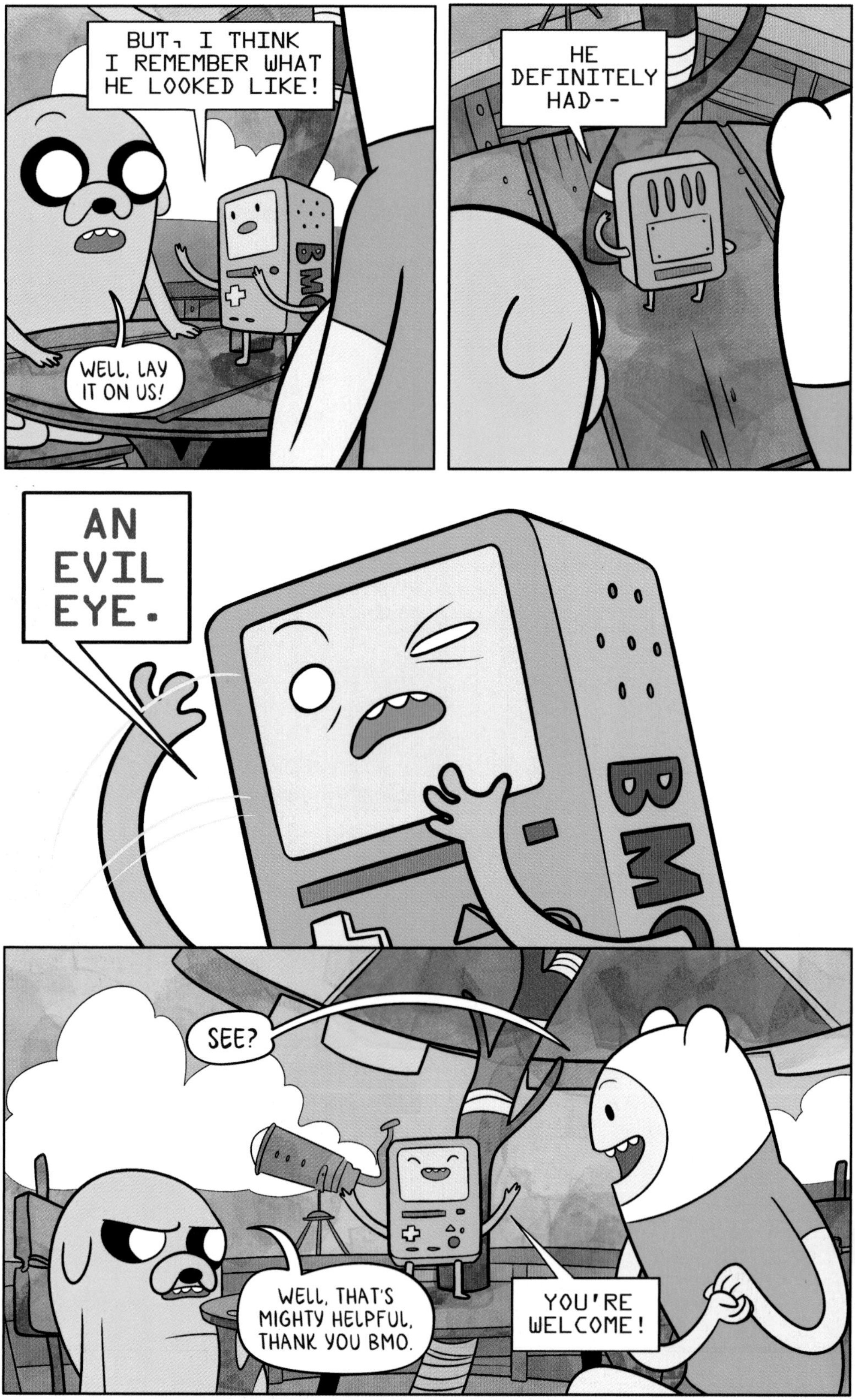
BUT, I THINK I REMEMBER WHAT HE LOOKED LIKE!
WELL, LAY IT ON US!
HE DEFINITELY HAD--
AN EVIL EYE.
SEE?
WELL, THAT'S MIGHTY HELPFUL, THANK YOU BMO.
YOU'RE WELCOME!

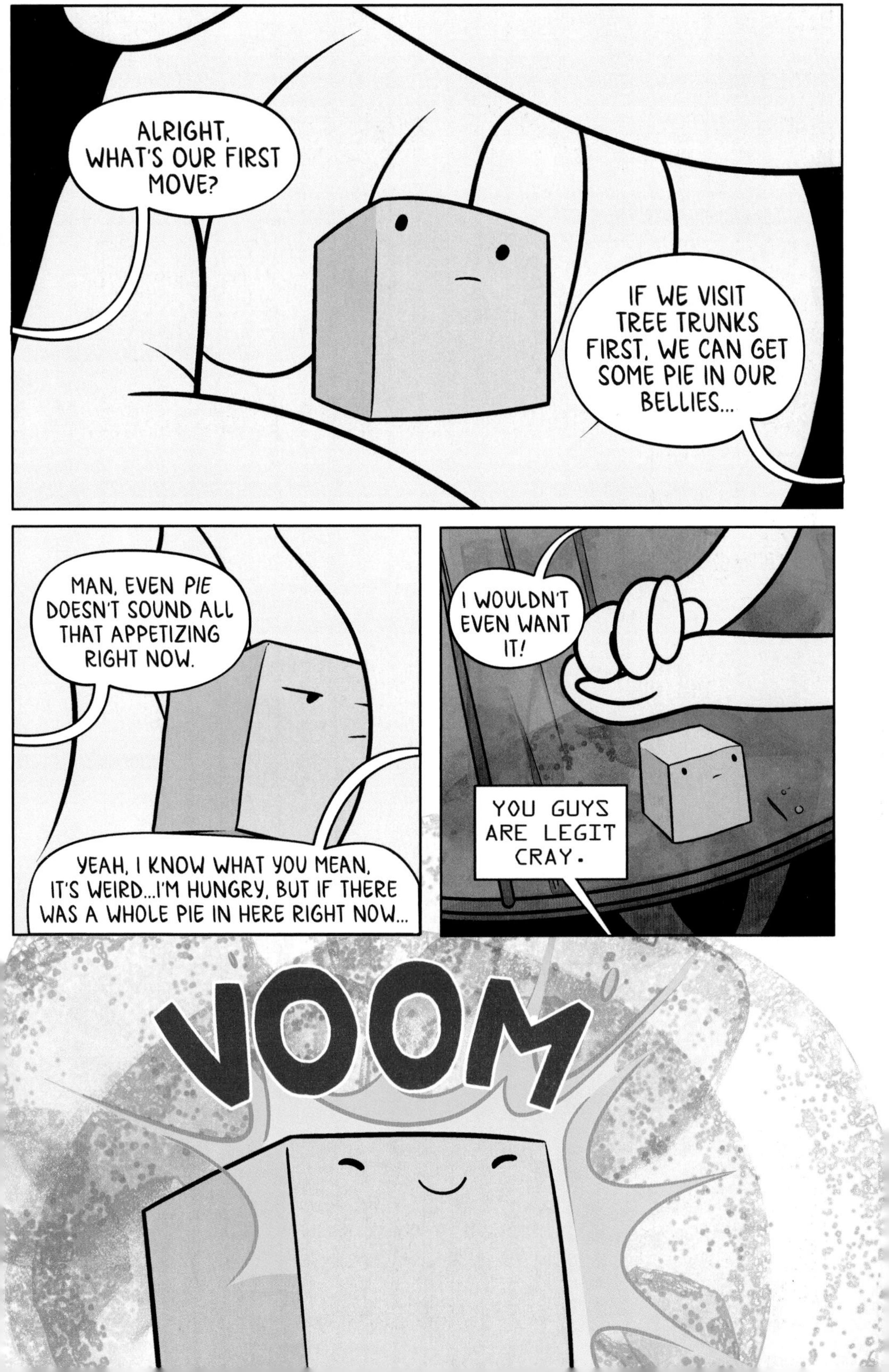
ALRIGHT, WHAT'S OUR FIRST MOVE?
IF WE VISIT TREE TRUNKS FIRST, WE CAN GET SOME PIE IN OUR BELLIES...
MAN, EVEN PIE DOESN'T SOUND ALL THAT APPETIZING RIGHT NOW.
YEAH, I KNOW WHAT YOU MEAN, IT'S WEIRD...I'M HUNGRY, BUT IF THERE WAS A WHOLE PIE IN HERE RIGHT NOW...
I WOULDN'T EVEN WANT IT!
YOU GUYS ARE LEGIT CRAY.
VOOM

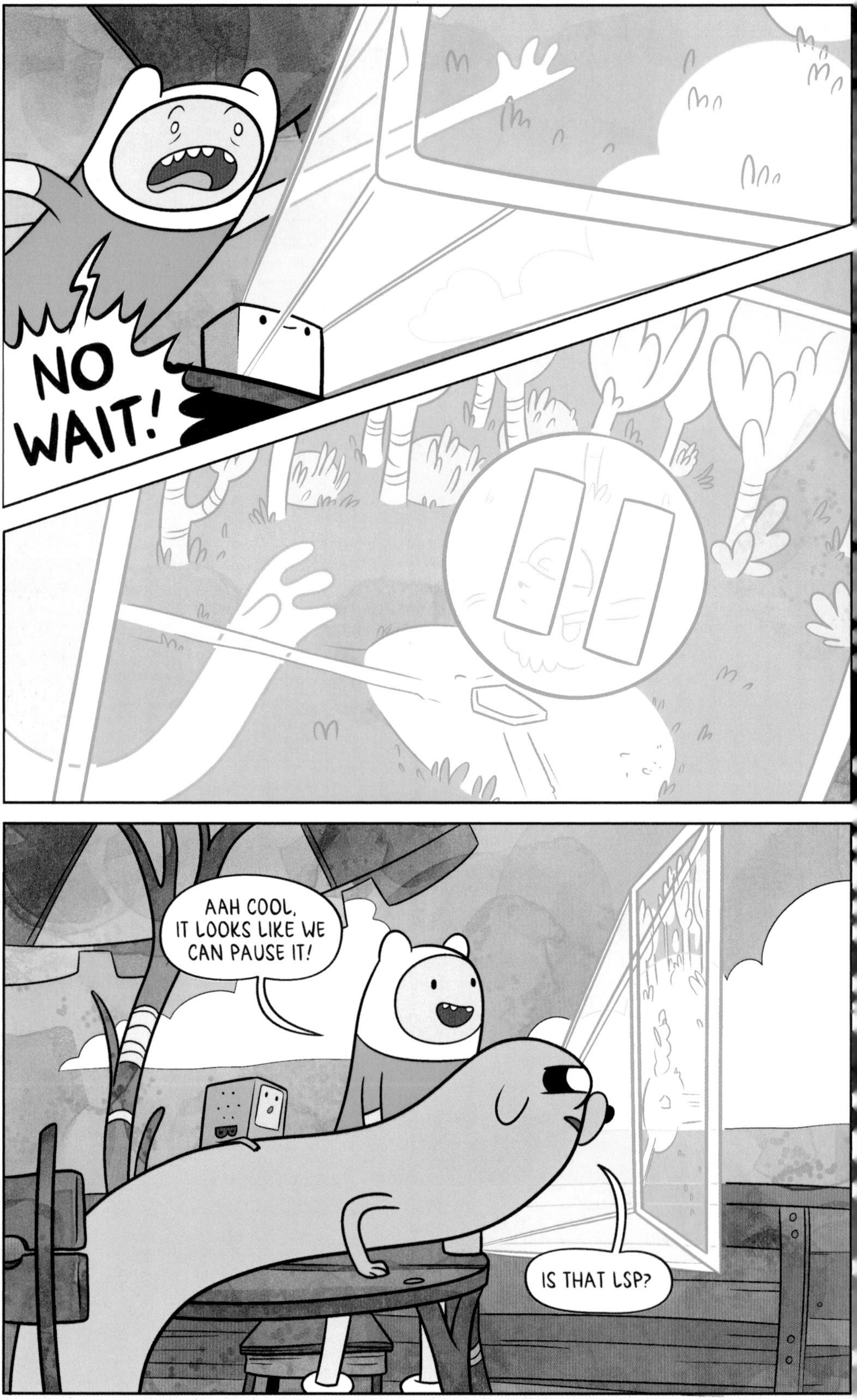
NO WAIT!
AAH COOL, IT LOOKS LIKE WE CAN PAUSE IT!
IS THAT LSP?

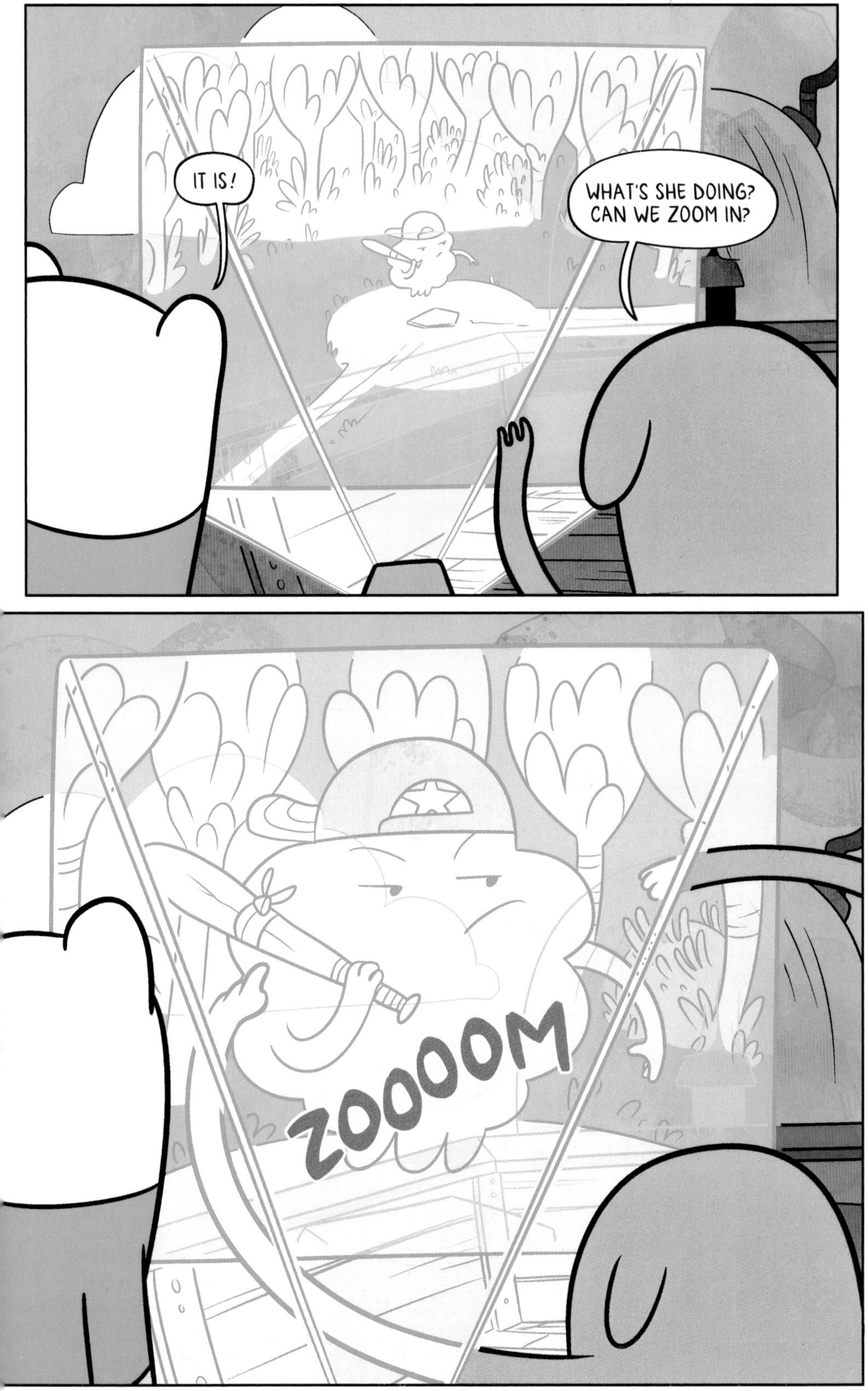
IT IS!
WHAT'S SHE DOING? CAN WE ZOOM IN?
ZOOOOM

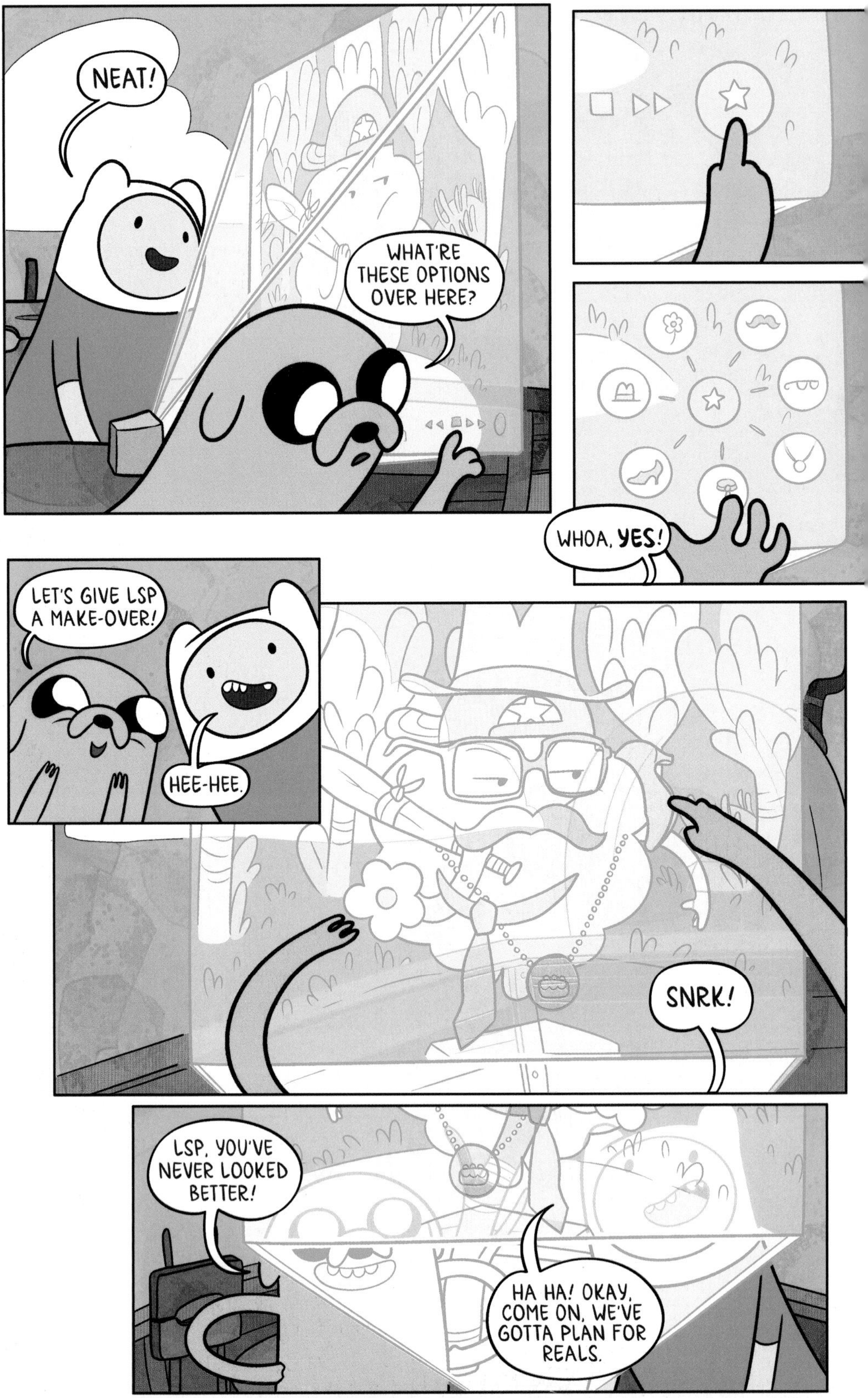
NEAT!
WHAT'RE THESE OPTIONS OVER HERE?
WHOA, YES!
LET'S GIVE LSP A MAKE-OVER!
HEE-HEE.
SNRK!
LSP, YOU'VE NEVER LOOKED BETTER!
HA HA! OKAY, COME ON, WE'VE GOTTA PLAN FOR REALS.

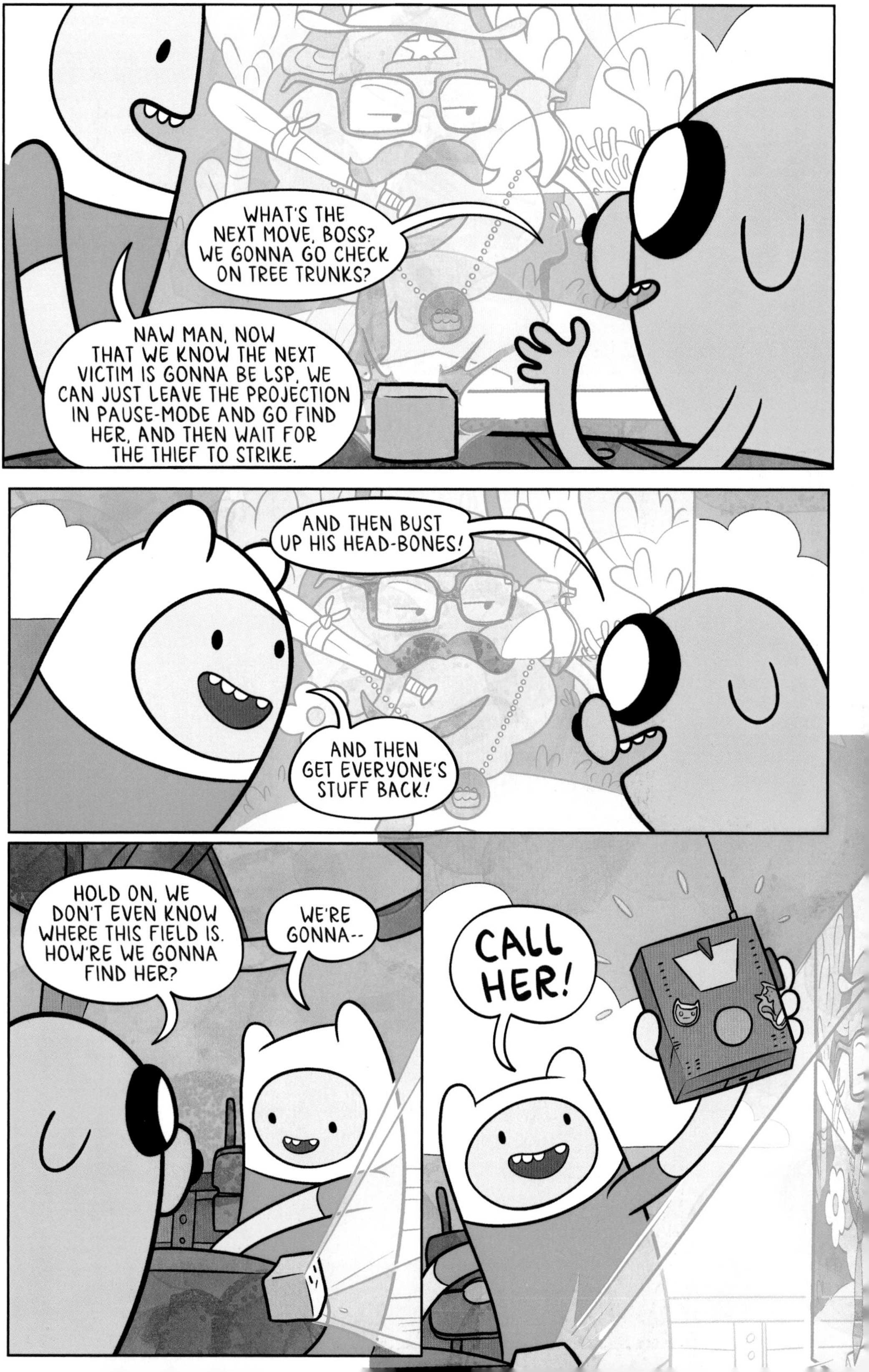
WHAT'S THE NEXT MOVE, BOSS? WE GONNA GO CHECK ON TREE TRUNKS?
NAW MAN, NOW THAT WE KNOW THE NEXT VICTIM IS GONNA BE LSP, WE CAN JUST LEAVE THE PROJECTION IN PAUSE-MODE AND GO FIND HER, AND THEN WAIT FOR THE THIEF TO STRIKE.
AND THEN BUST UP HIS HEAD-BONES!
AND THEN GET EVERYONE'S STUFF BACK!
HOLD ON, WE DON'T EVEN KNOW WHERE THIS FIELD IS. HOW'RE WE GONNA FIND HER?
WE'RE GONNA--
CALL HER!

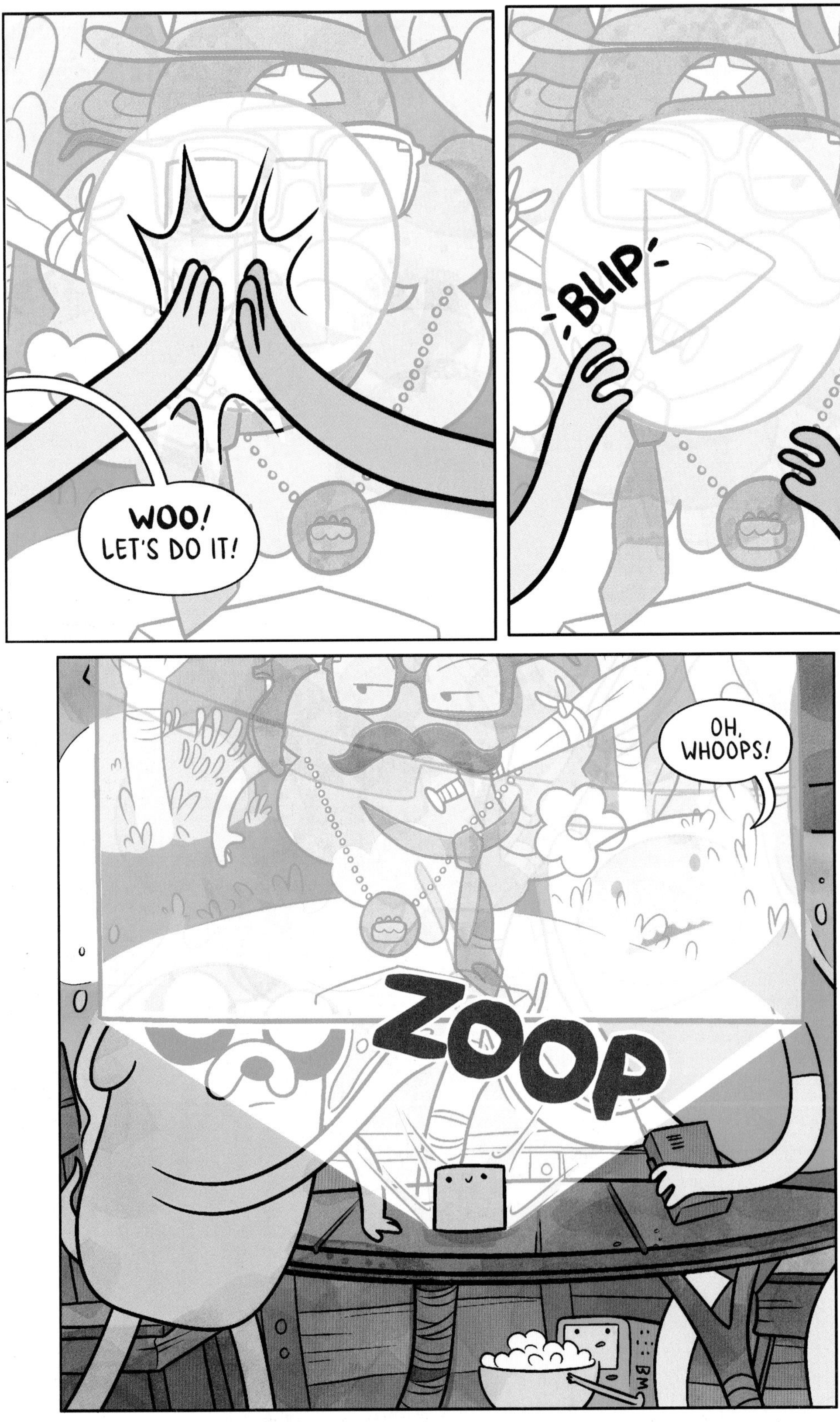
WOO!
LET'S DO IT!
BLIP
OH, WHOOPS!
ZOOP
BM

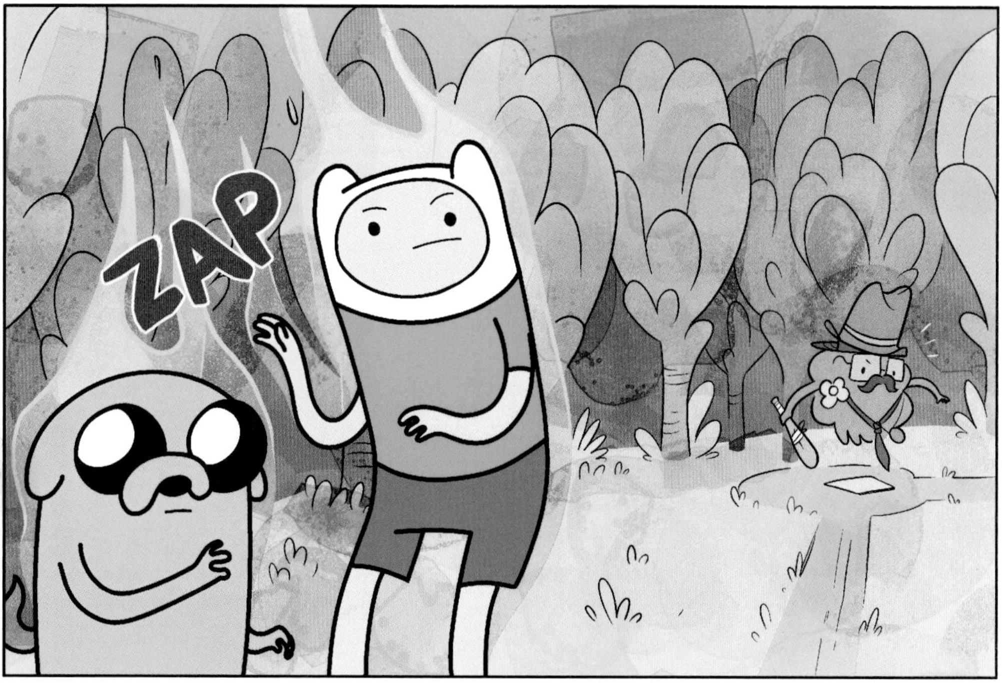
ZAP

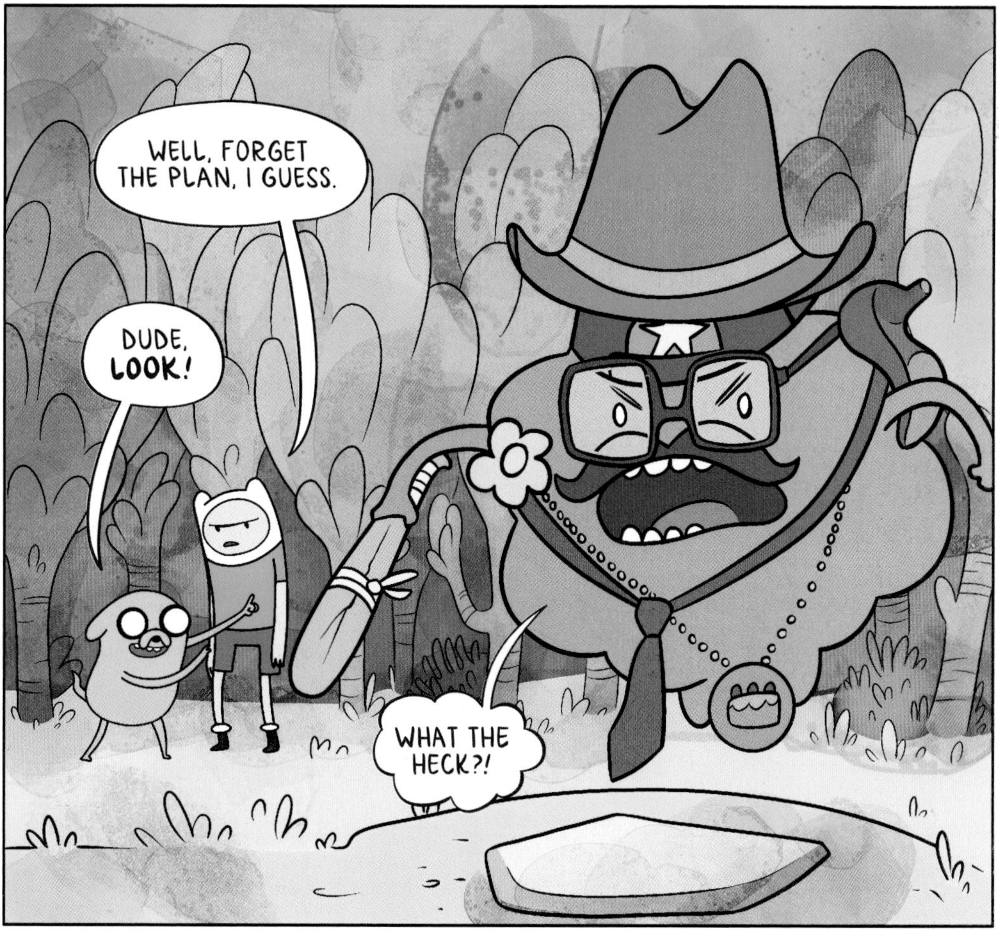
WELL, FORGET THE PLAN, I GUESS.
DUDE, **LOOK!**
WHAT THE HECK?!

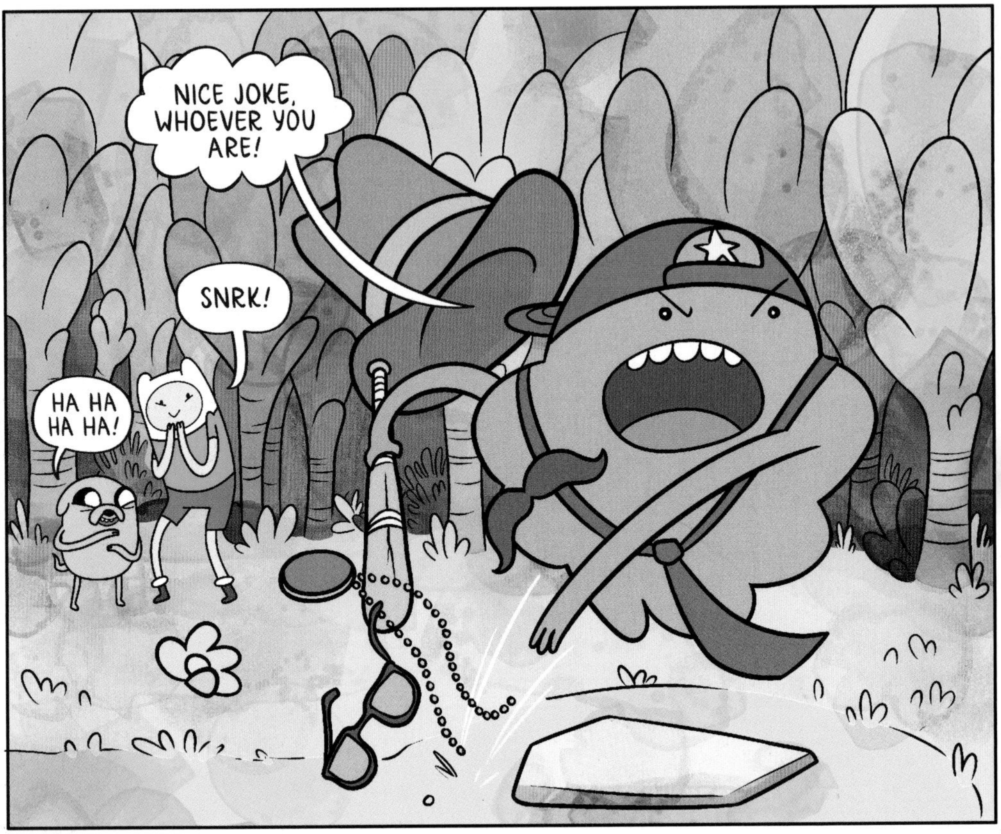
NICE JOKE, WHOEVER YOU ARE!
SNRK!
HA HA HA HA!
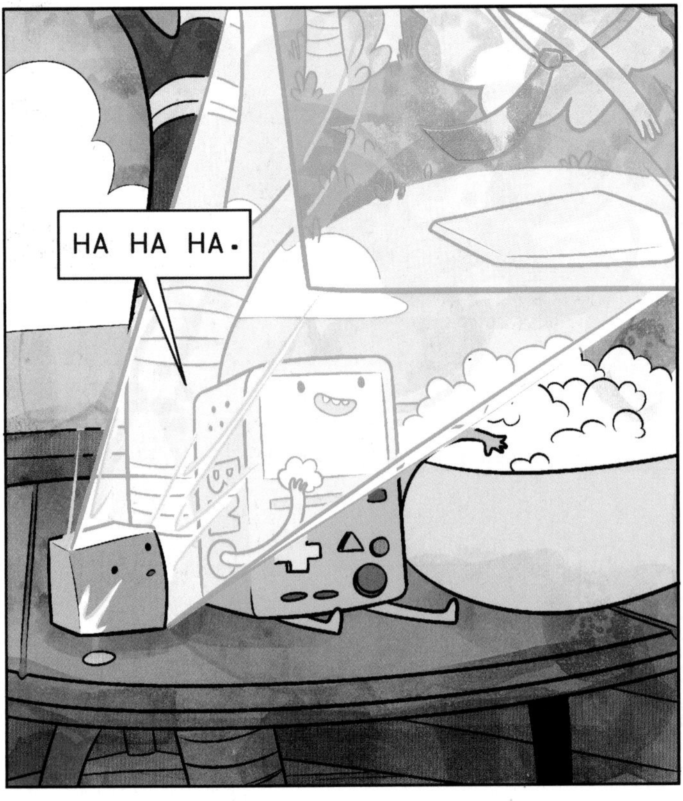
HA HA HA.
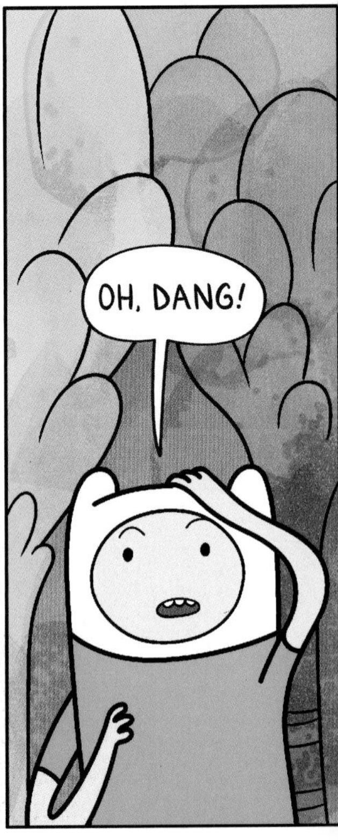
OH, DANG!

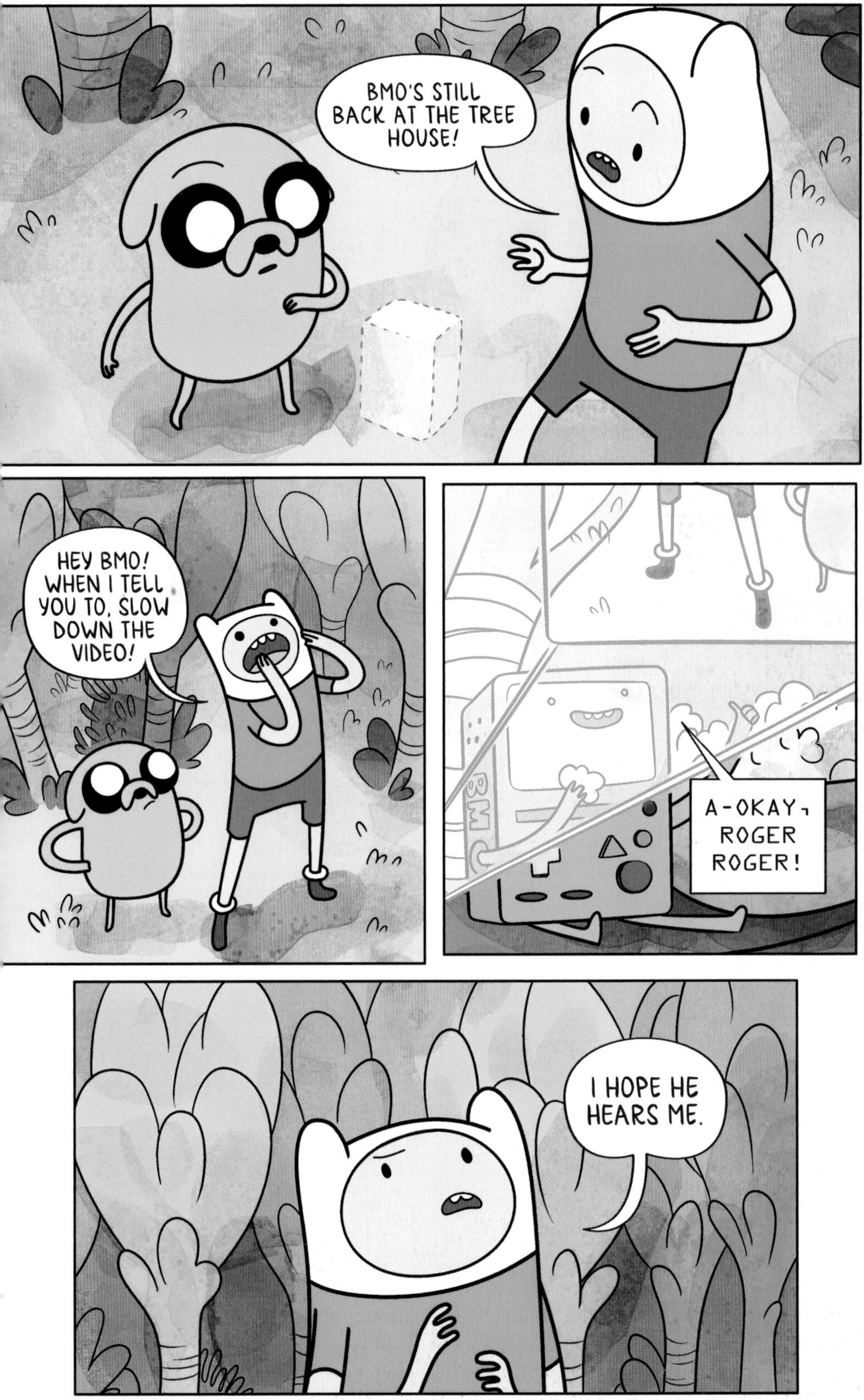
BMO'S STILL BACK AT THE TREE HOUSE!
HEY BMO! WHEN I TELL YOU TO, SLOW DOWN THE VIDEO!
A-OKAY, ROGER ROGER!
I HOPE HE HEARS ME.

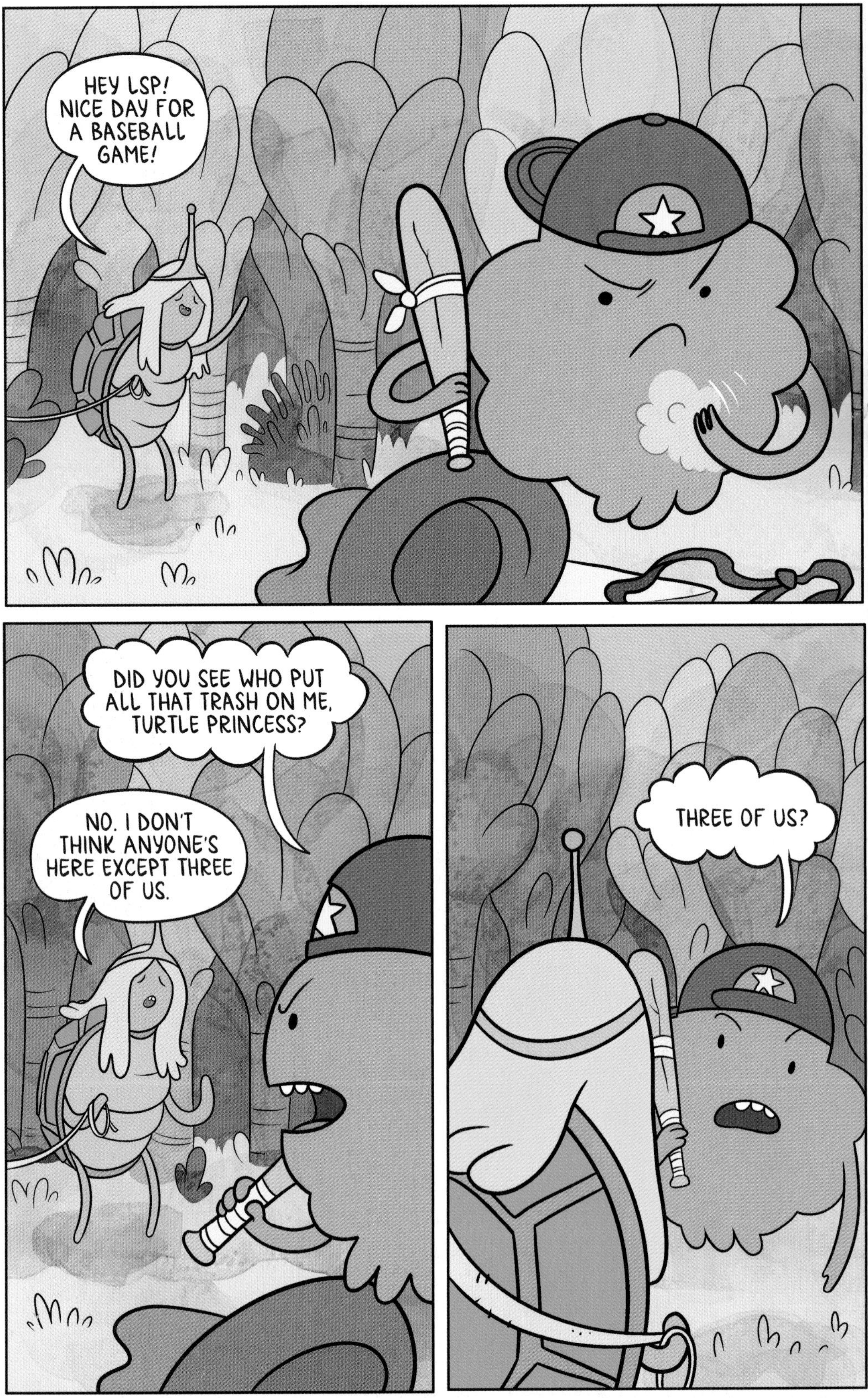
HEY LSP! NICE DAY FOR A BASEBALL GAME!
DID YOU SEE WHO PUT ALL THAT TRASH ON ME, TURTLE PRINCESS?
NO. I DON'T THINK ANYONE'S HERE EXCEPT THREE OF US.
THREE OF US?

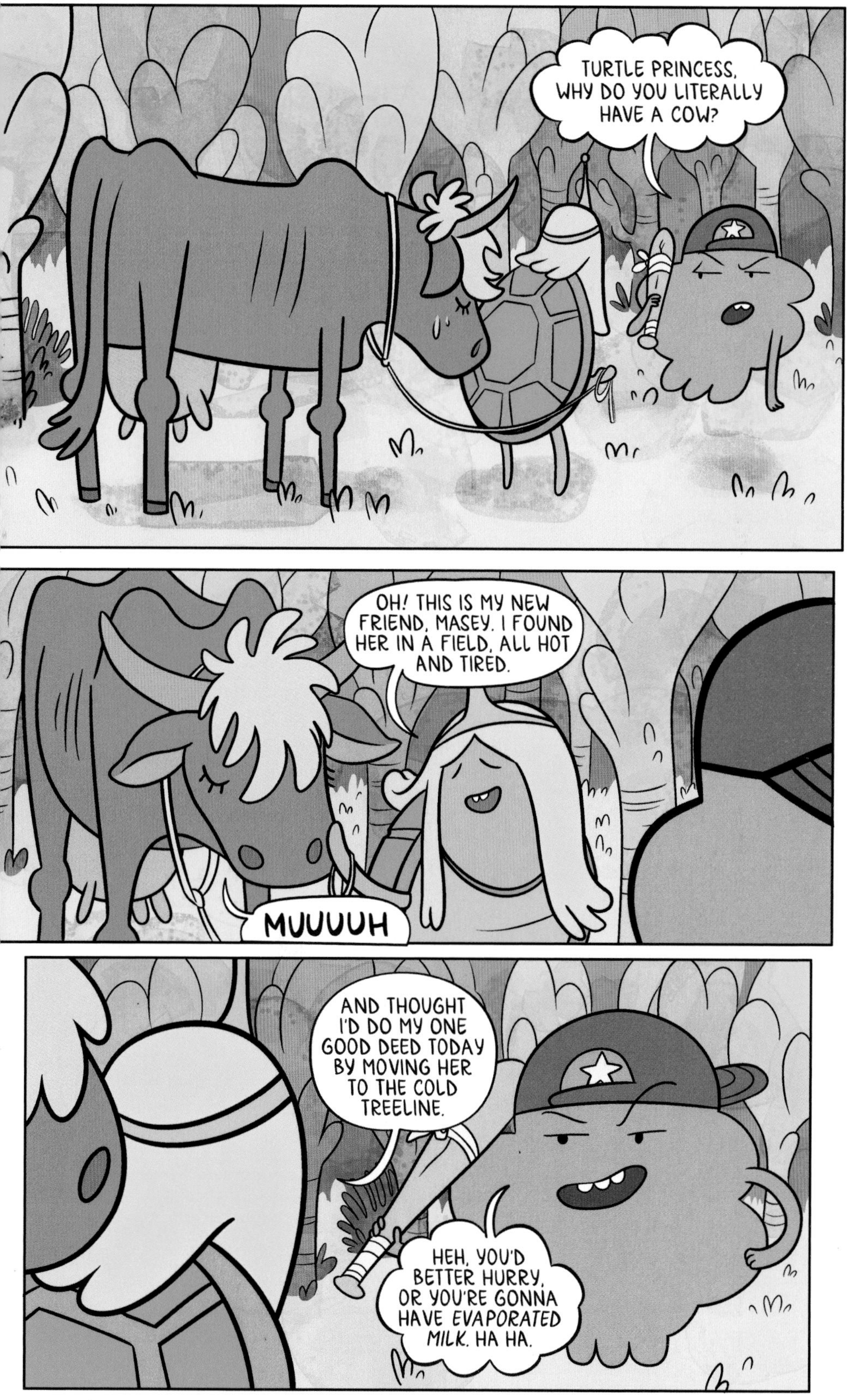

TURTLE PRINCESS, WHY DO YOU LITERALLY HAVE A COW?
OH! THIS IS MY NEW FRIEND, MASEY. I FOUND HER IN A FIELD, ALL HOT AND TIRED.
MUUUUH
AND THOUGHT I'D DO MY ONE GOOD DEED TODAY BY MOVING HER TO THE COLD TREELINE.
HEH, YOU'D BETTER HURRY, OR YOU'RE GONNA HAVE *EVAPORATED* MILK. HA HA.

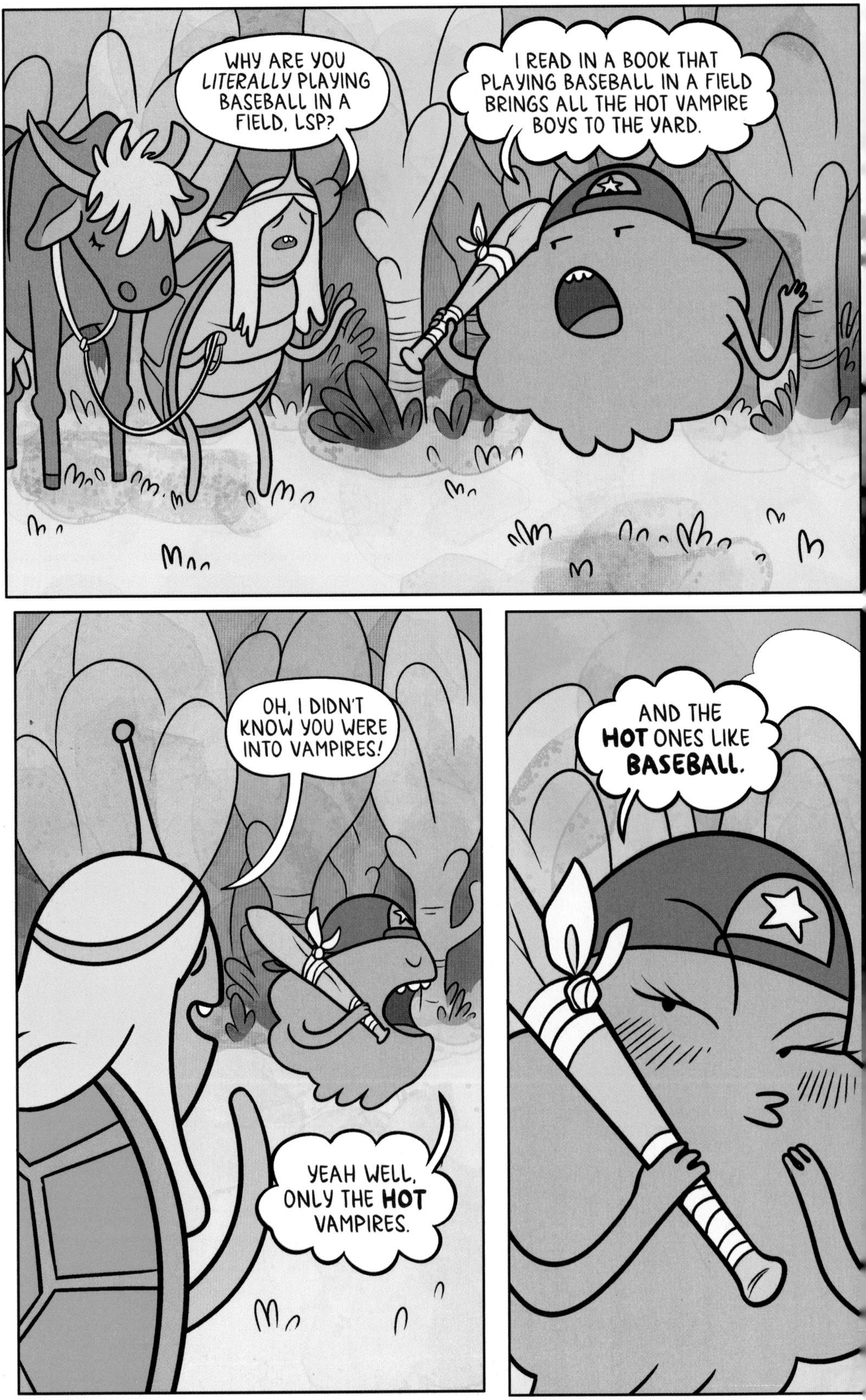
WHY ARE YOU LITERALLY PLAYING BASEBALL IN A FIELD, LSP?
I READ IN A BOOK THAT PLAYING BASEBALL IN A FIELD BRINGS ALL THE HOT VAMPIRE BOYS TO THE YARD.
OH, I DIDN'T KNOW YOU WERE INTO VAMPIRES!
YEAH WELL, ONLY THE **HOT** VAMPIRES.
AND THE **HOT** ONES LIKE **BASEBALL**.

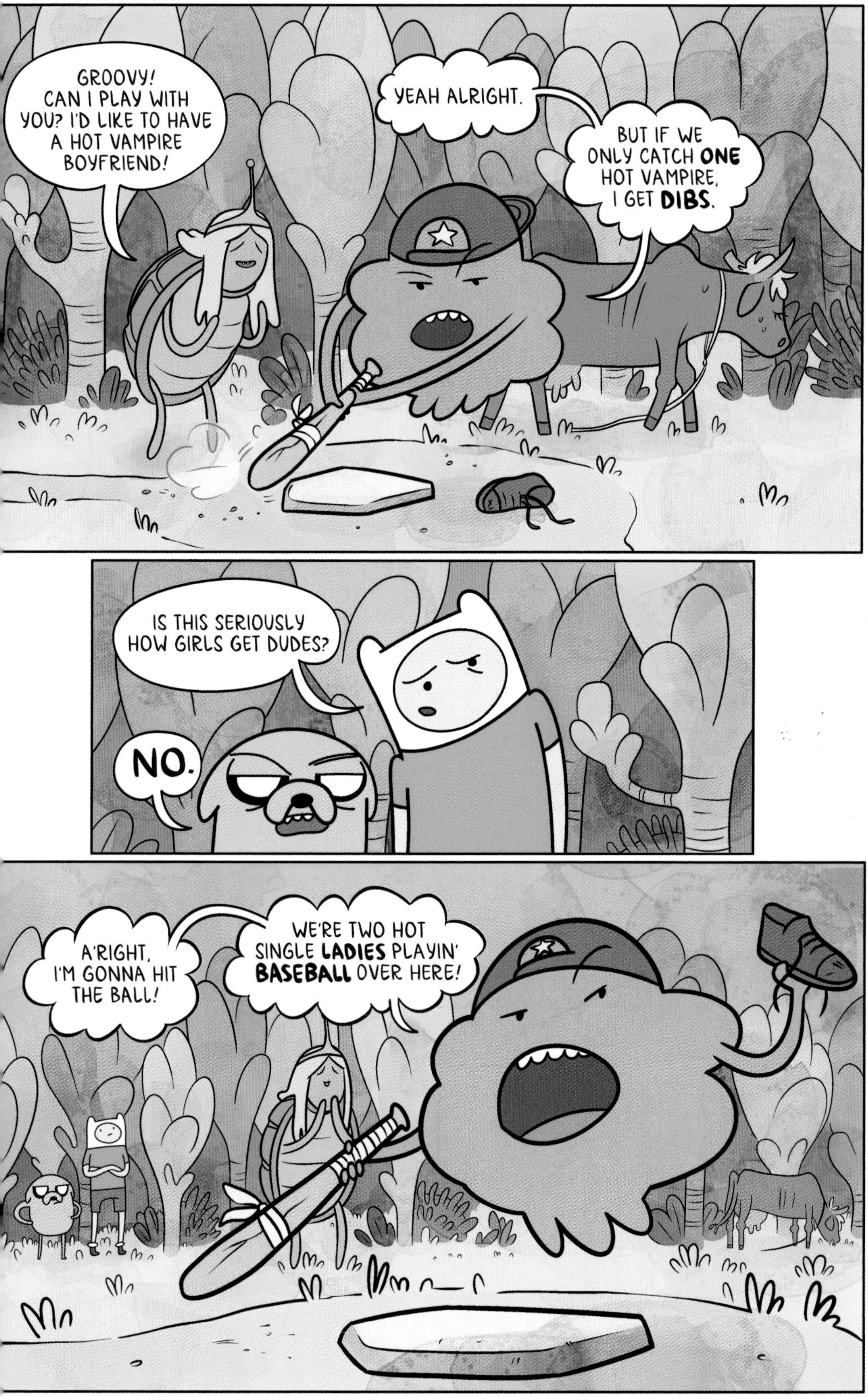
GROOVY! CAN I PLAY WITH YOU? I'D LIKE TO HAVE A HOT VAMPIRE BOYFRIEND!
YEAH ALRIGHT.
BUT IF WE ONLY CATCH **ONE** HOT VAMPIRE, I GET **DIBS**.
IS THIS SERIOUSLY HOW GIRLS GET DUDES?
NO.
A'RIGHT, I'M GONNA HIT THE BALL!
WE'RE TWO HOT SINGLE **LADIES** PLAYIN' **BASEBALL** OVER HERE!

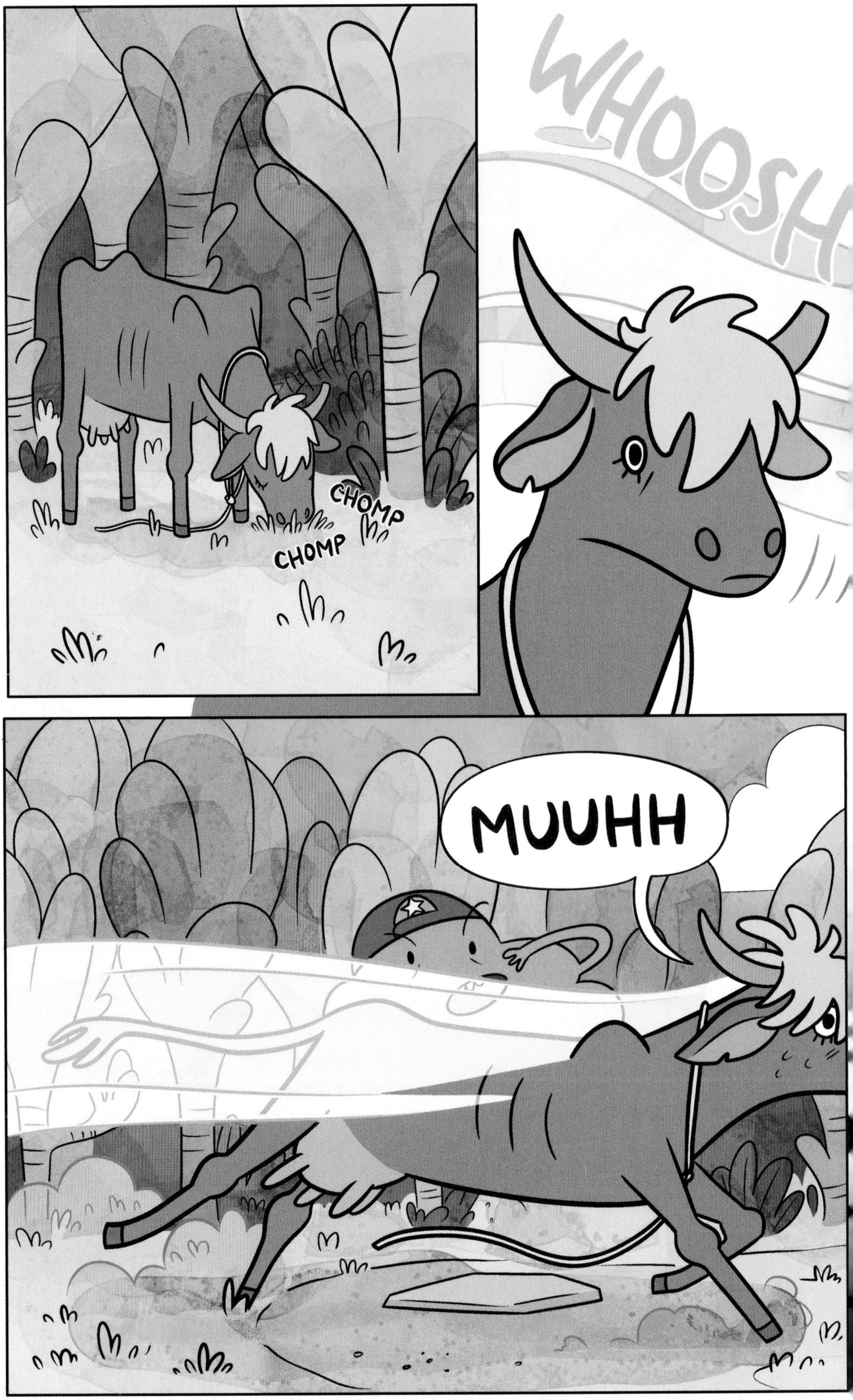
CHOMP
CHOMP
WHOOSH
MUUHH

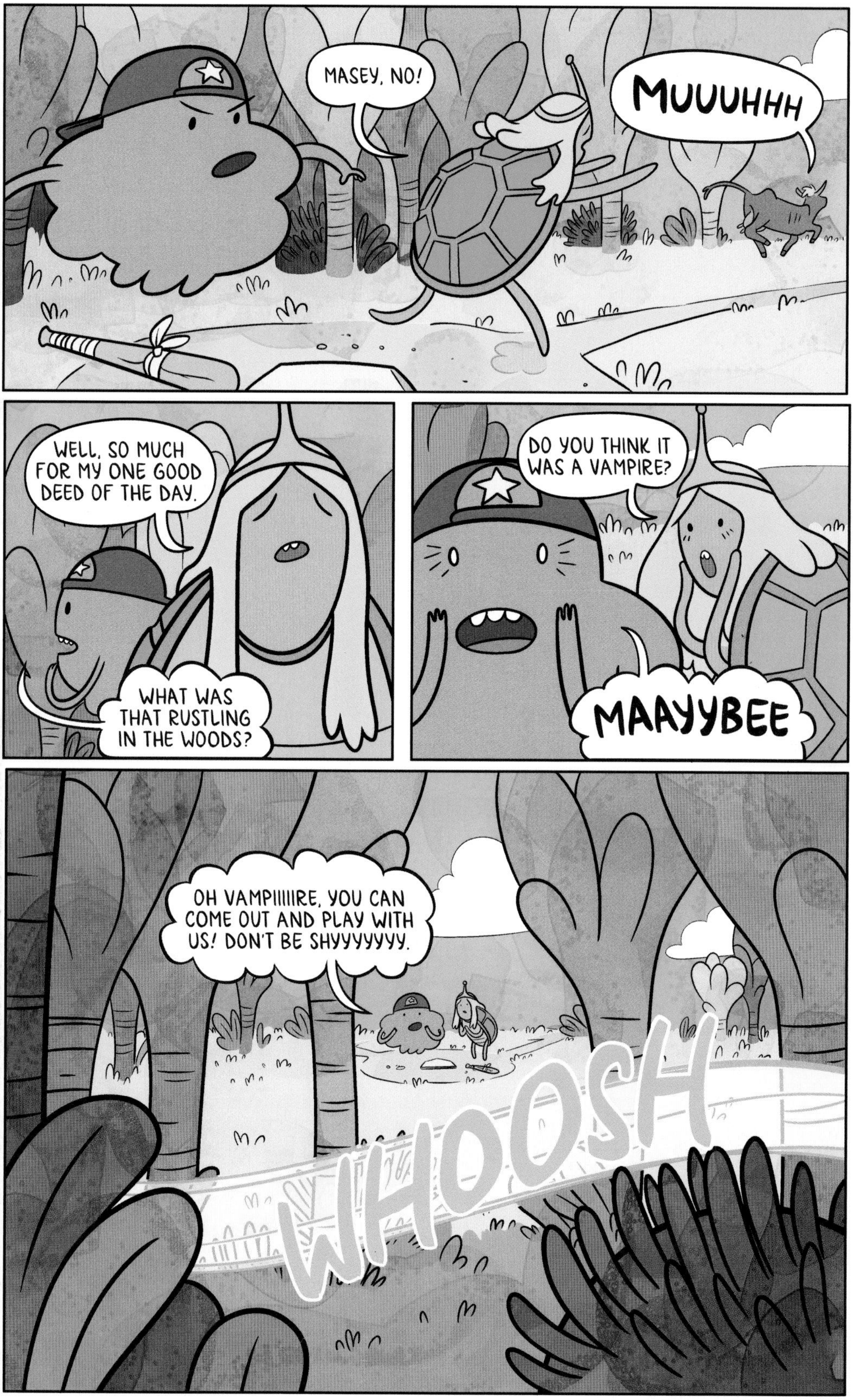
MASEY, NO!
MUUUHHH
WELL, SO MUCH FOR MY ONE GOOD DEED OF THE DAY.
WHAT WAS THAT RUSTLING IN THE WOODS?
DO YOU THINK IT WAS A VAMPIRE?
MAAYYBEE
OH VAMPIIIIIRE, YOU CAN COME OUT AND PLAY WITH US! DON'T BE SHYYYYYYY.
WHOOSH

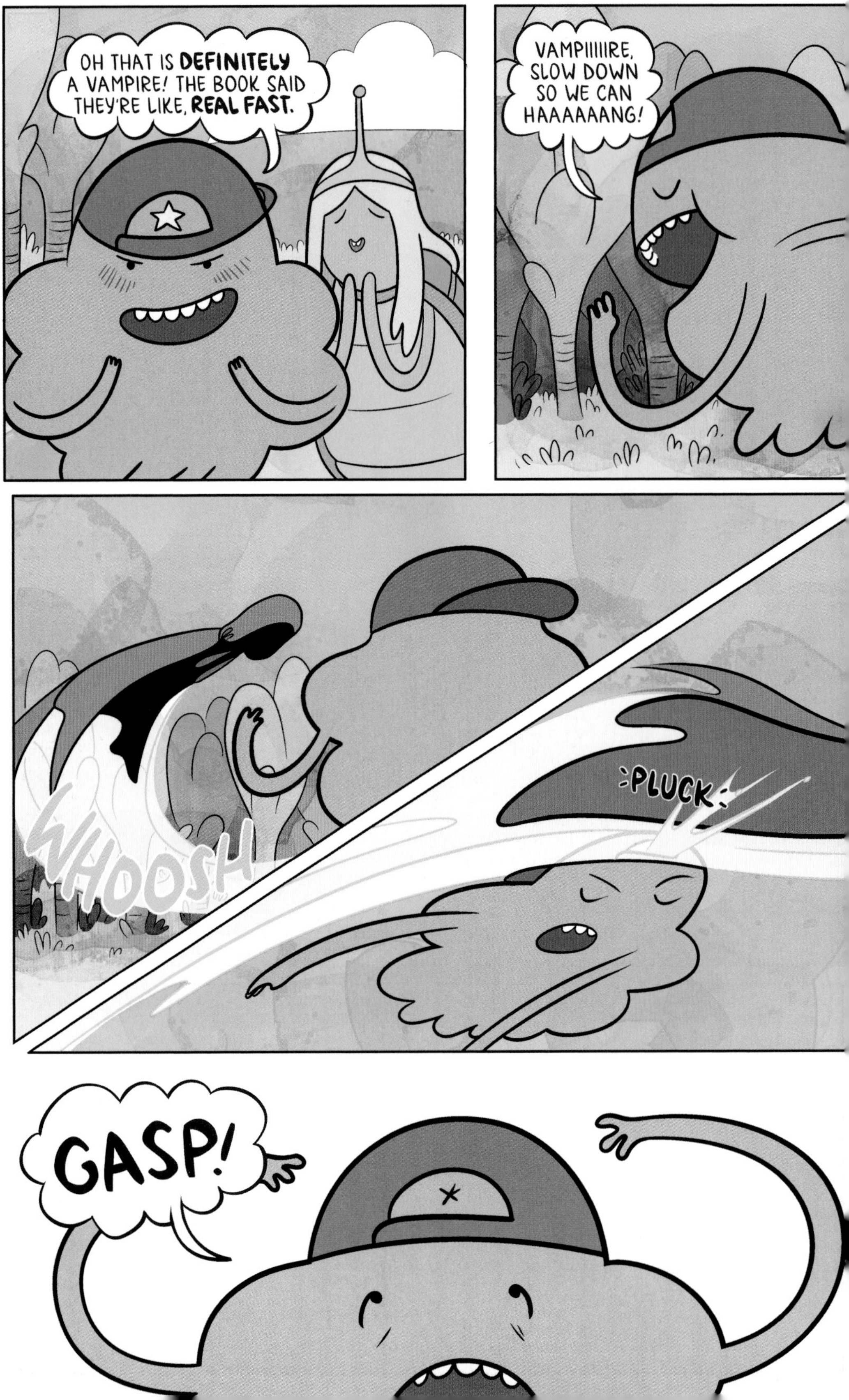
OH THAT IS DEFINITELY A VAMPIRE! THE BOOK SAID THEY'RE LIKE, REAL FAST.
VAMPIIIIIRE, SLOW DOWN SO WE CAN HAAAAAANG!
WHOOSH
PLUCK
GASP!

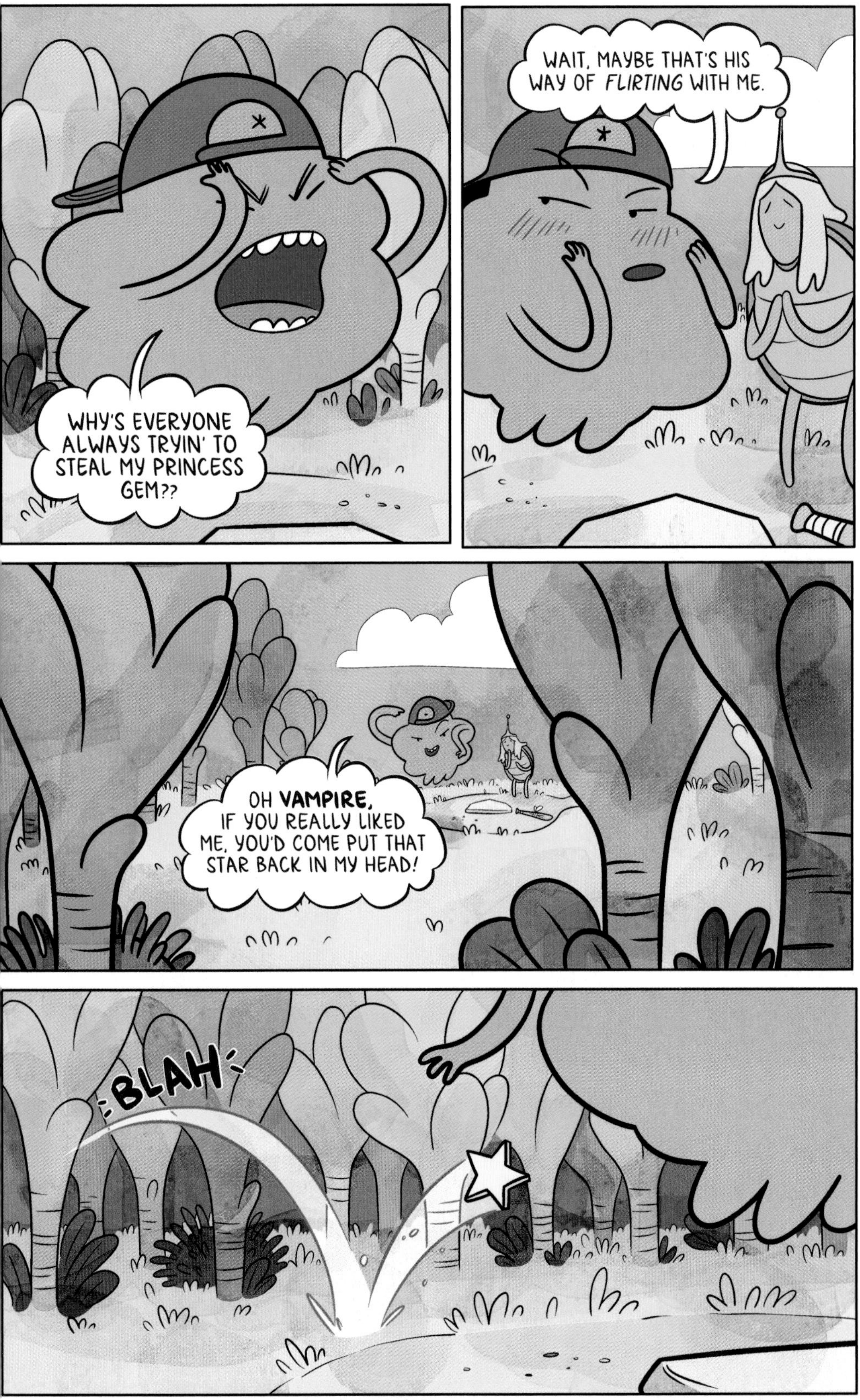
WHY'S EVERYONE ALWAYS TRYIN' TO STEAL MY PRINCESS GEM??
WAIT, MAYBE THAT'S HIS WAY OF *FLIRTING* WITH ME.
OH **VAMPIRE,** IF YOU REALLY LIKED ME, YOU'D COME PUT THAT STAR BACK IN MY HEAD!
BLAH

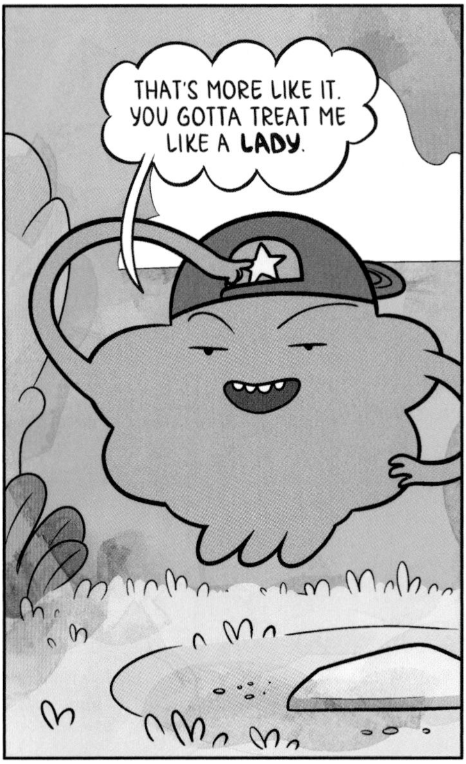
THAT'S MORE LIKE IT. YOU GOTTA TREAT ME LIKE A **LADY**.

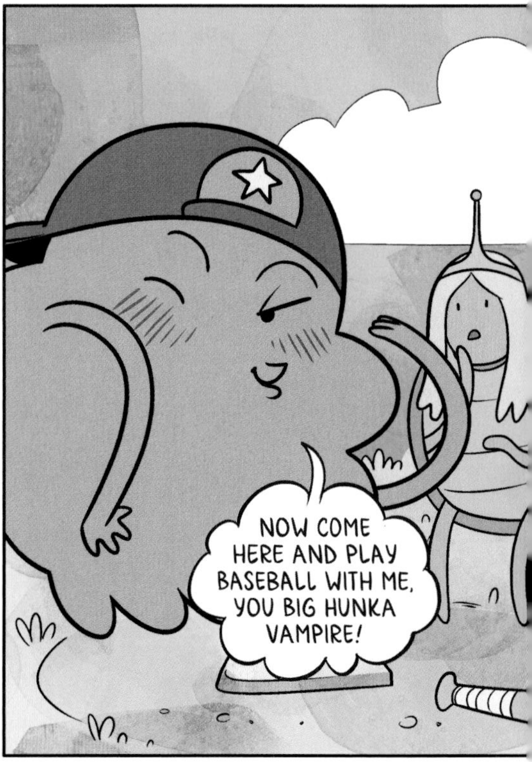
NOW COME HERE AND PLAY BASEBALL WITH ME, YOU BIG HUNKA VAMPIRE!

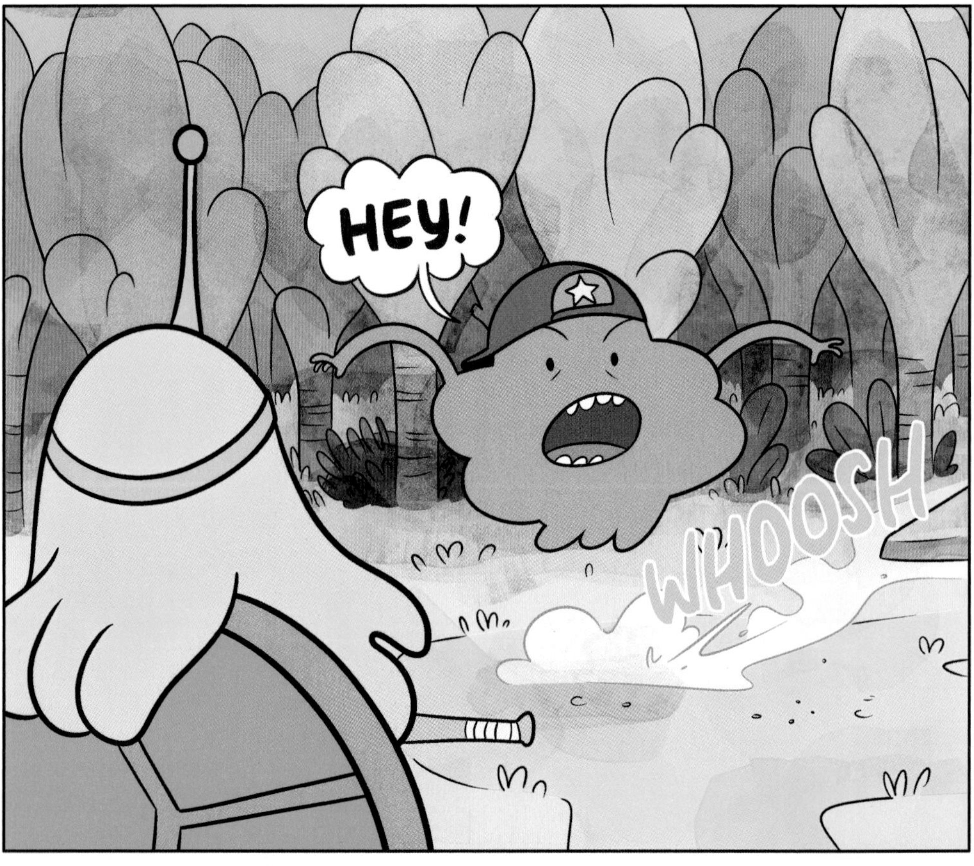
HEY!
WHOOSH

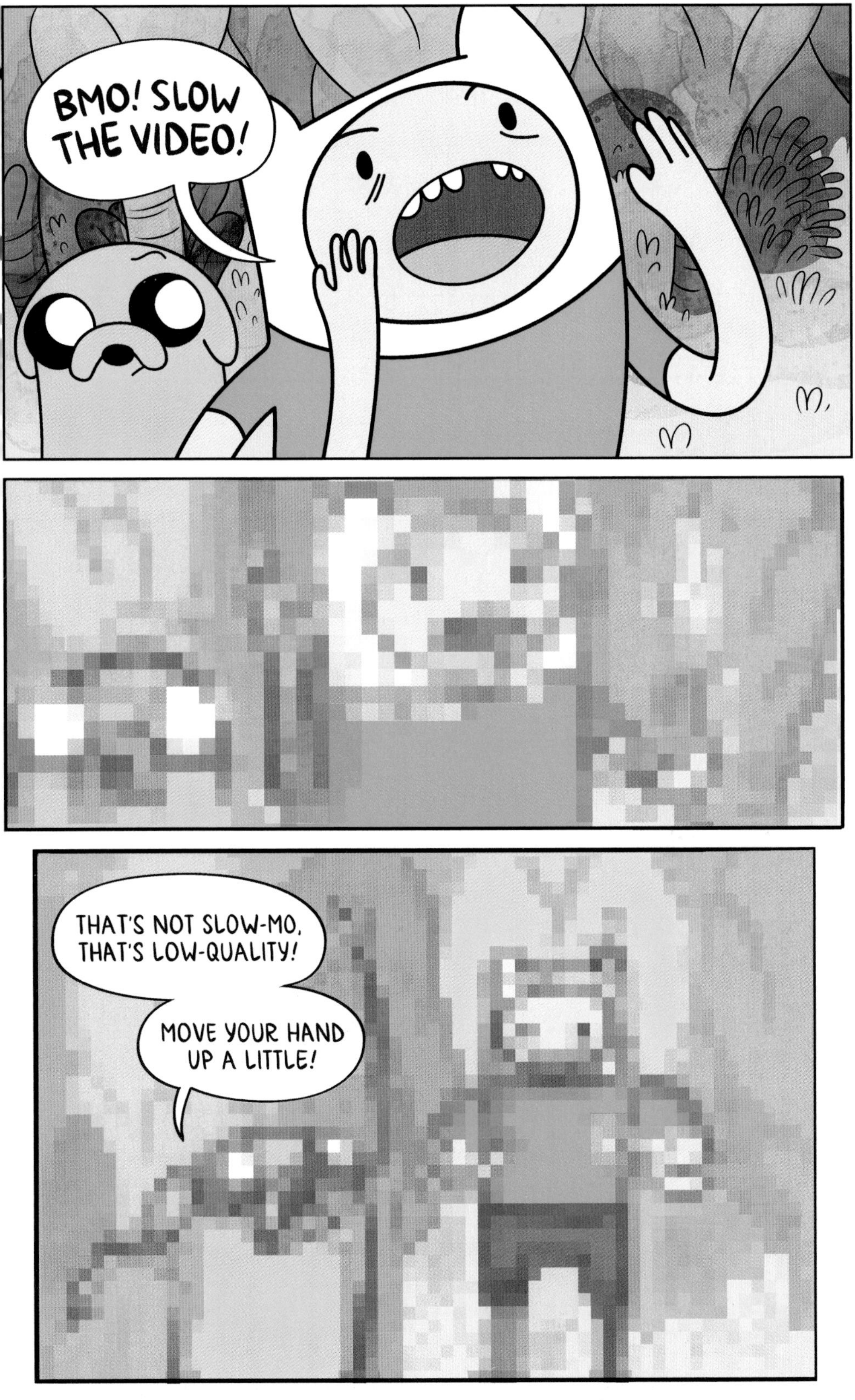
BMO! SLOW THE VIDEO!
THAT'S NOT SLOW-MO, THAT'S LOW-QUALITY!
MOVE YOUR HAND UP A LITTLE!

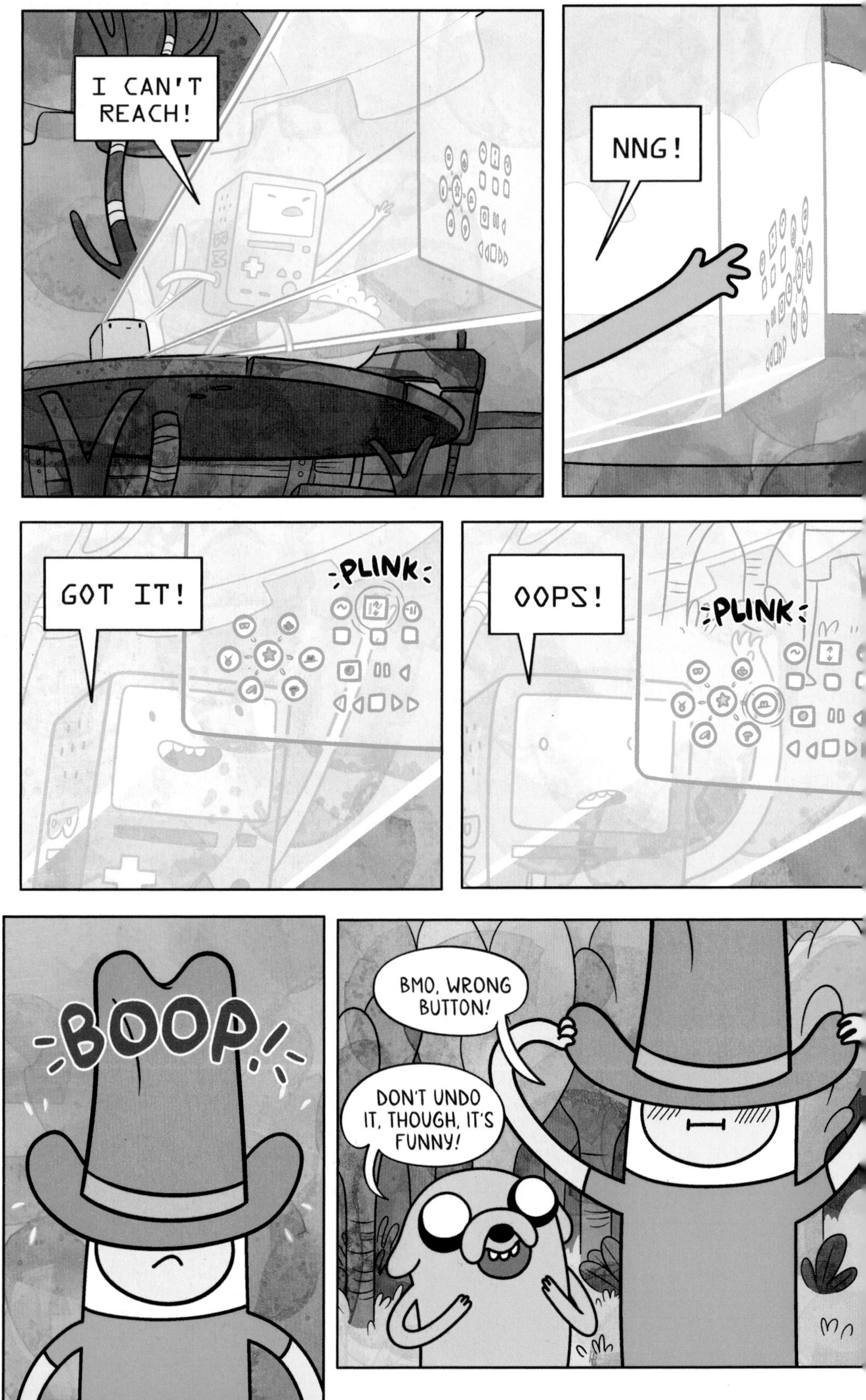
I CAN'T REACH!
NNG!
GOT IT!
PLINK
OOPS!
PLINK
BOOP!
BMO, WRONG BUTTON!
DON'T UNDO IT, THOUGH, IT'S FUNNY!

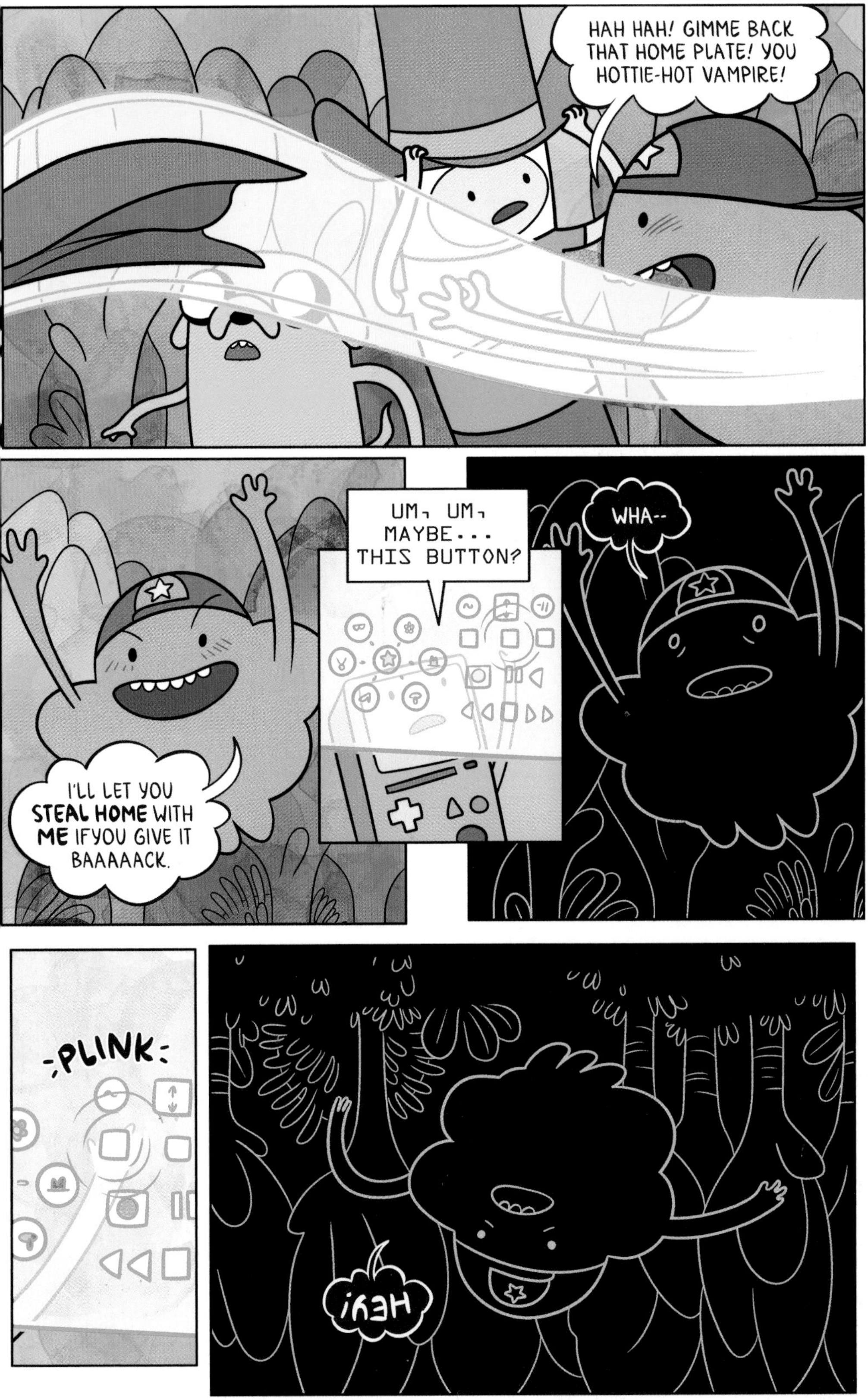
HAH HAH! GIMME BACK THAT HOME PLATE! YOU HOTTIE-HOT VAMPIRE!
I'LL LET YOU STEAL HOME WITH ME IF YOU GIVE IT BAAAAACK.
UM, UM, MAYBE... THIS BUTTON?
WHA--
PLINK
HEY!

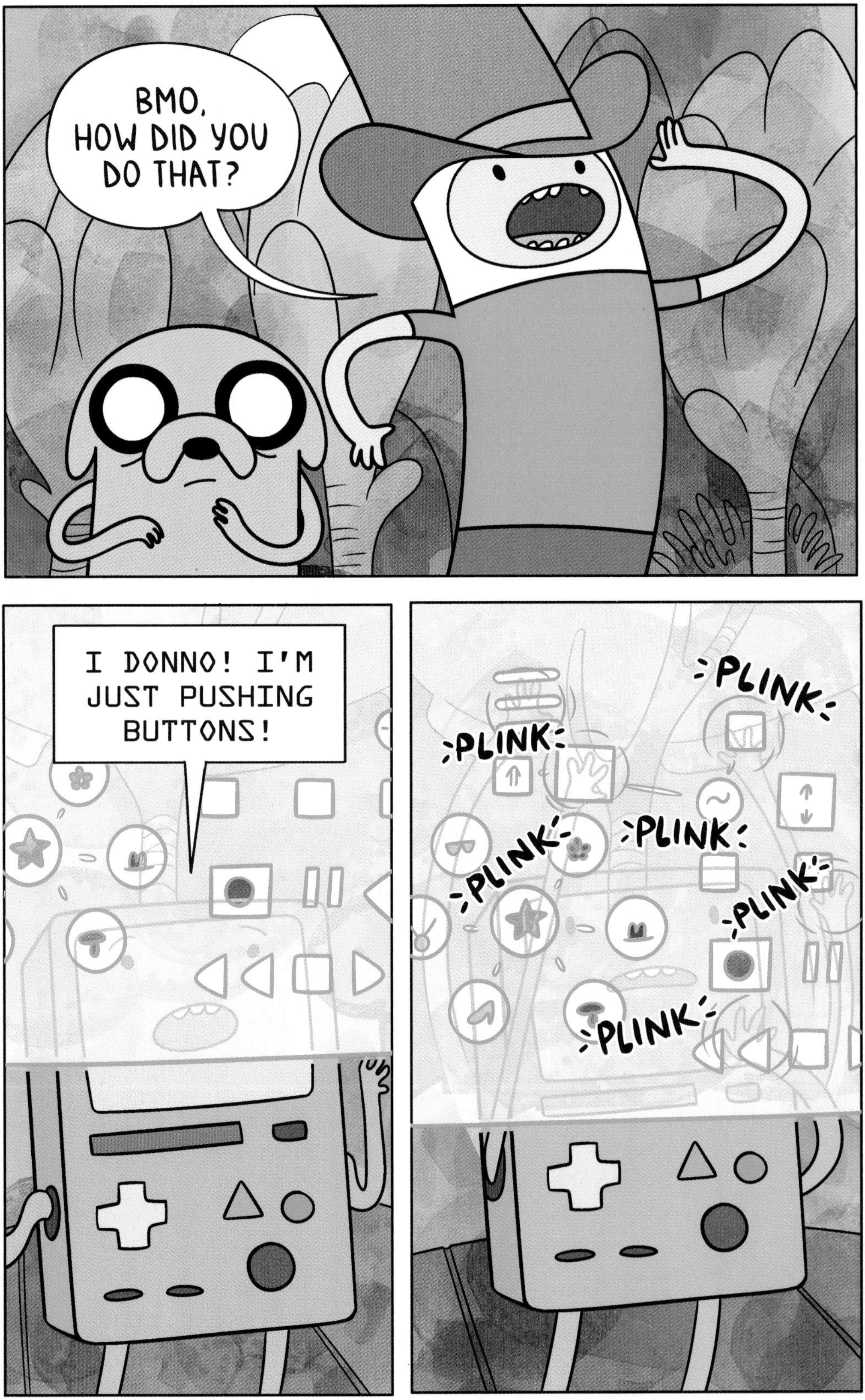
BMO, HOW DID YOU DO THAT?
I DONNO! I'M JUST PUSHING BUTTONS!
PLINK
PLINK
PLINK
PLINK
PLINK
PLINK
PLINK

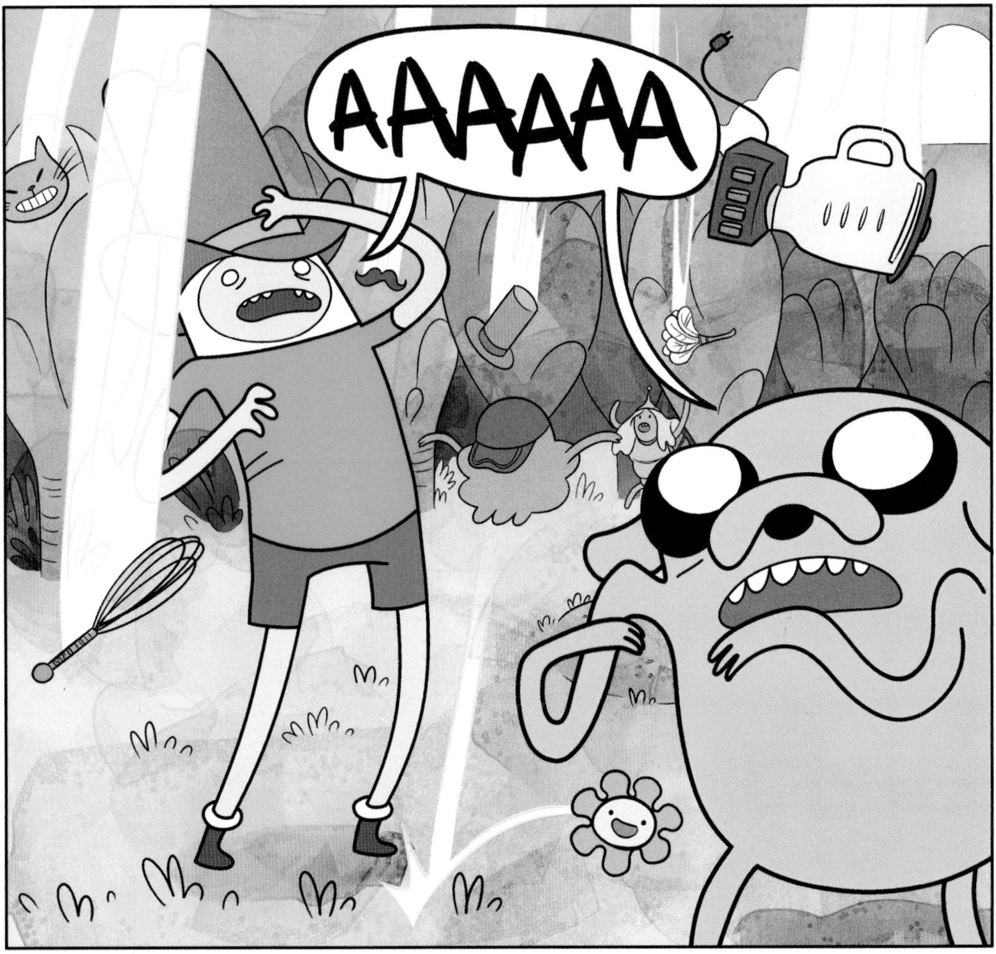
AAAAAA

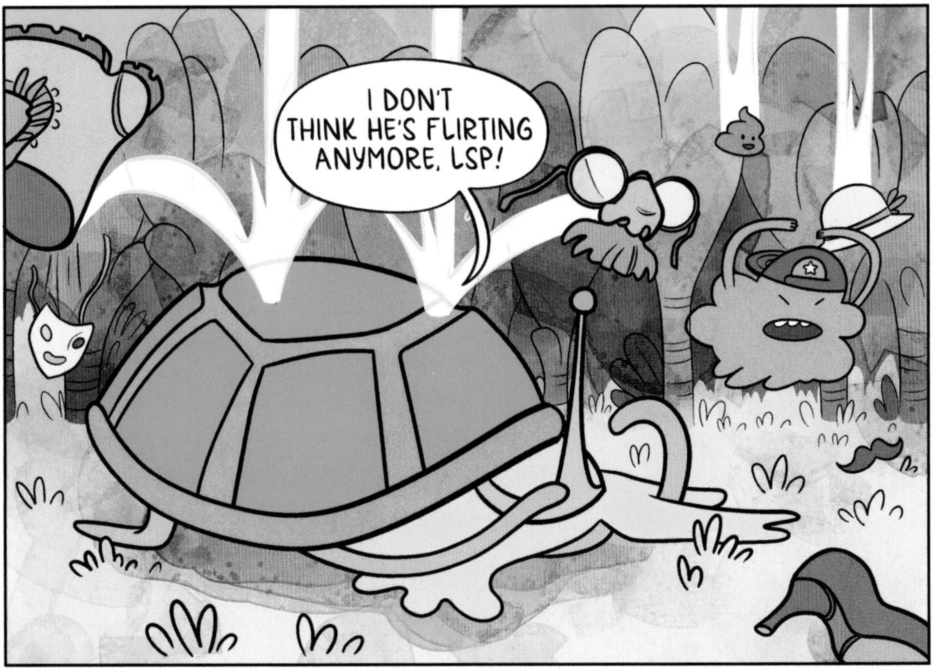
I DON'T THINK HE'S FLIRTING ANYMORE, LSP!

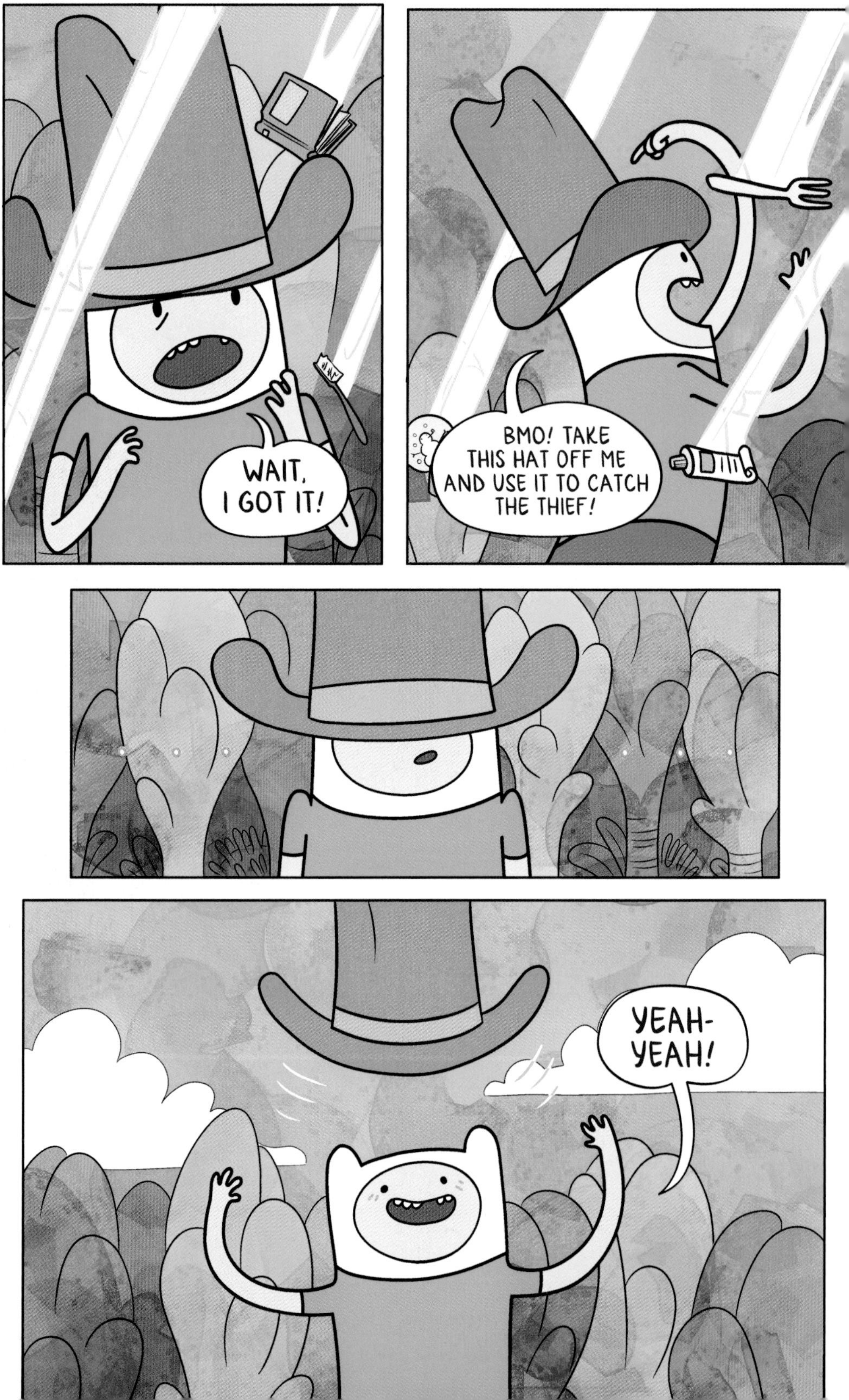
WAIT, I GOT IT!
BMO! TAKE THIS HAT OFF ME AND USE IT TO CATCH THE THIEF!
YEAH-YEAH!

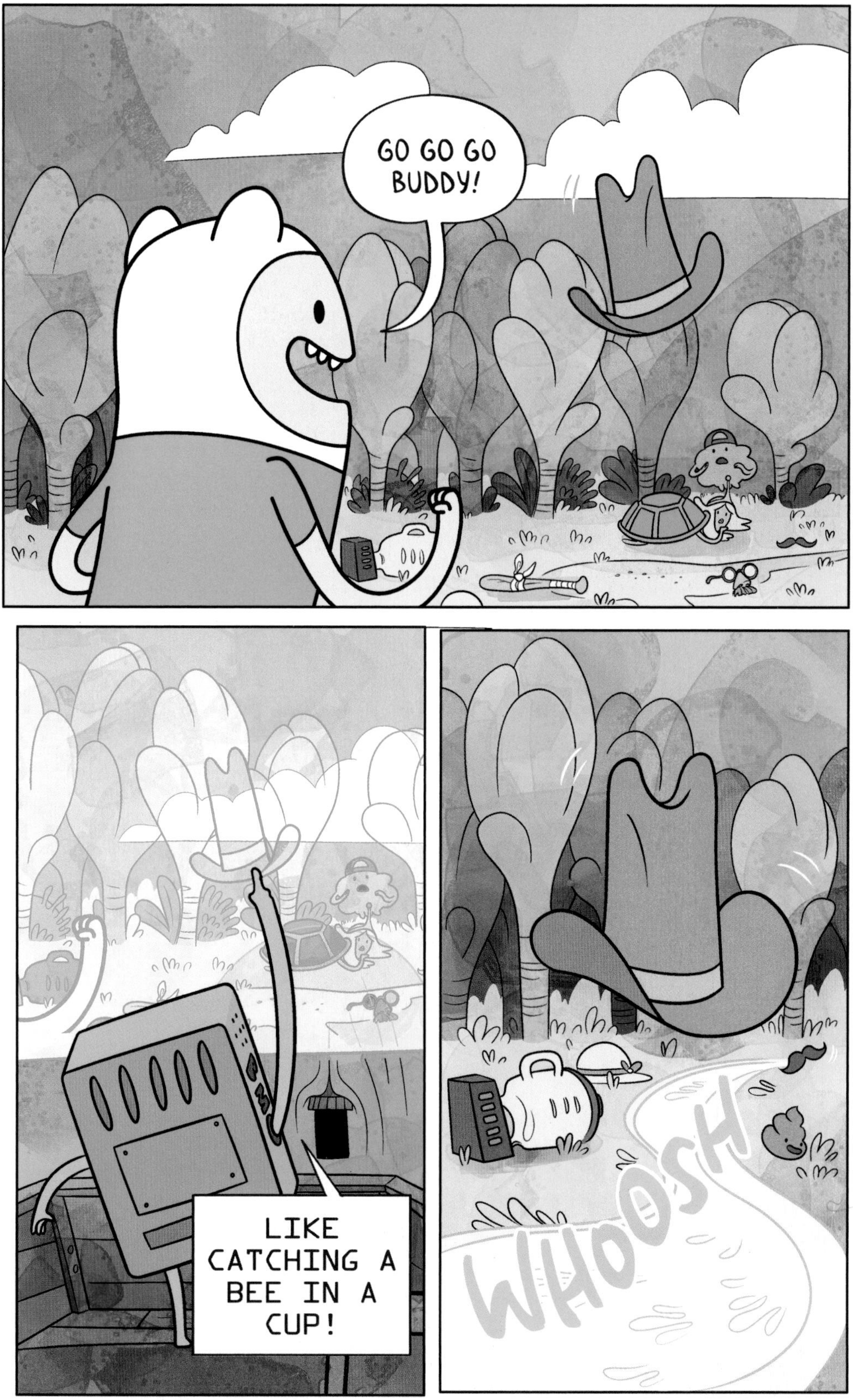
GO GO GO BUDDY!
LIKE CATCHING A BEE IN A CUP!
WHOOSH

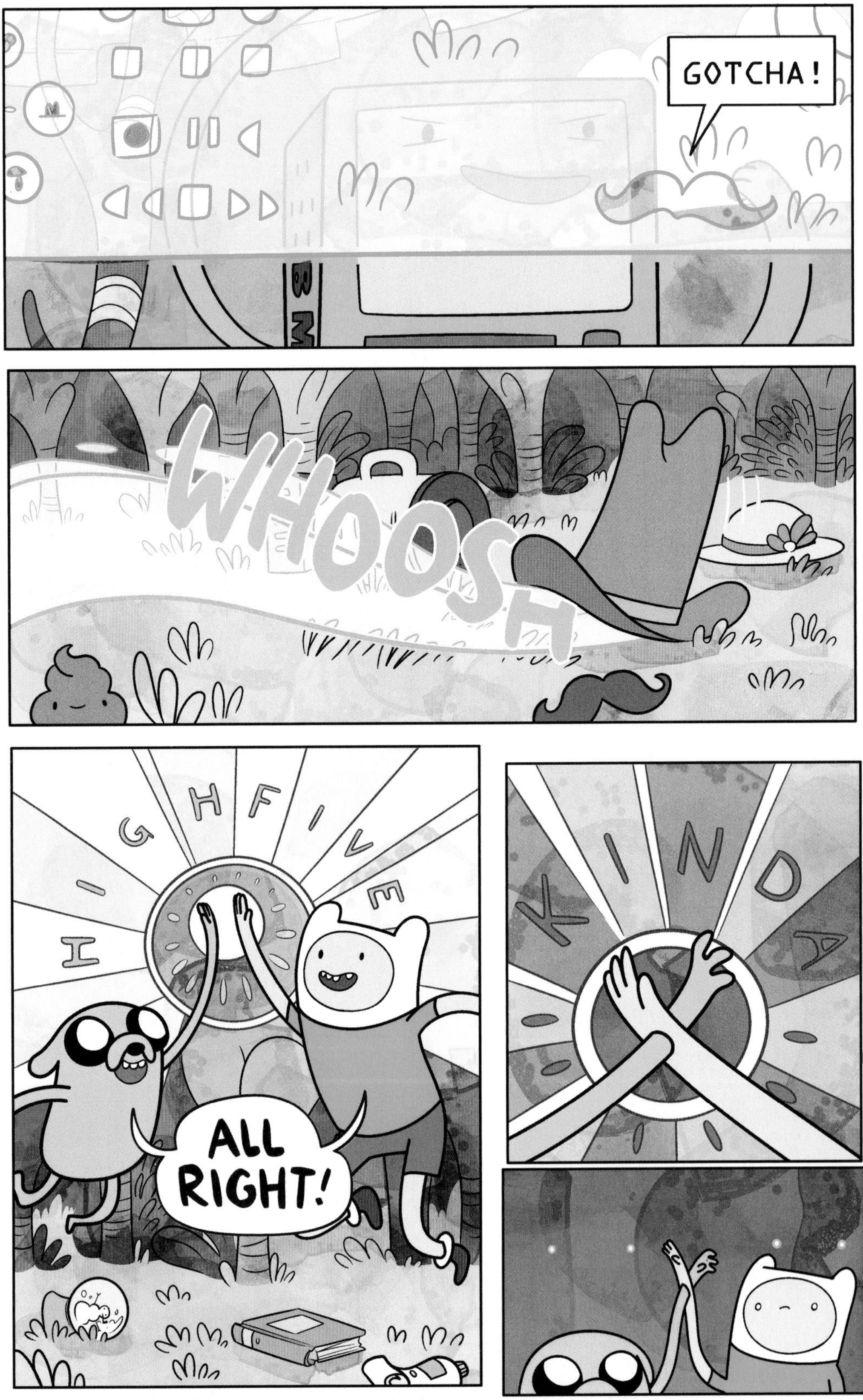
GOTCHA!
WHOOSH
HIGH FIVE
ALL RIGHT!
KINDA

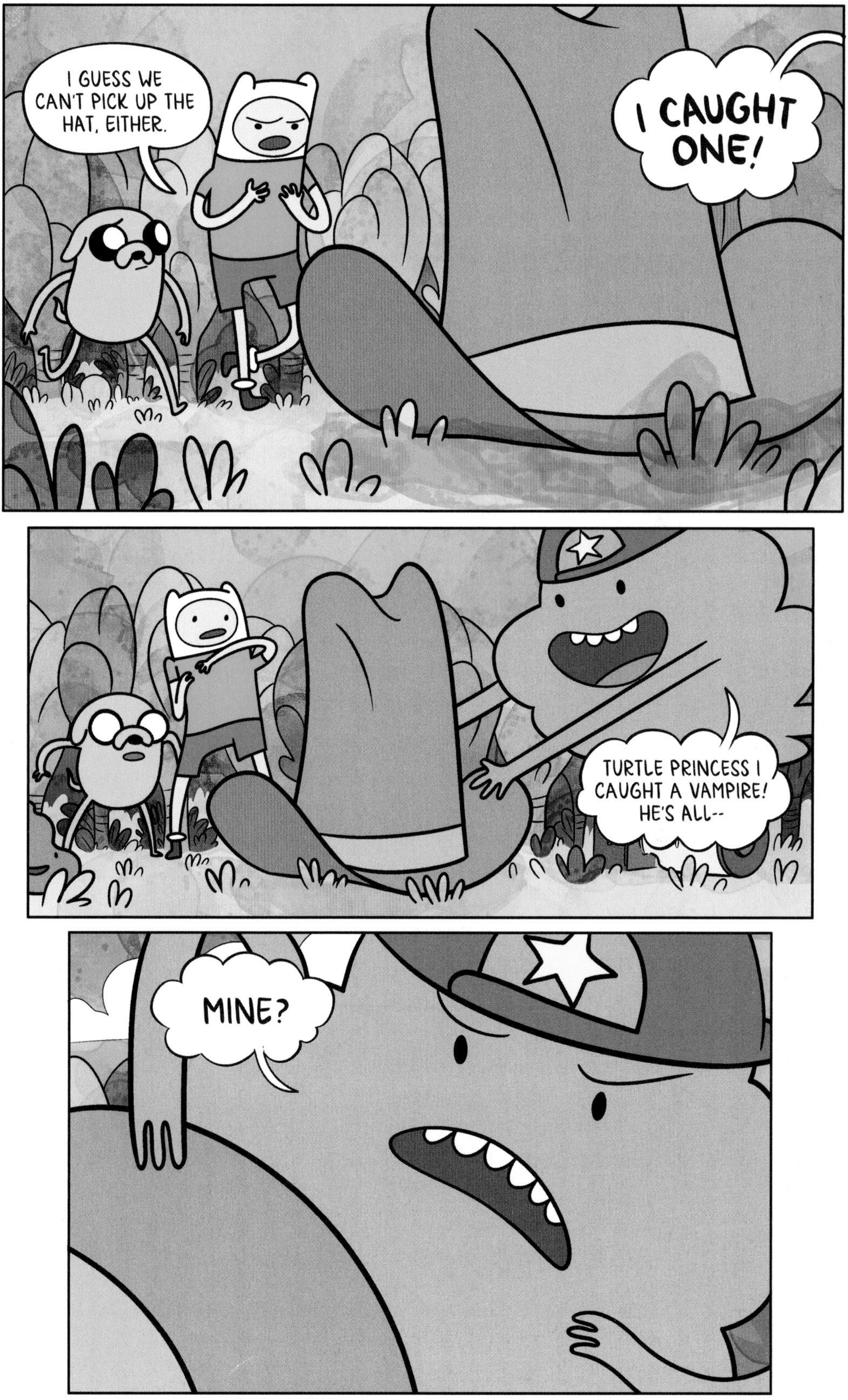
I GUESS WE CAN'T PICK UP THE HAT, EITHER.
I CAUGHT ONE!
TURTLE PRINCESS I CAUGHT A VAMPIRE! HE'S ALL--
MINE?

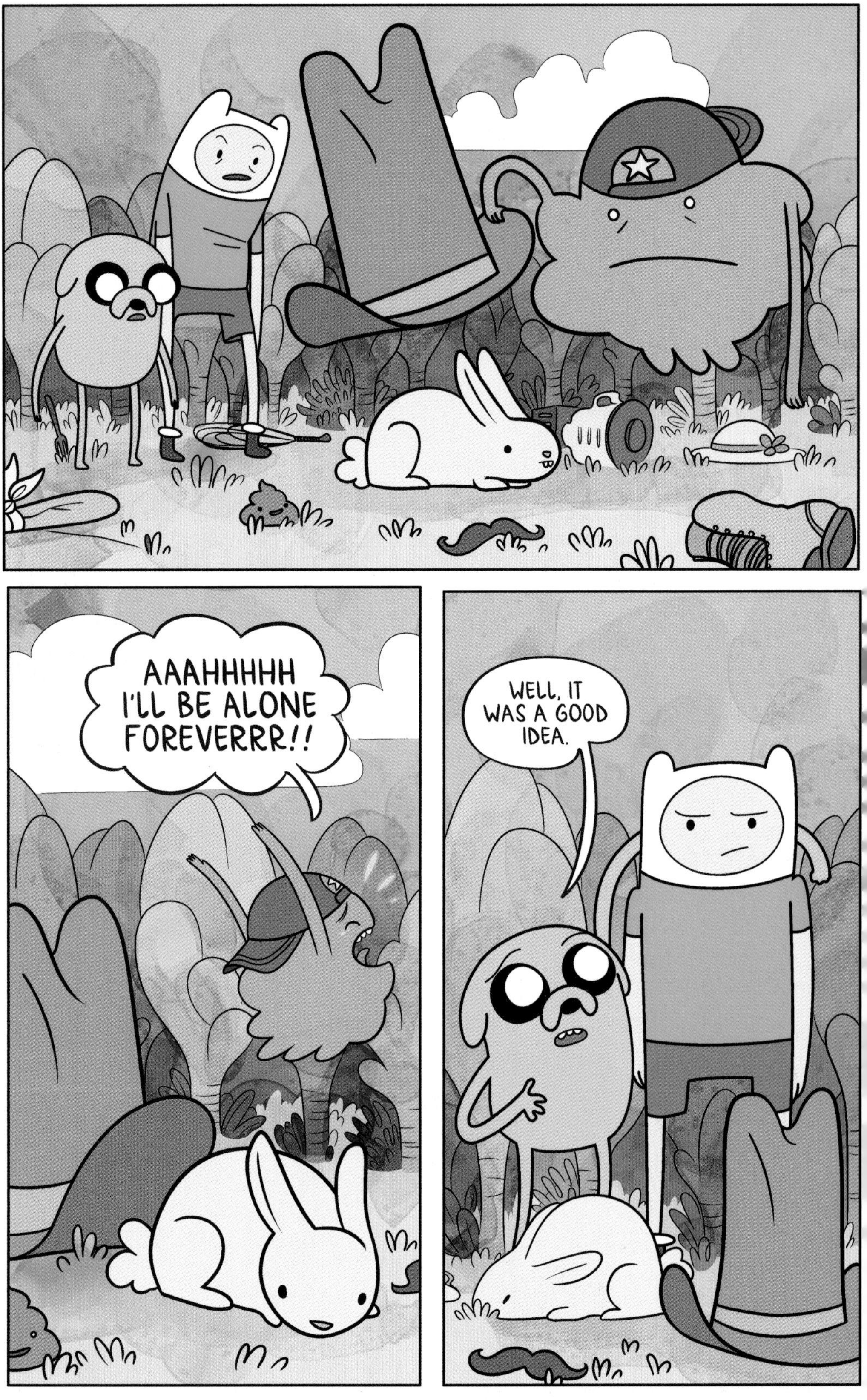
AAAHHHHH I'LL BE ALONE FOREVERRR!!
WELL, IT WAS A GOOD IDEA.

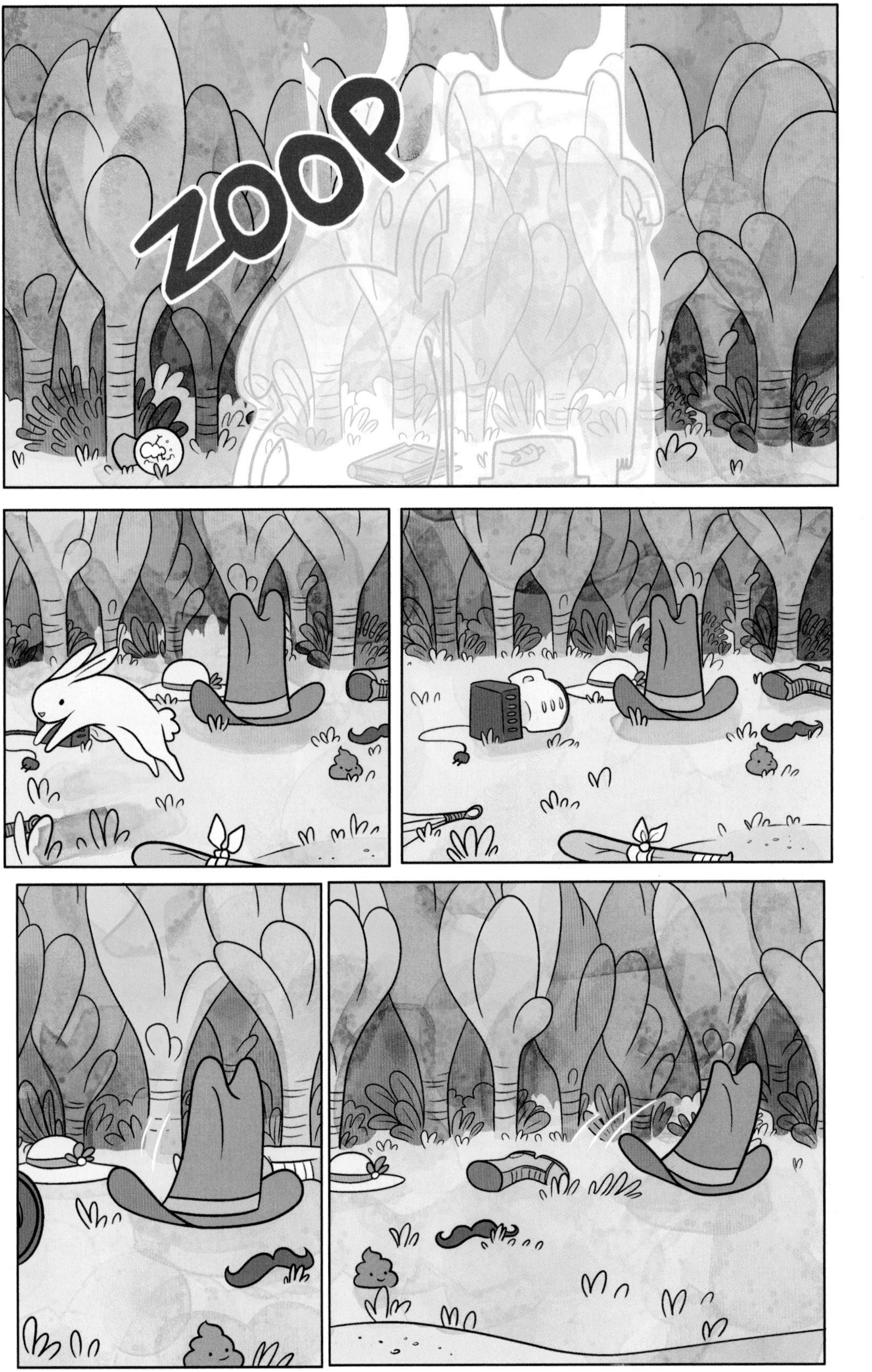
ZOOP

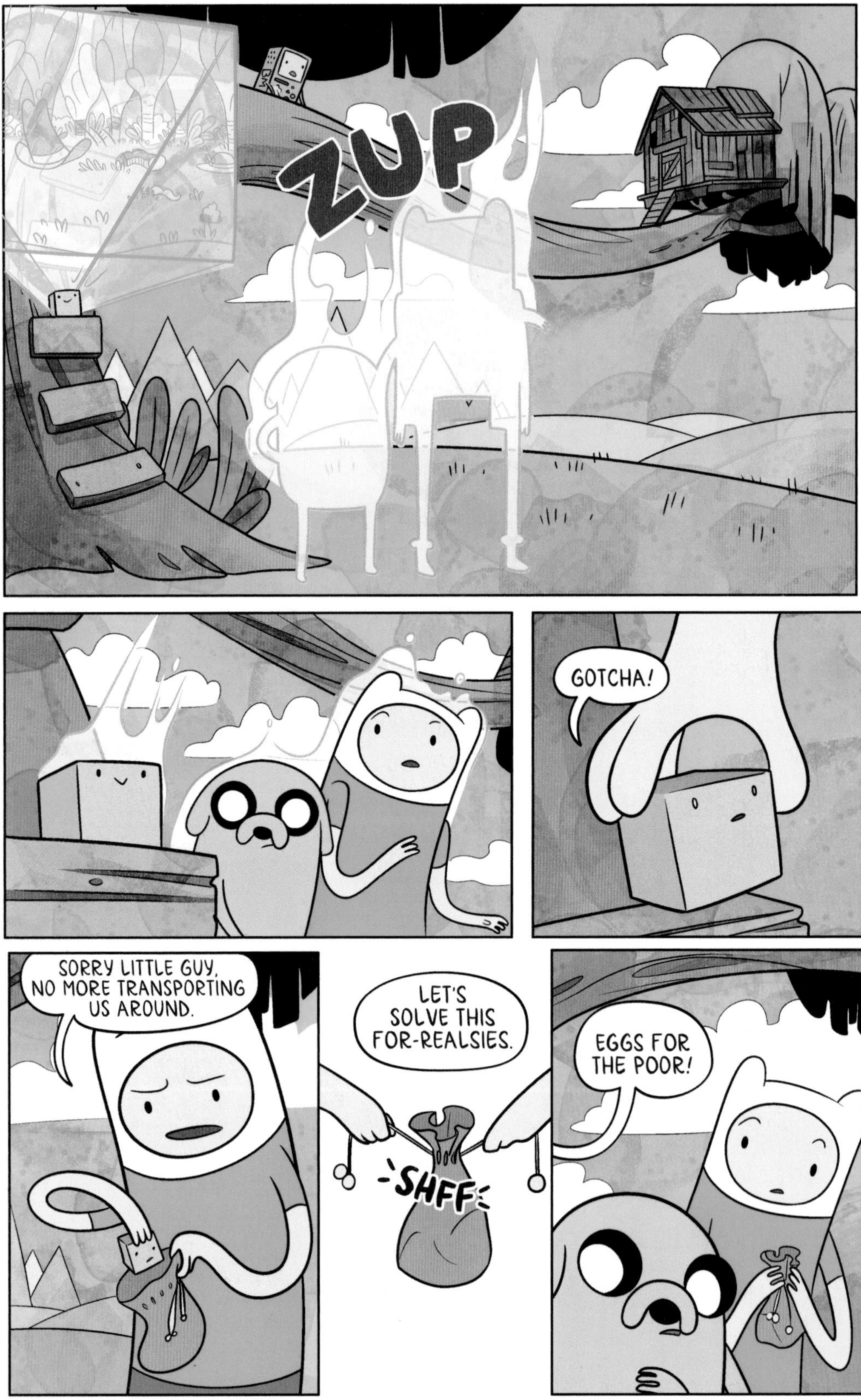
ZUP
GOTCHA!
SORRY LITTLE GUY, NO MORE TRANSPORTING US AROUND.
LET'S SOLVE THIS FOR-REALSIES.
SHFF
EGGS FOR THE POOR!

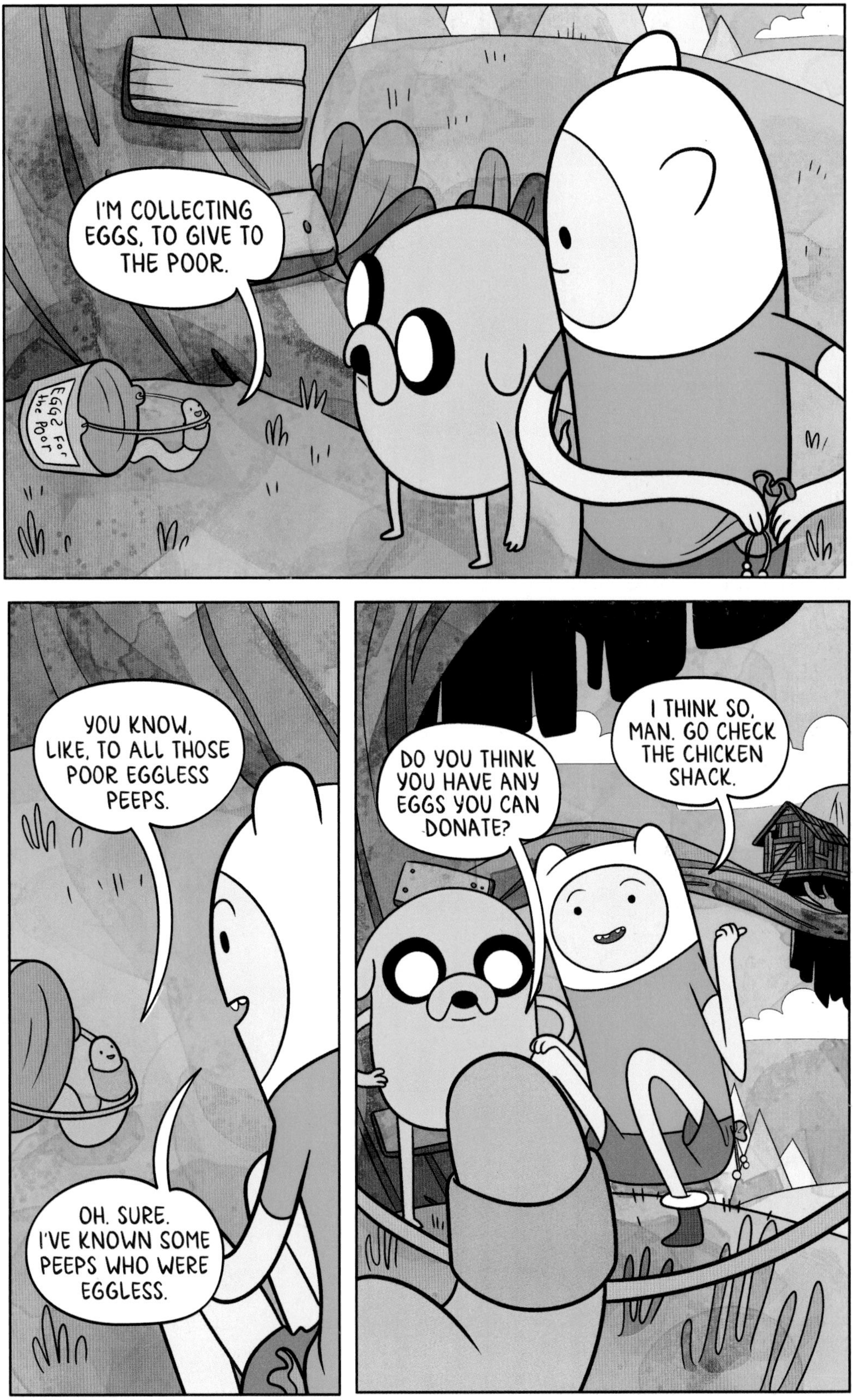

I'M COLLECTING EGGS, TO GIVE TO THE POOR.
EGGS For the Poor
YOU KNOW, LIKE, TO ALL THOSE POOR EGGLESS PEEPS.
OH. SURE. I'VE KNOWN SOME PEEPS WHO WERE EGGLESS.
DO YOU THINK YOU HAVE ANY EGGS YOU CAN DONATE?
I THINK SO, MAN. GO CHECK THE CHICKEN SHACK.

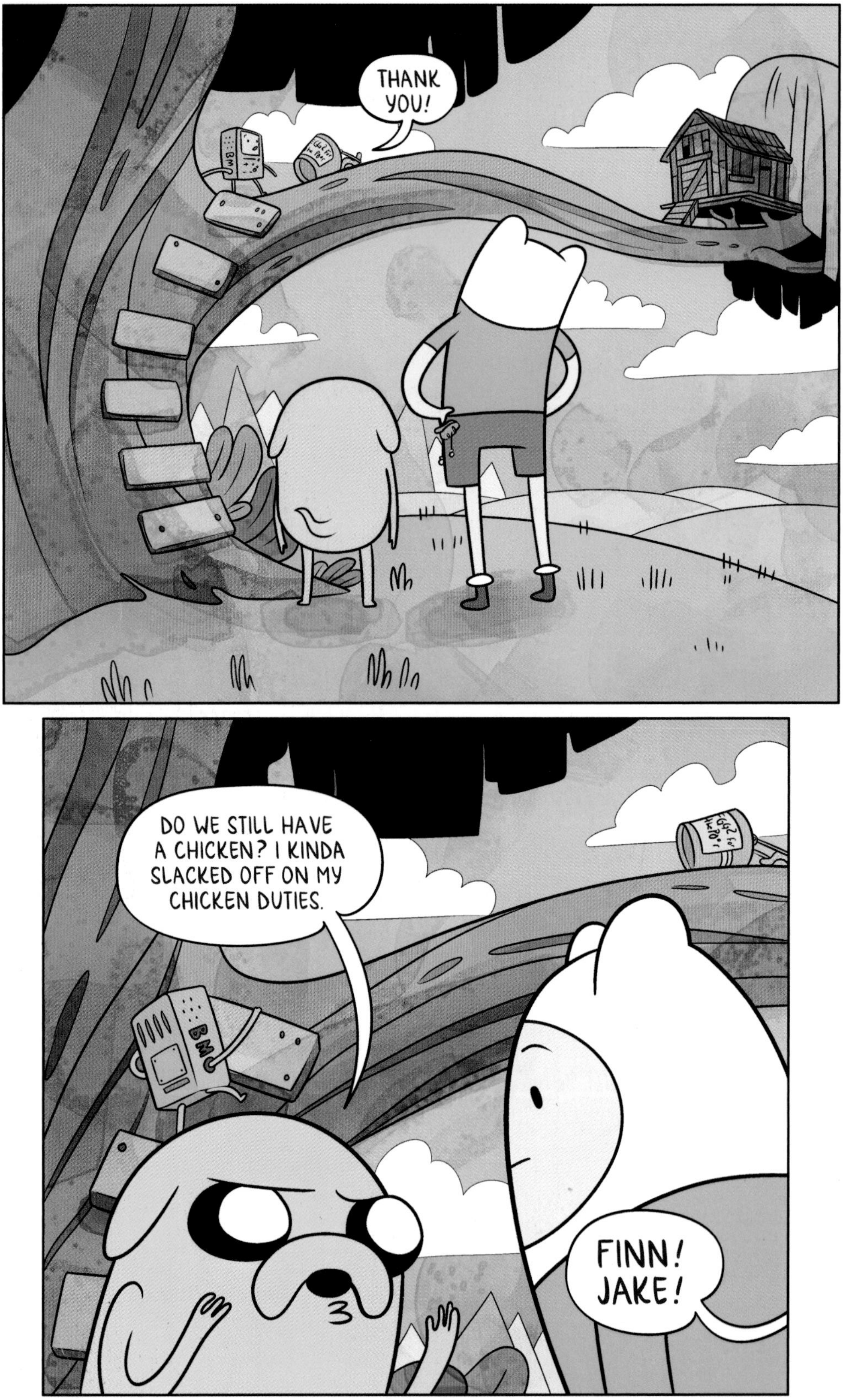
THANK YOU!
DO WE STILL HAVE A CHICKEN? I KINDA SLACKED OFF ON MY CHICKEN DUTIES.
FINN! JAKE!

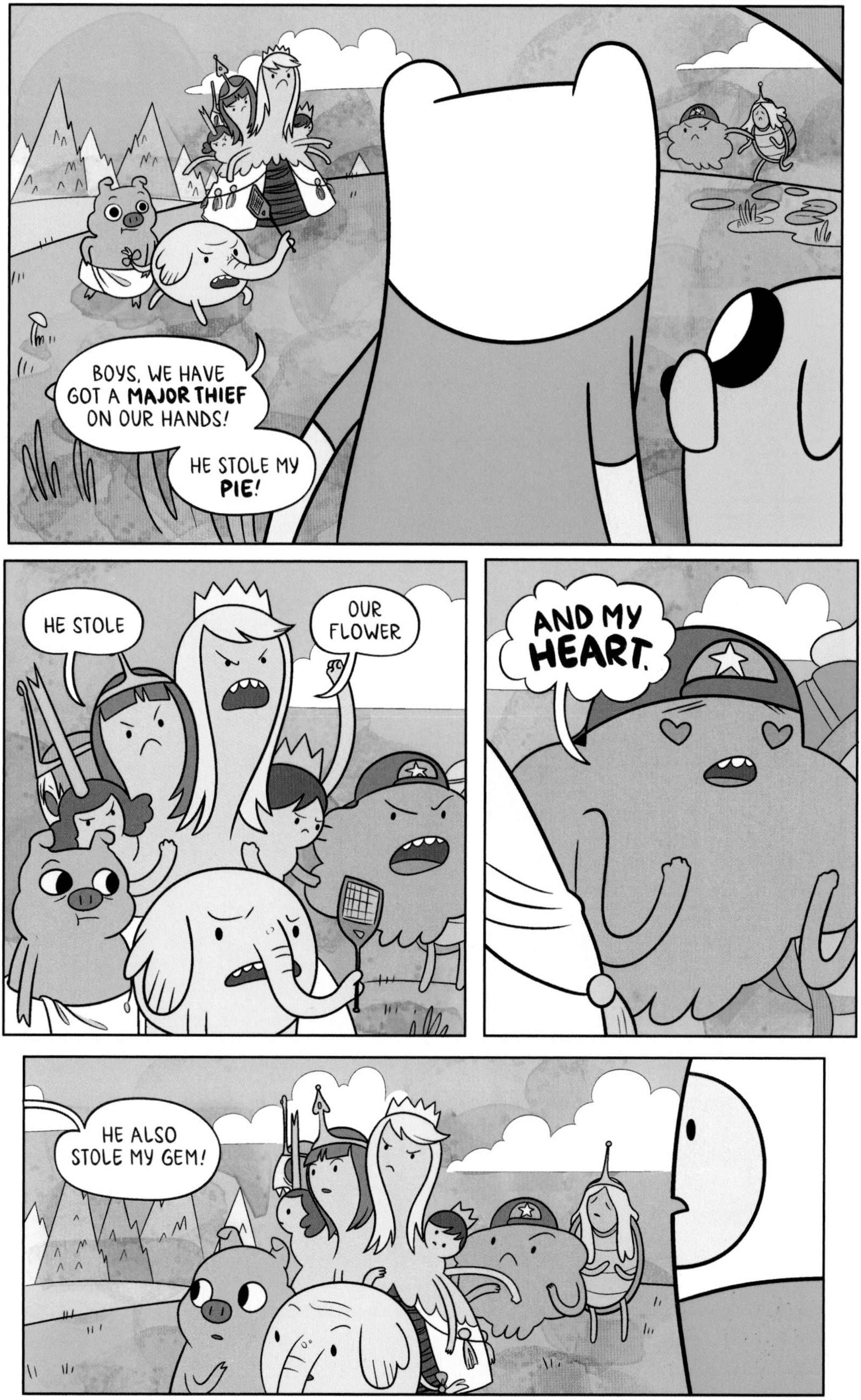
BOYS, WE HAVE GOT A **MAJOR THIEF** ON OUR HANDS!
HE STOLE MY **PIE**!
HE STOLE
OUR FLOWER
AND MY **HEART**.
HE ALSO STOLE MY GEM!

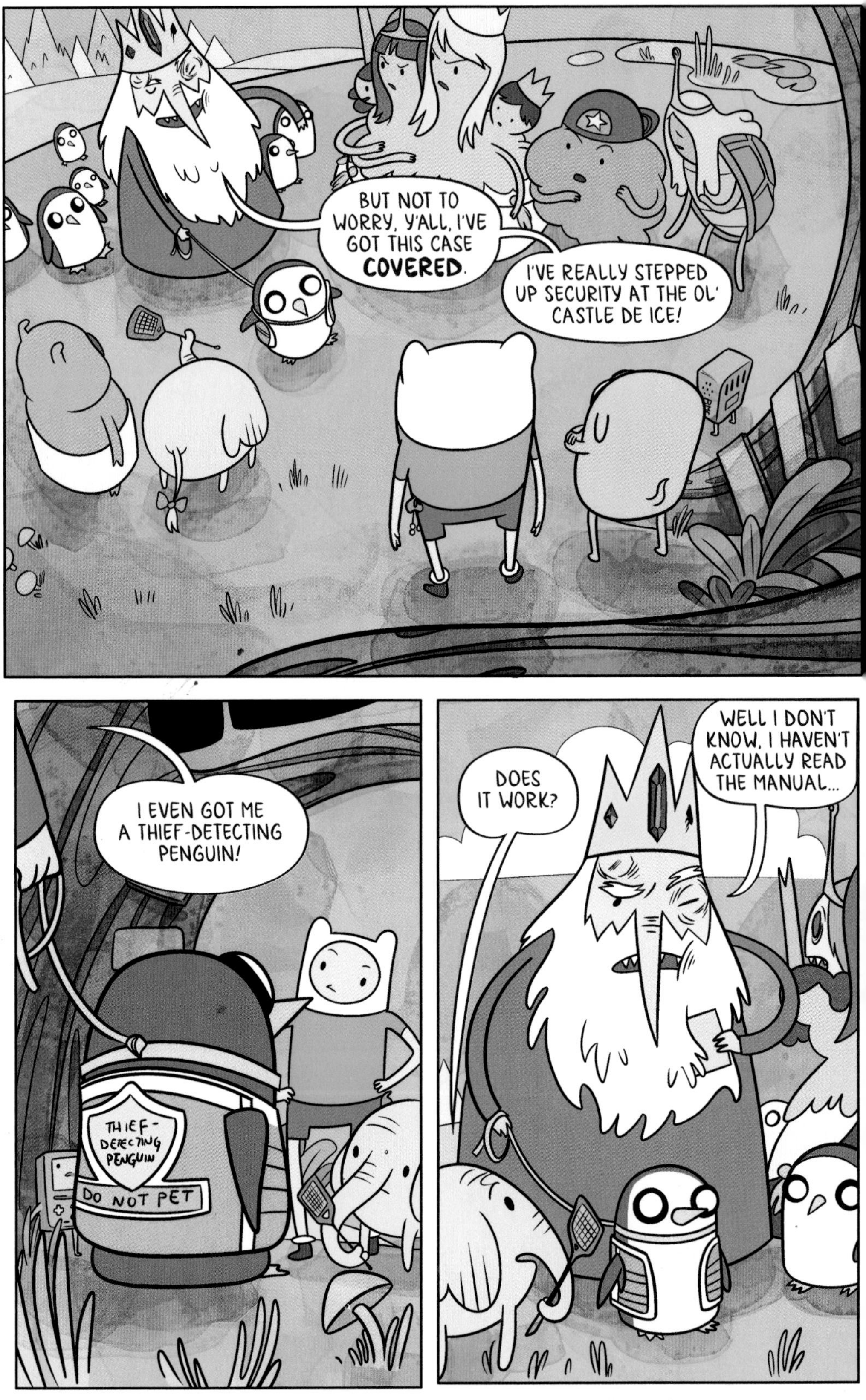
BUT NOT TO WORRY, Y'ALL, I'VE GOT THIS CASE **COVERED**.
I'VE REALLY STEPPED UP SECURITY AT THE OL' CASTLE DE ICE!
I EVEN GOT ME A THIEF-DETECTING PENGUIN!
THIEF-DETECTING PENGUIN
DO NOT PET
DOES IT WORK?
WELL I DON'T KNOW, I HAVEN'T ACTUALLY READ THE MANUAL...

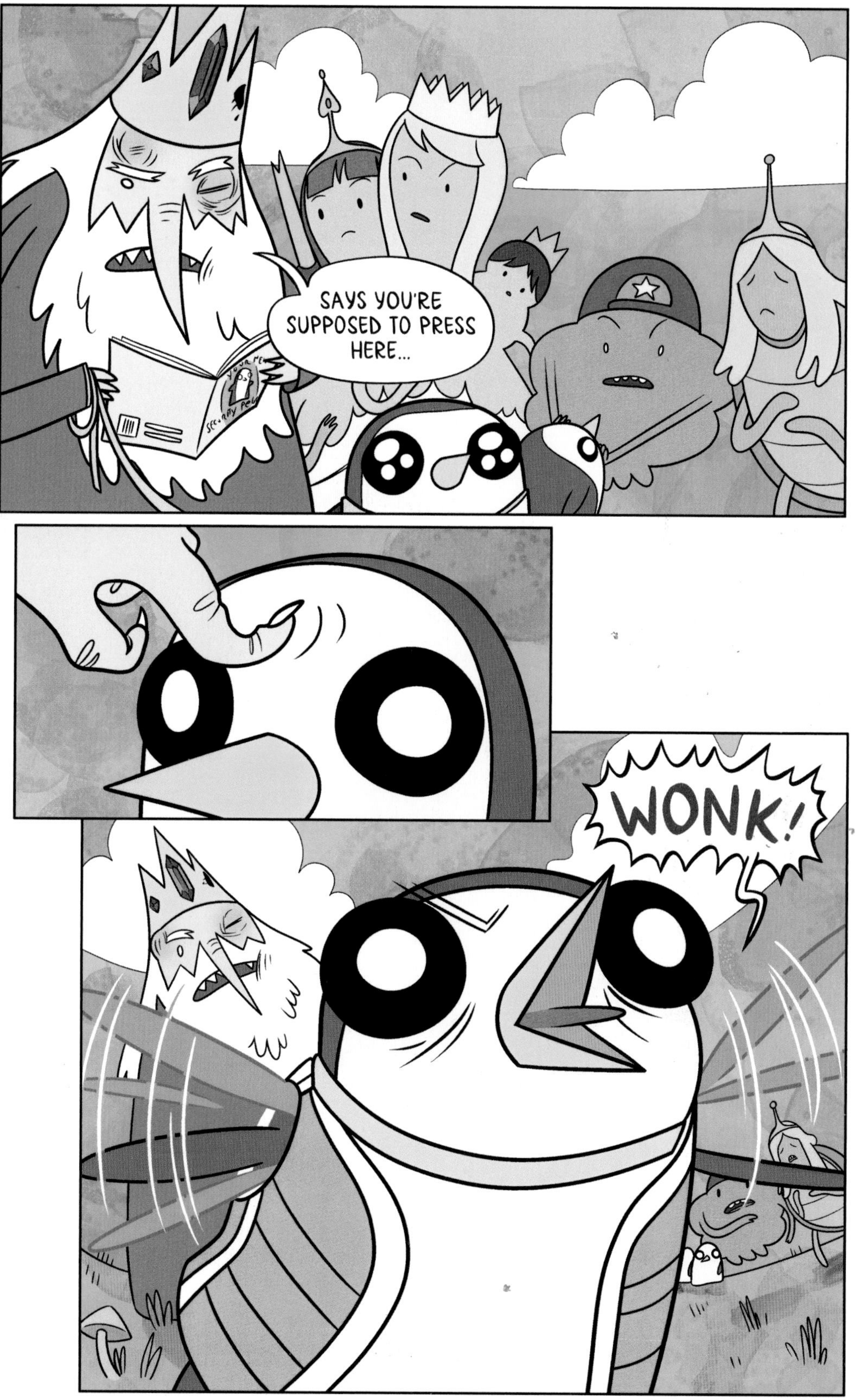
SAYS YOU'RE SUPPOSED TO PRESS HERE...
WONK!

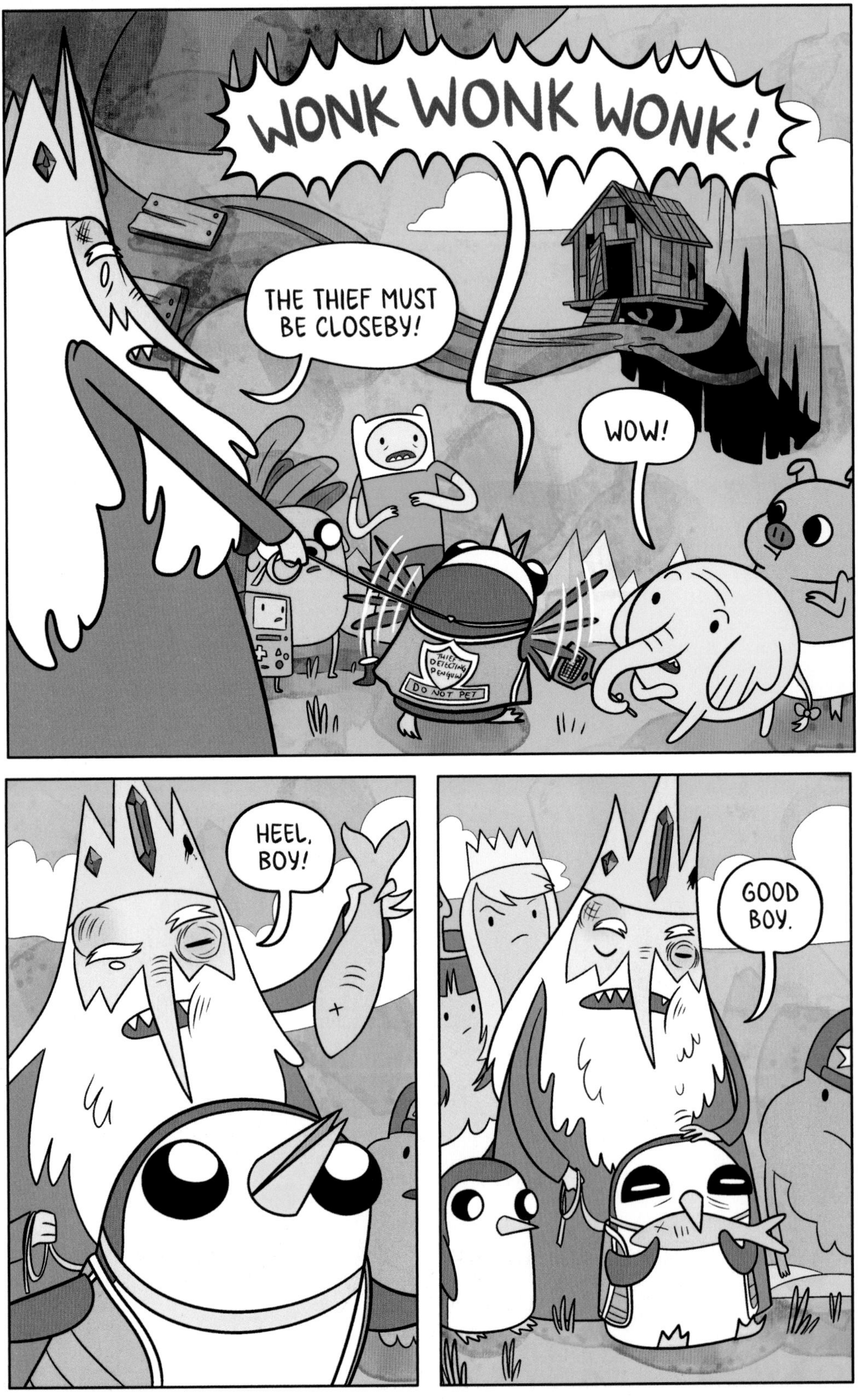
WONK WONK WONK!
THE THIEF MUST BE CLOSEBY!
THIEF DETECTING PENGUIN
DO NOT PET
WOW!
HEEL, BOY!
GOOD BOY.

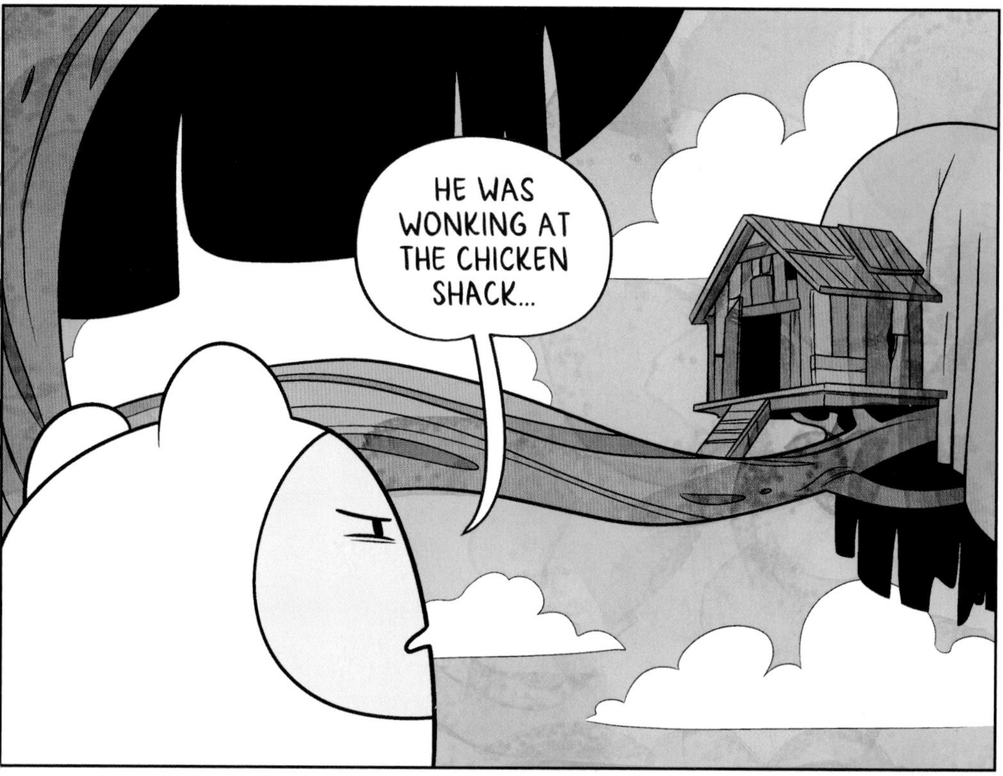
HE WAS WONKING AT THE CHICKEN SHACK...

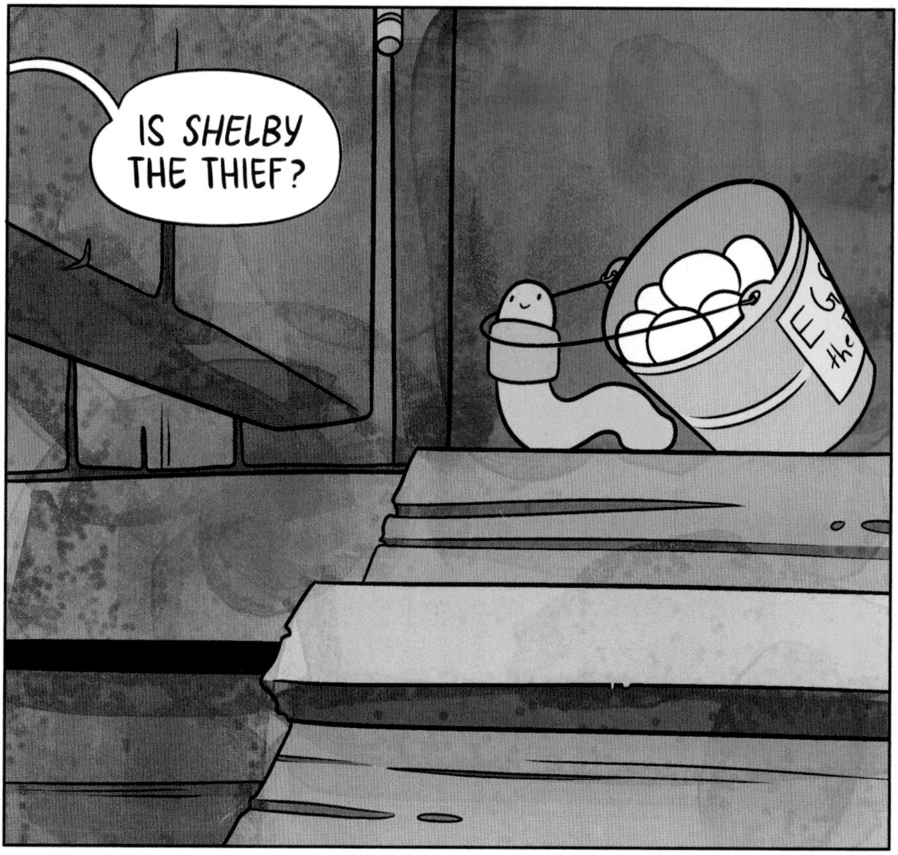
IS *SHELBY* THE THIEF?

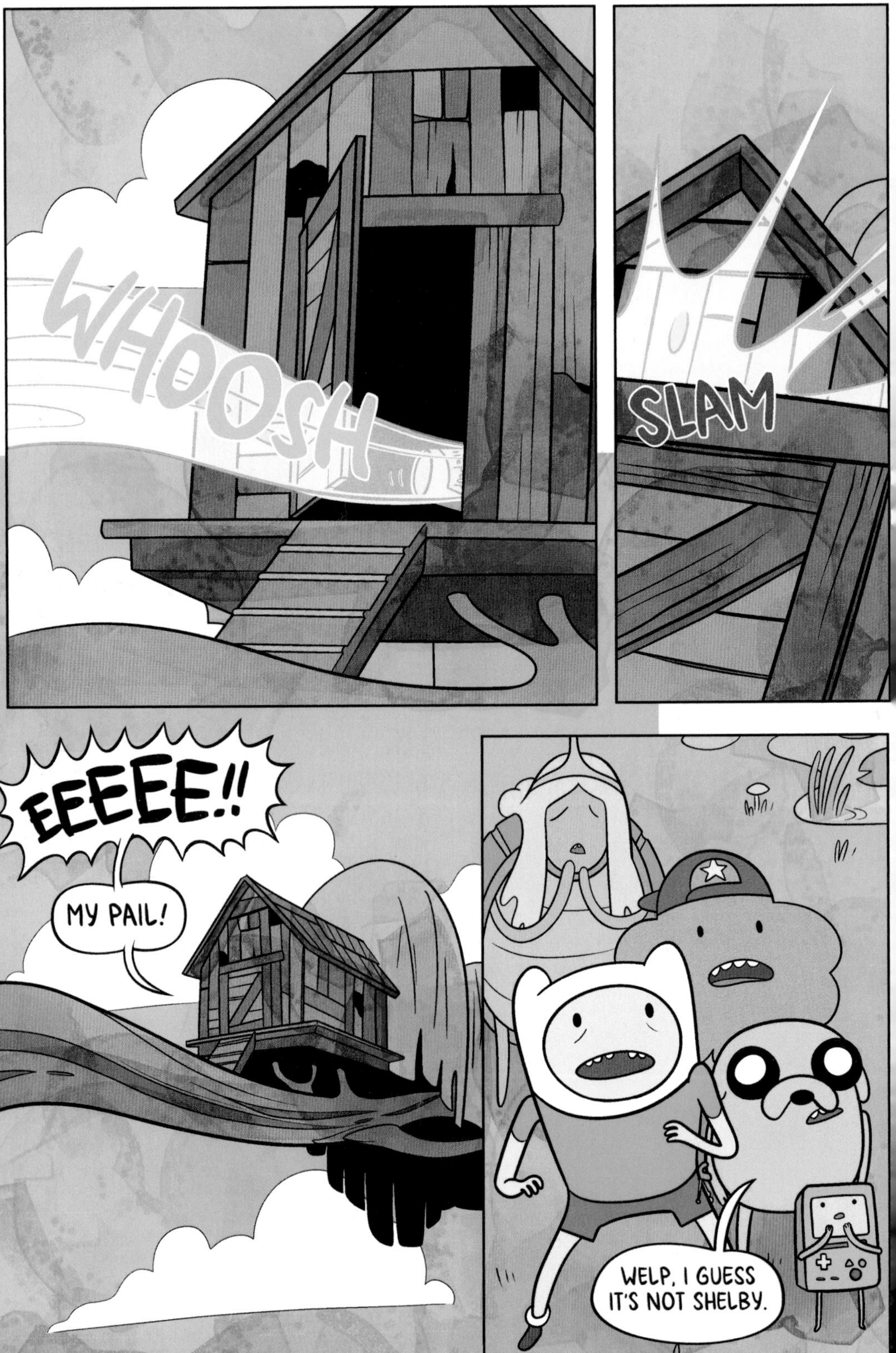
WHOOSH
SLAM
EEEEE.!!
MY PAIL!
WELP, I GUESS IT'S NOT SHELBY.

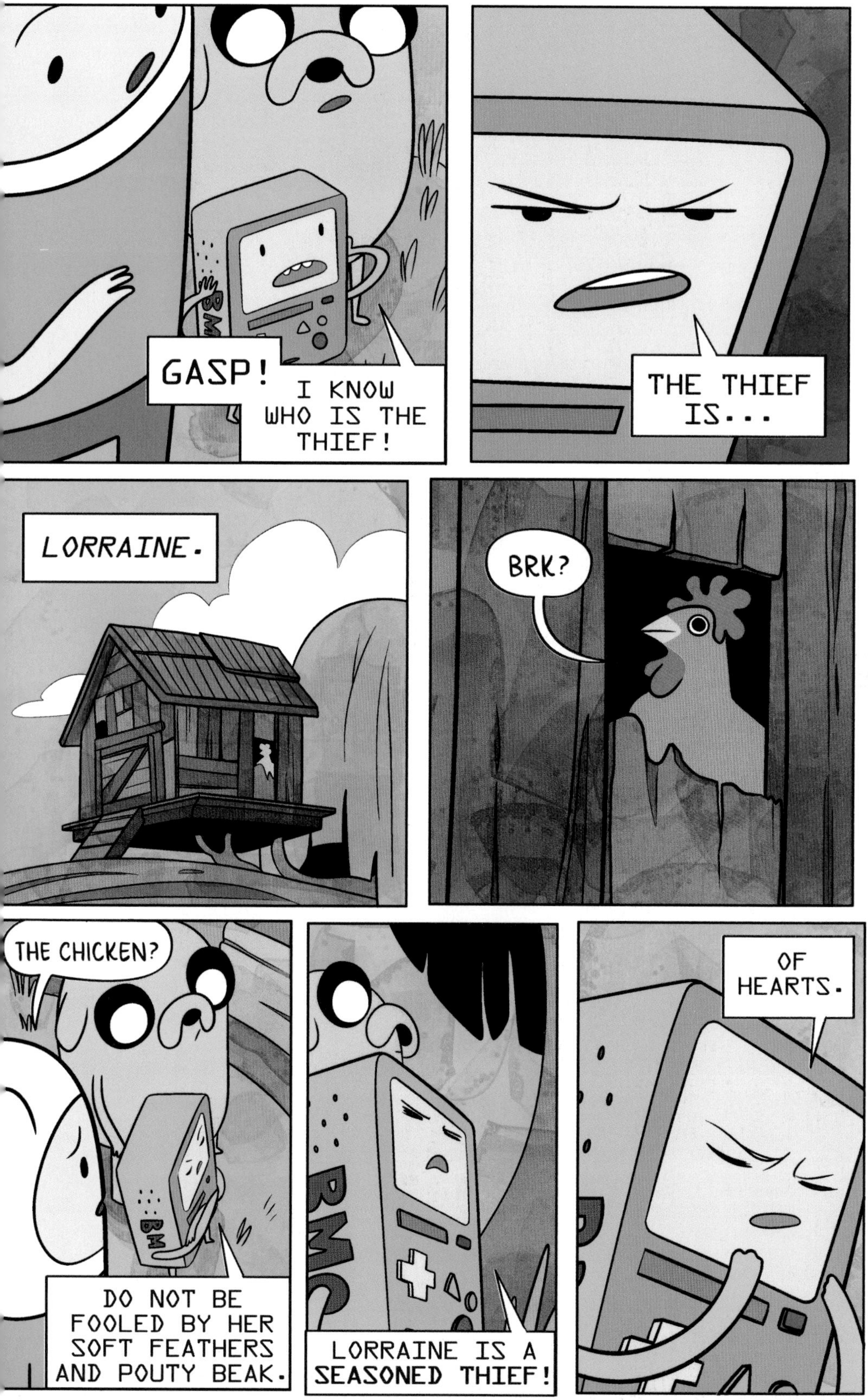
GASP!
I KNOW WHO IS THE THIEF!
THE THIEF IS...
LORRAINE.
BRK?
THE CHICKEN?
DO NOT BE FOOLED BY HER SOFT FEATHERS AND POUTY BEAK.
LORRAINE IS A SEASONED THIEF!
OF HEARTS.

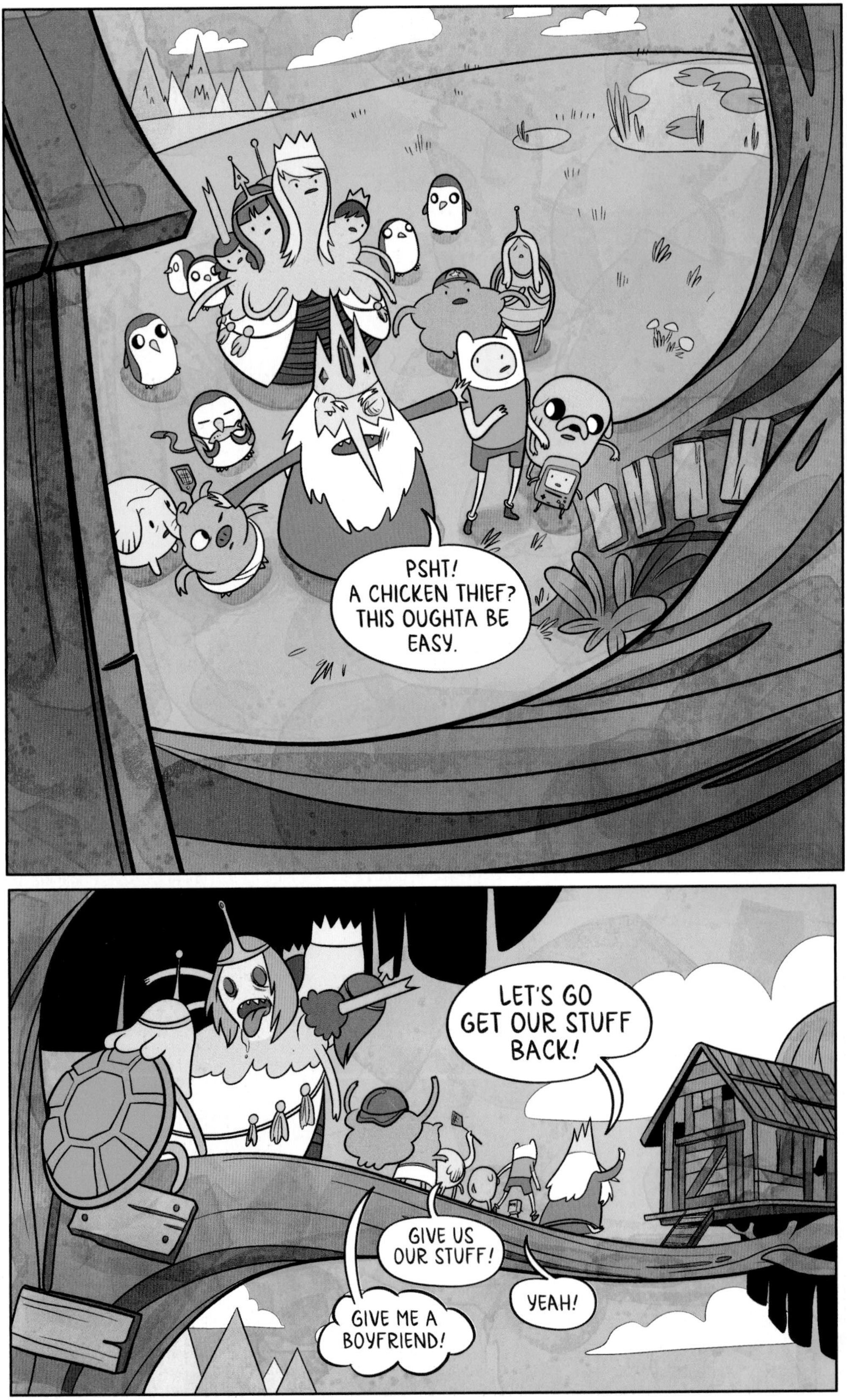
PSHT!
A CHICKEN THIEF?
THIS OUGHTA BE
EASY.
LET'S GO
GET OUR STUFF
BACK!
GIVE US
OUR STUFF!
YEAH!
GIVE ME A
BOYFRIEND!

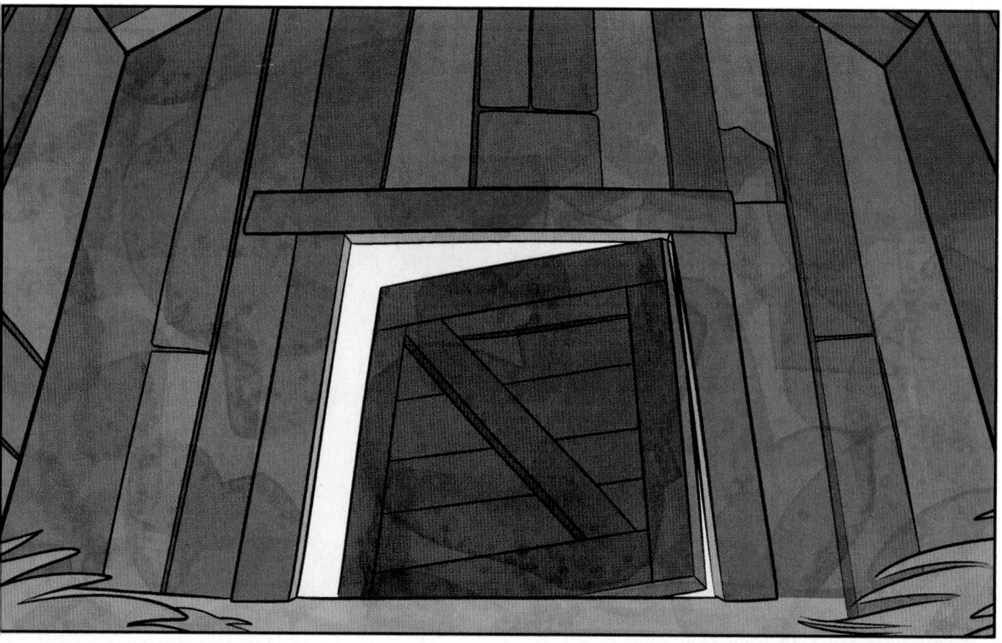

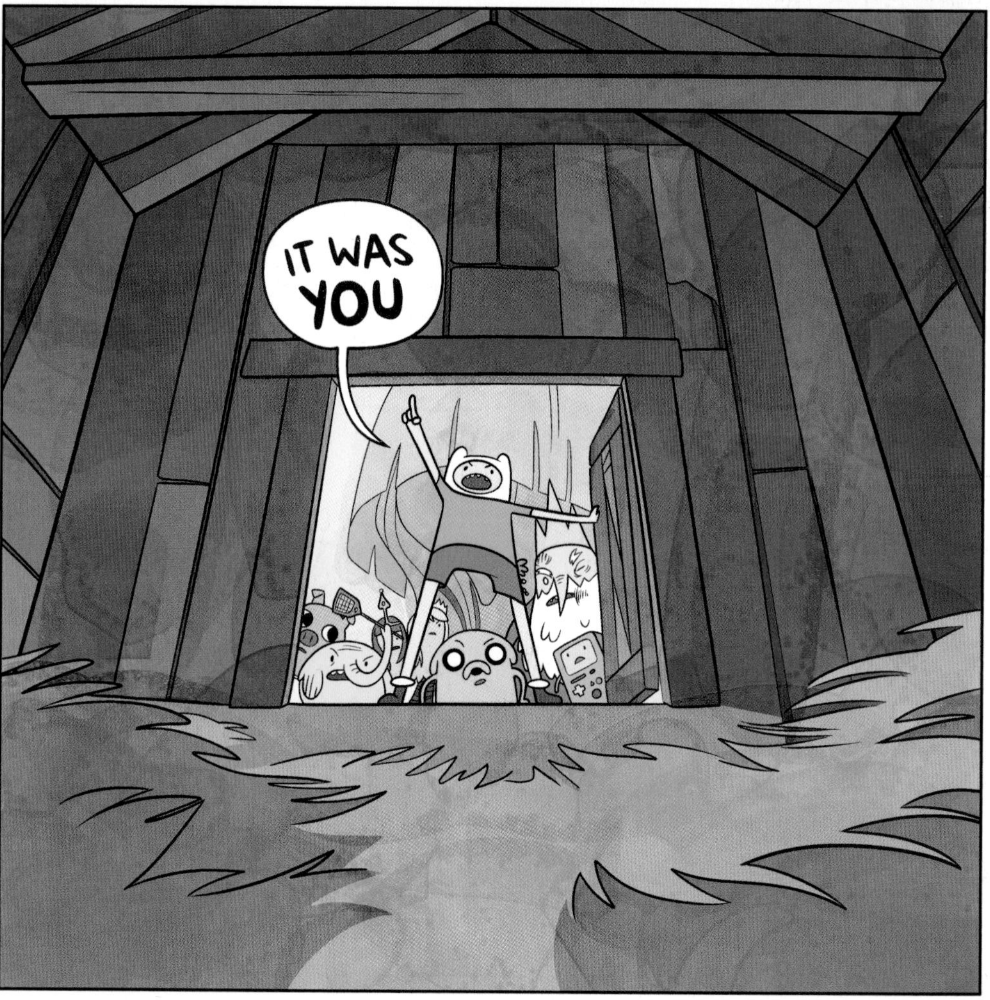
IT WAS YOU

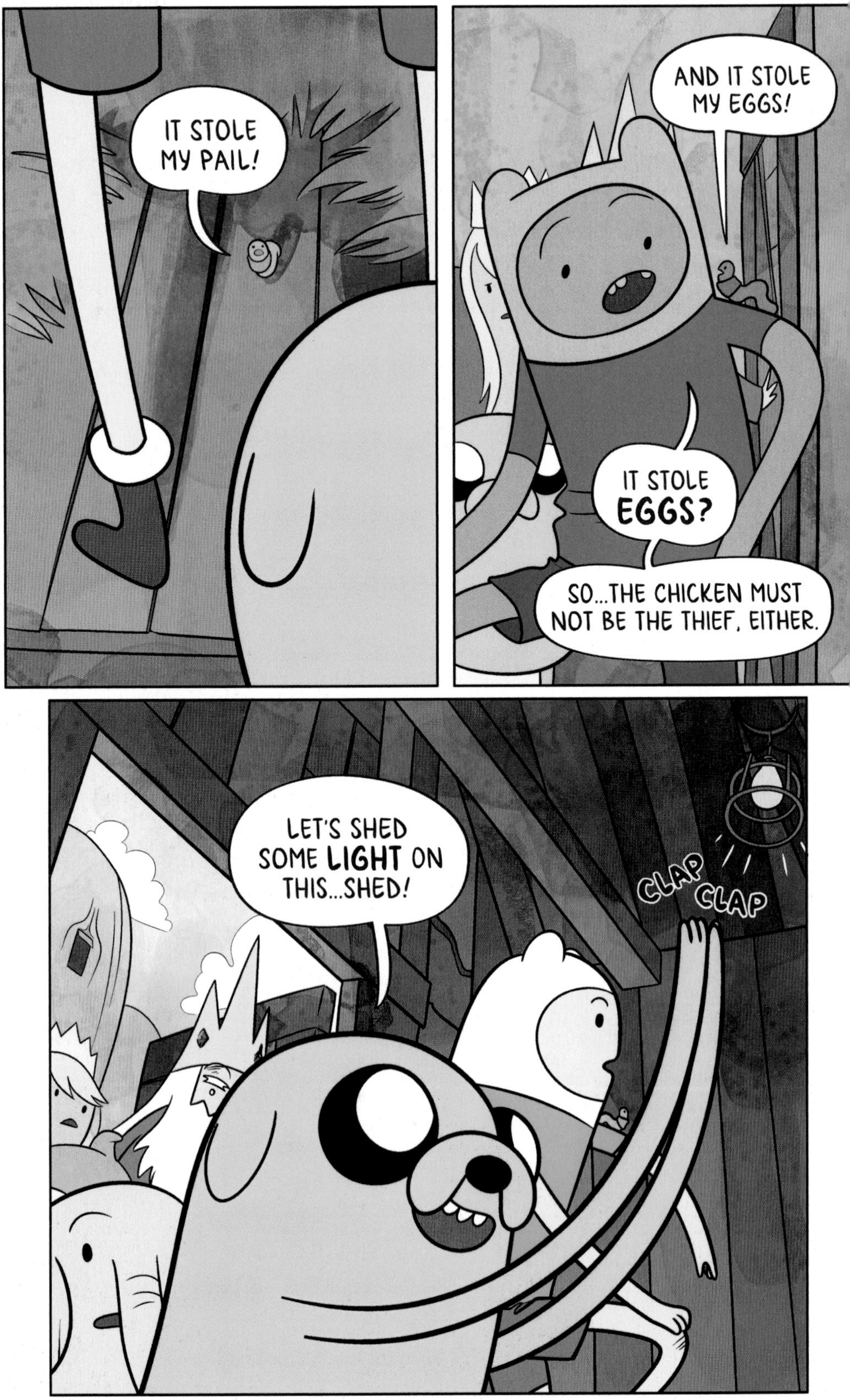
IT STOLE MY PAIL!
AND IT STOLE MY EGGS!
IT STOLE EGGS?
SO...THE CHICKEN MUST NOT BE THE THIEF, EITHER.
LET'S SHED SOME LIGHT ON THIS...SHED!
CLAP CLAP

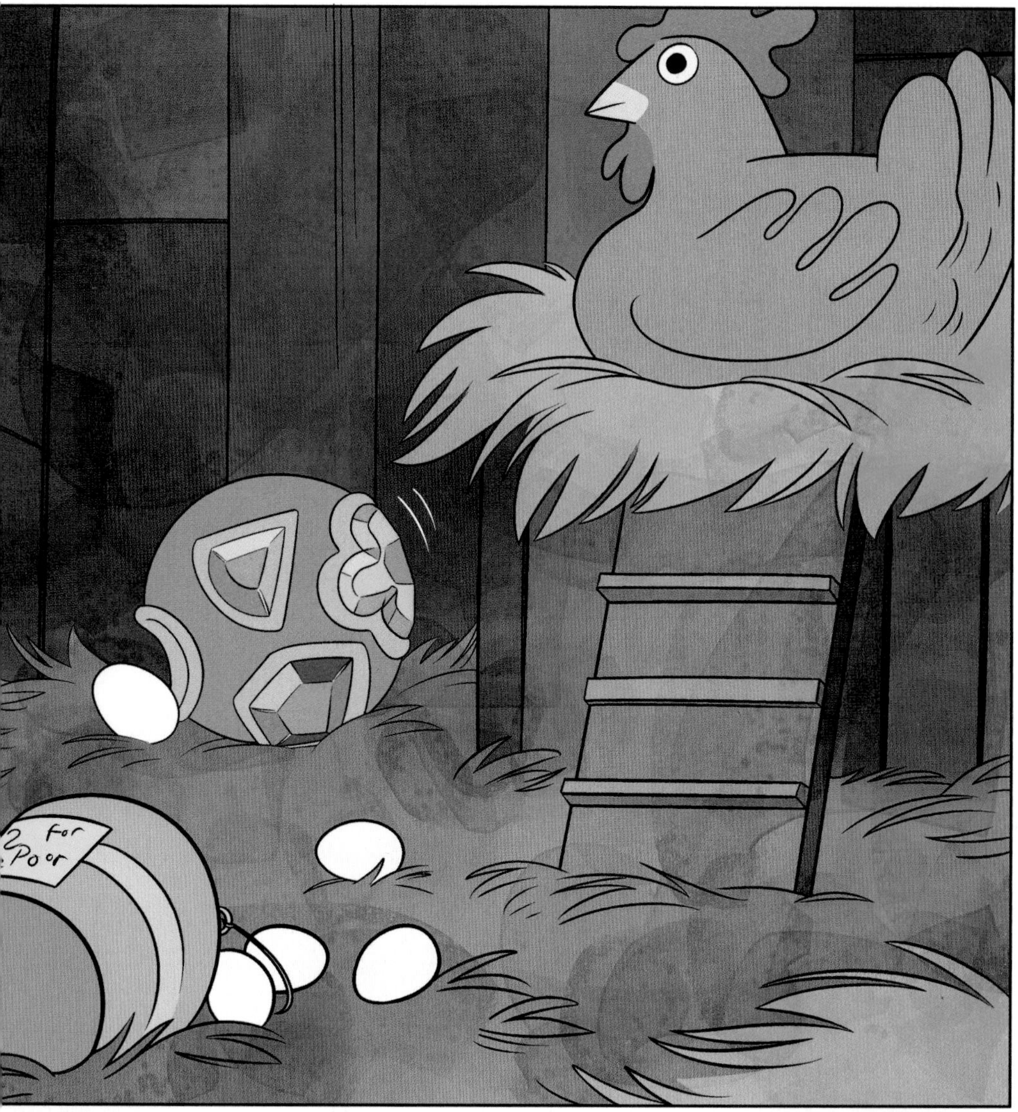

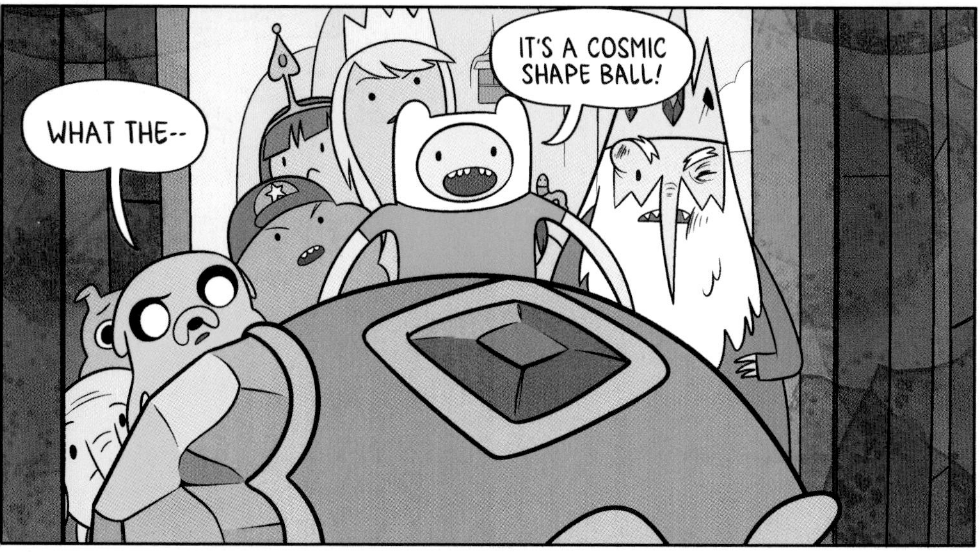
WHAT THE--
IT'S A COSMIC SHAPE BALL!

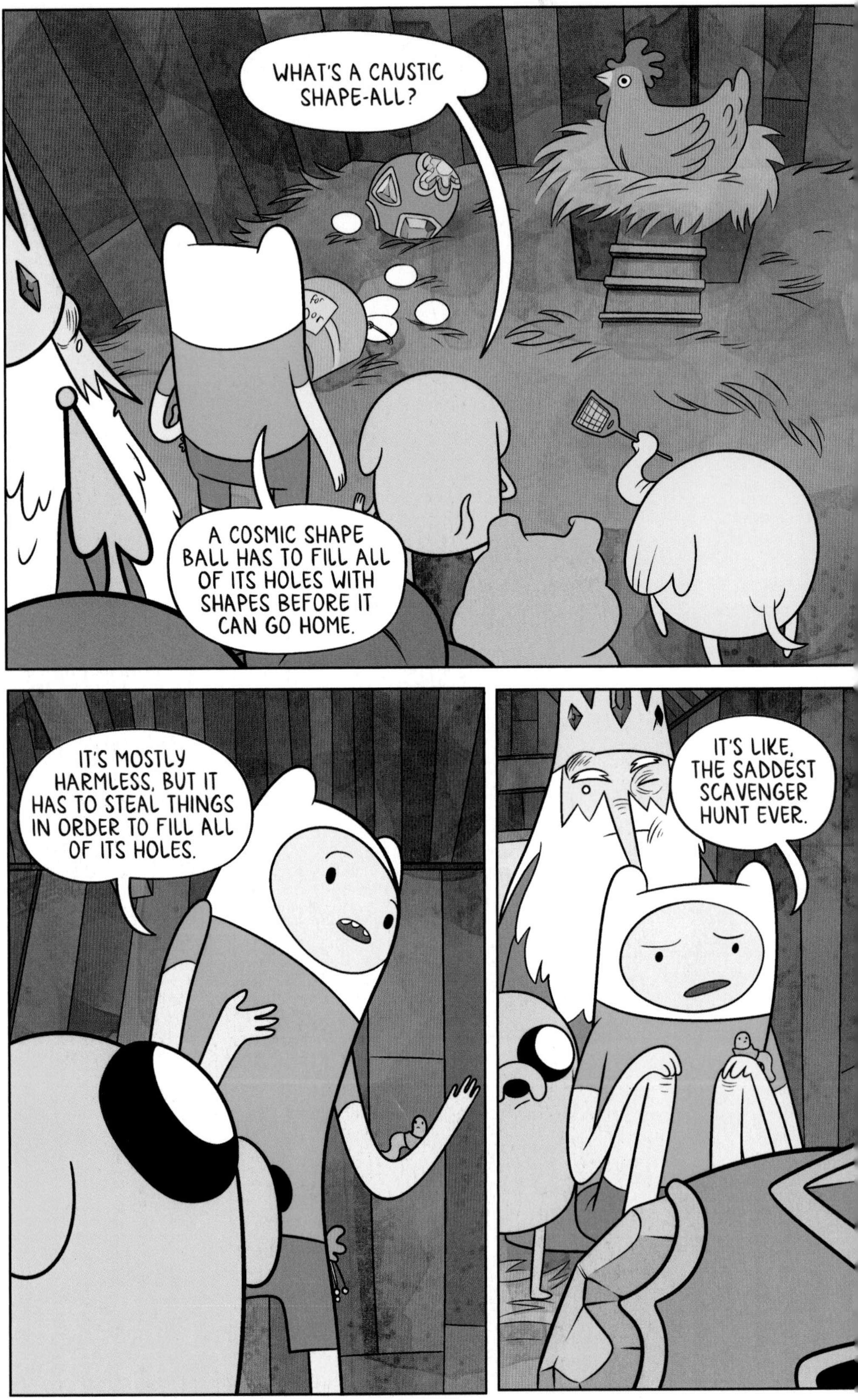
WHAT'S A CAUSTIC SHAPE-ALL?
A COSMIC SHAPE BALL HAS TO FILL ALL OF ITS HOLES WITH SHAPES BEFORE IT CAN GO HOME.
IT'S MOSTLY HARMLESS, BUT IT HAS TO STEAL THINGS IN ORDER TO FILL ALL OF ITS HOLES.
IT'S LIKE, THE SADDEST SCAVENGER HUNT EVER.

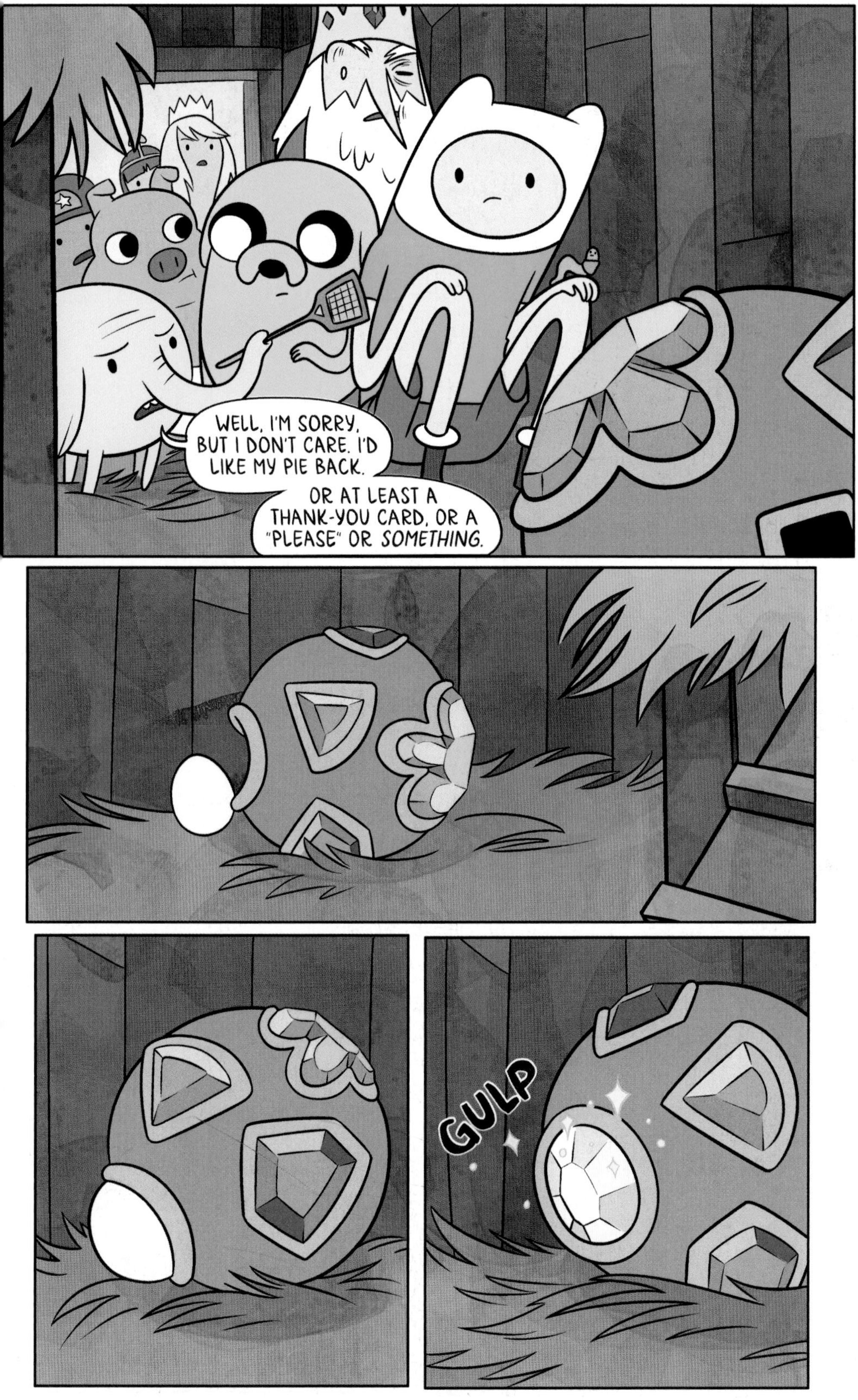
WELL, I'M SORRY, BUT I DON'T CARE. I'D LIKE MY PIE BACK.
OR AT LEAST A THANK-YOU CARD, OR A "PLEASE" OR *SOMETHING.*
GULP

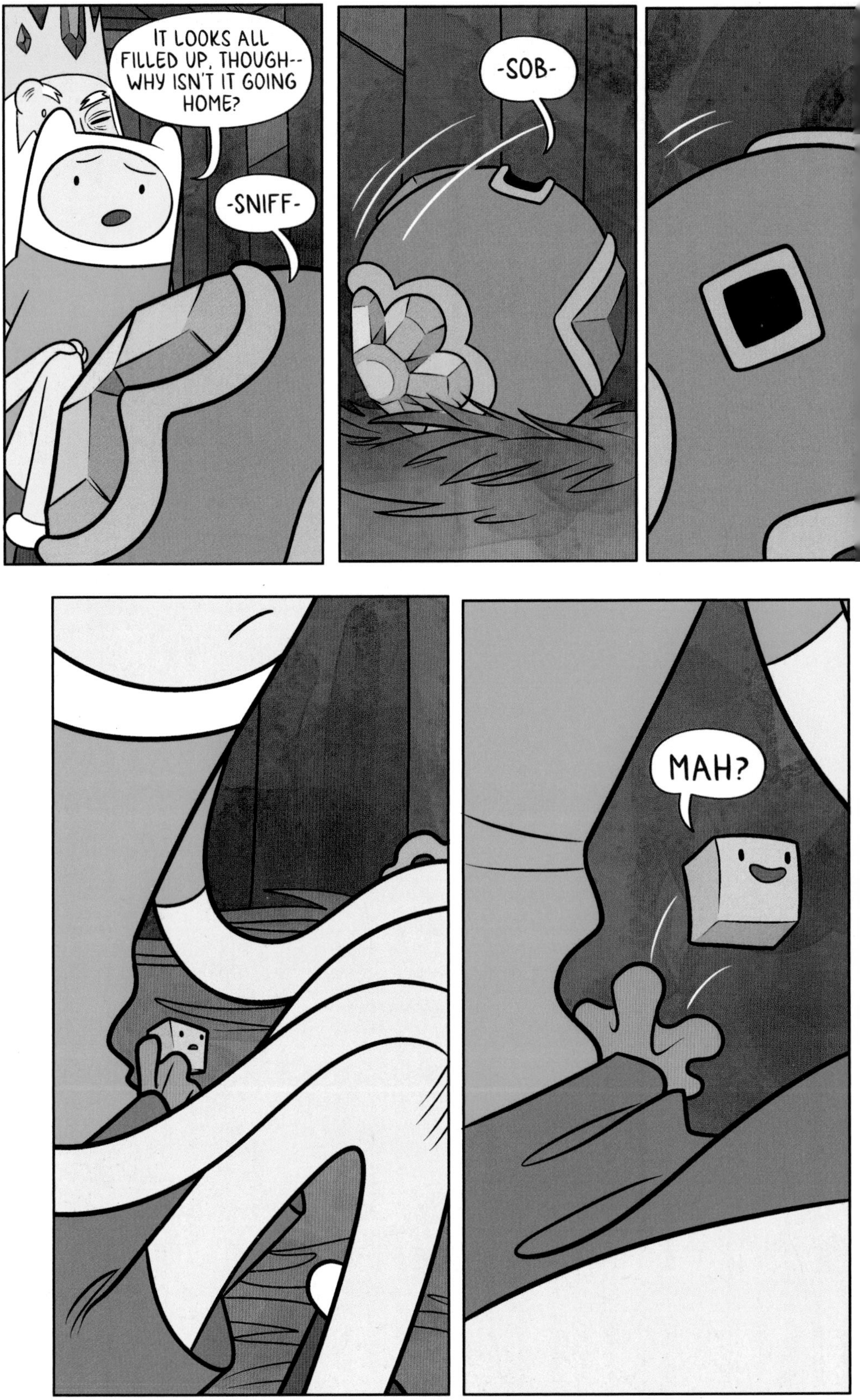
IT LOOKS ALL FILLED UP, THOUGH-- WHY ISN'T IT GOING HOME?
-SNIFF-
-SOB-
MAH?

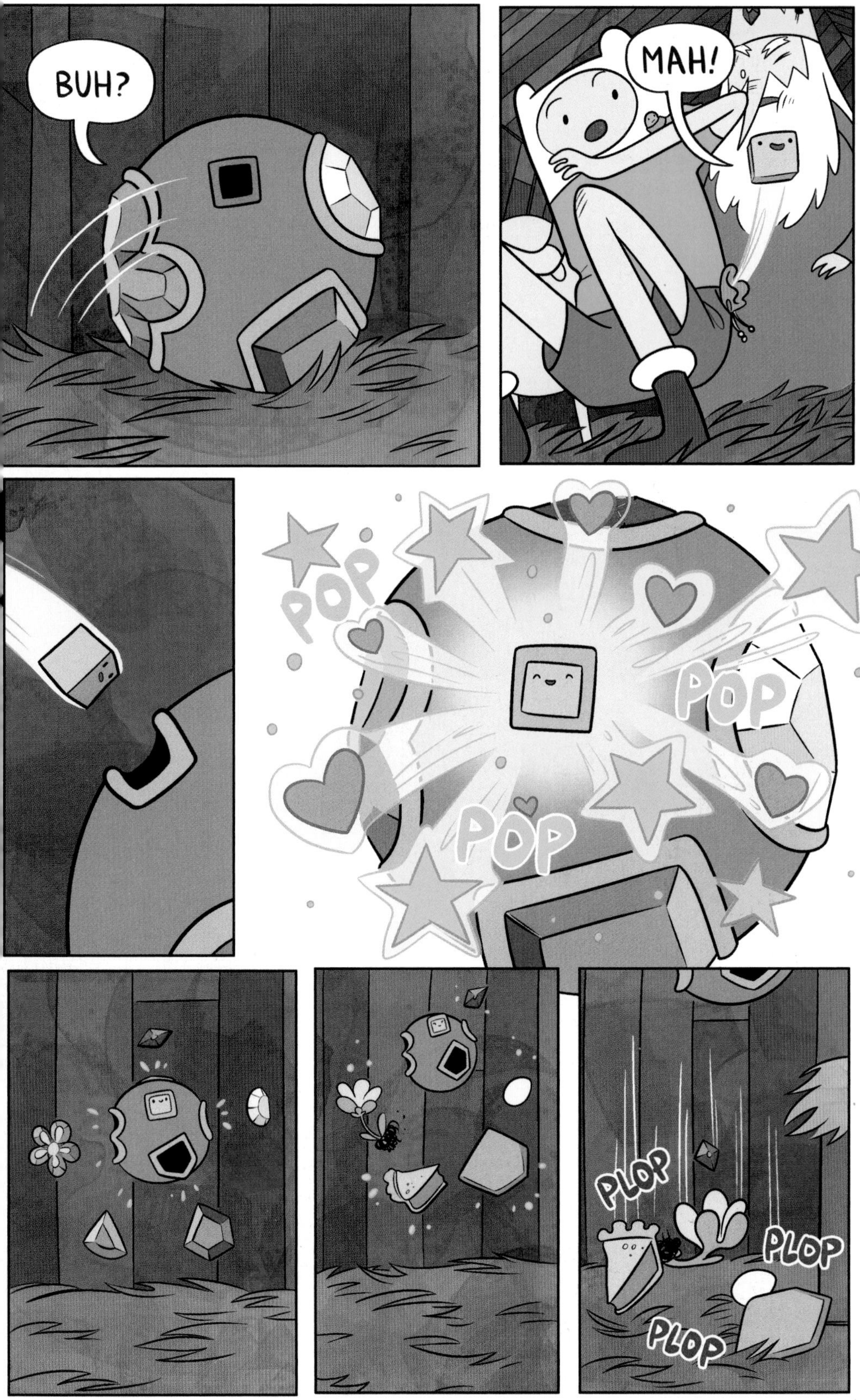

BUH?
MAH!
POP
POP
POP
PLOP
PLOP
PLOP

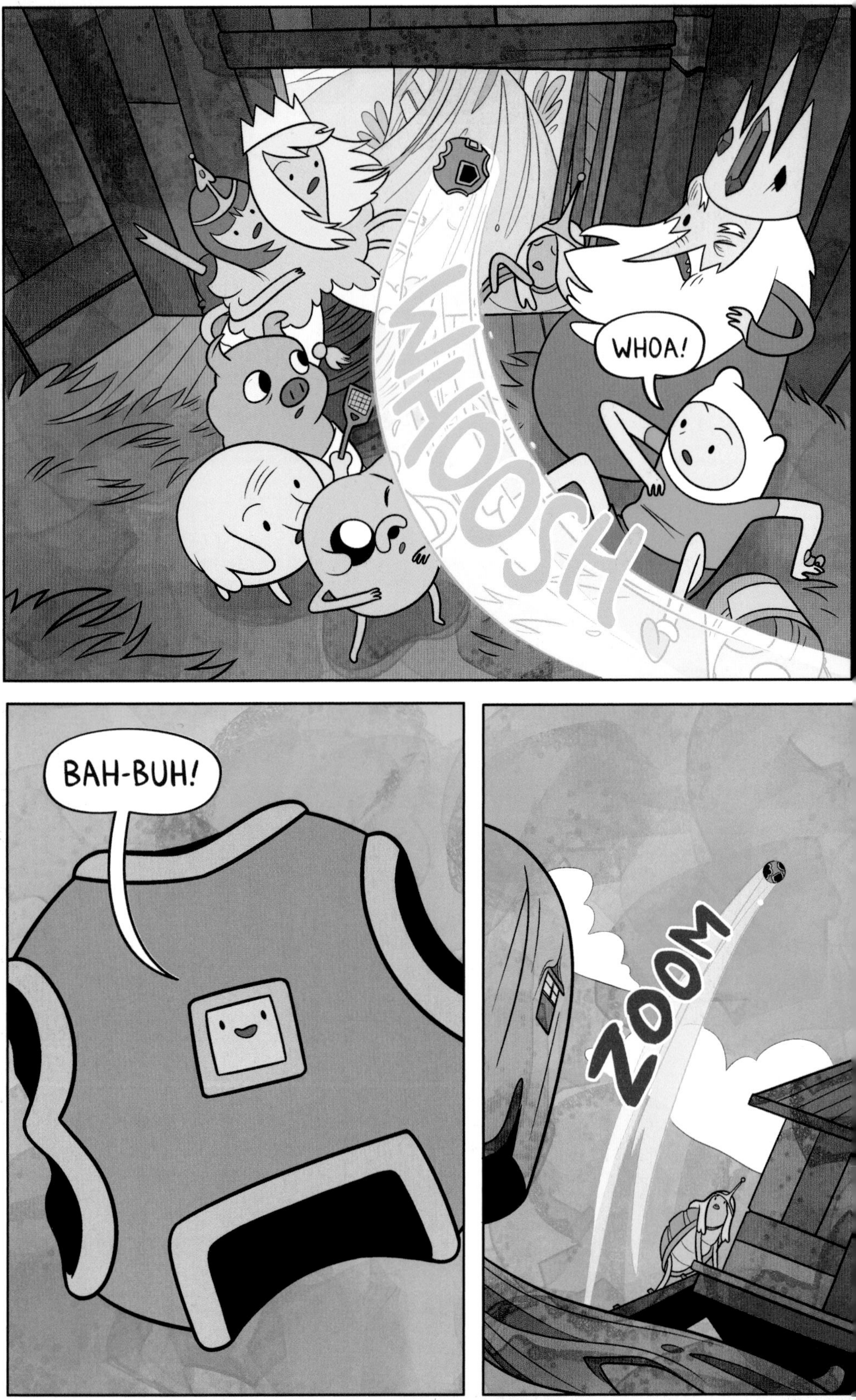
WHOOSH
WHOA!
BAH-BUH!
ZOOM

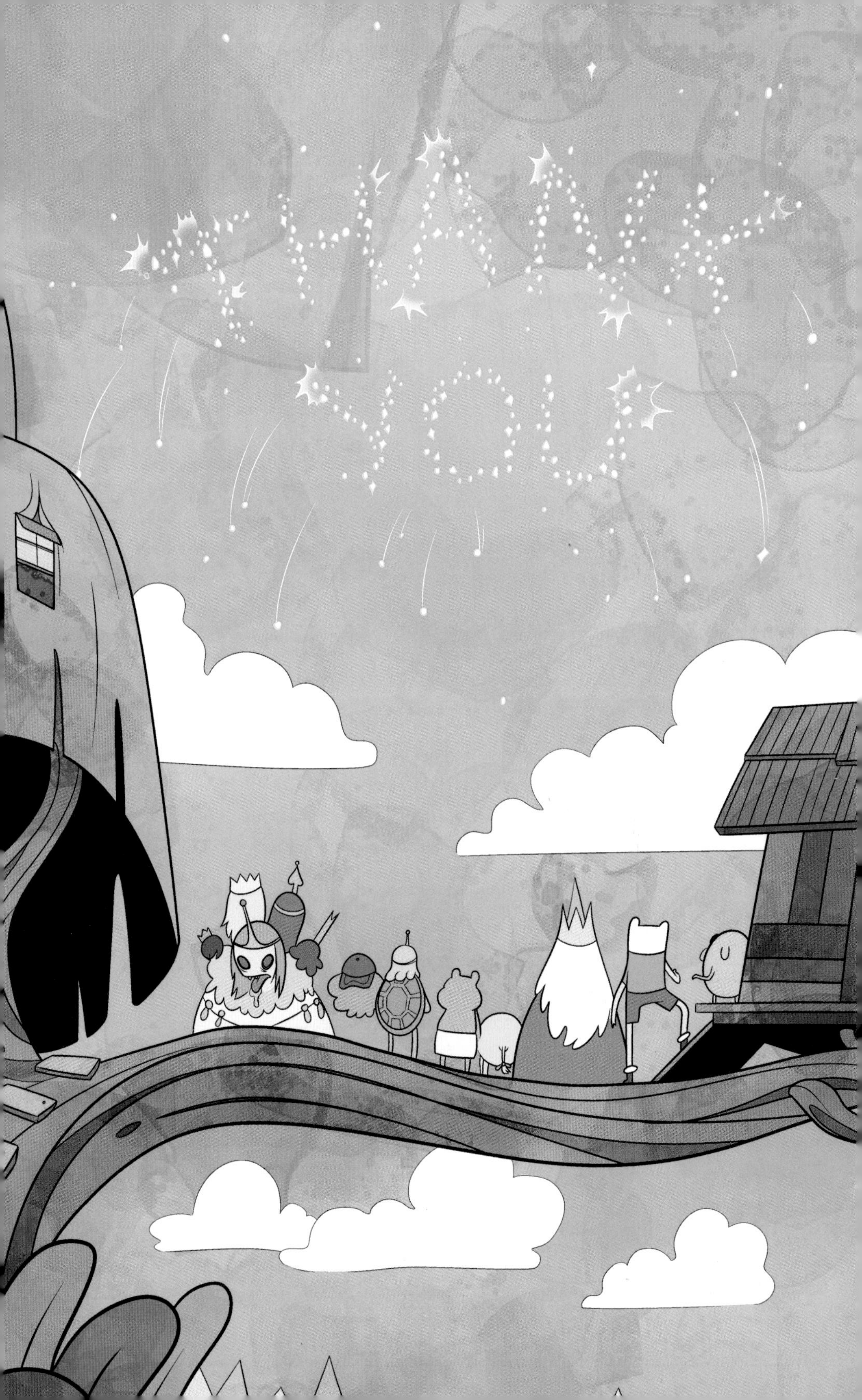
THANK YOU

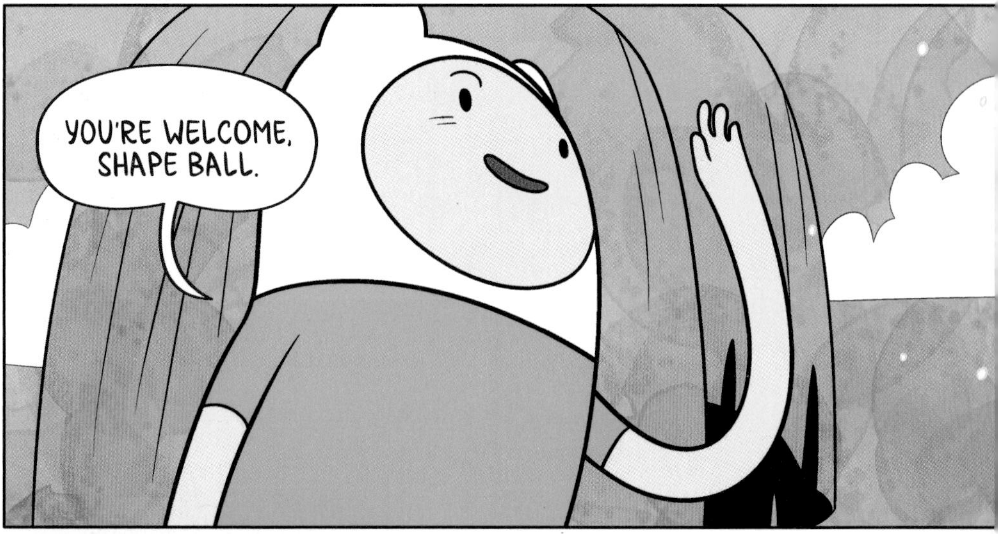
YOU'RE WELCOME, SHAPE BALL.

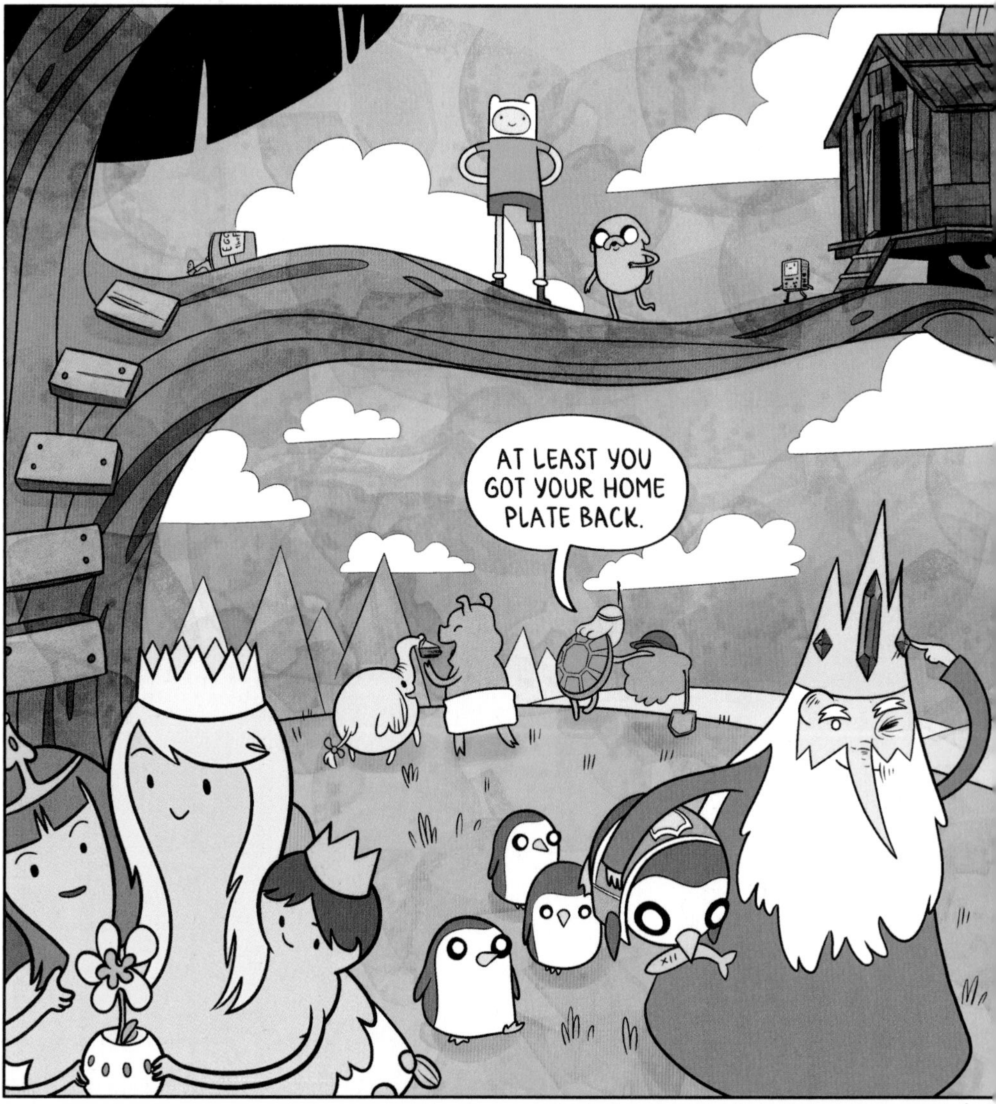
AT LEAST YOU GOT YOUR HOME PLATE BACK.

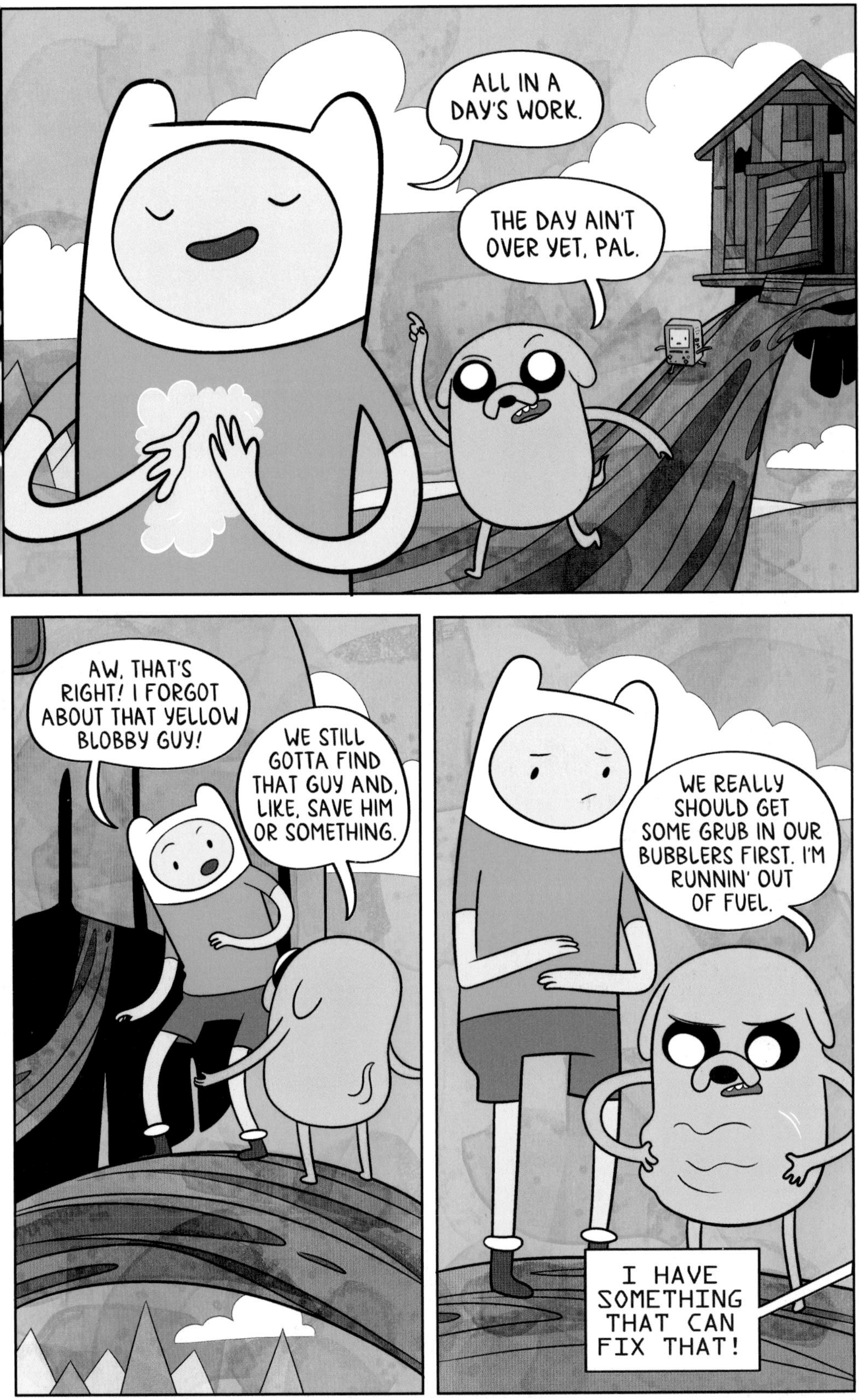
ALL IN A DAY'S WORK.
THE DAY AIN'T OVER YET, PAL.
AW, THAT'S RIGHT! I FORGOT ABOUT THAT YELLOW BLOBBY GUY!
WE STILL GOTTA FIND THAT GUY AND, LIKE, SAVE HIM OR SOMETHING.
WE REALLY SHOULD GET SOME GRUB IN OUR BUBBLERS FIRST. I'M RUNNIN' OUT OF FUEL.
I HAVE SOMETHING THAT CAN FIX THAT!

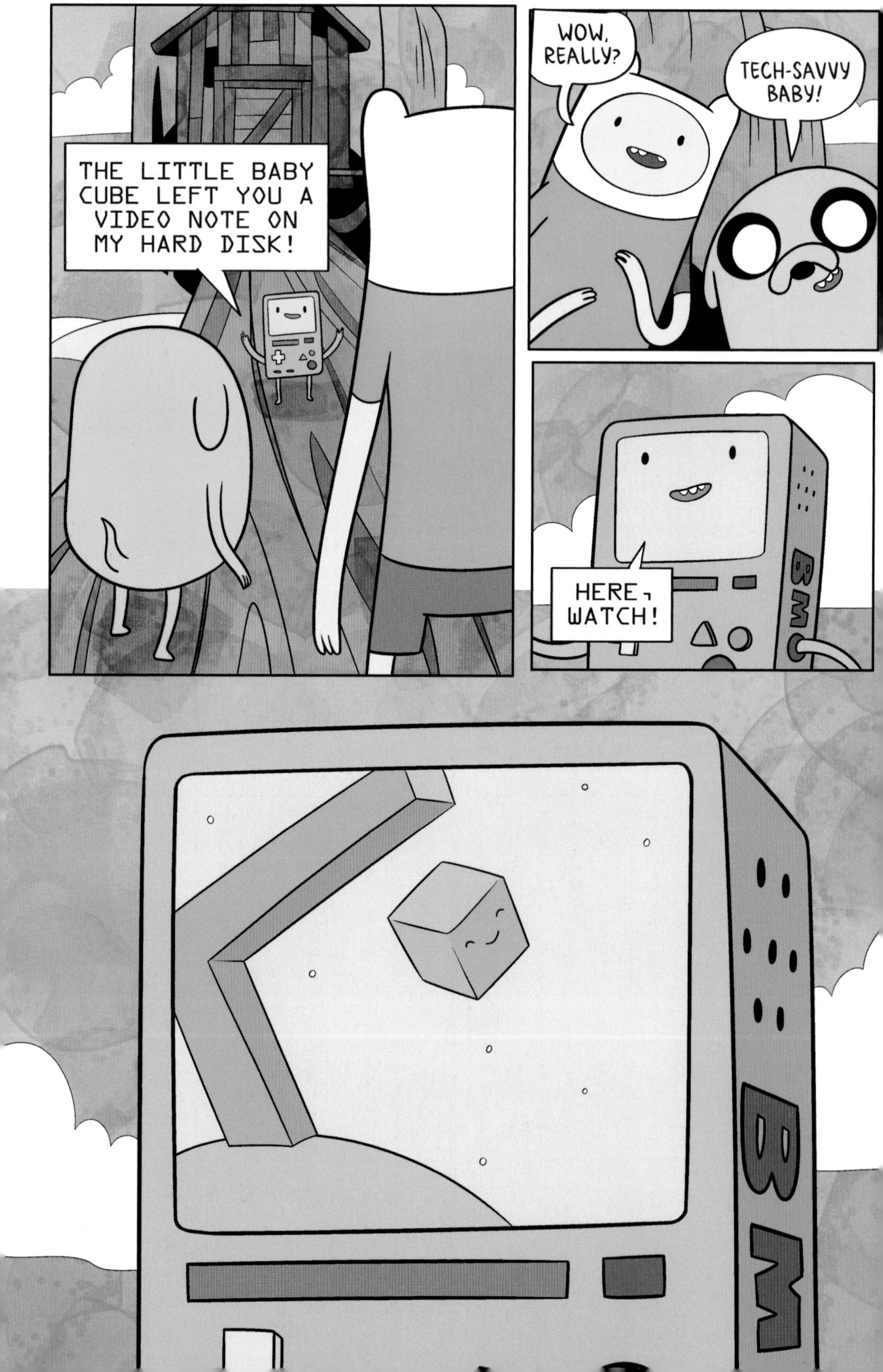

THE LITTLE BABY CUBE LEFT YOU A VIDEO NOTE ON MY HARD DISK!
WOW, REALLY?
TECH-SAVVY BABY!
HERE, WATCH!

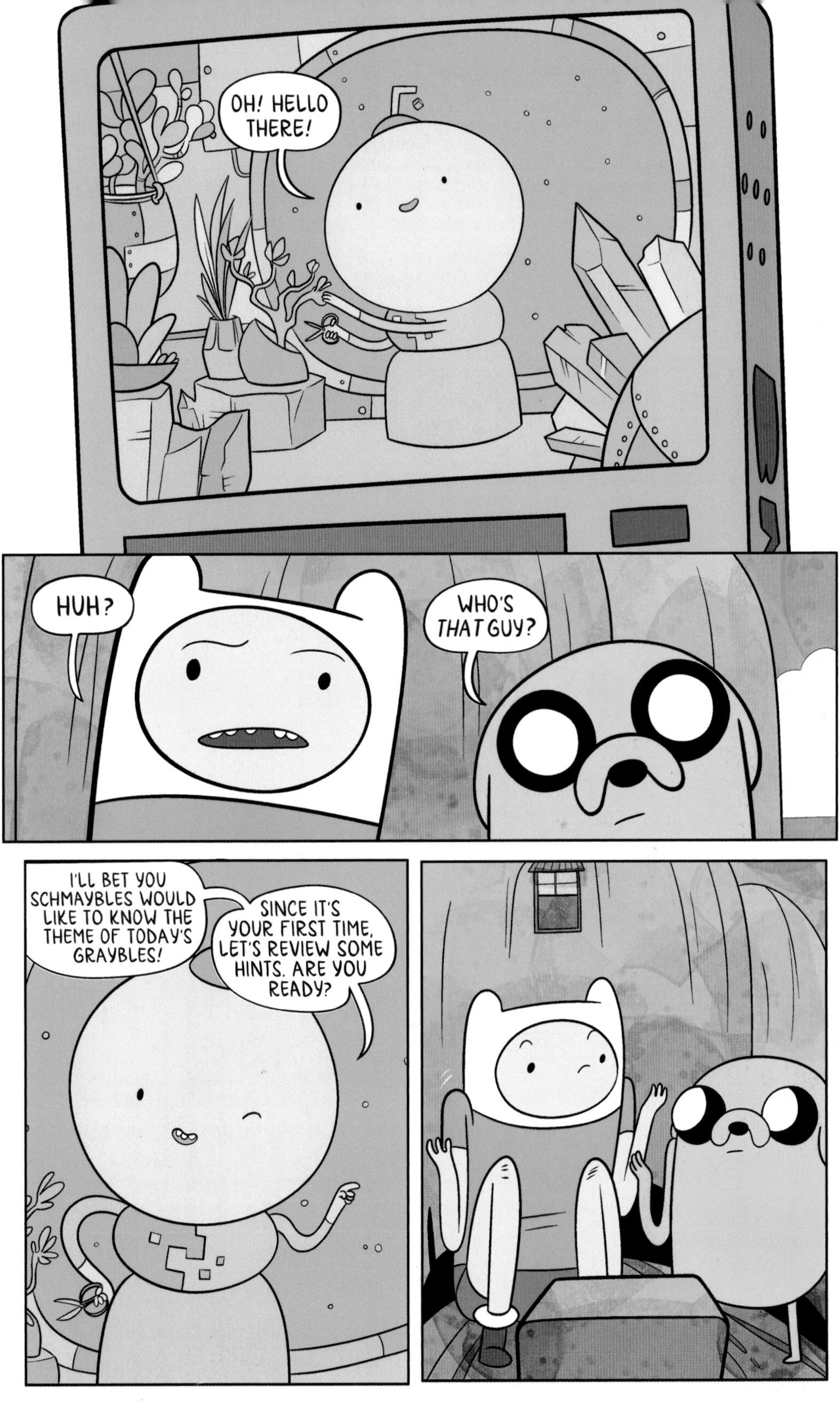
OH! HELLO THERE!
HUH?
WHO'S THAT GUY?
I'LL BET YOU SCHMAYBLES WOULD LIKE TO KNOW THE THEME OF TODAY'S GRAYBLES!
SINCE IT'S YOUR FIRST TIME, LET'S REVIEW SOME HINTS. ARE YOU READY?

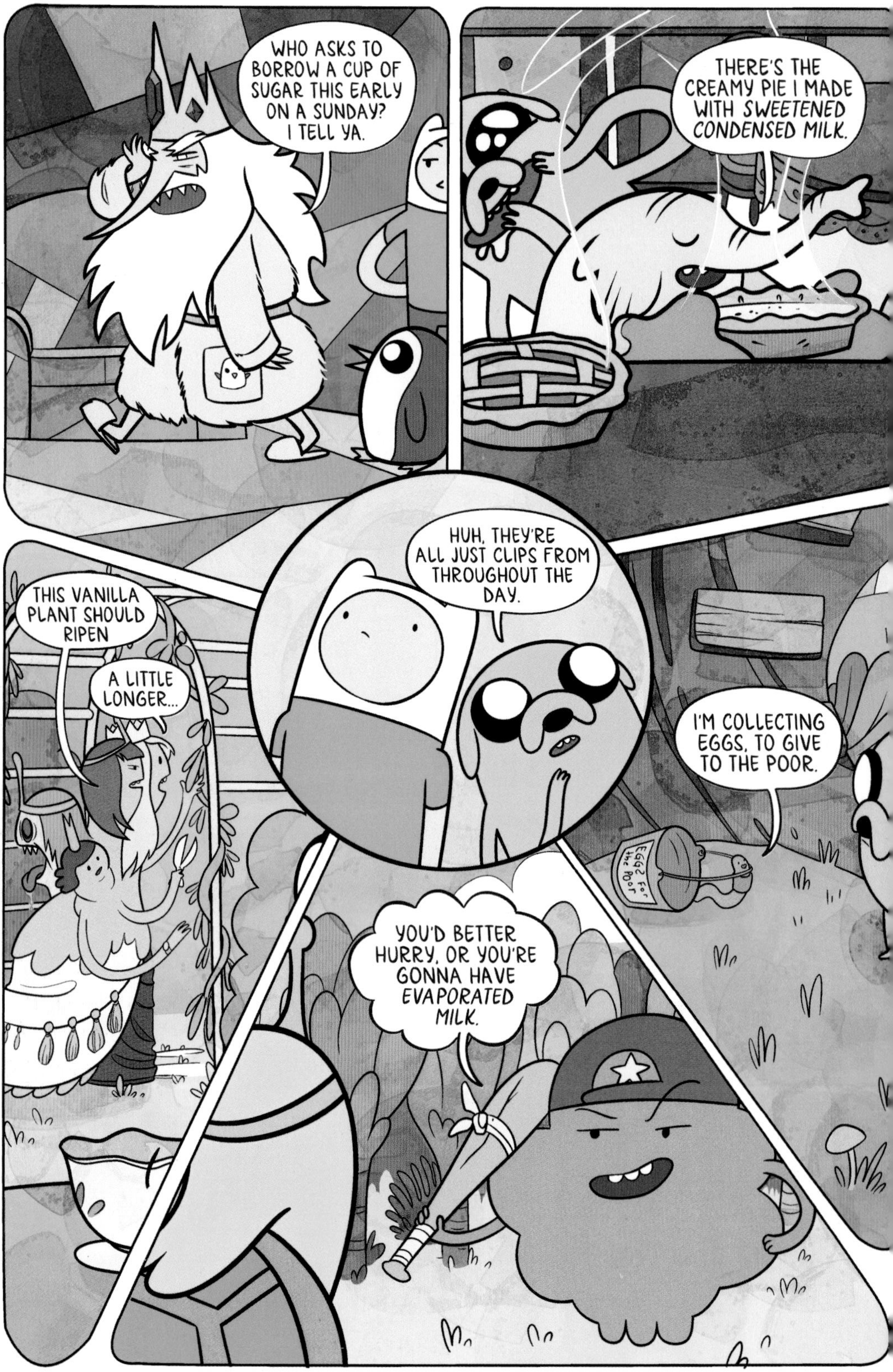
WHO ASKS TO BORROW A CUP OF SUGAR THIS EARLY ON A SUNDAY? I TELL YA.
THERE'S THE CREAMY PIE I MADE WITH SWEETENED CONDENSED MILK.
HUH, THEY'RE ALL JUST CLIPS FROM THROUGHOUT THE DAY.
THIS VANILLA PLANT SHOULD RIPEN
A LITTLE LONGER...
I'M COLLECTING EGGS, TO GIVE TO THE POOR.
EGGS For the Poor
YOU'D BETTER HURRY, OR YOU'RE GONNA HAVE EVAPORATED MILK.

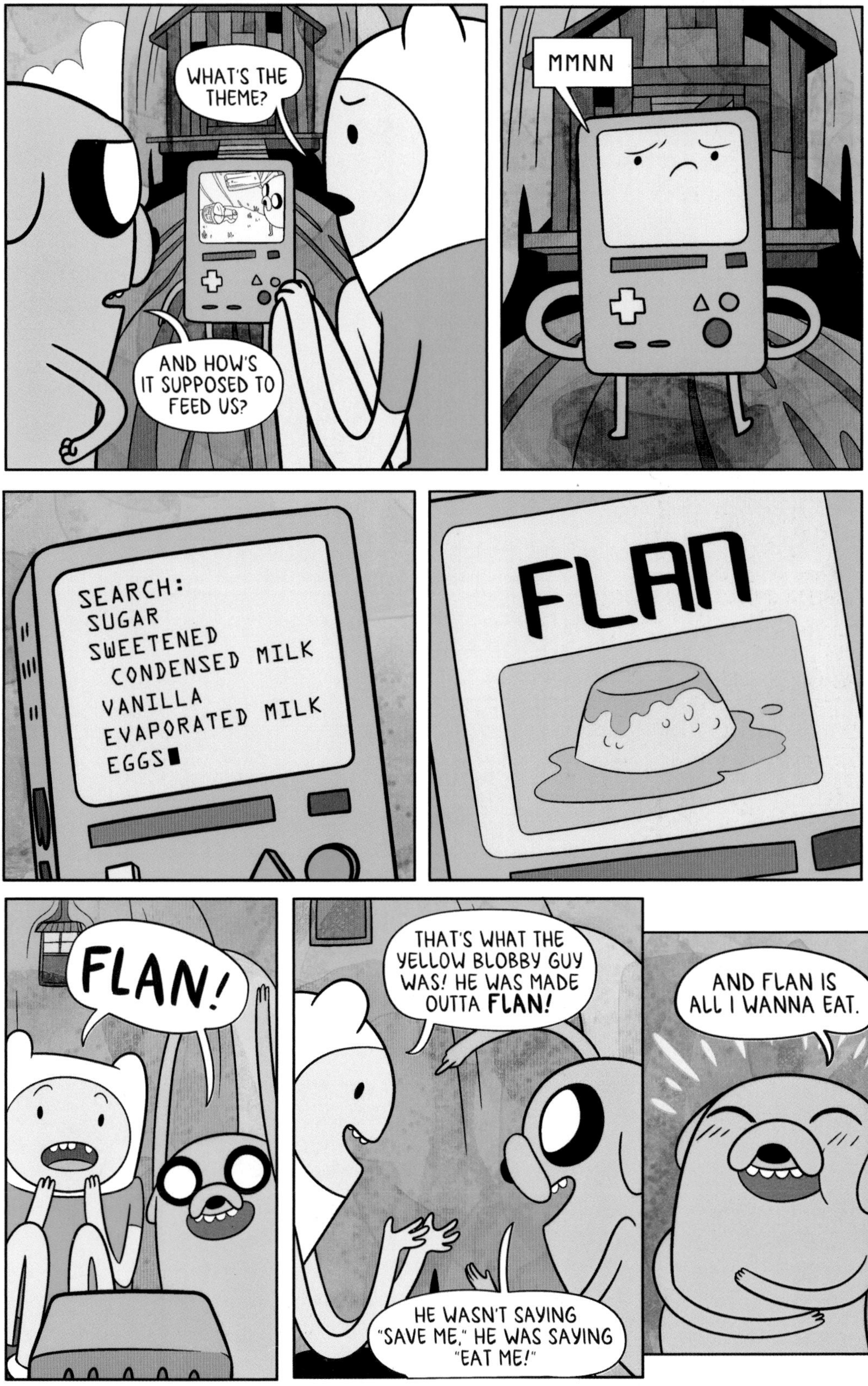
WHAT'S THE THEME?
AND HOW'S IT SUPPOSED TO FEED US?
MMNN
SEARCH:
SUGAR
SWEETENED CONDENSED MILK
VANILLA
EVAPORATED MILK
EGGS
FLAN
FLAN!
THAT'S WHAT THE YELLOW BLOBBY GUY WAS! HE WAS MADE OUTTA FLAN!
HE WASN'T SAYING "SAVE ME," HE WAS SAYING "EAT ME!"
AND FLAN IS ALL I WANNA EAT.

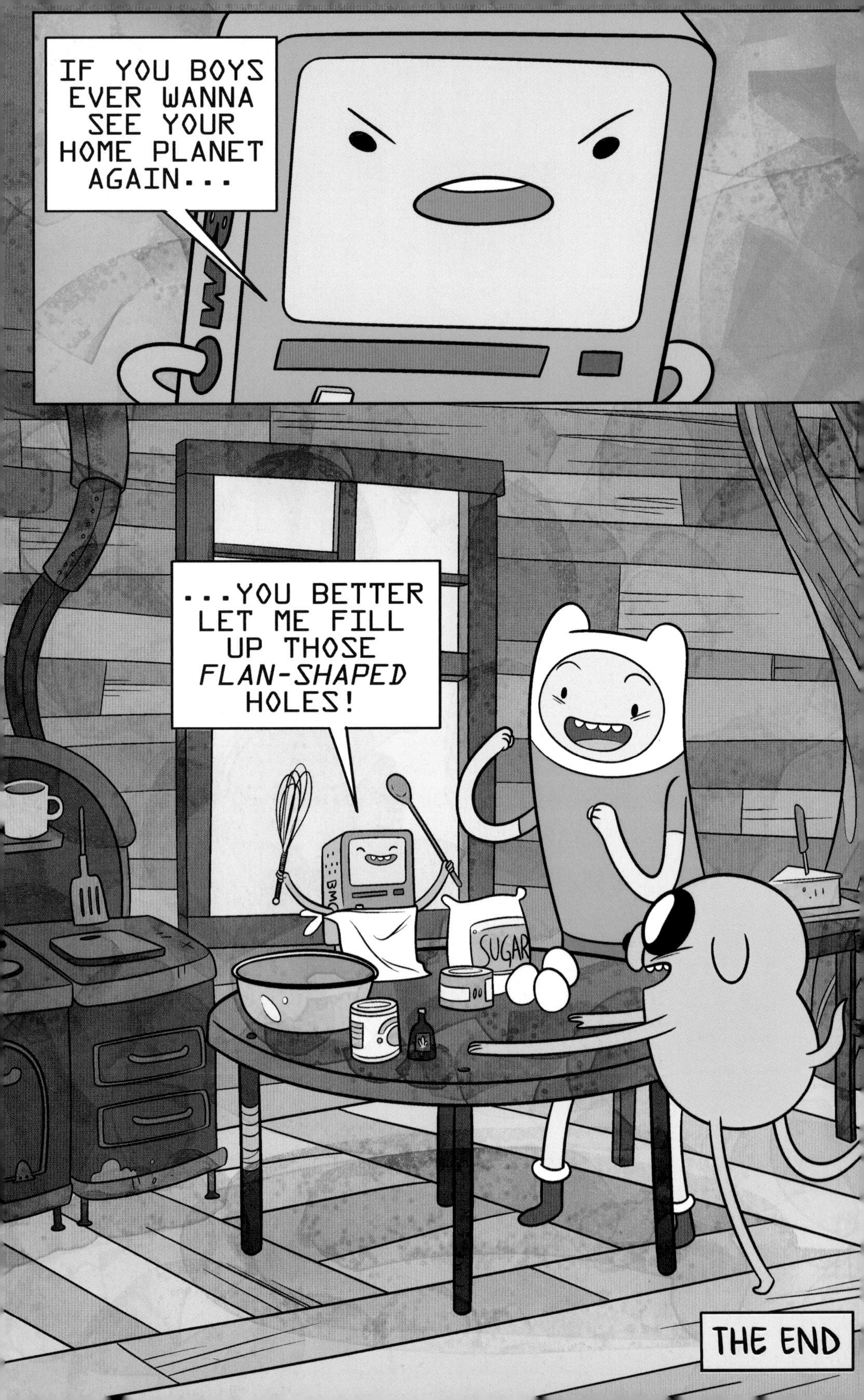
IF YOU BOYS EVER WANNA SEE YOUR HOME PLANET AGAIN...
...YOU BETTER LET ME FILL UP THOSE *FLAN-SHAPED* HOLES!
SUGAR
THE END

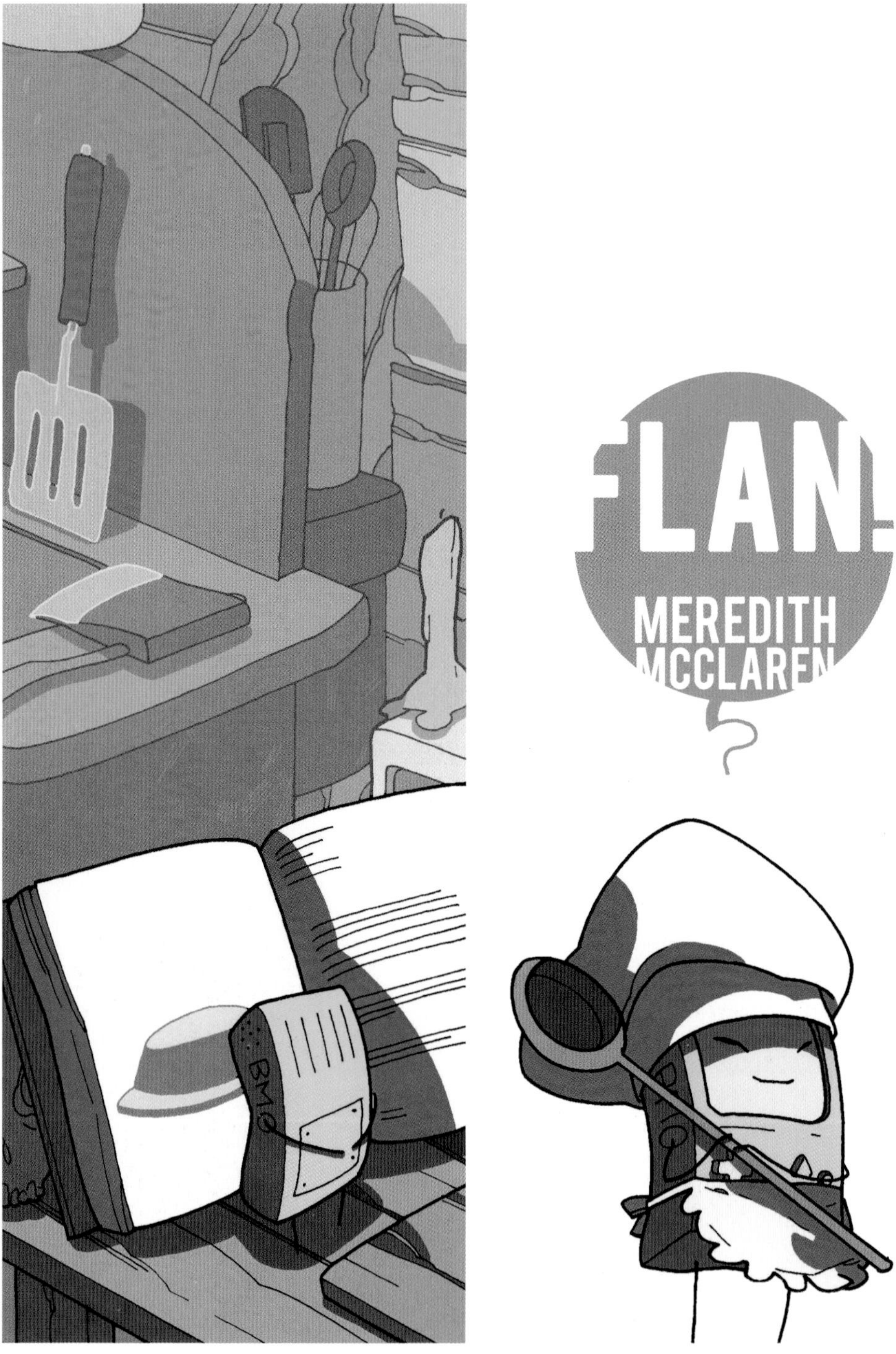
FLAN
MEREDITH
MCCLAREN
BMO

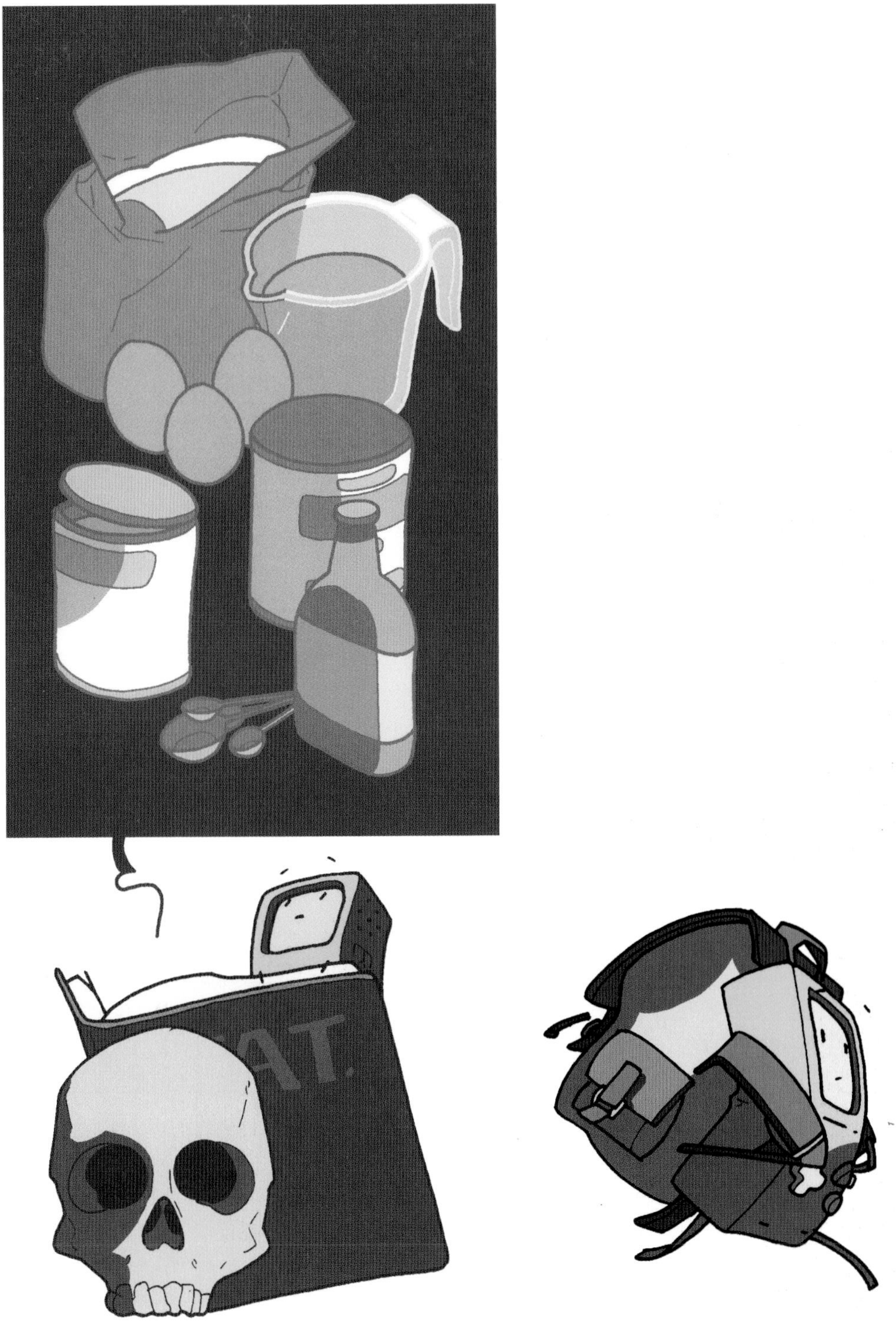
AT.

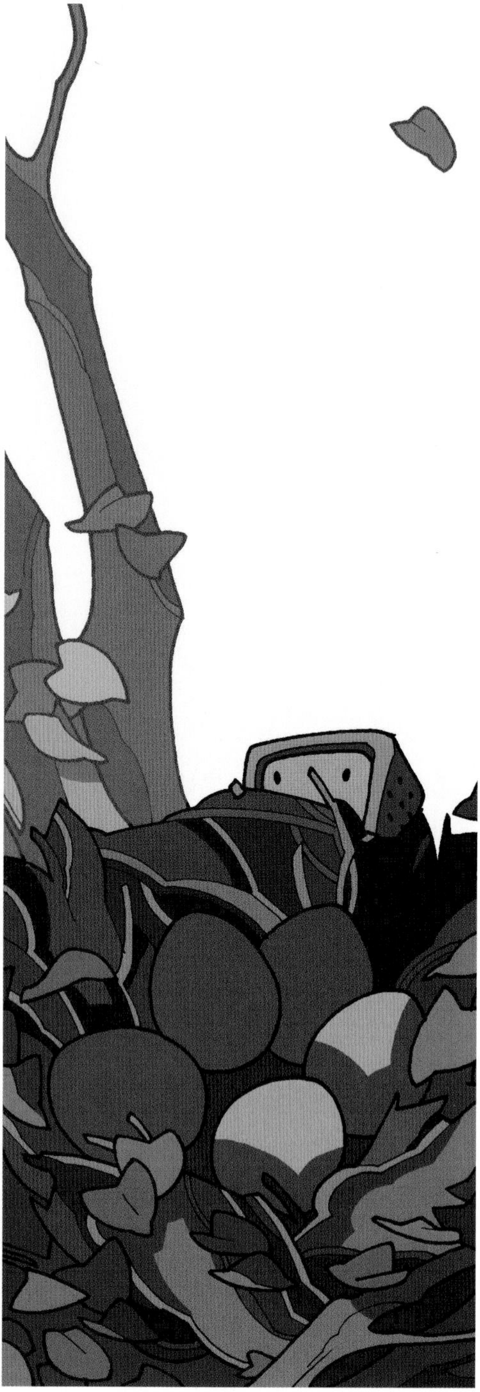

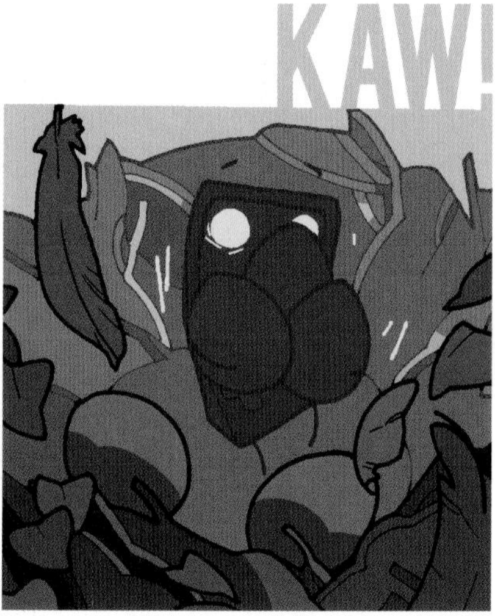
KAW!

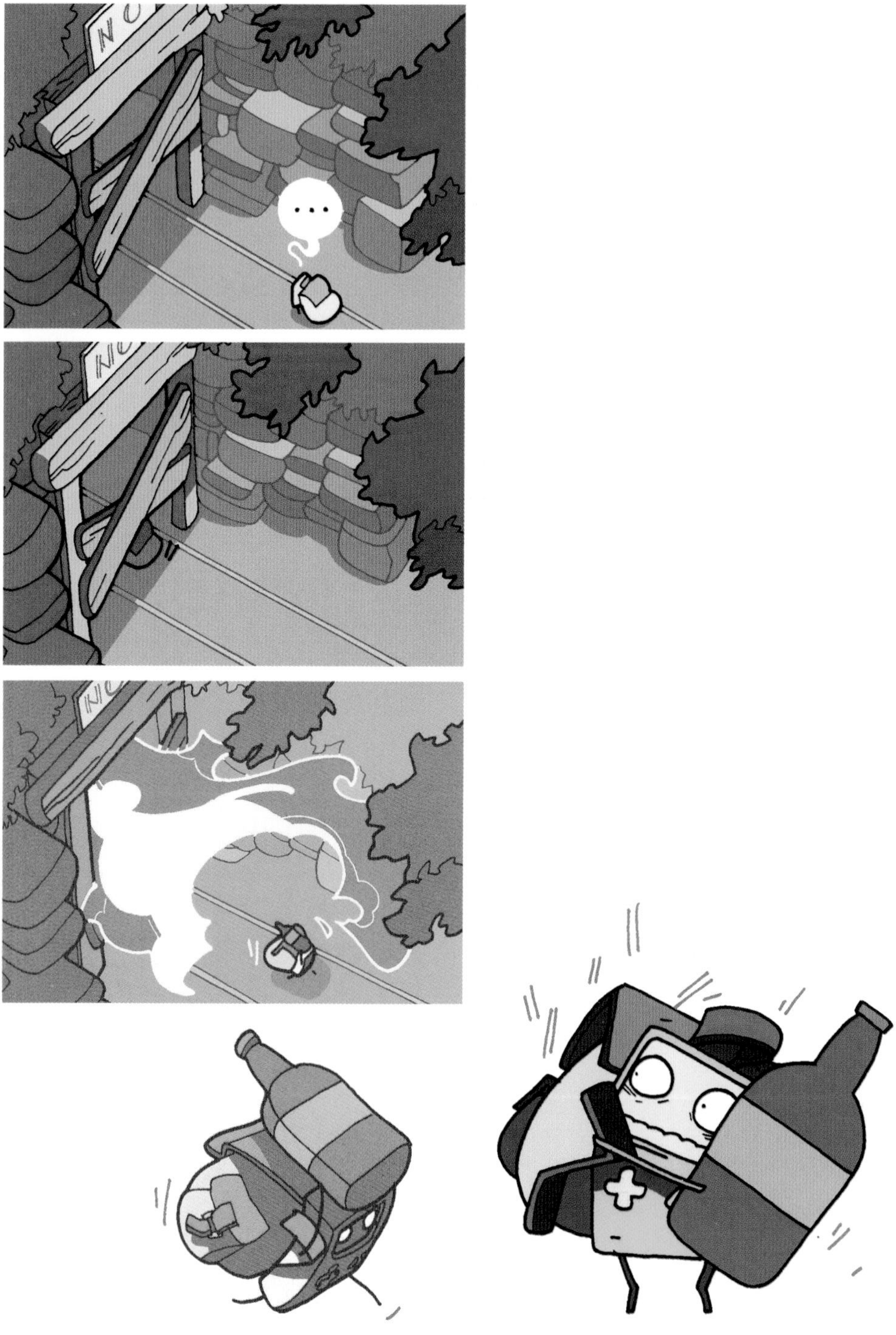
...

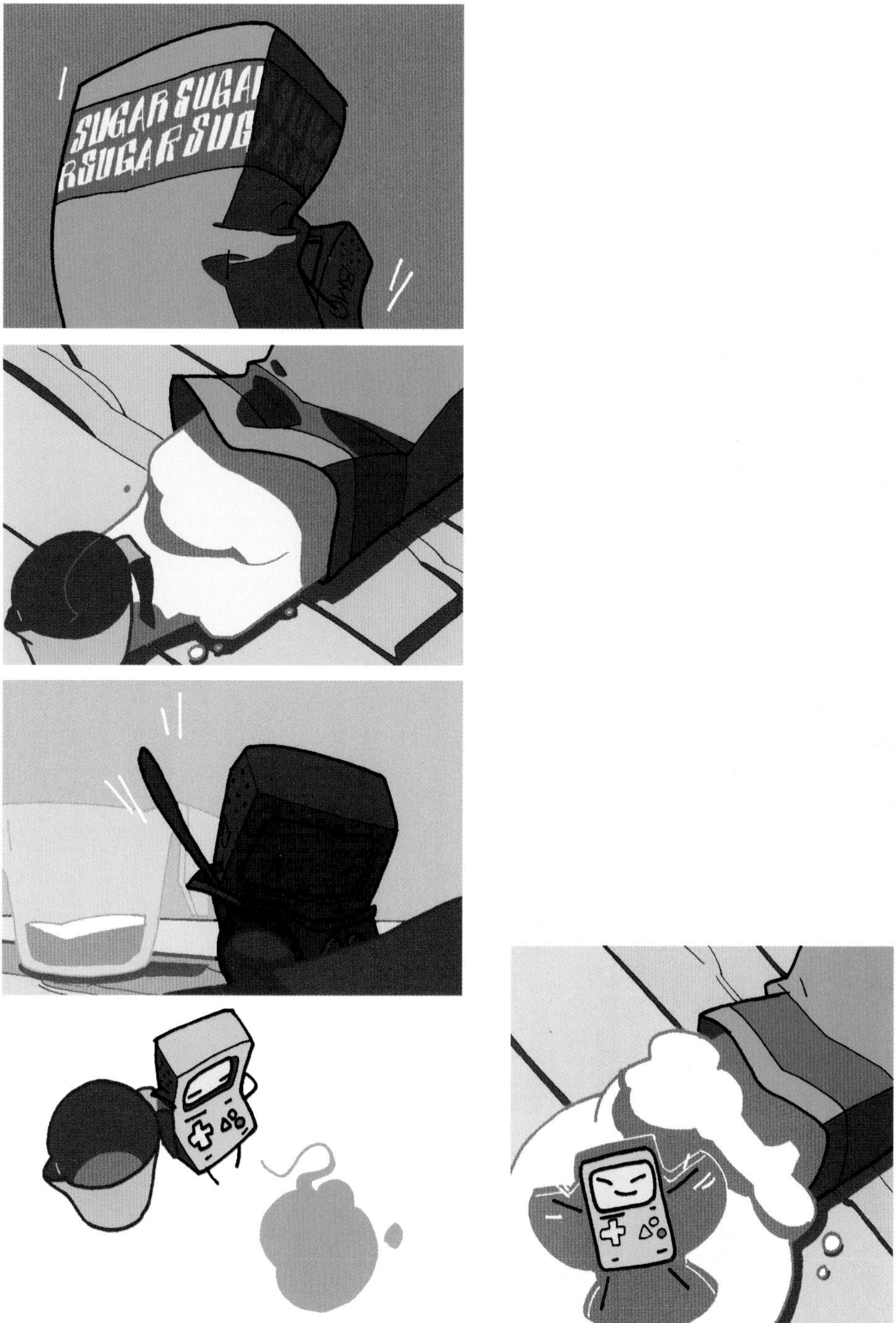
SUGAR SUGA
RSUGAR SUG

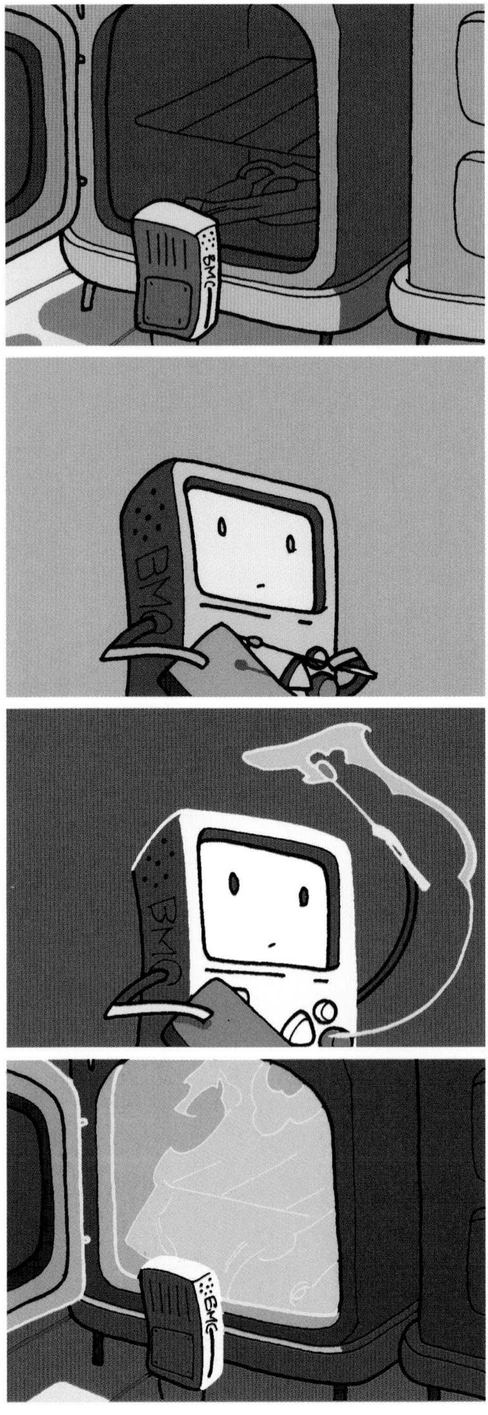
BMC

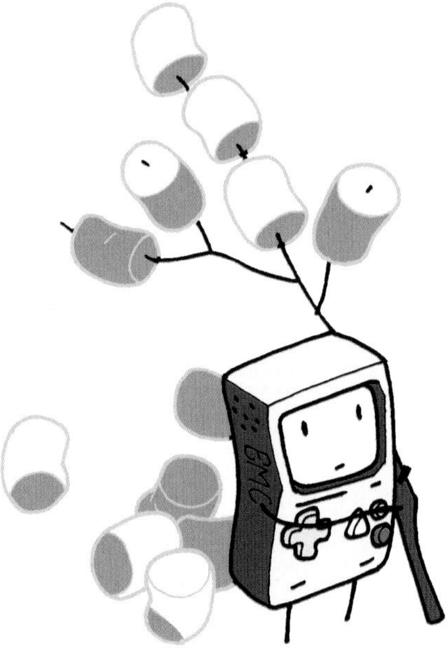
BMC

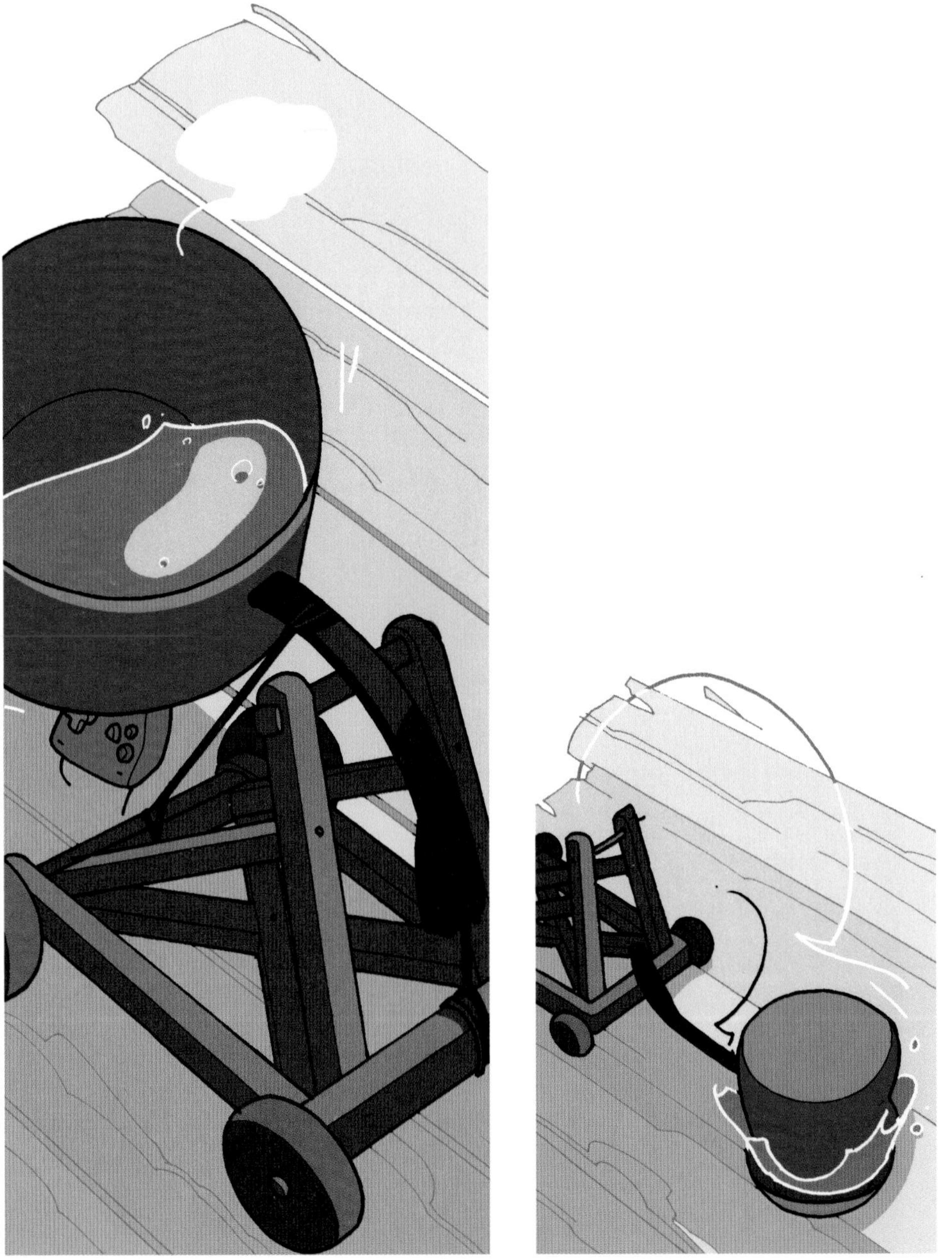

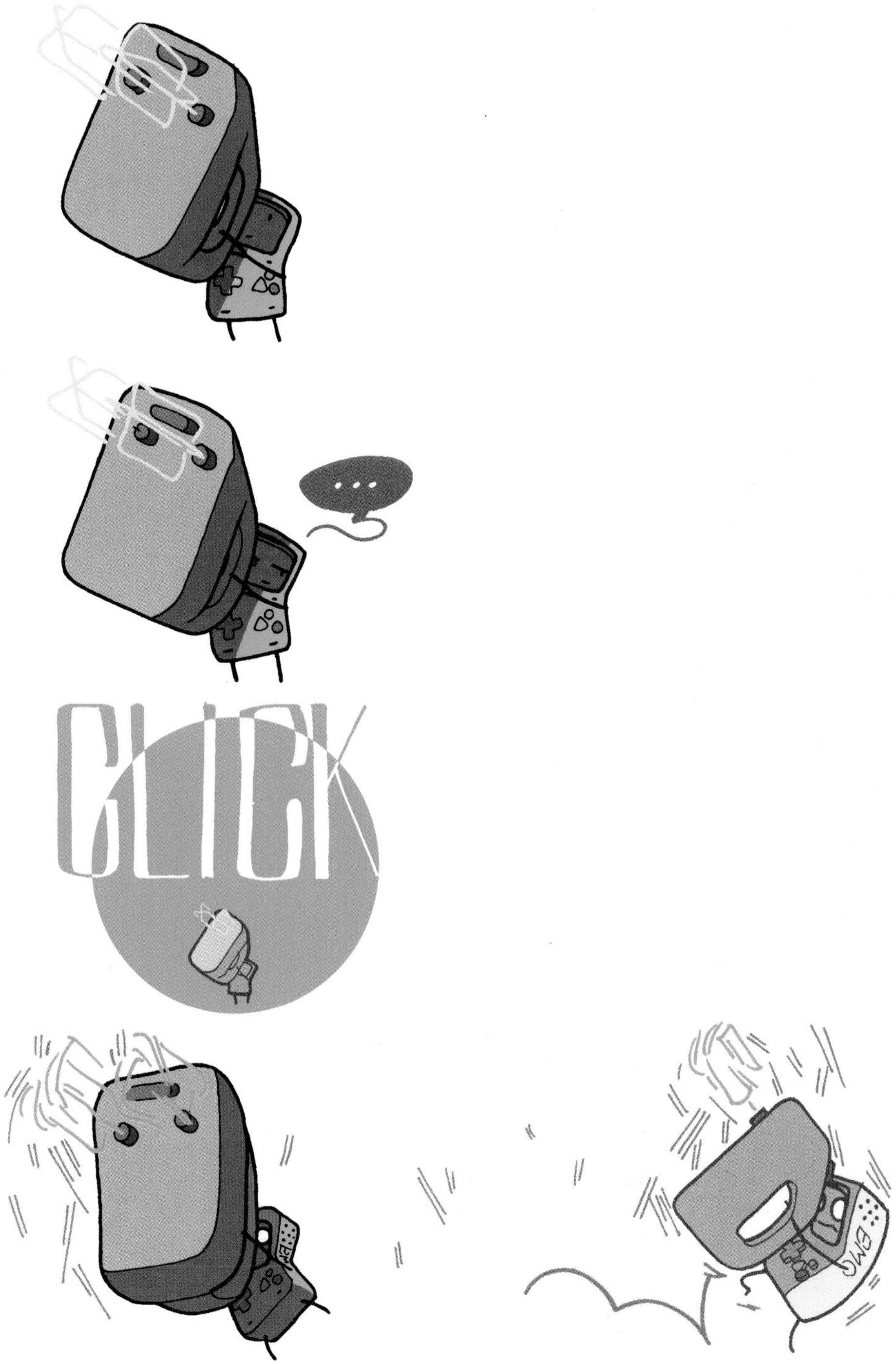
...
CLICK

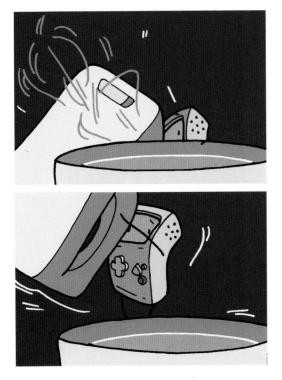

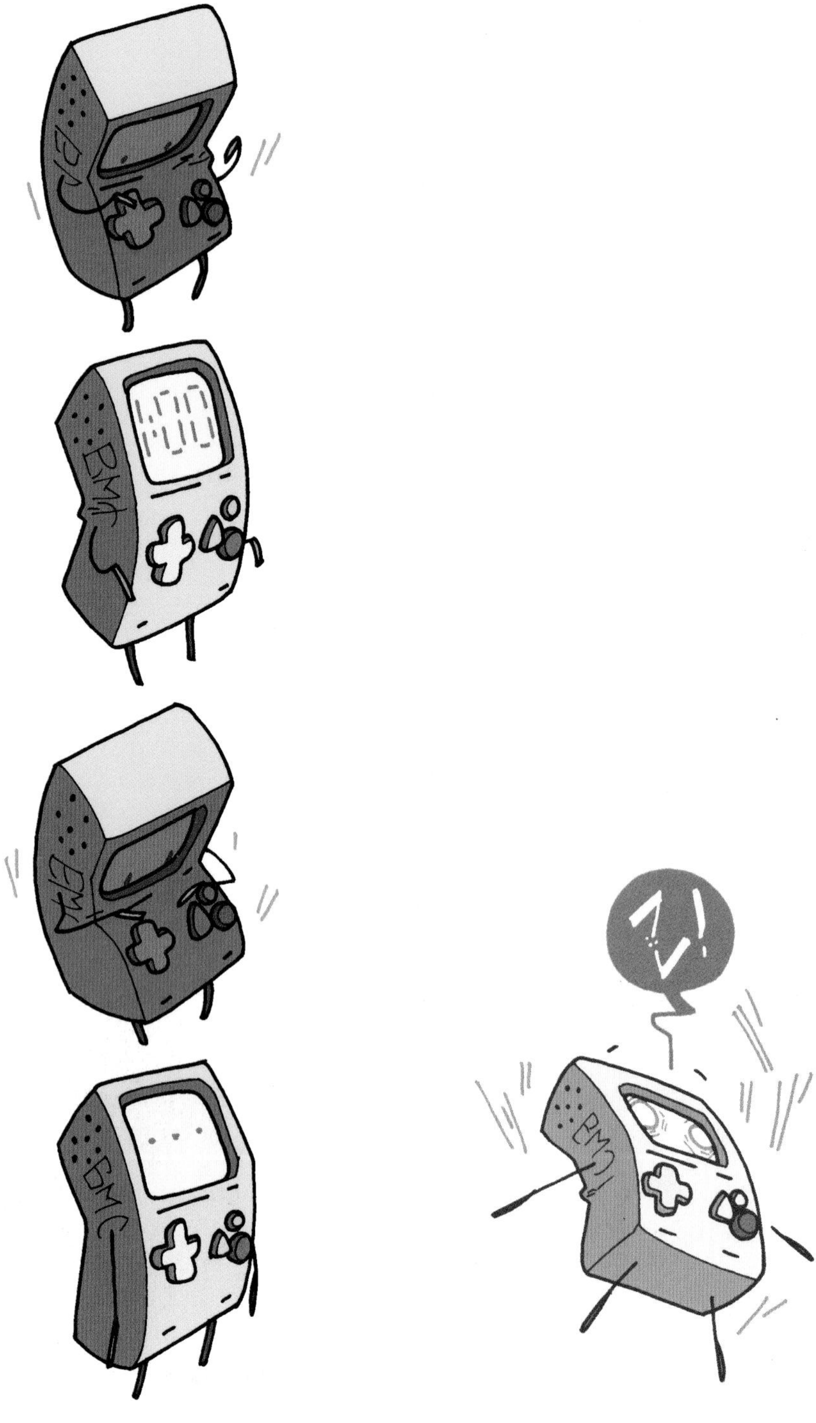
BMC
Z!

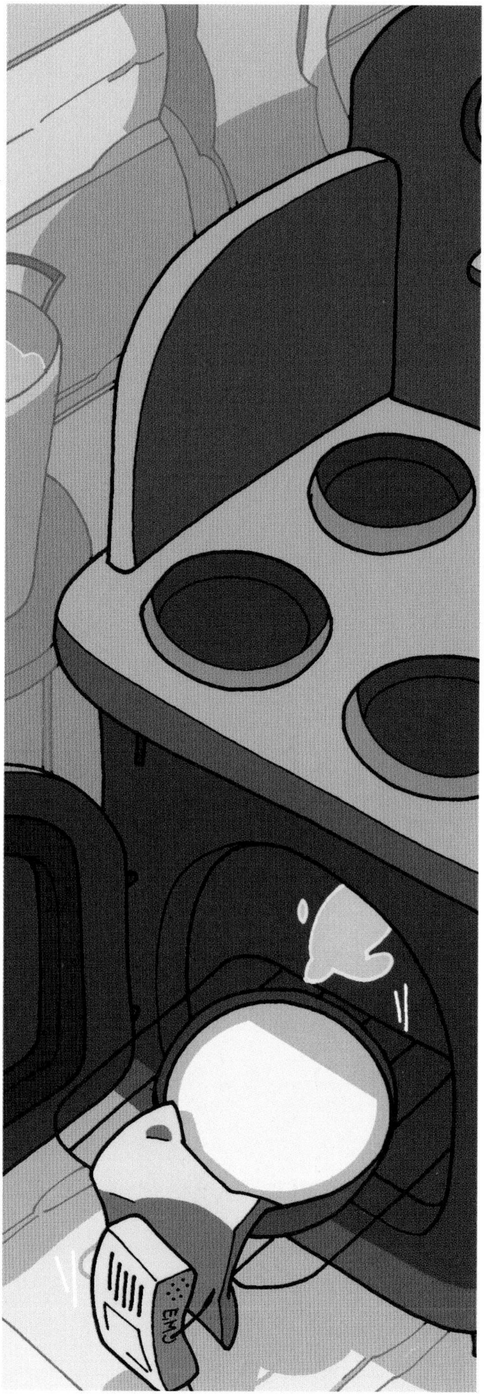
EMJ

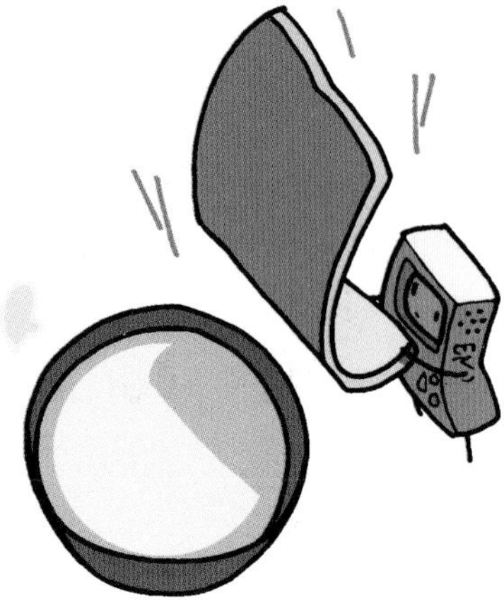
EMJ

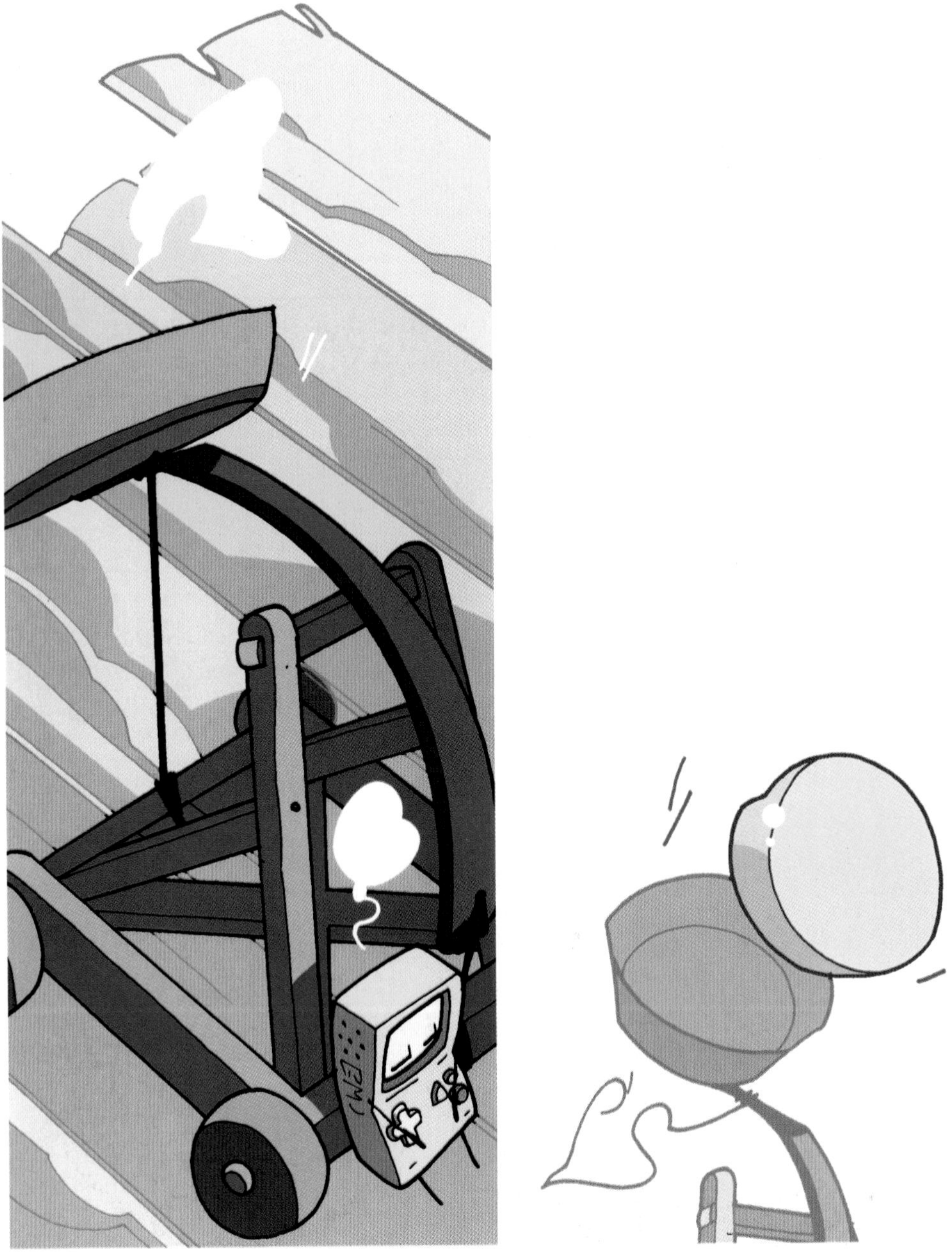

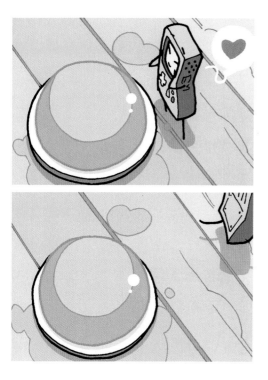

END.

ADVENTURE TIME ™

VOLUME 6

FALL 2015

Written by **Kate Leth**

Art by **Bridget Underwood**